IF WE COULD GO BACK

CARA DEE

If We Could Go Back

Copyright © 2019 by Cara Dee
All rights reserved

This book is licensed for your personal enjoyment and may not be reproduced in any way without documented permission of the author, not including brief quotes with links and/or credit to the source. Thank you for respecting the hard work of this author. This is a work of fiction and all references to historical events, persons living or dead, and locations are used in a fictional manner. Any other names, characters, incidents, and places are derived from the author's imagination. The author acknowledges the trademark status and owners of any wordmarks mentioned in this work of fiction. Characters portrayed in sexual situations are 18 or older.

Edited by Silently Correcting Your Grammar, LLC.
Formatted by Eliza Rae Services.
Proofread by Tanja.

WELCOME TO THE CAMASSIA COVE UNIVERSE

Camassia Cove is a town in northern Washington created to be the home of some exciting love stories. Each novel taking place here is a standalone—with the exception of sequels and series within the CC universe—and they vary in genre and pairing. What they all have in common is the town in which they live. Some are friends and family. Others are complete strangers. Some have vastly different backgrounds. Some grew up together. It's a small world, and many characters will cross over and pay a visit or two in several books—Cara's way of giving readers a glimpse into the future of their favorite characters. Oh, who is she kidding; they are characters she's unable of saying good-bye to. But, again, each novel stands on its own, and spoilers will be avoided as much as possible.

If you're interested in keeping up with secondary characters, the town, the timeline, and future novels, check out Camassia Cove's own website at www.camassiacove.com. There you will also see which characters have gotten their own books already, where they appear, which books are in the works, character profiles, and you'll be treated to a taste of the town.

*

Get social with Cara
www.caradeewrites.com
www.camassiacove.com
Facebook: @caradeewrites
Twitter: @caradeewrites
Instagram: @caradeewrites

A THANK YOU
A DEDICATION

To the guy who perfected the ketchup heart.
You're still there for me, and you show it every day.

CHAPTER 1

Bennett Brooks

Maybe you should try cocaine.
My mood soured as I opened my laptop and took a sip of my coffee. The train departed. I had an hour to kill but was more likely to kill myself.

"This seat taken?" someone asked.

I flicked him a brief glance and shook my head.

Bloody hell, I was only twenty-eight. Wasn't I too young for misery?

It was official. Sitting still for forty-five minutes every morning was giving me too much time to think—that was the problem. I tried to work and couldn't get into it. Forty-five minutes wasn't long enough to get settled, so it was time going to waste. I needed my cubicle that would hopefully soon turn into an office if I could get that promotion. I was driven and hanging on to a shred of hope that this summer would get me to where I wanted to be.

And if it doesn't…

I didn't want to think about it. I couldn't stomach it anymore.

Checking my watch, I chastised myself for being impatient. It never ceased to amaze me how spoiled we got. It was a new train, a two-stop route between my little town in northern Washington and Seattle, a route that'd shaved at least forty minutes off my commute. Yet, two months into this new transit, I grew restless after a few minutes.

I closed my laptop, giving up on the notion of getting anything done. The six-thirty train from Camassia was an express departure, so I was surrounded by men and women in suits working on their way to the city. They could get into it—work, or whatever they looked busy doing.

I completed the crossword puzzle I'd started last week instead. I made reservations and confirmed another, read the local paper, and drank from my travel mug. This had become my everyday life, starting in April when my boss told me there was a promotion on the horizon. I was getting close, though I knew how quickly a deal could fall through.

My hopes were almost as high as my expectations, no matter how hard I tried to keep my thoughts leveled.

I had to get out of here.

A promotion would fix my worries and shake up the dreariness of my regular routine.

Or you could try cocaine.

"No, sir, I'm on my way now." I jogged up onto the platform and held up a finger to the guy signaling that the train was about to leave. He spotted me and stepped aside so I could board the car.

"Close call, kid," the man commented gruffly.

"Let me know if you need assistance, Bennett," my boss told me. "I didn't expect you would be commuting daily."

Neither had I, to be honest. But there were bigger fish in Seattle, and out-of-towners preferred a meeting in the city over going all the way up to Camassia.

"I have it covered," I replied. "Did you follow up on the rumor I heard?" Because if Westwater Hotels was looking to launch their new brand of hotels, we'd want to get in on that.

"I did." Mirth seeped into his tone. "If I get a meeting with them, I'll send you."

Fuck yes. A surge of relief and anticipation flooded me, and I had to resist the urge to fist-pump the air. Instead, I calmly sat down in my window seat and wrapped up the call like a professional person. But holy smokes, this made my day. It certainly made up for the failure of yesterday when I lost a potential client to another agency's bid.

For the fourth day in a row, the seat across from mine was occupied. My brow furrowed, and I took in his uniform. He had to be one of those bike messengers. The long-sleeved black-and-neon-blue shirt was skintight, and I recognized the logo on his chest. I'd seen it around the city. Curious he was riding in business class.

With a shake of my head, I refocused and decided to start a new crossword puzzle.

I nodded absently in greeting to the same men I passed as I boarded the train most mornings, finding my seat in the last car.

A flash of black and neon blue caught my eye, and I looked out the window. *That guy again.* I narrowed my eyes, then shook my head and refused to—dammit, I was going to want to know regardless of how hard I tried not to.

The man stepped on right before we rolled away from the platform and took his seat across from me.

He nodded hello then got lost in a book.

I didn't pretend to work. Since the first time he'd sat down there two weeks ago, he'd become my puzzle. It frustrated me, and I knew my questions would sound elitist and judgmental, but he didn't *fit*. He was around my age, I was fairly sure, yet he wore ratty jeans and hoodies that belonged to a teenager. For the record, no, I didn't want to "Go fuck a Monday," as his hoodie had suggested one day, "because they're always hard."

When the sorry men and women wearing similar suits to what I wore guzzled their coffee and tried to work, he sat there in his uniform and a pair of headphones. Sometimes, he had a book, like today.

It was when the weather was particularly cold that he wore his holey jeans over his bike shorts. Or so I assumed, since the body-hugging uniform shirt was always there, with or without an unzipped hoodie.

Late August was giving us heat, so today it was all uniform and...form. The stretchy fabric showcased his physique and made my gut tighten with envy. I hadn't been that in shape since high school.

I sipped my coffee and discreetly smoothed down my tie. My stomach was showing the results of back-to-back breakfast and lunch meetings. There was no muscle definition, and I could stand to lose five or six pounds. The man across from me had definition everywhere. Nothing too much in a relaxed state, just enough to see it was very *there*. Biceps, abs, thighs...

He irritated me.

His hair was perhaps a shade or two darker than my own, and his streaks were disheveled where mine were neat. His eyes, even when he was visibly tired, were captivating. Even I could admit that. Green met deep blue and muddled with a little bit of gray. I couldn't say anything remotely interesting about my eyes. *Brown. They're brown.* The man had some scars too. A couple small ones on his jaw, more pronounced when he'd forgotten to shave. Another scar cut into his left eyebrow.

I shook my head. Perhaps one day I'd give up on my frustration and simply ask him. How would that go? I'd sound like an utter fool. *Excuse me. I was wondering...how does a bike messenger afford business class every day? While you're at it, can you tell me your life story? Much appreciated.*

No, I couldn't very well do that.

I started going to the gym the following week and blamed it on the bike messenger. Every time I was in Seattle, I vowed, I was going to visit the gym in the building next to the restaurant where I met with most of my potential clients.

I grumbled to myself as the strap to my gym bag got caught in something. The train station was packed with people, and it was the biggest downside to this exercise nonsense. The later departure was in the middle of when everyone got off work.

Juggling my gym bag and briefcase, I made it to the platform and stepped onto the train four minutes before we were to depart. My shoulder was stiff and sore, and I pressed a palm to it as I carefully rotated the muscle. I supposed I was shocking my system by lifting weights and dying on an exercise bike.

I entered the business-class section and found a—*He's here.* This was the first time we were on the same train going north. And this was certainly a surprise. I sat down across from him, eyeing the suit he wore. His expression wasn't as open and bright as it tended to be in the mornings. Now he fit in with the rest of us suited schmucks.

The plot thickens, I mused to myself.

He glanced up from his paper when I accidentally dropped my gym bag on the floor, and he seemed a little surprised to see me too.

"Bollocks. Sorry about that," I heard myself say. Frustration built rapidly, and it annoyed me. His appearance had thrown me. Now I knew even less how to place him.

"Don't worry about it." His voice was smoother and richer than I'd expected. An accent that didn't belong on the West Coast either.

That was that. I rearranged my bags before hauling out my laptop, and he read the paper all the way back to Camassia Cove. All while wearing a bespoke suit.

I couldn't concentrate, often casting looks his way. When his brow was furrowed, he appeared older. Now I couldn't even be certain we were the same age.

"You're late," Brianna pointed out.

"Sorry." I dipped down and kissed her cheek, then took my seat and opened the menu. "I haven't much time. I'm meeting with Ashley around the corner in..." I checked my watch. "Fifty-five minutes."

"Has she given up on competing against you for the promotion?"

"I hope so." I decided on a salad because I'd be having dinner with Ash. "Christ, what is this place?" Everything on the menu was vegetarian. "Anyway. How was your own meeting?"

"I signed the contract." She smiled widely, and I was

genuinely happy for her. She'd worked hard to flesh out her studies and turn them into a book. "Right now, we're just negotiating minor details."

"What?" I frowned. "You don't sign anything until all those minor details have been settled."

She was dismissive about it, and she ran a hand through her short hair. "My agent said there was nothing to worry about."

"Bullshit," I blurted, but come on. I worked with contracts on a daily basis. She needed to be careful. "What are the details?"

She disapproved of my foul language, though I'd stopped caring. She wasn't my mother.

"Go on, then." I sat back while a waitress came by to take our orders.

She rolled her eyes but answered nonetheless. "I want us to publish before Christmas, and I suppose the publisher is looking at next fall. Or early spring. Anything to avoid summer."

"That's not a minor detail." I shook my head. "You're talking of negotiating a whole year before you go to print, and it's almost September. I can guarantee they're done editing everything they're putting out before the holidays."

I'd flustered her, not to mention rained on her parade a bit, and I was sorry for that. However, she knew what I did for a living. She could've come to me.

"You got the deal," I said and reached across the table to squeeze her hand. "I'm very happy for you. We'll have to celebrate."

That seemed to thaw her slightly, and she launched into the more exciting aspects of the contract, such as PR and royalties. I managed to keep quiet when she revealed she was going to speak at universities and that there would be a marketing team to help her with branding. Again, it was what I did for a living, and no one could blame me for having opinions.

It was of no use to try to sway her. My sister was fiercely independent, and I was damn proud of her accomplishments. The first time one of her studies was published in a medical journal, I'd bought a copy and shown it to my coworkers.

I envied her sometimes. I did realize she was six years older than me, but I couldn't imagine I'd be where she was today in six years. My future was straightforward and predictable. Meanwhile, Brianna was always off to some conference in New York, seminar at Oxford, or convention in Shanghai.

Our food arrived, and I asked what she was working on at the moment—other than her book deal, and she became excited all over again.

"I'm helping a colleague, actually," she said. "He's researching escapism—how far we go to get away from our realities and what tools we use, such as film, literature, and online role-playing." She lifted a shoulder and took a sip of her wine. "Catfishing, cheating, et cetera. Where the lines are drawn between addiction and indulgence."

"So...normal, average stuff," I deadpanned. "Sounds fun."

She nodded, ignoring my sarcasm. "You'd be a wonderful candidate, little brother."

"What the fuck?" I was insulted, I was pretty sure.

She gave me a dismayed look for the cursing before diving into a ramble on why I should be part of their study.

For the record, I was doing no such thing.

I managed to squeeze in half a session at the gym after seeing Ashley. Then I had to hurry to make my train. I'd rushed out of the shower at the gym, so my hair was still bordering on wet when I got to my platform. The train was already there, and I had to run the last bit, all while juggling my gym bag, briefcase, and one stack of papers I'd been reading in the taxi toward the station.

I was breathing heavily by the time I made it onto the train and found my spot in the business-class section. The enigmatic suit moonlighting as a bike messenger—or vice versa—was here too. Just lovely. Collapsing into my seat, I dumped the papers on the table between us and tried to untangle my bags. *That's it.* I was buying a new bag; this one was absolutely useless.

Perhaps I should get a messenger bag that could hold my workout clothes as well as my laptop. Then, if my papers got wrinkled or damp from the towel... To hell with exercising, I wanted to say. It was that guy's bloody fault. His and his physique's.

"Rough day?"

My head snapped up at the sound of his voice, and I narrowed my eyes. *He's talking to me. He looks amused. And tired.* I straightened automatically and adjusted my tie.

"I've had better," I admitted.

He let out a low chuckle. "Usually how it goes."

I tilted my head, then nodded once, even though I wasn't sure I agreed. For now, I was stuck on his voice. Growing up all over the world had made me sensitive to dialects, and with more than "Don't worry about it" to go on, I could finally place him on the East Coast. I guessed Boston, though there was a hint of a drawl somewhere too.

I'd spent my high school years in North Carolina, muddling the London accent from my time in England. I wanted to say this man had spent time in Georgia or one of the Carolinas.

I decided that I was, in fact, older than him. Unless his eyes were deceiving me. The color was unforgettable.

"Friday tomorrow, thankfully." I wanted to learn more about him, and mindless chitchat was safe. "I hope to get friendly with one beer too many."

He smirked a little and nodded. "I hear ya."

There wasn't much more to say. Our mindless chitchat died out, though it was enough conversation for us to start saying good morning to each other when we got on the train from then on out.

CHAPTER 2

Jake was showing promise. I watched him work on something in his cubicle, while the others were more interested in deciding what to do for lunch. The bullpen outside my boss's office held twelve cubicles, and I knew how difficult it could be to concentrate here.

My regular team and I shared a smaller area on the other side of the elevators.

"You can go on in, Bennett."

I snapped out of my musings and rose from the little sofa outside Mr. Hayes's office.

"Cheers, love." I passed his assistant and entered his fishbowl of an office, the walls consisting of frosted glass. "Welcome back, sir," I said. "How was your vacation?"

To be frank, he looked like he needed another one. He both looked and carried himself like he was decades older than me, when in reality, it wasn't more than...two, three years? Or thereabouts.

He looked away from his computer and gestured for me to sit. "Thanks, Bennett, it was...all very fine. I have some good news to share with you."

Did I get the promotion? No, that was a ridiculous question. I'd landed three fairly large accounts this summer, but the hotel chain was what I assumed he'd base his decision on. We didn't have the account—yet—though I knew he'd gotten a meeting with them.

"First of all—" He reached for a folder on his desk and held it up. "This is wonderful." Oh, it was the contract for another account. "I take it the campaign isn't for anything seasonal? A little late to start the holiday promotions."

I shook my head and straightened. "Rebranding. I suggested commercials running on regional public transit. They're off shooting those now."

"Clever," he noted. "Unfortunately, I have to add more to your plate."

"Oh?" I was on the edge of my seat. *Tell me we have a shot.* I knew I'd be great at this. I burned for what I did, and I had ideas —if only I could get to present them.

He smiled faintly and opened a drawer in his desk. "I want you to put together a team, Bennett. You have two weeks to come up with a concept for your meeting with the reps of Westwater."

Holy fuck. I gusted out a breath as excitement filled me, and I nodded, doing my best to control my smile. No need to go megawatt on him. This was it. This was what I'd been waiting for. It was going to take me to the next level.

"Yes, sir." I accepted a folder from him, opening it briefly. It was his notes on the conversations he'd had with the hotel chain's marketing team, as well as notes for me. "Thank you for trusting me with this."

He waved that off. "You've earned it." Clasping his hands

on the desk, he gave me his full attention. "You're in for another few hectic weeks. I'll expect daily reports, and you have to tell me if you need assistance." He pointed at the folder. "You'll be delivering your pitch at their headquarters in Boston."

I nodded again, and it was getting hard to sit still. I wanted to shout from the rooftops, the relief was so overwhelming. "I'll be well prepared," I promised. "I want to be able to put everything into this. Can I get your advice on the Sportsmanship account and whether or not I give it to Ash?"

"She can join your crew," he replied. "I assume Sportsmanship is already used to discussing everything with you, so I need you to keep doing that. But do hand over some of the responsibilities to Ashley. It'll do her well to manage a team a little larger than her usual."

That made sense, and I added a mental reminder to bring her along to my meeting with them in Seattle next week.

"Dad!" I closed the door after myself and walked farther into his house, following the voices toward the backyard. I smiled instinctively as I heard Nate rambling about everything his teacher did wrong.

I found them on the little patio, my father sitting by the table under a large umbrella. Nate was near him, and he was munching on apple wedges.

Jess was running through the sprinklers, and he spotted me first. "Daddy!" Then my five-year-old was darting straight toward me.

I grinned and caught him when he jumped, neither of us caring he was soaked in cold water. "Hello, sweetheart." I kissed his cheek and situated him on my hip. "Did you have a good day with Grampa?"

"Yeah, we bought cookies after school," he laughed. "I had four!"

"Well, you're my cookie monster, aren't you?" I sat down next to my father.

"He actually didn't finish the last one," Nate said frankly. "So, he had three-and-a-half cookies."

"How about you give me three-and-a-half kisses?" I suggested.

My boys were polar opposites. Jess threw goofy grins and believed the loudest voice in the room was heard the best. Nate, my eight-year-old genius, was straightforward, quieter, and went for subtle sarcasm and lazy smirks. Unless he was in a cuddly mood; then I was given sweet smiles and Eskimo kisses.

"I don't believe that's possible," he muttered. "Half a kiss is just a small kiss, but a whole kiss nonetheless."

I snorted.

Dad huffed a chuckle and patted him on the bum. "Go kiss your father hello, you little nitpicker."

Jess wanted down, so I let him run back to the lawn where the sprinklers waited for him, and I got a moment with Nate. He offered me a hug, and I kissed him on the forehead and asked how school was.

"Mrs. Dillon is going to be a problem," he said. "She told me evolution is a *theory*." He looked positively scandalized, and I had to hand it to him. It was quite the issue. I winced internally and promised I'd look into things.

If I got this promotion, I'd be able to afford to get him into private school. The boy actually needed it. He was so far ahead.

"Thank you," he said, eyes showing his relief. It made me smile, and I touched his cheek. He was too adorable for words, this young adult. Both he and Jess took after me—brown hair, brown eyes, fair skin—but they could pull it off. What was recently making me feel subpar and forgettable, they aced. They were the most beautiful creatures I could possibly bring up in the world.

Nate excused himself to do his homework in the kitchen, which left me with Dad and his inquisitive expression.

"What?" I loosened my tie and shrugged out of my suit jacket. It was warm for September, though I wasn't complaining. Fall would follow soon, and then we'd have another dreary winter.

"You're happy about something," he said.

"Yes, sir." I couldn't contain it. "My boss put me in charge of the pitch to Westwater Hotels. If they accept our bid, I think the promotion is mine."

"Attaboy, proud'a ya." He nodded and sat back, lighting up what was left of a cigar. Despite being the gruff, retired army veteran from another generation that he was, he was as generous with affection and rewards as he was with structure and punishments. He'd brought up my sister and me without help for the most part, and he had high morals and, in my opinion, great wisdom.

There was no one I'd rather leave my kids with after school than my father. Unfortunately, his physical strength wasn't what it used to be. Shrapnel in his leg, a bad hip, and a knee that was mostly metal made him rely on a cane, and PTSD-related anxiety tired him out quickly. It was one of the reasons we'd eventually settled down in Camassia, where he was from. He was happiest here, where he could sit in his backyard, choose when he was mentally prepared to face crowds, and flirt with the neighborhood ladies who stopped by with casseroles and cookies.

"How are you feeling today?" I asked. He looked okay, but his pillbox was on the table.

He waved a hand and took a puff of his cigar. "I'm on the right side of the grass, so I can't complain."

My mouth twisted up. That was what he always said.

"You let me know if it gets to be too much with the boys—"

"Quit it," he grunted. "Picking up those boys every day is the only thing I have that gets me outta the house. I'll make you suffer if you take that away from me."

"No need to resort to threats," I replied, amused. "I still remember the lashing you gave Brianna when she tried to take away your crossword puzzles."

"She's too high tech, that girl," he grumbled. "I don't know where I went wrong with her. Electronic crossword puzzles?" He made me laugh. Brianna had given us PDAs for Christmas. I actually enjoyed mine. "What's wrong with the old-fashioned way, huh? Not a damn thing, that's what."

He'd already complained about it a few times.

"She converted me," I admitted. "I do my puzzles electronically now."

"Yeah, well," he huffed. "Maybe I do too."

I chuckled.

"Don't you tell her," he warned.

"No, sir." Wouldn't dream of it.

Unlike my sister who jet-setted between her townhouse in Seattle and her condo in Chicago, I lived a few streets away from Dad. This was Downtown in Camassia, and most houses were modest Victorian homes or brick painted in pastel colors. There were picket fences everywhere and two cars in most driveways.

Jess ran inside to go play his video games, Nate stumbled over some outdoor toys because he had his nose stuck in a book, and I walked behind him to pick up said toys. I left them in the wicker chest on the porch, then entered the house to get started on dinner.

Sleeves rolled up, tie thrown over my shoulder, I did the dishes while I waited for the pasta to boil. The upside to doing meal prep once a week was that I always had ready-made marinara in the freezer. It would only need a few minutes in the microwave.

I threw in a few hamburger patties for good measure and pulled together a salad from leftover vegetables, and then I told the boys to get ready for dinner. *What's next...?* I surveyed the kitchen, and it hit me. Setting the table might be a good idea. I had to prepare their lunches for tomorrow too. I had a work lunch, so I wouldn't need to bring anything.

After dinner, I helped Nate with his homework while Jess watched TV. He was trying to impress his big brother, which might explain why he was watching the news. Helping them with their baths came next, and we'd gotten good at this. We had our own routine, and my boys made it easy for me.

Of course, shit shot straight to hell some days too. The next morning, we were running late. I dropped a fussy Jess off at Dad's because it was too early to take him to kindergarten at six-fifteen, and then...then I forgot Nate. Sometimes I couldn't believe myself.

"I'm sorry, son," I said for the fourth time.

He yawned and shouldered his backpack higher. "It's okay."

No, it wasn't. Who the hell forgot that his son was in the car? After dropping off Jess, I always drove Nate to his friend's house. I had a deal with his parents; Nate ate breakfast with them, and I took the boys to soccer practice on Sunday mornings.

I would have to improvise today. On the way up to the platform where I took the train, I called my sister, who, thankfully, was home.

"Wait, I just woke up. You did what?" she asked tiredly.

"I may have forgotten to drop off Nate," I sighed.

My son snickered.

"Can he be with you today?" I asked her, stopping to buy him a ticket.

"You're taking him to Seattle?"

"Yes, we're waiting for the train now," I replied. "I have meetings in the city all day."

Nate was the most well-behaved child I knew, so if Brianna was busy, it wasn't a huge obstacle for me. It was for his sake. He'd be bored out of his mind tagging along with me.

"Bring him over," she said. "Or do you want me to meet you at the station?"

"I'll bring him to you," I said, relieved. "Thank you, sis."

"Anytime, love. Although, one might wonder why his mother can never be there."

I wasn't going to get into that with Brianna now.

The train rolled in a few minutes later, and I directed Nate to where I always sat.

Right as we got seated—Nate stealing my window seat with a sleepy grin—a certain man in black and neon blue followed.

"Good morning," I said, taking the aisle seat next to Nate.

"Morning." He nodded and sat down and stowed a duffle under his chair. He eyed my son curiously, then slid his tropical blue-green gaze my way. "I thought you'd found a better train. Been a while."

Oh. He'd wondered about me?

"I usually work here in town," I explained. "It's just this summer that's been different. And autumn, I suppose." I closed my mouth before I could overshare.

I missed having mates. From time to time, I had a beer with coworkers. Otherwise, my interactions were limited to people I was related to.

"My dad meets with important people in Seattle so he can get promoted," Nate elaborated.

I flicked him an amused look.

"Ah." The man gave him a smile. "You helpin' your father with the important people today?" The way he spoke—and it had to be a Boston accent—made father sound like *fahtha*.

Nate smirked slightly. "No, he forgot I existed until he arrived at the station and noticed I was in the back seat."

"Nathan," I chastised under my breath.

The man let out a laugh. It was a warm, infectious sound, one I couldn't help but smile at.

"That happens sometimes," the man admitted, eyes full of mirth.

Did it happen to him? Did he have kids, too?

I could no longer count on my son to carry the conversation, because he only snickered in response and then dug out his Nintendo. The man got comfortable and propped his foot on the vent under the table, and he grabbed his book that he'd put on the seat next to him.

I supposed I could go through my plans for my breakfast meeting...

It wasn't until we reached Seattle that the man joined in on a conversation again. I was telling Nate we'd take a taxi to Brianna's place, and I happened to refer to the neighborhood. The bike messenger who probably was a lot more than that weighed in, mentioning that the train would get us there faster at this hour. I'd never taken the public transit in Seattle, so I'd have to take his word for it.

I had an expense account, which meant I took a taxi or booked restaurants close to the train station.

"It's close to where I work," the man said. "I can let you know when to get off."

Okay, then. We followed him off the train, and I took Nate's hand so I wouldn't lose him in the morning rush-hour crowd. I figured I'd lost my head enough for one day.

Fifteen minutes later, we boarded the Link light rail heading north to U District.

Unlike our cushy Amtrak, the city transit was packed with people, and we ended up standing close to the doors. I grabbed on to one of the bars above me, and Nate found his grip on my leather belt since I had to hold my briefcase too.

"And I thought the underground in London was busy," I muttered.

The man heard me, and no wonder, we were as packed as sardines here.

"So you are British," he said.

Had he been wondering again?

I lifted a shoulder. "My mother was English. American father." She'd been a teacher where my dad was stationed in South Korea. It was how they met. My time in the UK had been restricted to a few years at an all-boys school before we moved to North Carolina. And after that, summers to visit Mum's family.

No need to get into the way army brats grew up.

"You're not from around here either," I noted.

"Quincy," he replied. "South of Boston." I'd thought as much. "Then I took a left and ended up out here."

I cracked a smirk. That was a far left.

The train jostled, and I gripped the bar tighter. It came to a stop, several people around us huddling while others pushed through to get off. Others came on. Nate shuffled closer and peered up and around him, visibly curious and fascinated by city life.

The air was stale and stuffy, and in a moment when we

stood still, I managed to loosen my tie a little. Then we were moving again. I felt bad for crowding the man, though I didn't have much choice. We were almost chest-to-chest, and it didn't look like I was going anywhere anytime soon.

"Kieran, by the way." His close proximity sent a whiff of mint and coffee my way.

I swallowed, feeling weird. My stomach grew tight. "Bennett."

I caught his smile in my periphery. Why I couldn't look him directly in the eye befuddled me. Possibly because I was a fan of personal space, and there was none here.

"Good. Now I don't have to refer to you as Oatmeal Guy in my head."

At that, I couldn't help but face him, and I frowned. "Pardon?"

He chuckled quietly. "I'm pretty sure you had oatmeal on your shirt the first time I saw you."

"Brilliant," I huffed. I couldn't say I was surprised. When you had kids, there was always a stain somewhere, and Jess was a thrower when he had a hissy fit. I shook my head and smiled ruefully. "Kieran." I tested his name. "I guess that tops Bike Messenger."

He offered a full-on grin at that. "Only until noon."

"And then?" I couldn't help but ask.

The train slowed as it approached the next station, and Kieran told me this was our stop.

"Cheers," I said. *Waiting*. I had to solve this mystery so I could move on.

"And then I'm the boss," he added.

I looked at him quizzically.

He nodded down to the logo on his chest. "It's my company."

"Oh." Huh. I didn't know what to do with that. He worked as a messenger at the company he ran?

Could the man be more frustrating? I loathed enigmas, yet they drew me in. Perhaps because I liked to figure things out, even when they drove me bonkers.

When the day was over, I turned to my sister. She was the best sounding board I had, but I planned on rethinking that after I'd vented and she laughed at me.

"That's rude," I accused.

She kept chuckling while she set aside the teapot, and I slumped back in a seat at the kitchen table. Nate was watching a documentary in the living room, so I had time to sulk.

"This is just so very you, Bennett," Brianna said. "It's why I wanted you to partake in my colleague's study."

"Will you stop seeing me as a subject to research?" I griped.

"Where's the fun in that?" She grinned and brought our tea over. "Make no mistake, the theory is not without flaws. But you, my dear little brother, are easy. You seek out mystery and suspense because you lack it."

"Ouch." I would never accuse her of mincing words, that was for sure. "You're saying my life is dull."

"No, Bennett." Her gaze softened. "*You* are. You haven't been happy in quite some time, and you continually beat yourself up for everything Allison does. It isn't fair to you."

I flinched at the mention of my wife.

"When is she coming home?" she asked.

"Ah—" I cleared my throat and focused on stirring the lemon in my tea. "Since she took classes over the summer, she said she'd try to make it home most weekends starting in a few weeks." I set the spoon on the saucer. "Can we change the topic now?"

I didn't enjoy discussing Allison. There were too many conflicting emotions. Most of the time, I was stuck between missing her and resenting her. The latter sparked guilt that weighed heavily on me.

My sister and I didn't have the best experiences with female role models, though she had certainly turned into one herself. Our mum left us when I was eleven, only to make that a habit. She would get bored and leave, come home when she missed us, then leave again. When I was fourteen, she died in a bus accident in Brazil.

Brianna didn't push it, thankfully. "You should ask this Kieran out for a beer. You need more friends in your life."

She wasn't wrong. The problem was I didn't know how to make friends as an adult. Was there a protocol? If I asked him to meet up for happy hour and he didn't have time, did that mean he wasn't interested or that he genuinely didn't have the time? I could always count on my father to watch the boys, but most men and women my age lived on a tight schedule.

"I'll think about it." I took a sip of my tea before checking the time. One cup, then I'd tear Nate away from the TV.

CHAPTER 3

This was a wonderful idea. I'd have to buy Dad a box of cigars as a thank-you. Not only was Jess at a good age to learn how to swim, but I got to meet new people. This was the second lesson, and I'd already spoken to three people I wasn't related to.

I grinned to myself as Jess jumped into the water with the other kids. Then I walked over to the corner of the pool where there was a modest café for parents and proud grandparents.

I ordered a cup of coffee, regretting that decision as soon as I sat down. In this heat and humidity, I should've bought a bottle of water.

"Rookie mistake."

I looked up to see a woman smiling ruefully.

"Mind if I sit?"

"By all means." I nudged out the chair next to me. "I was just thinking how foolish it was to buy coffee."

She laughed softly and pulled her blond hair back into a

ponytail. She struck me as a very ordinary mum—no makeup, unwashed hair, and perhaps she was lacking a bit of sleep. I found her all the more appealing for it. It was relatable. Maybe I wore a suit—because I hadn't been home yet today—but underneath it all, I was ready to fall asleep on my feet. I was hungry too.

"I'm Maggie." She extended a hand.

"Bennett. Nice to meet you." I shook her hand and smiled politely. "Which one of the little rascals is yours?"

She peered over at the pool and pointed. "Jaylin—the five-year-old goofball clinging to the instructor."

I smiled at the little girl, dark hair plastered across her face, as she expressed her excitement about something. Like my Jess, she loved the water.

"She's precious."

"What about you?" she asked. "I think I saw you last week. You have two boys, right?"

I pointed out Jess in the water, another one who fit the goofball bill, then loosened my tie. "Two, yes. Nathan's my eldest. He's eight going on eighty and wanted to spend the evening with his grandfather instead."

Maggie chuckled. "I know that feeling. My husband was going to take Jaylin to swimming lessons, but he not-so-subtly suggested this might do me good. I don't get out of the apartment much otherwise, and I crash at nine."

"Nine is *late*," I joked. "I could drop at seven."

"Right?" Her eyes lit up.

The second week of October quickly became the best week I'd had in a long time. The account with Westwater Hotels was mine, as was the promotion, and my new office next to my boss's had a much better view than I was used to. Gone was the alleyway behind the building. Now I saw cobblestone streets, trendy brownstones, and our little train station when I looked out the window.

The color of the trees had shifted to reds and yellows, and the awful weather couldn't dampen my mood. I even found myself smiling at the ridiculous number of carved pumpkins.

This was what I'd been waiting for. My life was going to turn around now. I could feel it.

As a thank you, I took my boss and his wife out for dinner that night. At my fourth use of "sir," he chuckled and told me he was just Ellis outside the office. He admitted to feeling weird about being a sir to me since we were practically the same age.

If you didn't have kids early, you didn't have to get a late start to your career. Around the time he'd started his business, I'd been wading through diapers.

When I came home that night, I put the boys to bed before crash-landing on the couch in the living room with my phone in hand. It was time to call Allison, and I was pretty sure she noticed my mood the second I said hello.

Next, she gasped. "You got the promotion!"

I grinned and adjusted the pillow behind my head. "I did. You're now married to the latest account exec at the Three Dots Agency."

"Aw, congratulations! I'm so proud of you, Bennett. We'll have to celebrate when I get home on Friday."

I sat straight up. "You're coming home?"

She'd told me she'd be home most weekends this fall, but she'd said similar things before.

"I'm coming home," she confirmed. "And no classes on Monday, so you'll be stuck with me all weekend."

I couldn't fucking wait. See? Things were already looking up. A few months ago, I'd jokingly suggested to myself I could try cocaine to shake me to life. Now everything was falling into place.

"I miss you." I couldn't even describe how much I missed human contact. I wanted to hold her, breathe her in, kiss her silly, and make love for hours. Or twenty minutes, at least.

"I miss you too," she replied softly. "Only two years to go."

I nodded, even though she couldn't see me. To me, there was no "only" about it. Since it was my fault she'd missed out on college the first time, I would never stand in her way. I supported her with every fiber of my being, but it *was* hard. Especially because we had the boys.

"I'm getting better at cooking," I said out of the blue. "I think. Nate doesn't hate it anymore."

She laughed. "I did notice you were better last time I was home." Yeah, four goddamn months ago. A surge of resentment rose quickly, and I had to fight it into submission. It wasn't the time to go there. "Remember when you tried to cook for our first date?"

How was I supposed to know you couldn't throw frozen chicken in a skillet?

"Best Burger King meal I ever had." I smiled to myself, thinking back. From then on, we'd ordered takeout for every anniversary. It was a silly little thing.

"Yeah," she said, and there was mumbling going on in the background. "I'm heading out with a couple girlfriends, but we can catch up on Friday, right? I'll make you your favorite."

I squinted at nothing. "Heading out" was probably the sentence I hated the most. Not that I told her that. I wouldn't begrudge her some fun with her friends while I sat at home and took care of every little fucking thing—Christ. I blew out a breath and repeated *"I just got promoted, I just got promoted"* in my head. It was a good day.

"I'll see you then," I answered.

"Okay, love you!"

"You too." I ended the call and slumped back against the cushions again.

I hadn't been to Seattle in a while, and I had three meetings there tomorrow. I should go to bed. I should shower. I should pack lunches for Nate and Jess. Maybe if I just closed my eyes for five minutes first.

The week continued to be cooperative. It was a bit touch and go when I woke up way too late—on the bloody couch—but Dad swooped in and saved the day, and I made it just in time to board the train.

Sans gym bag. I was in Camassia more often than Seattle now, so I'd bought myself a membership at a local gym.

Kieran was in his seat, dressed in a suit today.

"Good morning, Kieran." I sat down across from him and unbuttoned my jacket.

He looked up from his paper, half surprised. "Mornin', stranger." His eyes truly were something else. The depths of those blue-green pools caught me off guard every time it'd been a week or two since I'd seen him. "I was thinking about replacing you. At least Joy in 4A shows up every day."

I chuckled and let my briefcase stay on the next seat. I wasn't going to get any work done anyway.

"Definitely replacing you. You're in a good mood," he said. "You don't belong on my train."

"It's been a good week." I relaxed in my seat as the train departed, and I was happy Kieran seemed to welcome the chat this morning. "My boss promoted me."

"Well, hey. Congrats, man." He slanted a lazy smirk. "Does that mean more or less commuting?"

"Less going to Seattle, more going to Boston." I watched his features alter slightly, remembering him telling me he was from a place south of Boston. Now he struck me as a little wistful. "Do you miss it?" I heard myself ask. *Bollocks*. It probably wasn't something I should ask a virtual stranger.

He didn't seem to mind. "Sometimes. I wish I had the time to visit my family more often."

I didn't know how to respond. My curiosity about this man hadn't faded one bit, and it irritated me to go with a safer topic. "I noticed you're not the bike messenger today." I nodded at his outfit. "I take it the boss has a full schedule?"

"That, and I'll ride a bike in this fucking weather when hell freezes over."

I let out a laugh, surprised by his answer. I decided he was rugged, much more so than I could ever be. If I used the term, I'd go so far as to call him *street*. He hadn't been born with his bespoke suit on, that was for certain. And, of course, that sparked my interest further. Was he one of those great American tales of success? Did he come from nothing and build his own empire?

I wanted to know, and I didn't know why. Maggie didn't spark my curiosity as much, and I found her lovely to befriend. I'd have to ask my sister. She could usually fish out an answer after digging into my brain.

"Any fun plans this weekend?" Oh, so he wanted to talk more. I liked that.

"My wife is coming home for a visit," I replied, twisting my wedding band around my finger. "She got a late start because we had kids, so she's going to college now in Chicago."

Kieran didn't know what to do with that. His forehead creased. "Huh. Did you live there before or something?"

That was a polite way of asking why Allison didn't go to a local college, a question I asked myself every day.

"She's from there originally," I said. "It worked out since she can stay with her parents while attending school."

"Ah. Gotcha." He really didn't, and that was okay; I didn't get it either, but he dropped the subject. "Your weekend will be more exciting than mine, I bet. My in-laws are visiting, and I kinda wanna kill myself."

I grinned instinctively, and my sister's words came to me. About making friends, about going out for beers. I found myself hesitating, or maybe not hesitating, just...having doubts about how to ask him. Not to mention the tension it could create if he wasn't interested.

Hey. Backbone: find it.

I cursed internally and ran a hand through my hair. Happy hour—I could go with that.

"That's why we drink, isn't it?" It wasn't the worst way to broach this. "If you ever want to try this thing called happy hour that people keep talking about, let me know."

There. I left it up to him—without obligation, but with the offer right in front of him.

His brows lifted a fraction, and he pinched his bottom lip. "See, that's an offer no Irish kid from Quincy can refuse."

Thank goodness. My chest fluttered strangely, and the relief hit me harder than expected. Perhaps I wasn't entirely useless when it came to making friends.

Kieran dug out his wallet from the inside of his suit, and he retrieved a business card that he gave to me. "Shoot me a text when you wanna go out."

Hell, he was leaving it up to me again. I accepted the card and glanced at it briefly. *Jet City Express Delivery. Kieran Marshall, CEO.*

"I'll be in touch, definitely." I pocketed the card. Deciding that giving him my card in return would only say "Look, I also have a business card," I racked my brain for something else to talk about. My gaze landed on his paper, more specifically the section he'd left open on the seat next to him. "Are you and your family moving?"

He looked down at the listings for houses and inclined his head. "Hopefully. We're cramped in an apartment in the Valley, and I want a yard for my girl." Cedar Valley was where I worked and from where we took the train every morning. Ever since the community college had opened there, the population had become a lot younger. Old factories had turned into lofts that were shared by students who couldn't afford a place of their own. "Where do you live?"

"Downtown," I replied. "A couple minutes from the marina."

"That's the district I'm eyeing the most, but the wife has her sights set on Ponderosa." Fancy. He'd certainly find better schools there for his daughter. It was where I hoped to enroll Nate as soon as possible. Ponderosa was north of Downtown and had the only private school in town.

Real estate was a safe topic, and we discussed the housing market for the better part of the trip to Seattle. By the time we reached the city, I discovered I wasn't as insecure anymore. It was okay to unclench and just have a conversation with someone.

"You could've at least offered a challenge." Brianna tsk'd over the phone. "He's your cocaine."

I rolled my eyes inwardly and crossed the street as I flagged down a nearby taxi. "He's certainly not a drug. That would imply I'm addicted to him." I got into the car and said I was going to the train station. After a day of meetings and budget negotiations, I was ready to be home. "I'm only baffled about why I care to get to know him."

"You don't start out as an addict," she pointed out. "For recreational users, it begins with curiosity, doesn't it?"

I never should've told her I was considering taking up drugs as a hobby. For heaven's sake, it'd been a joke.

Brianna sighed and cut me some slack, at last. "You seek adventure, Bennett. There is nothing weird about that. For some reason, Kieran stands out. He piqued your interest, and now he's a puzzle to solve. I'm sure you'll be more at ease once you discover he's just another guy." She paused. "I, for one, think it's wonderful you're connecting with new people. I've been worried."

"I suppose I'm a bit rusty."

"Understandable. You've forgotten your social skills because parents have no lives."

Then there was that. My sister was never having children, and she often made remarks—tongue in cheek—how parents were tied down by macaroni jewelry and silly string. I would've taken her more seriously if she didn't often complain about how rarely she saw Nate and Jess.

Thanksgiving was coming up in a little over a month, so that was my answer when she predictably asked when she'd see her nephews again.

"Unless you want to come up for dinner on Saturday..." I let that hang there and smirked.

"Er, I'm terribly busy, I fear." She let her practiced American accent slip whenever she lied. "No, Thanksgiving is better. I'll spend the night and take the boys to a movie the day after." She just didn't want to see Allison, who wouldn't be home for Thanksgiving. Another hard pill to swallow, although she'd given me plenty of notice. "We'll have to celebrate your promotion too."

"I want cake," I told her. She knew which one I liked too. She laughed. "Consider it done."

The day after, I took Jess to his swimming lesson. Maggie was there, and we'd reached the stage in our developing friendship where she could tease me about the obvious excitement I displayed at seeing Allison tomorrow. Maggie even called me *cute*.

Then she smiled wistfully. "I wish my husband would be that happy to see me."

I chuckled and took a swig of my water. "I haven't seen my wife in four months." Come to think of it, it was the longest we'd spent apart since we met.

"Still." Maggie waved it off and smiled. "I bet the boys are excited."

Oh. Well... "I haven't told them yet," I admitted, to her evident surprise. "She's canceled last minute a couple times before, so I reckoned it would be best to make it a surprise." Just in case.

I worried about Nathan the most where Allison was concerned. Jess would scream at the top of his lungs and launch himself into Allison's arms. Nate was different. He'd grown quite guarded in the last year, and his welcome would be cooler.

"It must be hard, all of this." Maggie's eyes flashed with concern, reserved for my sons. "What are her plans for after graduation?"

That was an easier one. For as far away as Allison was now, her future would bring her much closer. "She already has a job lined up in Seattle." One of her closest friends worked at a local news station there, where she'd join the finance department. Said friend was also sleeping with one of the producers, but I wasn't supposed to know that. "Where do you work? I don't think you told me."

Maggie quirked her lips. "I'm a good little Catholic housewife. I volunteer sometimes, but for the most part, I'm just home."

"Ah." I couldn't imagine. "Do we have a Catholic church in Camassia?" We'd moved here the summer before I went off to college. I felt like I should know.

"Oh, yes. Up in Ponderosa," she replied.

She went on to tell me about the church activities, such as an annual coat drive and biannual fundraiser for veterans, and I listened with one ear while I snuck glances at what Jess was doing.

She's here.

I watched her step out of the cab with her carry-on and a thick scarf she threw around her neck.

"Boys, come down here!" I called. Closing the dishwasher, I smiled in anticipation and wondered how long my luck would last. This week certainly had been wonderful. I heard Jess stomping down the stairs, his brother following and sounding less like a little dinosaur.

"Is it dinner?" Jess asked and wiped his nose on his arm.

I snorted and washed my hands after dealing with the dirty dishes. "Not yet, but you can answer the door in...four...three..." Allison climbed the steps to the porch. "Two...one—"

A key wriggled in the lock in the hallway, and Jess flew out of the kitchen.

His shrill excitement followed. "Mummy!"

My gut clenched in a not entirely pleasant way, and I felt like a bitter son of a bitch. It wasn't fair of me to be jealous. I wondered if this was what Maggie felt, because right now, all I wanted was for Jess to greet me the way he greeted Allison. Then I reminded myself I saw Jess every day, and that did... nothing to dissolve the jealousy.

There was a pitiful voice in the back of my head that demanded acknowledgment from our sons that Daddy was a bit better because he never left.

As I wiped my hands on a towel, I spied Nate smiling hesitantly in the kitchen doorway, eyes no doubt trained on Allison and Jess.

"Nate," I said softly. "Go say hi to your mum."

He nodded jerkily and left the doorway, disappearing from sight. For a moment, all I heard was Allison gushing over the boys and Jess making plans for us this weekend. Each request was fired off rapidly, and my wife had to remind him to breathe.

I gave them a minute before it was my turn to lean against the doorframe, and my mouth twisted up as I saw all three of them on the floor. Allison was peppering Nate's face with kisses, slowly thawing him out.

Allison spotted me, hugged Nate closer, and beamed at me. "Bennett."

"Welcome home."

After making myself a cup of tea, I donned a jacket and stepped out onto the terrace in the backyard. It was my thinking place on sleepless nights. The neighborhood was quiet, and I was greeted by the stunning sky and its millions of stars.

My breath fogged in the cold.

I'd turned and twisted for hours, so I was done thinking on this particular night. Instead, I brought out my phone and sent the message I'd debated over whether or not I should send for the past half hour.

Was your weekend as awful as you predicted?

I didn't expect a response, given the hour, so I was surprised to see his text show up.

Who's this?

I took a sip of my tea and replied.

I'm not Joy in 4A with the perfect train attendance.

He sent a smiley, with a colon and a parenthesis, then sent another message.

Shame. I should give her my number.

I chuckled into the mug, and he texted me once more.

Worse than I predicted. How was yours? Shouldn't you be ravishing the missus before she's off again?

"You'd think," I muttered. My reunion with Allison on Friday had left a lot to be desired, but that was understandable. She'd been tired, and catching up with the boys was, of course, a priority. Saturday had been marginally better. Sunday too. Now it was technically Monday, and she was leaving in a few hours.

Sorry to hear about your weekend. Mine was all right, albeit exhausting. Back to normal tomorrow.

I took another swallow of my tea while he responded, and I looked down at my feet. My plain slippers were a keepsake from a hotel, and they didn't stand a chance against the damp floorboards of the terrace.

You going to Seattle this week?

Unfortunately not.

No. Between now and Thanksgiving, I have two work trips to Boston and one to Portland, and I

haven't assembled my team yet. It's going to be a busy month.

Conversation lulled while I finished my tea and peered up at the night sky.

It really was going to be a busy month. In fact, wasn't I always going to be busier now? The Westwater account would be my main focus for years to come, I hoped. I'd be making quarterly trips to their headquarters in Boston, leaving me one day a week for meetings with my regular clients in Seattle. Before Thanksgiving, though, a coworker would cover those for me.

My phone buzzed with a new message from Kieran.

When was the last time you did something crazy?

My forehead creased, and I reread the text several times. *Crazy* didn't have a spot in my life. Sort of like cocaine.

I was in college and remember it vividly. Because nine months later, we had Nathan.

Kieran ha-ha'd at that before typing another message.

Get some sleep, Ben. And text me when you wanna go out.

I *hated* being called Ben. I'd never been able to figure out why, only that it made my blood boil. Perhaps I was too tired to muster any anger now, though, because I ignored it and sent a last message.

Will do. Goodnight, Kieran.

CHAPTER 4

During the next several weeks, I often found myself wanting to go out with Kieran for a beer or four, but I just never had the time. We texted sometimes; he sent me a few updates on official train news, like the one time Joy in 4A wasn't in her seat. Kieran suspected alien abduction, until the next day when she was back.

He made me laugh.

Thanksgiving was a lovely holiday that I got to spend with my boys, Dad, and my sister. Despite missing Allison and believing she should've been there, it was relaxing, in a way, to be alone with my immediate family.

Wednesday the following week, I came to work early so I could get as much done as possible. I was heading out with Dad, Nate, and Jess later to pick out a tree, which would be our second year doing it. It was going to be my tradition, something the Brooks boys did together.

Being first in the office that morning was nice. The place

was quiet, and I stood by the window and had my first coffee in utter silence. No fax machines buzzing, no phones ringing, and no crowded cubicle area.

My eyebrows lifted, and I nearly coughed around a mouthful of steaming coffee. I hadn't realized that my view of the train station meant I could see Kieran, but there he was. He stepped onto the platform, briefcase in one hand, the morning paper in the other. He was too far away to detect his mood or features, though I could see it was him.

I sent him a text.

It's thirty degrees out. Wear a scarf.

He dug out his phone and read the message, followed by his head snapping up. I grinned, watching as he looked to see if I was nearby.

God? Is that you? Sorry about the porn mags when I was twelve.

I laughed and replied to him.

I'm in my office. Consider me the friendly neighborhood CCTV.

His response made me laugh again.

This is America, son. Keep that British Big-Brother bullshit across the pond.

The next time I saw Kieran wasn't until December 19th. I lingered in Seattle after just coming home from Boston, only so I could get on the train I knew he took home every day. I was tired as hell. My mood was sour. The text he'd sent me that one time—about when the last time was I did something crazy—had been going on a loop in my head for a solid week.

My promotion was supposed to turn my life around. Everything was supposed to be great now. I had more ups than downs, but I couldn't shake the feeling of being stuck. Did all people my age go through this? Possibly. I couldn't be the only one who constantly asked, "Is this it?"

Adventure seeker, my sister had called me. Right. I had to be the worst one of them, though the fact remained. I wanted to do something crazy. Anything to shake up the dust particles that had settled on my existence.

Spotting Kieran already in his seat, I made my way over and cut straight to it.

"We should go out and get smashed." I sat down and pushed my carry-on under my seat. "I'm talking ridiculous, can't-walk-straight drunk."

He looked at me in surprise in the few seconds it took him to process my popping up out of the blue, not saying hello, and then my statement. His trademark smirk followed. "Hey to you too. And sure. Say when."

"When," I joked. All right, I wasn't the funniest guy I knew. "Tomorrow?" Tonight was Jess's last swim lesson for the semester, and Allison was already home. We were all going to go see Jess and his group show off what they'd learned this year, and then...well, it was the holidays. With my wife home, we had plans. Dinners, preparations for Christmas, office holiday party, New Year's.

Kieran winced. "Dinner with the in-laws. How about Saturday?"

Fuck. Was this how it was going to play out? "Office party," I replied and ran a hand through my hair.

"And we're going to Boston to see my family on the 26th..."

"Being an adult bloody well sucks sometimes," I blurted out.

"No shit." He chuckled lazily and stretched out his legs under the table between us. "You know...it doesn't have to be an evening."

I quirked a brow in question.

He shrugged, weaving his fingers together across his toned stomach. "Next time you have work in the city, we'll hit up a bar before we go home."

So...Happy Hour to the Extreme. Because I was going to drink so much I passed out.

"After the holidays, I'll be in Seattle every Wednesday," I said.

"First Wednesday in January, it is." He nodded. "How's life otherwise?"

"Dull." I felt I could be honest with him. Perhaps I'd lost a few fucks in the past several weeks. Something had to give—soon. "What about you?"

He smiled and nodded once. "Same."

"Jesus, it's like Florida in here," Dad grunted.

Exiting the men's locker room, I told him to go find a seat so he could rest his bad leg. Allison and Nate were already waiting over by the café.

"You promise you'll watch every second, Daddy?" Jess looked up at me and extended a pinkie.

I hooked it with mine. "Of course. I promise, buddy." I guided him to the other side of the pool where his instructor and fellow swimmer kiddos were waiting for the last people to show up.

Maggie's daughter waved madly when spotting us and ran over.

"Hiii, Mr. Bennett! Hi, Jess!"

I grinned. "Hello, darling." Squatting down in front of Jess, I hung a towel around his shoulders and pressed a kiss to his forehead. "Mum and I will take so many pictures you'll be seeing them for years."

He giggled and nodded excitedly.

"Will you take pictures of all of us when we swim?" Jaylin asked. When Maggie had told me Jaylin was a goofball, she hadn't been joking. The girl was absolutely precious and had no idea what personal space was. "I can count to ten and not breathe under the water!" She beamed proudly, revealing two missing teeth, and played with my tie.

"That's very impressive." I brushed away a water droplet from her cheek.

"I can count to eleven," Jess boasted.

I snorted, and I wasn't even sure Jaylin had heard him. She let out a squeal and bounced off, shouting, "Daddy!"

I glanced over my shoulder—*holy shit*—and did a double take. Kieran was Jaylin's dad? Kieran was Maggie's husband?

"Hey, monkey, no running." He chuckled and caught her, picking her up to leave loud kisses on her cheeks. He'd spotted me before I'd seen him, I assumed. He was wearing his smirk as he carried Jaylin over to us. "Twice in one day, man. It must be Christmas."

I laughed under my breath and rose to a stand. "I didn't know you were Jaylin's father."

"Oh yeah?" He let the girl down again as the kids' instructor summoned them for a warm-up. "Funny, because I knew you were Nate and Jess's pop."

My brow furrowed. How the...

"Mags told me," he explained. "For the past few months, it's been Bennett this and Bennett that."

I didn't know what to make of that. "You can throw Joy in 4A in my face but not tell me your wife knows me?"

"And miss the surprise on your face when I showed up just now? Fuck no." He found this way too funny. With a chin nod, he took the lead to go to where all the other family members were gathered. "I think my wife has a crush on you."

I shook my head, baffled.

Okay, so it was time for introductions, then. In a second, we'd gone from two guys who may or may not become mates to...whatever this was. Two husbands, two wives, kids at a holiday swim meet. What was next, wine tastings and barbecues? For some reason, I wasn't a fan of this development.

I supposed I wanted something for myself, something that was only mine. I wanted a buddy I could meet up with every now and then without Allison being chummy with him too.

Maggie handled the introductions until it was my turn, and I introduced her and Kieran to Allison and my father.

"Very nice to meet you both." Allison smiled and shook Maggie's hand.

The place was crowded this evening, and we ended up standing by the wall on the short end of the pool. Dad had managed to grab a chair from the café, and he had Nate sitting on his good knee, both immersed in the game Nate played on his Nintendo. And when Allison and Maggie started chatting like they'd known each other forever, I felt like I'd lost something.

It was principle more than anything. Maggie and I weren't *that* close. But it was a reminder. Allison and I were married, and contrary to our current situation, we were sharing our life together. There was no mine and yours, only ours.

Kieran came to stand next to me, and he leaned in a bit. "Why do you look like someone kicked your puppy?"

I deflated and blew out a breath. I was being ridiculous, surely.

"Just a headache," I lied. Folding my arms across my chest, I kept my gaze fixed on the kids as they jumped into the water. "You have the most adorable daughter, by the way."

I caught his smile in the corner of my eye.

"She's the light of my life," he murmured. He was watching the children as well. "If it weren't for her, I don't know where I'd be today."

The frustration within me faded, and the next breath came easier. I knew what he was talking about; I knew that exact feeling.

Originally, I'd wanted Kieran to be an escape. Someone I could get wasted with and forget my day. My sister was right; I was looking for something. Something *other*. Something I didn't have already. Instead, we were bonding over our children, and that was okay too.

It was forty-five minutes of the children showing they could float, duck their heads underwater, take a few swim strokes, and jump from the edge of the pool.

"Honey?" Allison slipped her hand into mine and kissed my bicep. "I've invited Maggie and Kieran over for dinner after the holidays."

And there we go.

"Sounds great." I managed a smile and kissed her temple.

She went back to talking to Maggie, and I took another few photos of Jess.

"We're gonna be those people now," Kieran said under his breath.

"Yup. Trivial Pursuit Night, here we come."

"Fuck." His muttered response made me chuckle. "No offense, but—"

"Don't." I shook my head, only glad he got it. "That's why I looked like someone kicked my puppy."

I didn't want double dates and all that *couple stuff*.

"It's official," he told me. "If you cancel on me in Seattle, I'll kick your fucking ass."

I tilted my head and studied him, and I couldn't help but wonder if he needed the same thing I did—as much as I did.

Was he also sick of the mundane? We'd obviously made our choices, but it had to be okay to take a breather every now and then.

"First drink's on me." I nudged his side with my elbow.

"Deal."

That was how Kieran Marshall became my friend.

"Daddy."

Jess *never* whispered.

Rousing from sleep on a somewhat high Dad-alert system, I cracked one eye open to find both Nate and Jess staring at me. They'd switched on the lamp on the nightstand—oh, bloody hell, it was only four-thirty. I blinked drowsily and yawned, dragging a hand over my scruffy jaw. They wore matching sleepy grins, bed heads, and red PJs with snowmen.

I looked over my shoulder, seeing that Allison was still sleeping, then faced the boys again.

"What's wrong?" I whispered.

It was one thing to expect them to wake up early on Christmas morning. This was taking things too far.

Jess gestured with his hand, urgent. He wanted me to go somewhere. "Come, we hafta do the song."

"Like last year," Nate filled in quietly.

The little buggers drew an involuntary smile from me. God, how I loved them. Shaking off the exhaustion, I agreed and told them to meet me downstairs. Then I dragged myself out of bed without waking Allison and tightened the drawstrings of my sweatpants. After a quick detour to the bathroom, I was ready to head downstairs.

The sight that greeted me in the living room spread warmth in my chest. It was a stolen moment, one for only us as Allison slept on. The Christmas tree cast a glow over the living room, and I walked over to the fireplace to light a fire while the boys got comfortable under Nate's duvet on the couch. They'd somehow wrestled my old guitar out of the closet in the hallway and had taken it out of the case.

Before last year, I hadn't played since high school, and I hadn't touched it since last Christmas.

"Stop kicking me," Nate scolded Jess.

"You're in my space," Jess argued.

"Be nice, boys." I ruffled Jess's sleep-tousled hair and passed the couch to make a quick trip to the kitchen. If last year had started another tradition, the predawn morning wouldn't be complete without hot chocolate and whipped cream.

I went with an insta-mix and nuked three mugs in the microwave.

I must've forgotten my phone down here last night because I found it on the kitchen island while I waited for the cocoa to finish. I had a text from Kieran waiting for me. He'd sent it a few minutes past midnight.

Merry Christmas.

I brushed my thumb over the message, a smile tugging at the corners of my mouth.

Merry Christmas, Kieran.

I returned to the living room with three mugs topped off with too much whipped cream, and Jess's eyes lit up like the sun.

My place was on the floor, back against the middle spot of the couch, and I pushed away the coffee table a bit to get more room. Nate grunted and handed over the guitar, and he reminded me I had to tell the story too. It couldn't just be the song. It had to be accompanied by the story.

"Of course." I nodded and took a sip of the cocoa before doing my best to tune the old instrument. Dad had given it to me on my fifteenth birthday with a note saying, "Use it with reckless love more than tender care. It was the way Thomas lived."

The guitar had belonged to Thomas, Dad's closest friend who'd died a couple years after they'd returned from Vietnam.

Rusty would've been an upgrade for how I played, though this particular song came back to me fairly naturally. My dad had written the text, dedicated to me, without knowing they were lyrics. Brianna had her own page filled with Dad's words, which she'd chosen to frame as a picture.

"Once upon a Christmas," I started the story as I tinkered, "a young man sat up all night and watched his pregnant wife as she slept. His son would be born in a few weeks."

"That's Grampa, right? It's Grampa." Jess had already finished his beverage, and he leaned over to set his mug on the table. "He's old now."

I chuckled quietly and nodded slowly, finding the familiar, unhurried rhythm of the song I'd come up with when I was seventeen.

"The young man prayed for words of wisdom," I went on. "Words he could one day give his son. He prayed for advice, and then he remembered his best friend."

"That's Thomas," Jess whispered.

"Be quiet," Nate hissed. "I wanna hear."

I smiled to myself, feeling Jess shuffling around behind me. His head landed on my shoulder, and he started playing with my ear.

"He spent the night before Christmas thinking of his best friend and everything the young man had learned from him. He sat by the tree and wrote in his journal what he imagined his best friend would tell him now." I eased into the next bit, the first verse, and I hoped my singing voice didn't sound like shit. "Oh, but James, you have your own book in the Book of James...

As the body without the spirit is dead, so faith without deeds is dead, so my James..." I hummed quietly, a shiver of contentment flowing through me. "You tell your boy one day, what a good deed is."

Nate was next to cuddle closer once his hot chocolate was gone, the duvet rustling as he got settled. His head rested on my other shoulder, and when Jess stopped playing with my ear, Nate took over. His fingers walked absently across my neck.

"James, you tell your boy one day to...see not the color of a man's skin, not the clothes he wears on his body... My James, you tell him to share his bread and drink. Tell him to share his bread and drink."

"Does Grampa really have his own book?" Nate asked softly.

"No, sweetheart, the Book of James is from the bible." I'd never had the faith my father grew up with, not in a higher power. If I believed in anyone, it was Dad himself. The respect I had for him, he had earned over and over. When he spoke, I listened. And his words were never empty.

I continued strumming on the song, skipping a verse or two when Nate had a question. By now, I was fairly certain Jess had fallen asleep again.

"Have I met Thomas?" Nate wondered.

I shook my head. "I haven't either. He died many years ago." I'd only heard stories, countless of them. During a weird phase in high school, I'd questioned everything that happened around me, and I'd entertained the idea that maybe Dad and Thomas had been more than friends.

There was a photo of them at Dad's place, their cocky smirks dominating the picture. It was taken right before they went off to war. Arms flung around each other's shoulders, cigarettes in the corners of their mouths, and they were fully decked out in army greens. Thomas had been taller and stockier, more immense standing next to my gangly dad. His dark skin a stark contrast to Dad's lily-white complexion. Thomas had also had the kindest voice, according to my father. Wicked sense of humor and an answer for everything.

Over the years, Dad had bulked up, hardened, and accepted the scars life had given him. There was no trace left of the skinny kid in that picture, but I was sure Thomas would always be part of him. I'd sensed it more during my childhood, whenever Dad shared a story or when I asked questions. In an almost rigidly religious way, acceptance and open-mindedness had been demanded of Brianna and me.

"Finish the song, please," Nate mumbled through a yawn.

I did finish the song. I played it a couple times until I was sure Nate was asleep too, and then I carefully repositioned the boys on the couch so their heads weren't close to the edge.

"I love you, sweet boys." I kissed their foreheads, then made my way out of the living room. They'd wake up again soon enough and want to open presents—I stopped short, seeing Allison sitting on the stairs. My heart hammered in surprise.

She had tears in her eyes. "What you have with them...I don't have that. I'm missing out."

Yeah, you are.

"You can always come home and transfer to a school here." I knew she wouldn't. I dipped down and kissed the top of her head before climbing the stairs. I wanted another hour or so of sleep.

CHAPTER 5

The new year couldn't come fast enough, and by the time Wednesday rolled around, I was ready to cancel my meetings in the city and head straight to the nearest pub.

Kieran and I had taken the train together in the morning, and he seemed to be strung as tight as I was.

"I mean, I love my family," I said.

"I know, same. But sometimes—"

"You just have to get away."

"Before you break something."

"Exactly." I nodded and released a heavy breath. Then I gestured at his paper. "Have you guys found a house yet?"

"Not yet. There are a few I wanna look at." He showed me the listings, and color me surprised, because I had no idea the Dearborns were moving.

"That's the house next door to me." I pointed to a picture of a white Victorian with light green shutters and matching picket fence. My house looked the same, only our accent color was light blue. It was part of the image that represented Downtown. Everything had to look so bloody idyllic.

"I'm aware." Kieran smiled wryly and folded the paper. "Our wives talk. Allison told Mags about the listing."

I had no idea. Allison was back in Chicago and wouldn't be home again until spring break at the end of March. Our first couples' dinner had been postponed till then, and she would miss my birthday at the end of January.

"I'm torn between let's-do-this and please-pick-another-house," I admitted in a chuckle.

"I hear ya."

"We'd be attached at the hip in no time, all four of us," I said. "Plus the kids."

He nodded. "On the other hand, we could escape to the garage whenever and shoot the shit and work on our alcoholism."

"True." That was strangely appealing. To have an ally so close...

We were useless that day. Kieran texted me during his breakfast meeting and asked if it was too early to go. Around lunch, it was my turn to text him. I asked where we'd meet up, to which he told me about a hole-in-the-wall kind of bar close to his office. It sounded perfect to me, and I did the math. If I was meeting up with him at five, it was probably best to get a taxi around...now? I checked my watch. *1:02 p.m.*

I grimaced.

I swore time stood still.

On my way to my last meeting at three thirty, I messaged Kieran again.

The boys will be at my father's until I stumble

home. Did your ball give your chain a curfew?

His reply was instant.

Nope. I said I'd be late.

Thank goodness.

Maybe our subsequent Wednesday pub meets would be lighter, but for this one... I had no words. I was going all out tonight. And that thought was the only thing that got me through the day. I worked on autopilot and related to Jess more than ever. He was always restless and unable to sit still.

When my meeting was over, I buttoned my suit jacket and shrugged on my coat.

I could practically taste the first shot of whiskey as I got in a taxi.

Kieran sent me a message, saying he was done for the day.

So step on it. I'll be there in ten minutes.

Ten minutes became twelve because of the goddamn traffic, but no matter. Kieran was waiting outside the bar.

He led the way inside, and it was definitely a small place. The four booths were full already, so we made our way to the other side of the bar where we could share the corner. I hung my coat and suit jacket on a hook under the bar, then rolled up the sleeves of my button-down. The five other men who sat along the bar were just like us. Men getting off work, wanting a break before they went home.

"What can I get ya?" A woman our age walked over, her cleavage impossible to miss in that top. Was it actual leather? Either way, it pushed together her...well, her breasts. I cleared my throat and turned to Kieran.

"Three shots of Jameson, one Guinness," he ordered.

Well, then. "I'll have the same," I said as a song started playing. It made me notice an old jukebox by the bathrooms. There were a couple guys shooting darts, too.

The bartender lined up six shot glasses and poured the amber liquid.

"You might as well leave the bottle," I added.

Kieran clapped me on the back. "Now we're talking."

The woman smiled. "Starting a tab, I take it?"

I nodded and fished out my wallet, handing over a credit card before Kieran could.

He didn't look pleased.

"Next time." I tugged at my tie, loosening it.

He followed suit. "Fine."

Next, we grabbed two glasses and clinked them together. "Cheers."

"*Sláinte*," he said with a smirk.

Kieran Marshall was a good bloke. A great fucking guy. One of the best out there. He poured another round of shots, and I chased one down with a swallow of beer.

"Fuck, that's it," I hissed as the burn slid down.

I groaned and dragged my hands over my face. This was the life. This was the escape I'd needed for months now. I felt *so* good.

It'd taken us half an hour to get a buzz, and in that time, we'd gotten a few random topics out of the way. I learned we were the same age, only he was a September kid while I was turning twenty-nine in a few weeks. He'd gone to college in Savannah and dropped out after two semesters. It was in Georgia he'd met Maggie, who was apparently six years older than him, and she was from Seattle. In order to escape the city rents when they eventually headed west, they'd settled down in Camassia and never left, even as his company started doing really well.

It was a Kieran Marshall crash course. Hardly enough, but it was a good beginning.

"I have a question." I coughed into my fist, and Kieran waved a hand in go-ahead before downing another shot. "You said you worked three jobs and quit college. Today, you have a great job. Your wife, you said, earned a master's in anthropology, and now she's at home."

"Yeah." He pushed two shot glasses my way, both brimming with whiskey. "She's..." He exhaled a chuckle. "She's something else. Her mind—she's one of the smartest women I know, but once she became pregnant with Jaylin, she walked away. She doesn't wanna work."

"Huh." I took a swig of my beer, and by chance, I caught a glimpse of a snack menu over the bar. Hell. I wanted wings. My stomach snarled in approval, so I got the bartender's attention. "Can I have one of those, uh..." I pointed vaguely at the menu and squinted. "With all the snacks, a mix plate. Extra wings, thanks."

"Sure thing." The woman turned to Kieran. "Anything for you?"

"That sounds good—" He stifled a belch. "I'll have the same."

Glancing over my shoulder, I deduced the happy hour crowd had morphed into the group of lucky suckers who could go out on a Wednesday just like that. The music was a little louder, and everyone was a little drunker. My kind of people.

"Anyway." I faced Kieran again and blanched. "What were we talking about?"

He laughed and shook his head. "I have no fucking clue." He figured that was a reason to slide another shot my way, even though I hadn't finished the other two. I had to catch up. "How did you meet Allison?"

"College." I threw back a shot and made a face. "She had a

full ride at Northwestern when she started. I was already a sophomore." We were the same age, but Allison had taken a year off to plant trees in...some country where there were already trees everywhere. Okay, that was harsh of me.

Kieran let out a low whistle. "Good school. What did you study?"

"Marketing," I replied. "Allison was studying finance, but—well."

Kieran's mouth twisted, and I narrowed my eyes at the little movement. He had...a mouth. And a faint five-o'clock shadow. My own mouth ran dry.

"You knocked her up." His lips moved.

"That I did." I looked away and drained what was left of my beer. Much better. Thirst was awful, just awful. "It was my fault. And... Bloody hell, that poor woman." Sometimes I didn't know how she hadn't dumped me. "It was a rough pregnancy. She had to drop out a few weeks in, and she was on bed rest for the last two months."

"Damn." His eyebrows went up. "How was it your fault?"

I laughed—no idea why, but I laughed. "We were coming back to my dorm after a party. Positively plastered."

"Of course," he chuckled.

"She asked me if I had protection, and I did. We were fooling around like the kids we were, and she asked again right before I, you know. And I told her I was wearing a condom."

I hadn't been.

"Jesus Christ, Ben." He stared at me, incredulous and amused. I ignored the nickname. "You knocked her up on purpose?"

"No!" I nearly choked on my own spit. Clearing my throat, I tried again. "Hell *no*. But that was how smashed I was. I thought I'd put one on."

Kieran found that hysterical.

"Wanker," I slurred. Thankfully, our food arrived, which was a good thing. "Cheers, hon." My stomach was empty. Of things other than alcohol, that was. "Man, this looks great." I poured some hot sauce over the wings and pinched one between my fingers.

"Was Jess also your fault?" He was down to chuckles, the bastard, and he held up a finger to get the bartender's attention.

"No, that was both of us," I said. Before I spoke again, I waited until he had ordered us new beers. "I was ready, although I didn't actually tell her that. With the way she became pregnant with Nate, I didn't dare bring up children."

"Understandable." He laughed through his nose, eyes shining from his sadistic amusement.

"But she knew—I mean, we had a ten-year plan, and we both wanted more." I paused to lick some hot sauce off my thumb. "She figured we might as well get it over with so she could go back to school after."

"And they say romance is dead," Kieran deadpanned.

"It is!" Fuck, I hadn't meant for that to be so loud—or weirdly exuberant. It was nothing to be stoked about. No, a much better thing to find hilarious was how Kieran tried to grab a shot glass with barbecue-glazed fingers and watch it spill into his lap.

"Motherfucker!" He almost fell backward in an attempt to scoot back on the barstool, and he grimaced downward.

I all but howled in laughter. My vision blurred, and I slapped a hand against the bartop. "Can you spell karma, Kieran?"

"Fuck off," he chuckled. "Aw, man. Guess who's sleeping on the couch tonight."

"You can't shower when you get home?"

He snorted and wiped his pants with a napkin. "Doesn't matter. I was probably gonna end up there anyway. Mags doesn't like it when I have a beer with dinner, much less half a bottle of Jameson."

I crammed a jalapeño popper into my mouth. "She told me she was a good Catholic housewife. I assume you're Catholic too...?"

"Why would you assume that?" He balled up the wet napkin and dug back into his snack plate.

"Irish guy from Boston? Come on."

He chuckled around a few fries. "Touché. I guess I'm Catholic, but I don't go to mass. She does."

I remembered she'd told me about her work with the church.

"So now you're going to risk sleeping on the sofa every Wednesday."

That earned me one of his lazy smirks. "Are we doing this every Wednesday?"

I felt bold enough to quote him. "I'll kick your fucking ass if you cancel on me."

He threw a French fry right in my face, and I flinched and batted it away. "Don't worry, I'm game. I'll risk the couch and face my wife's wrath every night if that's what it takes."

"Oh, wow. It's like you don't even enjoy sex."

"What's that?" he asked with a straight face.

That was interesting. "And here I was, thinking I had the most depressing love life."

"Be happy you have one in the first place—unless you count ten minutes of 'Are you almost there?' every six months." He was quick to chug a good portion of his beer as soon as it was served. "At this...fuck." He belched and rubbed his chest. "At this point, I consider myself in an exclusive relationship with an adult store."

Really. "A what now?"

Kieran was hammered. His eyes were bleary and glassy, no

doubt a reflection of what he saw in my eyes too. And his grin was lopsided. "You never go to an adult store to get your rocks off? If I didn't, I'd lose my mind."

I leaned closer, intrigued. "You mean one of those seedy places with a movie theater in the back?" I'd bought handcuffs for Allison once—to spice things up, hoping at least one of us would get to try them—and that store had booths you could go into to watch porn. I always thought...I would never be one of those men.

Kieran nodded. "The private ones. I've never tried an actual theater. I like my privacy."

"Huh." I took a gulp of my beer, thinking about it. Then again, why would I go to such a place? I had a bedroom to myself. My problem, other than lack of passion, was that my wife was halfway across the country. "Is it exciting?"

He laughed and shook his head. "Why would it be exciting? It's sad as fuck." He lifted a shoulder. "I'm outta options. My imagination's run dry, and Mags freaked out and didn't talk to me for two weeks when she found porn at home."

Ah, those were the days. I remembered feeling horribly guilty once I started watching porn. So much so, I confessed it all in a rush to Allison. She'd stared at me as if I'd grown a second head before bursting out in giggles. In short, she had no issues with porn and had even admitted to watching it herself.

However, when I suggested we watch it together, she got angry. It was a tricky balance.

"I have a hidden stash of DVDs," I said.

"Yeah, well. I guess I'm paranoid she's gonna find out." This time, his smirk wasn't as confident.

Sympathy pierced my drunken bubble, and I felt for him. Once upon a time, Allison had been the adventurous one. I'd been awkward and adamant about everything being great simply because I was too afraid to admit I didn't know what I was doing. She'd helped me with that.

We hit these stages in life where things were different. After Nate was born, Allison went through a major adjustment; her body and hormones had changed, as had her needs. Much like me, she had highs and lows. I could go weeks without needing sex. It was normal, I hoped. Right now, I was particularly… needy, for lack of a better word. I wanted to explore, find the passion I recalled somewhat, amplify it…

I was sure Kieran and Maggie went through similar periods. Maybe they'd hit a low and didn't know how to get past it.

"Time to go home?" I had to concentrate harder to keep my focus.

Kieran checked his watch and squinted at it. "It's past eight. I guess we should."

I settled the tab before easing off my chair, and the vertigo hit me instantly. *Shit.* Having inhaled much more whiskey than beer, I hadn't needed to go to the bathroom until now. And I needed to go fucking ASAP, so I stumbled my way there and tried—and failed—to stand on my own without swaying.

Five minutes later, we left and stepped out into the cold of January.

Kieran took a piss in the alley next to the bar while I hailed us a taxi to take us to the train station.

"You should…" I held my phone closer so I could see the blurry screen. "The house, Kieran. Get the house—so we can be neighbors."

He came up next to me, zipping up his pants. "We should probably look at it first."

"Yes, but then you buy it."

He laughed.

CHAPTER 6

Wednesdays became ours. Thursdays kind of belonged to us too, once Kieran took over for Maggie bringing Jaylin to swimming lessons. But we didn't talk much at the pool because, more often than not, I was too hungover.

I started looking forward to Wednesdays the way Jess and Nate looked forward to the weekends. Kieran was a fixation; he represented the day of the week I could say fuck it all and be whoever I wanted.

The first Wednesday we reluctantly went straight home after work in the city was in late March. It was the day the Marshalls closed on their new house, and our wives were ecstatic. Allison was home for spring break, and she was quick to invite Kieran and Maggie over for dinner to celebrate.

The following weekend, we got together again for Allison's birthday dinner.

We were officially one of those foursomes that Kieran and I had dreaded. The first Pictionary night came when the

Marshalls moved in to their house in July. Allison was home for the summer, and it made it more important than ever to me to have my Wednesday away from everything.

July was also the month I started lying to my wife. Work was slow at the moment, but I told her I had meetings in the city so I could sneak off.

"You couldn't have just told her you need that one night off every week?" Kieran asked as we boarded the train that morning.

"Normally, sure." Not in the summer, though, and I didn't want another fight. I thought it was unfair of her to expect me to change everything only because she was suddenly home. We were on the third year of spending so much time apart that it was an adjustment every time we saw each other. "She wanted us to go to the beach today."

"I know." Of course he knew. Our wives had become best friends and talked about everything. "Tell me I shouldn't leave early to keep you company when you stroll around the city and do nothing."

I grinned. "I can't tell you that."

I'd suggested breakfast once when a client of mine was a no-show, and I'd learned Kieran was rigid about doing his four hours of bike delivery when the weather was warmer. He showed up at the station in his body-hugging uniform every morning unless the forecast promised a downpour. In other words, I knew I was on my own until lunch when he'd shower and change.

"You know what I'm gonna do while you're at work?" I relaxed back in my seat and smiled. "I'm going to go see a movie. I'm going to buy the biggest soda and popcorn, pour so much butter on that it'll drip, and I'm going to sit there and watch a movie by myself. No kids, no wife. Just me."

Kieran sucked his teeth and gave me a sharp look. "You fucking suck."

I laughed.

It was going to be a spectacular day.

"I can do *anything*." The more I thought about it, the more I realized I was a free man today. I wasn't a complete prick, so I wouldn't come home drunk. But everything wasn't about alcohol. "I can be one of those people who sits in a park for fun."

"You, potheads, and homeless people," he muttered.

I smirked at his envy. "I may even get ice cream."

"All right, enough outta you," he chuckled. "I'll make it an early day."

Perfect. "What do you wanna do?"

He hummed and stretched out his legs, crossing his legs at his ankles under the table. "Wanna do something crazy?"

"Yes," I answered without hesitation.

"Then leave things to me."

No problem.

"Hey, where do you think you're going?" Kieran frowned.

"Uh...this way?" I pointed toward the cabstand outside the station.

"Fuck that." He grasped my elbow and guided me toward the local transit he took to his office. "There's an AMC by my building if you wanna go see a movie."

So he *was* a sadist. He couldn't let me have my morning off without first making me suffer on a heavily crowded train.

I sighed and followed him—and the herd of commuters—to the train going north, and it was possible I bitched about it the entire time. Kieran thought that was funny. I didn't. The transit toward U District was always packed with college kids and, well, yuppies like Kieran.

I guess I was a yuppie too.

Much like the time I'd had to bring Nate to my sister's, we were packed in like sardines near the doors, and I shot Kieran a brief glare.

He grinned, grabbing the handlebar above him. This time, the envy was mine. His bicep flexed as the train jostled us, a reminder that I'd been slacking with the gym lately.

"Think about your ice cream."

"It would melt here." I pulled at my tie before finding a steady grip on a bar behind him. "I cannot believe you do this every day."

"You cannot, huh? Brit boy."

I rolled my eyes and was forced to move closer to him when people huddled to get off at the next stop. The car squealed and screeched, braking suddenly before slowing down to a more humane pace, but it was enough to send me flying into Kieran. There was no embarrassment as pretty much everyone bumped into someone. There was, however, a moment of disbelief.

"What the hell do you wear under your uniform?" I glanced between us and pressed a hand to his stomach. His abs were rock solid. Was that even *possible*? High school—I remember how I burned through food like it was nothing. I ran for an hour and built leg muscles. I ate pizza for a week and didn't gain an ounce. And college athletes, of course. They always looked ripped. As for the rest, I'd been hoping it was all photoshopped.

"All me, baby." His rich voice was thick with amusement, and I swallowed uneasily. My gut clenched, annoyance flared up, and so did something else. It didn't know what, only that it resulted in the weakest death glare ever. As if I lost all physical and mental strength.

My ears felt like they were on actual fire. "I need to exercise more often." I averted my gaze to get my act together.

"You look fine to me."

I narrowed my eyes at him. "Are you having a laugh?"

His eyes danced with mirth. "No, can't you tell I'm dead serious?"

I scoffed and looked away again. The doors opened, offering me a much-needed rush of somewhat fresh air. Unfortunately, more people stepped on than off, so I remained standing in Kieran's personal space. His body radiated heat, and I loosened my tie a bit more. I hoped I wasn't coming down with something. I was well when I left the house.

"Meet me outside the bar as usual," he murmured. "I'll leave at twelve-thirty."

"Are we drinking again?" I wasn't sure that was wise.

"Just a few shots." He steadied me with a hand along my side as the train rocked. "You'll need it to agree to what I have planned."

I looked down at his hand. Did he have a fever? "That sounds ominous." He was inside my open suit jacket, and his heat was searing through my button-down. *Bollocks.* Were we both coming down with something? I wondered what child I'd blame this time. Jess had brought home a nasty cold a few months ago, and I'd been useless for days.

His chuckle tickled my neck. "Trust me, Ben."

Sweat beaded at my temples. My collar felt too tight.

There was another stop, and it brought Kieran and me chest-to-chest. The unease grew, as did a sliver of panic. Because as a ball formed at the center of my being, dropping lower and lower, I could only describe it as something I tended to feel in more appropriate moments. Lust. *Hunger*. I swallowed dryly and thought back... When was the last time Allison and I had made love? Good fucking grief, I couldn't remember.

There was no way I'd embarrass Kieran with my inopportune urges, so I did my best to angle away from him. I couldn't believe myself. Was I so deprived that I caught an erection in the middle of a crowded train?

Coming down with something... I was an idiot. I wasn't coming down with anything other than horniness.

We were jostled once again, and I cursed under my breath.

Kieran gripped my side more firmly. "See? Isn't this fun? You get where you need to go, *and* you get a free ride on Seattle's finest roller coaster."

How could he think this was funny? Shooting him a scowl, I was unprepared to be assaulted by his charming smile and those eyes of his. I was standing close enough that I could see how the green at the center mingled with the blue. Were those flecks of silver or gold?

A waft of his aftershave filled my nostrils. That was something I shouldn't find appealing whatsoever. Wait, did we wear the same aftershave? No, it was slightly different. Maybe. I hoped it was different, because getting turned on by my own aftershave might make my sister cock her head curiously and wonder if I had narcissistic tendencies.

Time to cool down. The next stop was ours, and distance would clear my head in a heartbeat. Gut feeling. And tonight when I came home, I was going to walk up to Allison and...and what? Be shot down? Be called insensitive for implying she wasn't good enough when I suggested we try new things?

Funny how quickly those thoughts worked to quell my desire.

Quit bothering me at work.

I took a long pull from the straw, almost dropping my soda

as I replied to Kieran.

This is important. I have to tell you that there is at least a cup of butter on my popcorn.

I watched a little bit of the previews while I waited for his return text.

We need to work on your definition of important.

I snickered, and I felt better now, ready to forget the little... whatever it was that happened on the train. Scratch that, I felt naughty. My wife and kids were at the beach, thinking I was at work, and I *wasn't*. I was in an almost empty movie theater with a big soda and buttery popcorn. Kieran had kindly offered to keep my briefcase in his office, so it was just me.

It was just me...

I glanced down at my phone. Oh, fuck it.

If you leave now, you'll only miss the first ten minutes of the movie.

He replied after a minute.

Dude, I'm doing deliveries and working on the abs you felt up earlier.

I shifted uncomfortably in my seat and shook the memory, the feeling, of his muscles underneath my fingers.

But I bought Junior Mints too.

Everyone loved Junior Mints. Junior Mints were the best.

The lack of response from Kieran told me he was going to be a dull boy, and I gave up and pocketed my phone. To be honest, I didn't know much about the film I was about to see. It was the only one showing at this hour...and I was still giddy.

Retrieving the box of Junior Mints from the inside pocket of my jacket, I opened it and poured a handful of sweets into my mouth. The movie began with an action sequence that would've been "oh my God, so cool" in Jess's opinion.

The main bloke was buff and drove a cool car. The girl he wanted had an obvious aversion to clothes. It was as if I'd seen this movie a hundred times before.

I caught movement in the corner of my eye, and as I turned, Kieran slumped down into the seat next to me. What the—he actually... The surprise was no doubt evident on my face. He merely smirked and stole my Junior Mints.

"What did I miss?" he whispered.

A smile took over, and I relaxed in my seat, facing forward. "Not much."

We went for lunch after the movie, then trailed back to Kieran's office so he could shower and change into regular clothes.

If I thought my office was nice...

He had his own bathroom and a closet full of clothes, and he emerged from the bathroom in a pair of threadbare jeans and a vintage tee that hugged his torso. Ironically, I felt underdressed next to him, yet he was the one in street clothes.

"You ready to head out?" He threw the towel he'd had around his shoulders back into the bathroom, then grabbed his keys, phone, and wallet off the coffee table. That was right, he had his own couch and coffee table in here. Christ, I'd *lived* in worse places.

"Lead the way." I cleared my throat and gestured to the door.

Five minutes later, we were entering the bar we went to most Wednesdays. The bartender knew our names by now, and she'd shared her nickname—Roxy.

"You guys are early."

"Hey, hon. We won't be long today." Kieran slid onto a stool and drummed his fingers along the bartop, eyes scanning the menu above the shelves of bottles.

"You've said that before." Roxy snorted, amused, and pulled up a bottle of Jameson. "Quit pretending like you're going to order something else."

I took the seat next to him and decided to look less like I had a stick up my ass. I removed my tie and stuck it in my pocket.

"Fine. Three shots each." Kieran hauled out his wallet.

Roxy lifted a delicate brow. "No tab?"

"Apparently we're not staying," I drawled.

Kieran jerked a thumb at me. "I gotta liquor him up a bit, that's all."

In the end, three shots each became five, but Kieran stuck to his word. As soon as the fifth shot was sliding down my throat, he'd paid for the last drinks and left his seat.

Roxy watched us in amusement while we left, hollering, "See you soon" before the door closed.

My buzz was just settling in; in fact, I barely felt it. It would be a few minutes. My mouth was numb, my tongue was loose, but my mind was free of cobwebs.

"You're not gonna tell me where we're going?" I shrugged out of my suit jacket. It was a hot day, and the sun was currently beating down on us. It made me wish I had my own closet of clothes in the city.

"It's just around the corner." He smiled and donned a pair of shades, and in that moment, he looked more carefree than I'd ever seen him. I'd almost call him beautiful. Or maybe I would. I mean, it was okay to think that, wasn't it? It didn't mean anything.

I remembered a few months ago, he'd told me he liked my smile right after I laughed because my dimples were more pronounced then. We'd been wasted when he said it, but I hadn't forgotten the compliment.

"Can I just say I'm glad I have you in my life?"

Curiosity and mirth mingled in his expression, and I saw the smirk coming a mile away. "Is the booze setting in, buddy?"

"Maybe." I didn't think it was the alcohol talking.

He chuckled and threw an arm around my shoulder. "I can't believe I let you talk me into skipping work today."

I gave him a shove, which made him laugh more.

It wasn't long thereafter that he came to a stop, and I did a double take at the storefront.

"You've gone mad, Kieran!" This wasn't happening. He couldn't be serious. "There isn't a chance in hell—"

"But there is." He grinned.

As he passed me, he squeezed my shoulder and clapped me on the chest. "Come on. We gotta live a little, Ben." He pushed the door open, and I was immediately met by the scents of disinfectants.

What the fuck was I doing in a piercing studio?

It was a small shop with checkered floors and walls filled with photos and painted tribal patterns. Scrubbing a hand over my jaw, I followed him reluctantly, wondering if I could go through with *anything* they offered here.

The guy behind the counter would set off every alarm in an airport. I counted at least a dozen piercings in his ears alone. He wore ink on every visible inch of his skin, including his knuckles that read "Fuck Off!"

Okay, I'll be on my way.

"Oh no, you don't." Kieran grabbed my arm before I could turn away.

Where was my panic? My disbelief, my Bennett-sized hole in the door? There was a flat no I could deliver without a problem, but there would be no punch behind it. Because in the end, Kieran made me want to take that extra step closer to the edge.

"We're here to get pierced," Kieran told the guy.

"Right on, man." Goodness, the bloke was high. I could see it now in his glassy eyes. "Where do you want the steel?"

Kieran turned to me in question.

"What're you looking at me for?" I asked incredulously.

He laughed and faced our pierced stoner. "We'll each do a nipple ring."

"We will?" I think I just squeaked like a bloody fool. "No—wait, wait. Let's think about this for one goddamn minute, Kieran."

"That's the whole point of doing something wild, Ben," he argued with that Boston smirk. It had to be a thing there. It felt so...cocky, so rough, so untamed. "We're not going to think."

"We're not going to think," I whispered to myself, tearing my gaze away from his face. "All right, but..." I swallowed hard and forced myself to quickly do a mental scan of my body and the places one could get a piercing. Rule number one, and there was only one rule, it had to be concealable.

Slow whiskey waves of warmth rolled in over me.

We're not going to think.

I could be a yes-man with Kieran. I needed it. I needed this adventure with him.

Kieran's hand slid across my neck, and I shivered. "Nipple ring?"

I coughed into my fist and nodded, a war raging in the drunken swell of the alcohol. "Nipple ring."

"Excellent."

The guy who was going to put needles in our bodies introduced himself as Tom, and we were shown to a room in the back. One that could've belonged in a clinic, if it weren't for the checkered floor and gothic art on the walls. I stared at the examination table in mild horror.

Kieran stayed close to me. Maybe he sensed that I was a chickenshit.

"Want me to go first?" he murmured.

"Definitely," I replied.

He grinned. "Look, I was saving these till after, but maybe you need one now." He produced two small bottles of whiskey from his pockets, and I could've kissed him.

I grabbed both bottles while Tom prepared his station of needles. He seemed amused by my state of terror.

Kieran chuckled while I downed the first bottle. "I was thinking we'd each get one."

I licked my lips and opened the second. "We weren't going to think, remember?"

The second shot slid down smoothly as Kieran's eyes danced with laughter.

"Are you sure you want this, man?" Tom drawled. "I'm not supposed to work on anyone who's drunk."

"You're probably not supposed to work when you're high either," I pointed out. "Kieran, get on the bed. We're doing this."

A dark glint sparked up in Kieran's eyes. "Whenever you're ready." Then he pulled his tee over his head and got seated on the table.

I...I gawked. My throat felt thick—hell, the air around me felt thick. How sculpted could a man get? I had no words for the sheer perfection of Kieran Marshall. The summer had given him a slight tan, but otherwise, it was just pale complexion, abs, a dusting of chest hair, and a tattoo that covered the right side of his rib cage. I saw a shadowy street and brownstones, the silhouette of a man walking alone, with a low-hanging moon above him. It was hauntingly beautiful, only fueling my curiosity. It was a shame to call it curiosity these days, though. It was a burning need that only seemed to grow stronger.

CHAPTER 7

"All done," Tom declared, and my gaze flew to Kieran's chest. A silver barbell was pierced through his left nipple.

Other than his clenched jaw, Kieran showed no signs of discomfort. He straightened up and listened to Tom's scripted speech on aftercare for the next eight weeks, and his new piercing got a temporary wrap that would come off when he got home.

Nerves tightened my gut when it was my turn.

"Did it hurt a lot?" I asked hesitantly as we switched places.

He shook his head and put on his T-shirt again.

If it didn't hurt, why did he look so tense? Where was his happy mood from a minute ago?

I suppressed a sigh and unbuttoned my shirt. Thank goodness for the alcohol in my system. There was no deeper worry left, only nerves because bloody hell, that needle looked insane.

After draping my jacket and button-down over the end of

the examination table, I yanked my undershirt over my head and held it in my lap.

"Lie back a bit," Tom instructed. "Left or right?"

I flicked a glance at Kieran, finding him watching me, and cleared my throat. "Right."

I avoided Kieran's stare after that. He wouldn't find much to look at on my body.

I flinched as Tom cleaned the area around my nipple, and a new waft of disinfectant hit my nostrils. Then there was a needle. I gulped and gnashed my teeth, bracing myself for the agony.

As the needle pierced my skin, a sharp pinch blossomed into a hot, dull throb. I sucked in a breath and tensed up further, even though I could acknowledge that the pain hadn't been half as bad as I'd feared.

When all was said and done, a piece of metal was stuck in my nipple. It was unbelievable. I looked down at the barbell and wondered what my sister would say about this. Had I gone mad? Was I experiencing the beginning of a crisis? Thirty wasn't that far off.

I, Bennett Brooks, had just pierced my nipple.

I exhaled a shaky laugh at the absurdity, then pretended to pay attention to what Tom said. Something about letting the piercing breathe when I got home, something about cleaning it, something about eight weeks. I nodded dutifully, and he wrapped the pierced area in gauze.

I couldn't kill the smile.

Kieran must've noticed because he shook his head in amusement. Then we went to pay for our piercings, and it struck me that we didn't have any further plans. Was the idea that we were going home now? The thought snuffed out some of my buzz. I wasn't ready one bit.

As we stepped out into the summer sun, I rolled up the

sleeves of my button-down and tried to come up with something that would keep us in the city for a while longer. Every now and then, I winced when the sore area around my nipple brushed against my undershirt. It was almost worse than getting the piercing.

Kieran slid on his shades again and side-eyed me. "Wanna get a drink?"

I love you!

"I thought you'd never ask," I replied with a grin. "I have half a mind to text Allison and say I'm going to work late."

He laughed. "What's stopping you?"

Nothing, just wanted your seal of approval.

While I took out my phone to text her, Kieran admitted he'd already warned his wife he might be late.

Brilliant.

I had to schedule a late meeting and won't be home for dinner. Hope you guys are having fun at the beach.

"Should we try a new place or back to Roxy?" Kieran asked.

"Don't fix what ain't broke, to quote my father," I answered. "Roxy's place is perfect for us day drinkers."

"True," he chuckled.

So that was where we ended up again, and Roxy wasn't surprised to see us. We ordered chips and salsa with our beers, and this time, Kieran wanted a booth. They were usually occupied when we were here, but we were in luck now.

"I love this place," I admitted freely. Day was always night here. Despite being located on a fairly busy street, it felt secluded and...and ours. This belonged to Kieran and me. Sitting back with a sigh of contentment, I dragged a couple chips through the salsa and stuck them into my mouth.

Kieran had a faint smirk playing on his lips. "You liked getting pierced, didn't you?"

"I've never done anything like it." And I still couldn't describe the feelings that swirled around inside of me right now. "It was a rush. Which..." When I thought about it... "That's sad, isn't it?"

He clinked his beer bottle to mine. "We can be sad together, my friend. I feel more alive when I'm with you."

That piece of honesty made my day. My heart slammed against my rib cage, and I was overwhelmed by a similar rush to that I'd felt in the piercing studio.

I raised my beer. "To the sadness and stagnant lives that brought us together."

"I'll drink to that. *Sláinte*."

I took a swig and felt my phone vibrating in my pocket. "Just how Irish are you? I'm curious." I kept my phone under the table, having no intention of giving the outside world much of my time.

"One hundred percent," Kieran replied. "My grandparents on both sides go way back and came to the US together in the fifties."

I raised my brows, enjoying these puzzle pieces of history. "I'm surprised you don't have more of an accent." I lowered my gaze to read the text.

"You should hear me when I go visit my family."

Ok. Jess was fussy, so we came home. It would've been nice to have your help. See you tonight.

It would've been nice to... Was she fucking serious? I couldn't believe the gall of her.

"Why do you look pissy?" Kieran asked.

"Sorry," I said quickly, pocketing my phone. "Allison felt the need to tell me Jess has been fussy and that I should've been there."

"Ouch. Yeah, I'm not touching that one."

"Neither am I," I said, irritated with her. "I think it's time for whiskey, and then I wanna hear about your family in Quincy."

I knew he had six or seven brothers and sisters, but he didn't talk about them much.

At who-knew o'clock, we were the perfect amount of wasted, and we were laughing our asses off at shit our kids did when they thought no one was watching.

"Imagine if Jess and Jaylin end up in the same class when they start school. We'll be toast!" I exclaimed.

"Aren't we already?" Kieran laughed. "I thought Jaylin was bad with her cousins, but she and your boy might take the prize."

I grinned and threw back the last of my beer.

I wasn't in the mood to push for information, and while Kieran had no issues sharing stories about his nieces and nephews, he continued keeping things brief where his siblings were concerned. But we had a million other subjects to exhaust, and I was fine with that.

"You ready to go?" he wondered.

Go...? I blinked blearily and checked my watch. "It's only four."

"And we've basically been drinking all day." He smirked and rested his forearms on the table. "I could go for a burger and fries. I'm not saying we're going home yet."

"Good," I slurred, stifling a belch. "Okay, I can eat. It's not like I have the body of a Greek god to maintain."

Unlike some.

Kieran's shoulders shook with laughter, and his eyes brimmed with indecent amusement, something I was sure only he could pull off. In fact, there was always something indecent about Kieran.

Something forbidden.

I eyed him as my gut tightened painfully, but he was already on his way out of the booth.

"I'll settle our tab," he said on his way to the bar.

I felt tense all of a sudden, and I looked around to gain my bearings. The rock music blared as it always did, and at this time of day, more people began trickling in. A reminder that the outside world wasn't far away.

Kieran made me forget. He made me covet like a fucking addict. *What* I coveted was unclear.

My brain was powering down, bordering on useless, and I merely followed Kieran's lead. After he'd paid, we took a leak and then headed outside.

I blinked at the harsh light.

The fresh air was too fresh.

I wanted to go back to Roxy and her booze.

"I think this means I win," Kieran chuckled, draping an arm around my shoulders. "You can't hold your liquor, son."

"God," I muttered. The impressions were too much. People crowded the sidewalks, traffic was crazy, the sun was blinding, and the whiskey rolled in my stomach. "Where're we goin'?"

"Just a few stops on the train—"

"Fuck that! We'll get a taxi." The thought of getting on a crowded commuter train now made me sweat.

Kieran wouldn't have it, intent on steering me toward the station.

It was in sheer self-preservation that I shut down and let him guide me. I kept my double vision fixed on the ground and my thoughts fixed on the man walking so close to me. Why the *fuck* had I thought of him as forbidden? I shouldn't have. Other than lying to my wife about where I was today, my friendship with Kieran had been nothing but good for me. *He* was good for me. He was great for me.

"You're g-great," I told him.

I caught his smile in the corner of my eye. His arm stayed around my shoulders, maneuvering me between the crowds of people.

"I'm so pissed," I groaned.

"Pissed as in drunk?"

"Yeah."

He laughed under his breath. "Cute as shit is what you are. Come on, our train's coming any minute."

He had to take over when I was trying to scan my train card, 'cause I fucking couldn't.

The heat got worse and worse as we boarded the train, and I had to close my eyes the second we'd found a place to stand. Which wasn't an awesome idea. The world was spinning too quickly.

"Maybe it was good that we stopped drinking." I gripped the handlebar above us when the train departed. He and I were chest-to-chest, and I didn't want to embarrass myself this time.

"Only maybe?" His warm chuckle tickled my neck, and he steadied me with a grip on my arm. "We'll get some food in you, and you'll be ready to go."

I hummed and lifted my gaze to his chest. I could see where his piercing was, hidden under soft fabric and a strip of gauze.

"I can't believe we pierced our nipples, Kieran."

"We need something unforgettable in our lives."

The truth of the day.

The train screeched and swerved on the tracks, slowing down before the next station.

"Have you ever gotten an actual seat on this train?" I asked.

He grinned. "Once, I think."

I didn't mind how we always seemed to end up by the doors,

though. As people packed themselves tighter to get close to the exit, I had Kieran to lean on. By the time the train was rolling again, his hand had shifted to my side, and I closed my eyes once more.

His heat felt good. It probably shouldn't. No, it definitely shouldn't, and I shouldn't be calm about this. I shouldn't enjoy it. Or get goose bumps.

Fuck, I was drunk. Drunker than I had been in...well, ever?

"You with me, Ben?" he murmured. "Don't pass out on me."

"I'm here." I opened my eyes and found myself stuck in his concern. It wasn't the first time we were mere inches apart, yet I drank in the sight just as greedily now. His brow furrowed, maybe because I was fucking staring, but I couldn't stop. I didn't want to.

I caught a bead of perspiration trickling down slowly from his temple.

I swallowed dryly.

Did his eyes seem darker today? Or maybe only now. He'd stuck his shades in the neckline of his tee.

There are people everywhere. Yet, I couldn't hear them. A low rush invaded my ears, and I couldn't hear much of anything, except for the occasional screech from the train.

"Fuck." Kieran clenched his jaw, and the look in his eyes was almost that of a warning. For what, I didn't know.

"Why do I always wanna get closer to you?" I asked under my breath.

He still heard me, though he didn't answer. Instead, he screwed his eyes shut, his fingers flexing at my side.

The train jostled us, not for the first time sending me flying into him, not that there was much space between us to begin with. But now...I felt him everywhere, and an explosion set off inside of me. I flushed all over and shuddered violently, and a bolt of wild desire shot straight to my cock.

I exhaled shakily, half in panic, half in *I don't fucking care*, and found him looking at me the exact same way.

I want more.

"Kier—"

"Don't say a word." The words were rushed out of him, and he swallowed hard. "We'll take the next stop."

For what? Burgers and bloody fries? I couldn't. My body was a live wire, and I couldn't think properly. I was so goddamn turned on I thought I was going to shatter, and it was *Kieran* who turned me on.

It should've terrified me.

Maybe I was too wasted, and the fear would hit later.

Probably.

I didn't move away from him, and he didn't act like he wanted to get away. If anything, his grip tightened, and I felt him against my thigh. He was getting hard too. It wasn't just me. Holy shit, it wasn't just me. He was turned on as well. By *me*. Two blokes.

A strangled sound of disbelief tried to escape my throat, but I managed to push it down.

Holy fuck, holy fuck, holy fuck.

The train slowed down again, and we stared at each other. The lust in his eyes all but tore me apart. Stripped me down and shoved away the last shred of sanity.

We were the first two off the train when it stopped, and then he took the lead. I wiped some sweat off my forehead, my heart thundering, and followed him through the station. I had no clue where we were, and it didn't matter.

I could sense when we were getting near the exit. Fresh air, a few degrees cooler, blanketed us but did nothing to quell the burning need inside me.

We were met by the sound of heavy traffic outside, and I was glad Kieran seemed to know where he was going. Up one short street, a sharp left, then into a narrow side street. The city noise faded, the sunlight lost its brilliance. Next to an old building with a closed storefront, Kieran dragged me into an alley and didn't stop until we were hidden next to a dumpster.

My pulse went through the roof, and then we were on each other. My back hit the brick wall as his mouth covered mine in a brutal, hungry, savage kiss. There was no easing into things. I ignored the pain from the piercing and yanked him closer to me, and I swallowed his groan.

The sharp bolts of lust were unlike anything I'd ever felt, and they continued firing in every direction. One set off another, raging with shivers and tremors. I deepened the kiss and pushed my tongue around his, one of my hands coming up to cup his cheek. The rough shadow of scruff only turned me on even more.

"Kieran," I gasped.

"I gotta feel more of you," he panted. Then he slipped a hand between us, and he palmed my cock. My knees nearly gave out, and the neediest sound I'd ever heard came out of my mouth. "Jesus Christ, Ben."

I moaned into a kiss as he stroked me outside my pants, his hand firm and greedy on me. I couldn't stop myself from pushing into his hand.

Just as I thought the hottest experience in my life couldn't get hotter, Kieran gave me another drugging kiss and sank to his knees before me.

"Wh—" I choked on my question, not entirely sure what I was going to ask anyway, when he inched closer, undid my belt, and pulled out my cock. The shock rendered me completely rigid and speechless, and then my cock was sliding into the wet, tight heat of Kieran's mouth.

Oh my God.

Pleasure exploded within me, white-hot and overpowering.

His tongue swirled around me, he cupped my balls and stroked two fingers over the sensitive crease underneath, and a fever broke out as my cock hit the back of his throat.

Staring down at him, I saw he was stroking himself off while working me over like a professional.

Erotic.

It was too much for my brain to handle. It short-circuited, and I gave in to the mind-blowing sensations. I bucked my hips to go deeper, and I watched myself weaving my fingers into his hair and gripping it firmly. His groan sent a vibrating hum up my shaft. My chest heaved with the gasp that left me. I was fucking gone.

I moaned hoarsely, the orgasm slamming into me, and shoved my cock far enough to feel his throat squeezing me. I came in several bursts, and each one left me a little more listless than the one before. I was vaguely aware of Kieran's fingers digging painfully into my thigh, and then I didn't really know what was happening. He sucked me hard and long until I had nothing left to give.

"*Hnngh.*" I swallowed against the dryness.

I didn't know whether to laugh or cry. Maybe a bit of both. Emotions were surging completely out of control, and the waves of euphoria were something else entirely.

I was alive.

"Bloody hell," I exhaled.

Kieran rose and tucked me back into my boxers and zipped up my pants. Then I felt his shaky breath ghosting across my throat, where he gave me a quick nip with his teeth.

"Don't overthink it."

I was going to overthink it. When the shudders stopped flowing through me like electric currents, I was going to overthink this like never before.

"Did you finish?" I rasped.

He nodded and wouldn't look me in the eye.

I couldn't have that, not for a second, so I cupped the back of his neck and pulled him closer, covering his mouth with my own. His lips were warm, and he tasted of me. *That's...that's fucking hot.* I kept it unhurried, just wanting to...I wasn't sure, but keep him close.

"Don't pull back from me," I told him quietly. I knew absolutely nothing about what was going on, with the exception that this was one of those things I could picture people running away from. I couldn't take that from Kieran.

"All right." He broke the kiss to catch his breath, and he rested his forehead against mine. "You're gonna wanna talk about this, aren't you?"

"Oh, you bet."

He sighed. "Then let's get it over with before you sober up and freak out."

I didn't think that was going to happen, but was that why he looked so uncomfortable? Unsure, even. It was incredibly uncharacteristic of him.

"I don't feel like I'm gonna freak out," I said.

He quirked a brow and snorted. "You're still three sheets to the wind."

Yeah, but funny how a blow job could clear one's head.

My God, Kieran had sucked me off.

I shivered violently.

CHAPTER 8

We took a taxi to a diner where Kieran said we would have privacy.

It was a small place, very Americana, and while we ordered a couple burgers and fries, I realized my mind was still at ease. Questions had definitely begun piling up, but there was no sign of panic. The only true worry I had was ruining anything between Kieran and me. He'd become my lifeline this year, and I wasn't sure I could cope if that went away.

The waitress returned with drinks before leaving us alone in our booth again, and I stayed quiet as Kieran sat there and fiddled with the wrapper from his straw. Something was going on inside his head, something big.

"Look," I said, clearing my throat. "I'll be honest. Whatever it is, I just—I can't go back to before we knew each other."

"Couldn't you?" He pinned me with an intense stare, but, at the same time, he looked so tired. Mentally, emotionally. Wrung out and tense. He wouldn't be able to hold it very long. "More accurately, wouldn't you? If you could go back—to before we met on the train—"

"No." I shook my head.

"You just cheated on your wife with a man," he said pointedly.

I flinched and glanced out the window where the people of Seattle were on their way home from work.

I cheated on Allison.

I never thought that would be me. If anything, I'd worried about her. Maybe not recently, but the thought crossed my mind every now and then.

As a ball of guilt dropped into my stomach, my priority didn't change. I couldn't *not* know Kieran. I couldn't go back. I *wouldn't*. I wouldn't live only for my sons.

"I have to have you in my life." I felt extremely vulnerable admitting that for some reason, and I shifted in my seat. "I understand if you don't feel the same—"

"I do." Eyes downcast, he clenched his jaw and kept fiddling with that wrapper. "But it can't happen again."

I...hadn't even thought that far down the road. There was no opinion whatsoever, so I said, "Okay."

Kieran had some demons I hadn't gotten a glimpse of before. I could tell by his unease and how he was unable to sit still.

Had it happened before? Was he hiding someth—

"I'm gay," he said.

Shit. Right on the money, then.

"Fuck." He scrubbed his hands over his face, visibly strained and frustrated. "I haven't told anyone that in ten years. You're..." He sighed and sat back, and he shook his head. "I guess it makes you the fourth person to know the truth."

Why, I wanted to ask. Badly.

He was about to say something else, only our server arrived with two big plates.

Despite all of it, I was starving. I'd never understood when people felt down in the dumps for whatever reason and couldn't eat. Allison was like that. *Allison, whom you cheated on.* Damn it all.

"I will never judge you, Kieran," I said quietly when it was just us two again.

One corner of his mouth tugged up slightly, though it was anything but a humorous smile. It was filled with whatever it was that haunted him.

"My family would," he murmured, picking off the tomatoes from his burger. "I came out to Angie, my eldest sister, when I was fourteen, and she told me never to speak of it again. She said it was probably a phase. Everyone is confused sometimes. And she spared me a lot of grief."

"By hiding who you are?" I couldn't believe it. Anger flared up, as it always did when I read about these things. To have a similar case happening so close only made it worse. It felt personal.

"I get your reaction," he chuckled. "It was torture to hide when I was a kid, and yeah, I thought there was something wrong with me." He lifted a shoulder. "I didn't lose my family, though. I grew up, and I heard more homophobic slurs than I could count from most of them. It was 'fag this,' 'fag that.' And I kept thinking, if they'd aimed that at *me*..." He shook his head. "No, I'm glad my sister warned me."

That pained me. Genuinely, truly, it hurt. He'd sacrificed so very much, all because he didn't want to lose people who might be against him.

"Did you laugh?" I wondered, dreading the answer. "When your family cracked ignorant jokes about gay people, I mean."

He shot me a brief glare that spoke volumes.

I couldn't imagine the pain he must've felt in that situation. The level of betrayal, the shame.

An urge to comfort and protect seared its way through me, and I had to look away before I joined him on his side of the booth and...and what? Held him? I was a fool.

Instead, I cleared my throat and took a bite of my burger.

"Maggie knows," he admitted.

That was a bit of a fucking shock, to be honest. And it probably showed.

He nodded. "The second person who knew about me was a guy in Savannah. It was through him I met Maggie—when I was... I wouldn't say I was *with* him...? But we hooked up from time to time when I wasn't scared shitless someone would see us." He paused, maybe trapped in a memory. "One day, Maggie knocked on my door and gave me an earful about how I was hurting her friend by stringing him along."

Wild guess. She and that guy probably weren't friends anymore.

"She came to defend her friend and ended up falling in love with you?"

He laughed, his mouth full of burger. It wasn't a funny moment, yet he made it seem so effortless to look happy.

"That would be a long story very short, but kind of," he replied. "She picked a morning before class when I was at my lowest, and I word-vomited to her—this stranger. I told her everything." He reached for the ketchup on the table. "We became friends, and I could tell she had a crush on me after a while. Then she agreed to pretend to be my girlfriend one Christmas when I went home to see my family. My folks were on my case about bringing home a girl sometime, so..."

Pretending was always easy. Even I knew a thing or two about that.

"So, did you strike a deal, you and Maggie? I mean, it's unlikely she forgot you're into guys."

"And yet..." He sighed and stared at his burger. "It started out that way. She wanted a family, and I—"

"Wanted to make your parents happy," I said with a hint of bitterness. I didn't know where that came from.

Kieran frowned. "I wanted to belong somewhere and not have my family hate me, aye. The truth isn't worth everything, Ben. I never understood why staying true was this optimal end goal. Sometimes, the cost is too steep."

"I'm sorry." I wasn't sure I agreed with him, but I hadn't walked in his shoes. I didn't know what it was like.

"It's all right. I'm not saying my decision was brilliant, but I wouldn't change anything. Without..." He exhaled and put down his burger. "I have Jaylin. She's my world."

That part, I understood.

Kieran went on to explain that the situation at home became strained sometimes, because of who he was and that Maggie had lived under the illusion that she could change him. She'd thought, over the years, he would somehow forget and fall in love with her. He did love her, he said, just not in that way.

I, for one, fully understood now why she'd freaked out the time she'd found his porn stash.

Kieran and I were back in Camassia a little before eight, and we walked toward our cars in silence.

It was a lovely summer evening here tonight. The smell of pine and ocean salt in the air mingled with the scents of tree blossoms and food. With the train station so close to one of the popular restaurant avenues in the Valley, the craving for barbecue and seafood hit me on my way home from work more often than it should.

"So, our story for today?" Kieran asked as we reached the parking lot.

"We had one too many after work and got piercings." I knew very well how stupid that sounded, but it was what we had.

"We're gonna fight with our wives tonight, aren't we?"

"Oh, that's a certainty," I replied.

"Great." He sighed and unlocked his car. "We should get together this weekend for a barbecue."

"You smell the food too, don't you?"

"God, yes."

I laughed and told him I'd let Allison know. Then we went our separate ways, except we drove in the exact same direction and had the same destination. We should probably consider carpooling on the days I was in the city.

While I stopped at a light, I opened the glove box and grabbed a pack of gum. Time to do the last of my damage control before I faced my family. It wasn't the first time I'd chewed gum to improve my smell.

Leaving the Valley district, I followed Kieran through a patch of the forest that stretched from the ocean into the mountains. Thoughts about everything that had happened today threatened to resurface, which I couldn't allow at the moment. I was going to pretend. I wasn't losing my spot in Kieran's life, but we were standing on new ground now.

"It can't happen again."

Well, good. It was a wise decision. Being a cheater was horrible. I didn't even want anything to happen again! Most likely. All right, I could admit I disliked shutting doors so firmly; a small part of me evidently enjoyed playing with fire. Nevertheless, it was my friendship with him that needed to remain intact, nothing else.

What had happened was a momentary lapse of control. It'd been utterly thoughtless.

You were intimate with a man.

I shuddered and aimed for the same exit Kieran had just taken.

I'd never wanted a man before, even for a second. Objectively, I could find both men and women attractive, though that didn't mean I was aroused or *attracted*. This thing with Kieran was... I didn't know what it was. Brianna could tell me, I was sure.

"Like I'd tell her any of this," I whispered to myself.

She'd psychoanalyze me until I couldn't tell what was up and what was down.

Nothing had changed, though. I wasn't attracted to men. I was attracted to—actually, *was* I? Was I attracted to Kieran? There was undoubtedly a strong pull, but how did I know if that was physical?

I could list a hundred things that *weren't* about gender that drew me in where he was concerned. So, no, nothing had changed with me, and that didn't mean I wanted to jump into bed with Kieran. I only did that with my wife. Allison. Her name was Allison. I'd married her.

By the time I reached my street and parked my car in the driveway, Kieran had already disappeared inside his home.

There was no time to mentally prepare myself for Allison's questions tonight. Jess was standing in the living room window waving to me, and I mustered a smile and raised a hand.

That's why I can pretend.

At his goofy grin, revealing the gap between two teeth, it hit me how easy it would be to pretend like nothing had happened today. I didn't want anything to change at home, and I was going to make sure it didn't.

With that thought, I left my car and smoothed down my tie. I was back to looking like a respectable businessman, though Allison would definitely be able to tell I'd had alcohol today.

"Daddy, you're late!" Jess shouted as I entered the house. He came running from the kitchen in only a pair of pajama bottoms. "We went to the beach today!"

"I heard." I squatted down and smooched his cute face. "Mum also told me you were a whiny little thing." I poked his belly.

He widened his eyes. "Only a minute."

I chuckled. "How long is a minute?"

A crease appeared in his forehead, and he held up nine fingers. "Like this?"

"I fear we've been slacking about teaching you how to tell time, young man." I grinned and touched his cheek, then stood up again. "Where's your brother?"

He shrugged. "I dunno. His room."

That was good. One set of little ears was enough.

After shrugging out of my suit jacket, I removed my shoes and followed Jess into the living room. Allison was on the sofa, and one of her shows was on. *Survivor*, I believed. She recorded them while she was in school, then binge-watched here and there when she was home.

"Hey." I dropped a kiss to the top of her head, then sat down in a chair.

"Hello to you." She quirked a brow, studying me. "You look tired. Long day?"

I inclined my head. "Very." Something was off. I cocked my head and eyed her—oh. "You dyed your hair?" Her regular light-brown tresses seemed slightly more reddish.

"I did." She smiled. "You like?"

"It's pretty," I answered honestly. I did like this look on her. It was more laid-back, and it wasn't only her hair. During shorter breaks from school, she never truly relaxed. She got dressed for the day as soon as she woke up, and she rarely showed her face without makeup. Now, though, her face was clear, and she looked comfortable in yoga pants and one of my tees.

Jess, who stood by the table and ate from a bowl of grapes, looked at his mother and scrunched his nose. "It's the same."

She smirked and leaned forward to tickle him. "You're as observant as your father, I see."

Pardon?

Allison's phone dinged on the table, and she picked it up to read a message. When her gaze sharpened and flew to me, I could only guess it was from Maggie.

"Jess, you can go brush your teeth," she said. "Daddy or I will check on you in a bit."

Oh boy.

Jess was a second away from arguing, so I cleared my throat and gave him a pointed look of warning.

He blasted us with a high level of sulking before he stomped up the stairs.

"Gossip from Maggie?" I guessed.

Kieran worked fast.

"You went out drinking with Kieran?" she asked accusingly.

I remained calm, not ready to turn this into a fight. Not for this. "Yes, after work, we met up for drinks. We had more than a few."

She scoffed and pinned me with another look. "You don't look very drunk."

"We had burgers afterward. It sobers you up surprisingly well." Especially if you were discussing heavy topics. "Is there a problem, Allison?"

"Of course there is." By her tone, it was as if she couldn't believe I didn't see the issue. "I was under the impression you had meetings all day, and then, while I'm taking care of our children, you go out and—"

"Are you fucking kidding me?" I blurted out. She could *not* use the children in her defense here. Out of the goddamn question. With those few words, she had my blood boiling. "You know what? After we got positively smashed, we went and got piercings—for the fuck of it. I was off work earlier than I thought, but I wasn't ready to come home."

"Excuse me?" She sat back, shocked and angry, and her face turned a color that almost matched her hair dye. "First of all, you got *pierced*?"

"We got nipple rings." Okay, I felt like an idiot saying that. I wasn't seventeen, for chrissake.

She shook her head, dazed, and pressed forward. "I can't believe you. I'm barely home, and when I am, you feel the need to—"

"Oh good, you've noticed you're barely around."

"Don't throw that in my—"

I glared. "Lower your goddamn voice. I don't want the boys to hear."

She huffed and rolled her eyes. "As if they haven't gotten used to hearing us fight this summer."

"And isn't that bloody terrible?" I replied incredulously. "Nate gets withdrawn easily as it is."

She glowered at that. "I'm well aware of how my own son reacts, Bennett. I'd really fucking appreciate if you stopped behaving like this is my fault. Because if I remember correctly, I wanted to go to school when I was eighteen, but—"

"*Enough*," I growled. "You can't keep using that against me, Allison. No one forced you to go to a school halfway across the country. You could've had both—you could've attended a school in Seattle and come home every night. But that wasn't enough for you, and now you're trying to make me feel guilty for taking *one* day for myself? And you're bitching about taking care of the children all by yourself? *Fuck that*," I spat out. My heart thundered in my chest, and a quiet voice stirred within me, one that told me to shut up before I said something I couldn't take back. "I take care of the kids every single day you're not here. I love nothing more than being their father, but don't think for a single second that I will feel bad for wanting something for myself too."

"You mean one college experience wasn't enough for you?" she whisper-shouted. "Please do let me know when you're satisfied. Perhaps a tattoo will get you there?"

I gnashed my teeth and noticed I was halfway out of my chair. Taking a deep breath, I sat back again and scrubbed my hands over my face.

A second college experience, huh?

"Are you honestly comparing my years in college to yours?" I asked tiredly. "I can count the times I went out with friends on one hand, because I had to make money and take care of you too. College is nothing I look back on fondly. It was four years of running between classes, our flat, and work. Whenever I had an exam, I had to hope it was a slow day at the Xerox place so I could study. Think of that next time you head out with your girlfriends."

She stared back at me with venom but said nothing, and I caught her blinking back tears before she turned away.

I felt numb.

It hit me that Allison might never let go of the bitterness she'd felt since I'd gotten her pregnant. I'd been trying to redeem myself for nine years, and nothing appeared to work. It wasn't enough for her.

I could pretend, though. I could pretend everything was fine, and we'd become one of those couples who talked but never communicated. Had we not already reached that point? We could go through dinners and evenings on the couch talking about insignificant everyday matters. A lot of it revolved around the boys. Then there was work and school and whatever we'd read in the paper or heard on the news.

When was the last time we talked about deeper things? Really connected and existed on the same page in life.

I could pretend it wasn't years ago.

CHAPTER 9

I felt like all of us pretended for the rest of that summer. We had barbecues with the Marshalls, we did summer activities with the kids, we had dinner together every night, we talked but not really, we laughed but not really, and we loved each other but not really.

Before Allison went back to Chicago, we took the boys shopping for school supplies.

We'd finally gotten Nathan into the private school in Ponderosa, much to his excitement. He'd cleared the shelf above his desk in his room for new books, and he was very particular about the setup. He needed a new holder for his pens, a new ruler, and he didn't like his bookends.

"I need new name tags for my books too, Dad." Nate took the lead in the store and walked ahead of Allison and me.

Jess was clinging to the cart Allison drove, more interested in his toy from McDonald's than browsing for a new lunch box.

"We'll find you some tags, buddy," I said. My phone

vibrated in my pocket, so I retrieved it and smirked at a message from Kieran.

Steaks are marinating. Jaylin wonders if she can sit next to Jess. I told her no.

There would be so much trouble when they went to the same school. Three options for kindergarten became only one alternative when it was time for first grade in our district. And we didn't think they'd build a new school within the year.

I replied to Kieran while Allison encouraged Jess to pick out a pencil case.

You can't fight Jess's charm forever, my friend.

His response flew up on my screen.

Watch me.

I chuckled.

"Dad," Nate hollered down the aisle. "There's no space theme. I informed you I want the space theme we saw in the magazine."

"Yes, I received the memo, son. Loud and clear. We can always order something if you don't find it here."

"Just make sure it gets here before he starts," Allison cautioned.

No, I was going to delay the process so our son didn't have supplies for when school started. Christ.

A few hours later, we headed over to Kieran and Maggie's for another barbecue.

It was a nice day, one of summer's last ones. It was as if the day were squeezing all the warmth it could from the sun.

Allison made a beeline for the kitchen where Maggie was,

whereas I aimed for the backyard and had two hungry boys following me.

What Jaylin called "Daddy's music" was blaring from the speakers in the living room, and Nathan was not impressed. Jess got an energy boost from the Irish rock, though. He bolted through the open sliding doors and out onto the deck Kieran had spent the past few weeks building.

Seeing Kieran never ceased to offer a bit of relief. There was a sense of *everything will be okay* when he and I were in the same place.

The feeling struck a little harder today, probably because we hadn't had our Wednesday this week. Kieran had been at some work conference in Denver.

"Where's Jaylin?" Jess shouted. Because that was what he did.

"We say hello first, son," I reminded him.

Kieran threw us a smirk over the shoulder before returning to flip the steaks and hot dogs on the grill. A brand-new monstrosity that Kieran had bought the day after they moved in, along with new patio furniture. And the table was now packed with side dishes and condiments.

Maggie went all out with food. Allison had a dozen recipes in her head that she recycled over and over, and the one time I hinted she try something new... Well, that didn't go very well.

"Oi, Brooks boys," Kieran said. "She's probably in her room, Jess. You can go get her. Dinner's ready."

Nathan sat down where he usually sat and became immersed in his book. I walked over to the grill where a beer was waiting for me.

"This looks fantastic." I eye-fucked the thick steaks on the grill and felt my stomach rumbling. "Is that the rub you bought at the festival?"

There was an annual festival in town at the end of summer,

and we'd taken our families there together this year. Kieran and I had gone on rides with the kids, given them too much ice cream and funnel cake, then handed three fussy children over to our wives so we could go to the beer tasting. When fourteen breweries made it to Camassia, you had to be there.

"Aye, the last of it," Kieran replied. "How was your day?"

"Busy," I said. "The boys got new clothes but couldn't decide on anything they needed for school. I think I'll have to order off the internet."

He nodded and took a swig of his beer. "Well, let me know when Jess decides. Jaylin needs a new backpack, and when Mags asked her what she wanted, she said the same as Jess."

I let out a laugh, and as Kieran grumbled under his breath, I threw in some mock-sympathy and rubbed his shoulder. "You poor, poor man. Your little girl is best friends with a boy. How on earth will you survive?"

"This is just the beginning," he argued. "Today, it's a backpack. In ten years, it's condoms."

I shook my head, thoroughly amused. "A kid asking for condoms? You're doing something right, then."

He rolled his eyes and plated the meat.

The man made me smile. Every time I saw him. Taking a deep breath, I savored the feeling and looked out over the yard. Unlike ours on the other side of the fence, they didn't have toys scattered about. Jaylin had a swing set and an inflatable pool on the lawn, but someone was good at putting the little things away.

Other than that, there were a couple apple trees with a hammock strung up between them. Lastly, Maggie's flower beds that would next year become her garden. She'd told us of her plans to grow herbs and tomatoes. In great detail.

I needed to mow our lawn…

My backyard wasn't a complete disaster compared to theirs,

but it needed some maintenance. We had a hot tub on our porch that we hadn't used in four years, and the boys had a sandbox. Which didn't get much action either these days.

"This was amazing—as always." I wiped my mouth with a napkin and reached for my beer.

"You're always so kind, Bennett," Maggie said with a smile. "I enjoy cooking for you guys."

Out of the corner of my eye, Allison's own smile became a little forced.

"Can I take credit for the steaks, at least?" Kieran lifted a brow at his wife.

I laughed under my breath.

We were two happy, unhappy families pretending to have our shit together. Everything looked great on the outside, but little digs and sideways comments spoke of issues that ran deep. Buried under years of convincing ourselves this was how life was supposed to be—and some passive-aggressive behavior. As an extra spice.

While Maggie and Allison started clearing the table, Kieran and I brought our beers over to the hammock, and it didn't take many seconds before we had three children bouncing over.

We'd just sat down in the hammock when Jaylin shouted for us to make room.

"Don't jump, monkey," Kieran warned. "I don't know how much weight this will hold."

I had Jess put my beer on the lawn before he crawled up into my lap.

"I like it when you're cuddly, my boy." I hugged him to me and kissed the side of his head. "Do you think I can convince your brother to sit on my lap too?"

Nathan looked up from his book and shook his head quickly. "I don't think it will hold."

Kieran chuckled as Jaylin got comfy in his arms. "We might as well test the theory, buddy. Get over here."

Nate could not look more dubious, but I was glad he came over anyway. He'd already reached that age where being affectionate wasn't a given anymore, and it sucked royally. Standing in front of us, no doubt listening to the squeaking and creaking, he blew out a breath and glanced at the rope tied around the trees.

"There's a spot for you right here, son." I was thigh-to-thigh with Kieran, and Nate could plant his butt right in the middle of our laps. Jaylin and Jess were climbers anyway, leaving more lap.

"Ouch, watch the jewels, baby." Kieran hissed and removed Jaylin's foot from his crotch.

I wouldn't dare laugh, because Jess would be my karma.

"At least if we go down, you two are at the bottom," Nate mumbled.

I smirked and helped him up. Then we all waited in absolute silence while the hammock protested noisily.

"Eeep, we gonna crash!" Jaylin giggled madly.

"We're not going to crash," I chuckled.

It seemed to hold well enough, and I found myself needing this moment. Jess was full and tired, therefore in an excellent mood for being quiet and snuggled up in my arms, and Nate was leaning against me and reading his book. Even Jaylin seemed to calm down after a minute or so.

The backyard flooded with peace. The music had stopped, so all I heard was birdsong and the occasional neighbor.

"This is nice." I kissed the top of Nate's head and lolled my head to face Kieran. The sight made me smile. Jaylin was pretending to text on Kieran's phone, and he was playing along.

In low murmurs, he asked her to text Nana and tell her to send cookies.

"Okay, I'm doing it," she said seriously. Her little fingers flew over the buttons. "'Nana, Daddy wants oatmeal cookies and I also want some, but can you make mine with chocolate?' Now I'm sending it."

I grinned.

"Perfect." Kieran smiled and brushed some hair from her face. "I guess we wait now."

She really was his world.

In the year I'd known little Jaylin, she'd grown a lot. The chubbiness of her cheeks was disappearing, and she looked more like Kieran for every day that passed. Her hair was lighter and her nose was a lot cuter, but other than that—she had those eyes. The same as her father. His smirk too. You could see she would take after him immensely one day.

"Can you flip it with one hand?" She extended the mobile to him.

Kieran dutifully shut the phone, only to flip it open and earn a generous dose of excitement from Jaylin. Kids were easily impressed and viewed us as heroes for the littlest things. It was the best time.

"Hello Moto," she mimicked.

Kieran's shoulders shook with silent laughter. "Too fucking cute."

Jaylin blushed, resuming playing with his phone. "Bad word, Daddy."

"So don't tell Mommy."

"I'm no snish," she whispered.

"You're definitely not a *snitch*," he said and took a playful bite of her nose.

Seeing those two... That particular sight... My chest constricted painfully. I had no clue why. But self-preservation told me to bottle that shit up fast. I didn't want to go there, wherever *there* was.

Too comfortable to move an inch, I closed my eyes and threw out a mental anchor to keep me in the present. I had my boys with me, the sun was getting low, the late-summer air smelled of barbecue, and life was good. Life was okay. No, I was blessed. Life was good.

"Don't fall asleep on me, Ben."

I sighed through a chuckle and opened my eyes again.

Shit.

My stare flitted across his features as he watched me too, our positions mirrored. Kieran didn't get very tanned in the summer, I was learning. He got freckles instead. Tiny dots you could only see up close. Like now.

We shared something, didn't we? Something that scared me shitless. Something that made breathing easier. Something that could bring an insurmountable volume of pain. Something I craved more of nonetheless.

I'd done my best not to think of him in a way that was remotely close to what we'd done in that alley.

Sometimes I failed.

"Daddy?" Jess asked sleepily.

I swallowed hard and tore my gaze away. "What is it, sweetheart?"

He let out a big yawn. "I gotta pee."

Of course.

I didn't see the Marshalls the next day, and it was probably a good thing. As much as spending time with Kieran was my heroin, I needed a bit of distance at times too. He was intense; he was someone to get lost in. Evidently also on a platonic level.

I couldn't even imagine the hearts he'd broken over the years. He probably didn't even know, but people were drawn to him.

The time I had left my briefcase in his office while we were out, it hadn't escaped my notice that women gawked blatantly.

No, today was all about family.

We drove down to Seattle to drop Allison off at the airport. Nate was quiet; Jess was upset. And he'd started asking Allison why her school was so far away, to which she had bullshit responses that pissed me off nowadays.

She could pretend she hadn't willingly chosen a school in Chicago, knowing full well it would put hours between her and her sons.

I could pretend to understand her while I comforted Jess.

After we'd said goodbye to Allison, we drove to my sister's for dinner. Not the best place to be when your mind was at war, but I was in no mood to cook tonight.

"This is tearing at you, little brother," she told me. "I honestly can't believe her."

I sighed and peered into the living room to make sure the boys couldn't hear. They seemed to be distracted by the movie playing, thankfully.

"I don't need you to talk more shit about my wife, Brianna," I replied.

"Of course, always defending her," she muttered and checked on the rice. "Do you do it because she's not here to defend herself? She's literally leaving you to raise two kids on your own."

"I don't want to get into this now," I said firmly. "Please respect that."

She nodded shortly. "Fine. Let's talk about you and Kieran—"

"Oh, for the love of—"

"No, hear me out!" she laughed. "I swear, I won't go into

research mode. I'm genuinely curious. We haven't seen much of each other this summer, and I want to catch up. That's all."

I eyed her skeptically.

"I promise, Bennett."

I sighed again, figuring it couldn't hurt to just mention that Kieran and I got along well. I sure as hell wouldn't go deeper than that.

CHAPTER 10

"Don't talk to me," I muttered, rubbing my temples. The humidity and the children screaming in the pool didn't help my headache at all, and the last thing I needed was Kieran's gloating. He so very rarely got hungover the way I did.

The bloody Irish.

Yesterday, we'd had more than a happy hour after work. We'd both had late meetings in the city, so our Wednesday together had become a night out—in a regular bar. With truckloads of people, a rock band playing live music, and no Roxy.

It'd been a mistake. From now on, I would always make my way to U District and meet up with him there.

"You know what you need?" Kieran said. "You need a camping trip with me and the kids."

I flashed him a hard stare because that wasn't funny at all. "I cannot tell you how much I don't need that."

Good fucking grief, it would snow any day now. They'd been warning us every day since Halloween last week.

"Oh, come on." He sat forward and cracked his knuckles absently. "Jaylin's been asking all fall."

"And it's fucking freezing now," I pointed out in disbelief. I couldn't believe he was considering this. "Normal people go camping in the summer, not when the weatherman is telling us about a snowstorm in Canada's interior that might come our way."

He rolled his eyes and sat back again. "You're being ridiculous. We both have good gear."

Hardly because of my love for nature. I enjoyed a good hike every now and then, and I even liked taking the boys camping when it was warm—okay, I liked it somewhat. But heading out now? The two of us and three kids? Christ.

Nate would probably stay with my father, come to think of it. There was no way he'd spend a night in the woods this time of year when he barely tolerated it otherwise. My eldest was quirky about camping. He could get preposterously excited to go—Jess-level excited—and then we'd hike for an hour before he changed his tune entirely.

Jess would love it, though.

I wasn't considering it, was I?

"I didn't know Jaylin cared for the woods that much," I said with a frown.

Kieran gave me a flat stare. "But do you know a little boy who happens to love it? One my daughter just has to copy at every goddamn turn?"

I pressed my lips together to contain my laugh.

"Listen," he said, "we can head out early this Saturday. Chances are they'll find it too cold, and we'll be home for dinner the same day. Either way, I gotta go. I can deny her a twentieth Barbie, but I can't say no when she wants to explore nature. No matter where she got it from."

I squinted and scratched my chin. "She has twenty Barbie dolls?"

I was suddenly extra happy to have boys.

"Nineteen," he sighed exasperatedly. "Ben...don't leave me hanging here. I'll bring whiskey."

"Don't—" The mere memory of the number of drinks we had last night made me want to throw up. No, on the way home when I slurred about doing a dry month and Kieran had guffawed, I hadn't been joking. I needed to drink less, regardless. "I'll go. Fine. I'll talk to the boys when we get home—just, no alcohol."

He chuckled like the devil he was. "How about I ask Mags to make you those lemon bars?"

Now, I could nod. "See, you should've led with that. They're wonderful."

We'd see how wonderful they were when we froze our asses off in a tent this weekend, though.

"It might snow, son." Dad peered out from the door and up at the overcast sky.

I shot Kieran a look over my shoulder. Not that he could hear. He was in the car with Jaylin and Jess. "Yes, and we're still going. Like fools."

"I'm so glad I'm staying with you, Grampa." Nate gave me a swift hug before entering Dad's house.

"I'll have Ben and Jess returned to you in one piece, sir!" Kieran hollered from the car.

Dad's face crinkled with his amusement. "He's funny, that one."

"He's a bloody comedian," I muttered under my breath. "All right—Nate, have a nice weekend. I love you."

He smirked up at me. "Love you too. I'll think of you when my feet are toasty warm from the fire and my stomach is full of hot chocolate and marshmallows."

I narrowed my eyes. "You've been on the phone with Aunt Brianna a lot lately. Her attitude is rubbing off."

He laughed. Hell, Dad laughed too. I was getting no support here.

We said our goodbyes, and I trudged back to Kieran's car. He'd rolled up the window after delivering his oh-so-funny message to my father, and now I was greeted by the very loud soundtrack to the latest Pixar movie. Jess and Jaylin were bouncing in the back as much as their seat belts allowed.

"Okay…I was promised lemon bars," I said. "We're not leaving civilization before I devour at least one."

Kieran snickered and nodded at the glove box. "She made a dozen just for you."

Splendid. Who wanted defined abs anyway?

We went up, up, up the mountains, to the very last parking lot for outdoorsy people who wanted to go up to Coho Pass. It was split into two lots, so you could see day hikers who'd parked and would soon return to their vehicles and go home. The lot for overnight guests was understandably empty.

Kieran and I shouldered our backpacks, and that was when I realized how geared up he was for this. Was he a hunter? Because he had a rifle attached to the side of the pack. All I had was a couple knives. And bear spray…

"I didn't know you hunted," I said.

"Huh? Oh, I don't. But this isn't Boston, son. We have bears here."

I laughed. "That's why I have bear spray."

His brows rose. "I ain't planning on getting that close."
He had a point.
"Daddy, why can't I have a backpack like you?" Jess asked.
I bent down to zip up his jacket properly. "Because you'll get tired after five minutes. Maybe next year. How's that?"
He shrugged and made a face, then forgot the whole conversation when Jaylin said she wanted to "go nowww."
Passing a clearing with a bunch of picnic tables and nature-loving families, we began our trek on the blue trail, and Jess and Jaylin ran ahead to inspect pinecones and dead critters along the path.
"So you won't drink anything tonight?" Kieran asked.
I side-eyed him. "No... Why, did you bring anything?"
"I want whiskey and Bailey's with my cocoa tonight," he replied.
Damn. That did sound lovely. But I'd promised myself.
"Daddy!" Jaylin hollered. "Can we bury it?" She was pointing at something on the ground. A bird.
"Just leave it, monkey," Kieran answered.
She pouted.
"Come see this beetle, Jaylin!" Jess shouted up the path.
She darted off, the dead bird forgotten, and the hike continued. We stopped after an hour or so for snacks and hot cider that Maggie had packed. Since it was only the four of us, I'd brought my tent for us to share, and it had resulted in Maggie filling Kieran's pack with enough food to feed an army.
Dark clouds loomed above us all day, but so far, no rain or snow. I was still glad we'd packed my tent, though. Not only was it big, despite being lightweight, but it was an expensive four-season affair that would hold against storm winds and heavy snowfall.
I'd bought it a few years ago when I'd thought it'd be a fun thing to take the whole family camping.

Allison had laughed and shaken her head at me.

"Jess, don't go too far," I called.

We'd been at it a few hours at this point, and I envied my boy's energetic behavior. He just didn't get tired.

Jaylin was starting to struggle, which she didn't want to admit, and that made her a bit cranky.

"Daddy, I need a bathroom," she complained.

Kieran furrowed his brow. "There are no bathrooms out here, baby girl. I told you about this, remember? I'll help you, though. You wanna go now?"

"No toilet?" she squeaked. "Fuck."

My eyes widened, and I had to suppress my laugh.

Judging by the look on Kieran's face, she didn't curse often. "You know that word is off-limits to you, Jaylin. You'll be dropping a dollar from your allowance in the swear jar when we get home."

I smiled and continued ahead to catch up with Jess.

Studying the map, I deduced we were about an hour or two from the summit when the first raindrops started falling. So we decided to stop at the next clearing we saw and set up camp. Tomorrow, the weather would have to decide our route. If it got too cold or the rain wouldn't let up, it might be easier to reach the summit rather than head down all the way to the parking lot again. Because at Coho Pass, there was a tram we could take down.

Kieran barely looked winded, so I wasn't going to mention that my legs were dying on me. My thighs had been protesting for at least two hours, and now my calves felt stiff and sore too. As if they were constantly on the verge of cramping.

"It'll be fun trying to find firewood that isn't soaked." Kieran wiped some raindrops off his face. "But hey, at least it's not cold enough to snow. That's something, right?" He smirked.

I peered up at the sky, where the clouds seemed almost to sink into the treetops, and decided I would prefer snow. "If it snowed, the wood wouldn't be wet yet."

He chuckled. "You're so negative today."

I frowned to myself. There was no question about whether or not he was right; I'd been bitching all day.

That ended now, goddammit. I was spending the weekend with some of my favorite people. If Nate were here... My father and Brianna... That would be basically everyone. "Christ," I muttered under my breath. It probably wasn't a good sign that I forgot to include my wife.

Twenty minutes later, we found a decent spot to set up camp. Others had obviously been here before, and there was already a fire pit dug out with rocks surrounding it. The ground wasn't awesome; we'd have to clear the tent area of twigs and branches. On the other hand, we had a fucking view.

"Look, Jess!" Jaylin hollered excitedly. She was pointing to where the trees parted and offered a fantastic view of the bay. We were high up and could see the marina in Downtown, all the way out to the Chinook Islands.

"Talk about picture-perfect," Kieran murmured. "Yeah, yeah, I know, if the weather were better."

"I wasn't gonna say anything," I laughed.

"Good." He smiled wryly. "Let's pitch the tent."

"I'll do it," I said. "You can look for firewood."

"You sure?"

I nodded. "I'll help when I'm done. The guy at the store—when I bought the tent—guaranteed it wouldn't take more than five minutes to set up. It takes ten, but close enough."

"Ah, one of those fancy ones." He smirked.

"Don't add it to your shopping list," I told him, shrugging

out of my backpack. "You're one purchase away from being a shopaholic."

He laughed. "You sound like Mags."

Well, if the brand-new boots fit...

Kieran often had new gadgets delivered to his house. He said it was a way of curing boredom.

After digging out the tent from my backpack, I got started with the two bendy poles—wait, wrong one, no, this went to the left... Oh right, they would form an X. It was coming back to me. Nate had been my helper this summer. If he didn't grow up to become an engineer or something, I'd be surprised.

The dome-shaped tent was in place by the time my jacket was beginning to fail on me. It'd been advertised as rainproof, and I could officially call bullshit on that one.

We had dinner when darkness fell over Camassia. The rain had thankfully stopped, giving our fire a sparkling boost. Embers danced in the pillar of smoke. The kids were happy, munching on hot dogs and drinking lemonade.

Kieran and I had both brought our cameras, so they got some exercise too.

"Daddy, can I have more ketchup?" Jaylin held up her hot dog. She hadn't left her father's lap since it had started to get dark.

Kieran's forehead creased, and he shook his head in amusement as he reached for the ketchup bottle. "You're not supposed to lick the ketchup off the hot dog."

"It's yummy," Jaylin giggled.

As if on cue, Jess, who was seated next to me, began licking the ketchup off of his own hot dog.

I grinned at the little doofus.

Deeming my third hot dog sufficiently grilled, I withdrew the stick from the fire and grabbed a bun. Unlike the kids, Kieran and I went all out with condiments. Ketchup, mustard, roasted onion, and relish.

Everything was packed in to-go bottles or mini containers, and merely hot dogs weren't enough for Maggie. She'd made mozzarella sticks that were wrapped in foil in the fire right now, and for tomorrow, there were wrapped potato skins with bacon and cheese.

"Is there anything Maggie can't do in the kitchen?" I asked with my mouth full.

It was simply impossible not to notice the effort she put into everything.

Kieran smiled faintly. "She's pretty good."

I'll say.

"Mommy likes to make food?" Jaylin asked.

Kieran nodded and handed her a napkin. "A little. Anyway, there's dessert too. My backpack's gonna be empty when we go home tomorrow, so eat up."

"This isn't me being negative, but everything has gone too smoothly today," I said.

Kieran grinned and threw another log on the fire. "I was just thinking the same thing."

That was a relief.

It would be interesting to see how balance was restored. Either we got mauled by a bear in the middle of the night, or we all came down with food poisoning. Because the way things were right in this moment...way too perfect. Jess and Jaylin had fallen asleep within ten minutes after we'd inflated the air mattresses and rolled out the sleeping bags. The only thing we had to promise was not to leave them, and we'd vowed to sit right outside.

I'd caved on the Bailey's, though... Saying no to a shot of whiskey in my hot chocolate hadn't been difficult, but the mild and sweet burn of the Bailey's was too much to resist. It left a trail of chocolaty warmth on its way down.

Add a couple lemon bars to that? I was in heaven.

"I'm glad you dragged me up here, Kieran," I admitted. "It's great for Jess too."

He held out his tin mug and smiled a little.

I clinked my own mug to his and took a swig.

Everything that wasn't illuminated by the fire was as dark as it could get, except for the glittering lights down the mountain. Between the trees, Downtown's modest nightlife was in full swing. Not that we could see specifics from up here, but one part had more lights. The marina and the small boardwalk there were all restaurants and pubs.

Kieran and I sighed contentedly at the same time, and we chuckled.

"Daddy..." That was Jaylin's sleepy voice. "No, stop it. Nana says it's okay."

I peered into the tent, then lifted my brows at Kieran.

He grinned. "She talks in her sleep."

"Oh." I smiled and glanced inside the tent again. I could barely see her, despite the dimly lit lamp we'd strung up. She was buried in her sleeping bag, with only her cute face visible, framed by a hat with fuzzy earflaps. "She might be the most adorable girl I've ever met."

Kieran smirked, eyes on the ground, and wrapped his arms loosely around his knees. "Mags and I actually talked about kids the other day."

"Really?" I straightened quickly and frowned. It felt... strange. "Are you thinking about expanding?"

"She is." He cleared his throat, the humor in his face fading. "Your boys actually made me consider it, but I don't know. Christ. Bringing another little one into a family like ours...? Doesn't feel right." He side-eyed me hesitantly. "You think you and Allison will have another?"

I shook my head. Not a chance in hell. Raising two boys on my own was enough. "If I did want to... No... No, I couldn't. Allison and I aren't where we should be—on any level."

Kieran nodded slowly and watched the fire. "Do you see yourself spending the rest of your life with her?"

Jesus, what a question. I blew out a heavy breath, feeling weighed down. Truth be told, I didn't want to think in those terms. Once upon a time, it had been a given. Of course it would be the two of us until we died. Of course it would. But that was before...well, everything.

"We have another year," I said, phrasing myself carefully. "After she graduates and starts working in Seattle, there must be a change. It can't go on the way it is now."

I felt lonely—and had for a long time.

Most days, I was fine. The boys and I had created our own routines, and we did our thing. Sometimes, I even preferred to be alone with them. Then there were times, often after the boys went to sleep, that I yearned. I wanted someone next to me on the couch, someone to connect with, someone who spoke my language, someone who—

"I know that feeling," Kieran said quietly and finished his beverage. "But who am I kidding? It's not like I'm gonna leave her. I made my choice a long time ago."

That was another heavy thought I didn't want running around in my head tonight.

I threw back the last of my cocoa and Bailey's, then set down the mug. "Listening to us, no one would think we're only turning thirty next year."

He snorted. "Only? I think I've been stuck in a midlife crisis since I was fifteen."

I wanted to tell him it wasn't a midlife crisis. It was regret and bitterness because he couldn't be himself.

I knew because it'd been slowly building up in me too. The past few years, I'd kept hoping the next small thing would create big changes. Last time, it'd been my promotion. How daft could a person be to believe it would magically make me happy?

Maybe you should try cocaine.

CHAPTER 11

When we wanted something we couldn't have, we bargained. It happened every day, big and small. Allison bargained every time she went on a diet. If she had salad all day, she could have cake in the evening. If she exercised on Monday, she could order pizza when she studied on Tuesday, Wednesday, Thursday, and Friday.

I bargained as well. I gave myself an excuse—that I justified and validated in my head—to postpone things I needed to do right now. Such as dust off my gym membership, learn to cook better, get up earlier in the morning so we didn't have to rush on the way to school, and...such things as finding happiness. Or creating it, maybe. Either way, I constantly postponed it.

I didn't know what I wanted at the moment. What I did know was that the weeks leading up to Christmas were dreadful. I was genuinely unhappy with myself.

Was this the payback for the camping trip? There'd been no

food poisoning or bears, but both Kieran and I had been low on energy since we got back.

As the cherry on a shit sundae, my sons were sick, so I had been home with them all week. No puking or diarrhea so far, just nasty coughs, sore throats, and low-running fevers that didn't want to ease up.

Thankfully, we'd been given antibiotics today, so I hoped the worst was over.

I was bloody exhausted, and I hadn't even put on real clothes today. I'd worn sweats and a stained hoodie when I took the boys to the doctor, and they likely weren't coming off anytime soon. I couldn't be bothered.

The microwave beeped, and I took out the bowl of soup I'd reheated from Panera. Cooking was out of the question and had been since yesterday. Takeout would have to do. At least Panera had some good comfort food for when children were sick and their fathers were running on fumes.

With my luck, the boys would be back to normal just in time for Allison's homecoming this weekend.

I divided the broccoli soup into two smaller bowls, put them on a tray with two potato rolls and some tea, then carried it into the living room where the boys had lived this week.

It was actually a relief they didn't want to be in their rooms. Less running back and forth and up and down the stairs for me.

Before they spotted me in the doorway, I took a deep breath and appreciated the pitiful yet so beautiful sight. My boys all cuddled up on the couch under my duvet, both with bed heads, matching pajamas, and weary gazes glued to the cartoons on the TV.

I wasn't as good as Allison at putting up Christmas decorations, but I'd done my best. The tree was in place, the gifts were slowly piling up, and all the holiday knickknacks Nate and Jess had made over the years were placed on the shelves.

Walking over to the couch, I set the tray on the table and reached for their medication.

"I'm not hungry, Dad," Nate mumbled.

"You have to try, sweetheart." I sought out their feet under the covers so I didn't sit down on them. Then I made the middle spot mine and felt Nate's forehead. "We'll try a few spoonfuls, okay?"

He let out a breath and forced himself to sit up.

Jess followed suit but ended up coughing so hard his eyes welled up with tears, so I gathered him to me and rubbed his back.

"It'll be over soon, baby," I murmured. "I promise."

He whimpered and tucked his head into the crook of my neck. While I waited for the soup to cool, I administered their medication. Nate could swallow his pill with water, but Jess wasn't there yet. So I took a spoonful of soup, blew on it a little, and put the pill in the food.

"Remember not to chew this time." I smiled in sympathy at his cute huff.

Jess opened his mouth, and in the soup went. He swallowed it quickly this time, and he made a soft "ah" sound.

"I like the warm," he croaked.

I nodded. "Feels better on your throat, doesn't it?"

"Yeah."

That encouraged Nate to try his soup too, and he had the same reaction. Only, his words were, "Marginally soothing."

What nine-year-old used the word *marginally*?

It felt good to see them eat. Jess even ate half his potato roll, though both were in agreement that the soup was best.

When they didn't want any more, I bribed them to drink some tea before they went back to resting. I could take them to go see a movie next week, no problem.

Jess required more sugar than should be legal, but he

drank it. That was all that mattered. Nate was actually fond of tea, so he didn't struggle as much. Then they returned to dozing on and off and watching cartoons, and I retreated to the kitchen.

If I sat down with them much longer on the couch, I'd fall asleep. Although, at this rate, I could probably fall asleep at the kitchen table too. Only the lamp in the window was switched on, and the dark welcomed sleep.

There were a couple quiet knocks on the door—a welcome distraction, whoever it was. I guessed it was Dad, but a look out the kitchen window told me it was Maggie.

I should've known, I mused on the way to the door. She'd been with her parents for a few days.

I opened the door, and she walked in like a mild summer storm. All business, always with a step-by-step plan, yet there was a softness to her nature that prevented her from coming off too strong.

"I'm so sorry, I didn't know the boys were sick." She marched straight for the kitchen, and she hadn't arrived empty handed. She carried four Tupperware containers. "You should've called me," she scolded. "I had to hear it from Kieran, and that man lives in his own time zone."

Tell me which one; I'll join him there.

To be honest, I missed him. Today was Wednesday, our day, and we wouldn't even see each other next week or the one after that. The Marshalls were heading to Boston for the holidays, and when they returned, Allison and I were flying to Chicago with the children to see her parents.

"You didn't have to bring the boys anything." I sat down at the table, too tired to pretend to have manners. "I appreciate the help, but I have it sort of covered."

She sent me a quick smile before opening my fridge. "This isn't for them, hon. I'm sure Nathan and Jess have everything they need. You, on the other hand? When was the last time you ate?"

I leaned back in my seat and scratched my elbow absently. I'd had breakfast, I knew that much. "I finished the soup they didn't eat for lunch," I offered.

"Case closed," she replied wryly. "So. There's a chicken casserole and rice in this one." She held up one of the containers and put it in the fridge. "Kieran's mother's ziti in here. This one has..." She lifted the lid. "Fried chicken with biscuits and gravy."

My stomach snarled in approval. The last one sounded diabetically delicious.

She put the last container in the fridge too. "Lastly, I borrowed Kieran's recipe and made some lemon bars. I hope they're as good as his."

She did what now? I cocked my head. "Kieran's recipe? They're not yours?"

"No? Well, I mean, technically, it's another recipe of my mother-in-law's, but he makes them." She closed the fridge again. "I like to cook, but Kieran and his family take things to a new level."

I didn't understand a word of what Maggie was saying. I distinctly remembered the first time I tried the lemon bars. Kieran came over with a container and specifically said "the wife sends treats."

"...swear most time is spent on cooking or being in the kitchen when we're visiting them..." Maggie was in the middle of rambling about Kieran's family. "Oh! Before I forget—again—I wanted to give you these." She picked up an envelope from her tote bag. "They're pictures from summer that I thought you'd like copies of. Some are from your camping trip a few weeks ago too."

I accepted the envelope and opened it. "That's kind of you.

I haven't developed anything from our camera yet, but I can make copies as well. I know there are a couple good ones of Kieran and Jaylin on there."

She smiled. "I appreciate that. Now—eat, rest, and repeat. Maybe a shower too?"

I chuckled and dipped my chin. "Yes, ma'am. Thank you for the food."

"Thank Kieran," she sang on the way out of the kitchen. "He cooked this week."

I snapped my mouth shut and frowned.

That Kieran didn't have any struggles in the kitchen was no news. The lemon bars, though... That was befuddling. Why would he say Maggie had made them?

Knowing there were leftovers in the fridge caused my hunger to flare up, so I nuked the fried chicken with biscuits and gravy right away. Then I sat down at the table again and flipped through the pictures while I ate.

Maggie—or Kieran—had taken quite a few photos of Allison and me together with the kids this summer. Often mid-laugh or with smiles, but it was hard not to notice that our focus was always on the boys.

"Goodness," I muttered around a mouthful of food. Maybe Kieran should teach me to be more inventive in the kitchen, because this was fantastic.

I stopped at one photo and brought it closer. My smile was instant. The picture was of us in the hammock. It looked like Kieran and I were in the middle of a conversation that put grins on our faces. Nathan was in the middle, Jess was climbing on me, and Jaylin was climbing on Kieran.

Brushing away a piece of dust from Kieran's face with my thumb, I inspected his expression and wished Maggie had taken the photo closer.

That assertive grin of his, though. It was deadly. It put a rock in my stomach every time.

After finishing my food, I brought the container to the sink—the picture still in my hand—and I put on a fresh pot of coffee.

There was another knock on the front door, and I looked out the window again. *Gut punch*. This time it was Kieran, so I gave a nod to indicate it was open.

He appeared in the doorway, dressed similarly to me in sweats and a hoodie. "Hey."

"Hey yourself." I mustered a smile even though I didn't want to. Something was building up rapidly in my chest, and it weighed me down. There was a breaking point to which I was standing dangerously close, but I didn't know what was threatening to break.

Kieran walked a few steps into the dimly lit kitchen and rubbed the back of his neck. "So Mags may have mentioned that it seemed you were under the impression that she'd made the pastries."

"I wonder how that happened," I drawled. Staying by the counter, I leaned back against it and rested my palms over the edge. "What a weird thing to give someone else credit for, man."

He chuckled quietly, nodded, and looked down. "Yeah, maybe." He cleared his throat. "When you lie about big things, it's easy to lie about insignificant shit too."

"What do you mean?"

If he'd looked uncomfortable before, it had nothing on now, and it resulted in a blank mask that shut me out.

I fucking hated it. I didn't want to be on the outside anymore. Wasn't it enough I felt alone in my marriage?

"Forget it, I don't know what I'm saying," he said and shrugged it off. "How're the boys?"

I stared at him and didn't answer, waiting for the façade to crack, despite that I knew it wouldn't. He was a professional.

He'd been shutting people out all his life, successfully hiding who he was and choosing freely what some could be privy to. He drew the lines in the sand wherever he pleased.

As I glanced at the coffeemaker that was ready, I saw the picture that had landed on the counter, and I picked it up.

"Did you see the photos Maggie brought over?"

Kieran knitted his brow. "Some of them. Why?"

"This one stood out to me."

He approached with a sense of weariness and trepidation until we were close.

I held up the photo.

I needed him to see it. There was *something*. He had to identify it for me because I wasn't brave enough.

Kieran took a final step toward me as he studied the picture, and I was assaulted by the scent of his aftershave. *You've already identified it, you numbskull.* I swallowed hard. The forbidden thoughts were becoming impossible to keep locked up. Being near him like this stripped me of self-control and turned me into an addict again.

I could say no to whiskey. I couldn't say no to Kieran.

He didn't look away from the picture, but it wasn't because he hadn't studied it enough. He was scared too. He clenched his jaw. He didn't know how to flee, though he was trying to figure it out. If an escape route appeared, he would take it.

"What do you want from me?" he whispered.

With my heart thundering in my chest, I lifted a hand and tried not to let it tremble. He closed his eyes hard as I cupped his cheek and brushed my thumb over the stubble. At least he didn't move away. The opposite—he inched closer and settled one hand along my side.

My nerves got completely shot by the storm surge that welled over me. Tense and past desperate, I let out a shaky breath and felt the floodgates give way under the pressure.

Kieran pressed his forehead to mine, and I tilted my face to ghost my lips over his jaw. I breathed him in, felt my mouth water, and the yearning kept growing stronger.

Eyes closed and other senses wide open, I took exactly what I'd craved for months. I took my time too. So did Kieran. As I buried my face against his neck and tasted his skin, he shuddered and slipped his hands up my back, under my hoodie.

His hands on my skin set me on fire. I needed more. I shivered and trailed my lips up his jaw again, and he took over. He closed the last distance and kissed me, a searing kiss as he cupped my face in his warm hands, and I fucking broke. The way he touched me, the way he kissed, it was all overwhelming.

When his hands trailed down again, I wrapped my arms around his neck and deepened the kiss. I swept my tongue into his mouth and savored every millisecond. In return, he pressed himself as close as he could and responded with more passion. *Fuck.* He couldn't know how much he turned me on. More than that, how he brought me to life. Hell, I barely knew myself.

He let out a labored breath and fisted the sides of my hoodie. "I can't lose you, Ben."

God.

I kissed him again, with everything I was, to express how much I'd needed those words. My eyes stung behind closed lids for a brief second before I gained control of my emotions.

"Same." I was completely out of breath, but I couldn't stop kissing him. Touching him. Fuck, holding him. It was... There were no words. "I need this, Kieran. I need *you*. Like this."

He nodded and pressed our foreheads together. "Me too. I just... I-I didn't think you would."

I hadn't thought so either. We'd both been wrong. So very wrong. Because right now, everything felt right. I wasn't alone, and I wasn't faking it. This was where I was. With another man. Not my wife. Kieran. And I was helpless to stop it.

"You know nothing will change on the outside, right?" He swallowed and looked down between us, where he gathered my hands in his. "You gotta know what this entails."

"I don't care." I slipped my hands free and cupped the back of his neck, covering his mouth with mine once more. "You want me to say it? Fine." I spoke between quick, hungry kisses. "This is just between you and me."

We'll have an affair.

I couldn't say those exact words, even though that was precisely what I meant.

"You're willing to go behind your wife's back?"

I swallowed a burst of anger. Anger toward Allison. "What wife?" I whispered. "I don't wanna talk about her."

"Okay." He shivered and pinned me with an indecent look. His eyes brimmed with lust, a sight that derailed my thoughts to something much more physical. "Jesus fuck, you're sexy. I'll take whatever I can get."

I exhaled a laugh in shock and was momentarily overcome with childlike joy.

He smirked unsurely. "I can say that, right?"

Uh, *yes*. Given the rush that went through my body, he could say that every day. I'd forgotten the last time I felt so desired—actually, I knew when it was. It was in a back alley in Seattle.

"Tell me again." I smiled.

He chuckled and leaned forward, pressing a quick kiss to my jaw. "You're hot as fuck, Bennett."

I groaned under my breath and took his mouth with mine. And...huh. Interesting. After all my years of despising being called Ben, it'd become what I preferred from him.

"So are you," I murmured, feeling the heavy truth of my words rolling off my tongue with such ease. My gaze flicked from his eyes to his mouth, back to his eyes, his cut jaw, his nose, and his eyes again. A resounding god-yes, he was beyond words.

"Yeah?" He regained some of his confidence and kissed me again. "Is that weird to you?"

I chuckled softly. "I don't know. Maybe a little. I've never... well, before you..."

He hummed, his eyes flashing with something predatory. "I kinda like that."

I swallowed nervously. Good fucking grief, what was I getting myself into? I had no clue whatsoever, yet I'd never been so eager to jump in.

"So...what happens now?" I asked hesitantly.

"We live, Ben. We get through the holidays, and then we live."

CHAPTER 12

"Nice stress ball." My boss, Mr. Hayes, folded his arms over his chest and leaned against the doorway to my office, always with a polite smile on his face. "New?"

I caught the ball and set it on my desk. "A Christmas gift from my eldest." I smiled back. "What can I do for you?"

"I was wondering if you could take on a minor account." He walked farther in and sat down in one of the chairs across from me. "My cousin and his family just moved to town, and he's looking to start up a business in the city."

"Minor account..." I flipped open my planner, spotting three business trips to Boston this month alone. I usually only had one. "I mean, I can move things around, no problem, but wouldn't it be better for the interns to get their feet wet?"

He inclined his head. "Normally, I would at least let them sketch up their ideas, but I need discretion for this." He paused. "My cousin is trying to stay under the radar."

I frowned, confused. "Whose radar?"

He chuckled. "I apologize for speaking in riddles. He was once a famous musician, and his fall from grace was pretty severe. Now he wants to start fresh, without the attention of the media—until he's ready."

"Well, color me intrigued. I can do it." I shrugged and leaned back. "This month is going to be tight, but—"

"Oh, he's in no rush. Another month or two won't matter." He rose again and folded up the sleeves of his shirt. "I appreciate this, Bennett. I'll send him your information."

Hayes. My boss's last name was Hayes. I narrowed my eyes, my mind spinning. "Holy fuck—" Good job, foul language in front of the boss. I cringed, though I couldn't contain the surprise. "Are you related to Lincoln Hayes?"

His eyes flashed with amusement. "I've already warned him that he won't be able to stay incognito very long."

No shit.

"I'll be working with a rock star?" I smiled and pinched my lip. I'd have to impress the man for certain. All through high school, I listened to his band Path of Destruction. "Ah—" I put a hand over my heart. "Nostalgia."

My boss found me funny—and left me while laughing—and I decided to look up this alleged fall from grace later. Right now, I had more important things to do, such as stare at the clock until Kieran arrived.

His mother had fallen down the stairs over the holidays, so Kieran and his family had stayed longer. But now they were on the West Coast again. If they'd been on the plane I suspected, they'd landed a while ago and should be back in town any minute. And I'd told Kieran to get his ass to my office as soon as he could.

I missed him. So much had changed from last Christmas,

and spending weeks away from each other was a mental drain now. As neighbors, we at least got a hello every day. A quick chat in passing, usually on the driveway we shared. This year, we'd resorted to a couple text messages a day, and it was far from enough.

I'd watched gay porn since the last time we saw each other. Truth be told, it didn't do much for me. The thought of making Kieran lose it, however... I wanted to satisfy him. And *that* was an image I'd gotten off to more than a few times.

"Oh, you can go in," I heard my boss's assistant say. I supposed she was partly mine too, though my phone didn't ring off the hook the way Ellis's did. "When Bennett's door is open, he's available."

"A'ight, cheers." It was Kieran's voice, and I took a breath as my stomach flipped. His accent was thicker whenever he'd been in Boston, and it was...it was—what was the word? Smoking hot.

It was time to give a name to all these emotions I'd had virtually since meeting him. There'd always been a pull. I'd always been drawn to him, and now I knew it was attraction. Intense, burning-hot, ever-growing attraction.

Kieran appeared in the doorway and offered a cocky grin, and all I could do was tell him to close the door.

He was *beautiful*. Ruggedly handsome. Jeans, leather jacket, vacation scruff.

It was almost liberating to be able to think about him in those terms. Each one fit.

He winked and turned the lock in the door too. "You look like you wanna eat me, Ben."

I let out a laugh. "I kind of do."

He chuckled warmly and glanced around my office before he rounded my desk and planted his hands along the armrests on my chair, effectively bringing us face-to-face.

"I missed you."

I...I had too many feelings surging. "Me too." I drank in the sight of him. His eyes seemed clearer, and the cold outside had dusted his cheeks and nose in faint pink. "God, me too."

He grinned slightly and leaned forward more, until our lips brushed. I grabbed ahold of his hoodie under his open jacket and drew him closer, and he smiled into the kiss.

"I love that I can do this now," he murmured. His hands cupped my jaw, slowly sliding back to my neck, all while he reduced me to a puddle with that kiss. Slow strokes of his tongue, soft lips, firm kisses, and his fingers exploring my skin.

"I love your honesty." I had to get that out there because he had to know what it did to me, every time he admitted something like that. It was entirely new to me. Having always been the one to take any type of initiative in my marriage, doubt came very easily. Sometimes I wondered if I was a bother, if it was a chore to fuck, or—whatever. Not with Kieran. Even as normal friends, once we'd stopped tiptoeing around the fact that we really needed each other as mates, there'd been an openness I'd never experienced before.

Kieran hummed into a last, long, dizzying kiss, then drew back a bit. "I gotta behave today. For one, I don't wanna overwhelm you. For two, I have to pick up dinner."

I forced myself to sit back and gathered my thoughts. "Why, uh..." I cleared my throat and adjusted myself, something he definitely didn't miss, and he offered a smirk. "Why would you overwhelm me?"

"Because I want everything—right now." He straightened his clothes and returned to safety on the other side of the desk. "No one can see in here, right?"

I glanced at the frosted glass that separated us from the rest of the workspace, and I shook my head. "Nope."

He gave me a sly look and nodded at the chaise at the other

end of my office. "Then you could get a more comfortable couch in here."

Amusement and anticipation rushed in my bloodstream. "I could." It was impossible not to let my thoughts wander to his office in the city. His couch was big and cushy, something he'd purchased for power naps when Jaylin was little and didn't sleep through the night. "We could also have lunch in your office next week."

He cursed under his breath. "You can fucking count on it."

On Saturday, I invited my father and the Marshalls over for pizza. Cooking some elaborate dinner was setting the bar too high, but I'd actually made an appetizer from scratch. With Jess's help. He'd crushed tortilla chips like a pro, which we'd rolled string cheese in, added an egg wash and some spices, more tortilla crumbs, and then fried it to perfection.

Step one in learning how to cook better: everything tasted better deep-fried.

Step two: you couldn't go wrong with cheese.

Praise the internet.

The mozzarella sticks were gone by the time the pizza was here, and Jess was satisfied with the compliments he'd received for the snack.

After paying for the pies, I told Dad to get comfortable on the couch instead. The kids had occupied it so far, but they didn't have a bad hip. Nate grabbed a chair and sat down by me instead, leaving Dad with Jess and Jaylin.

Kieran passed me and clapped my shoulder. "Mind if I put on some music?"

"No, go ahead. There's a CD in the player already." I plated slices of plain cheese pizza for the two youngest while Maggie fetched sodas and beer in the kitchen. "I actually have an exciting topic from work—"

"There's no such thing," Dad grunted, a glint in his eye.

I chuckled. "There's a first for everything—believe me. Dad, you must remember my obsession with Path of Destruction when I was in high school."

He remembered it vaguely, I could tell, with good timing. The music came on, and the song opened with the same guitar solo I'd listened to all day. A live album of Path of Destruction from '97.

"Good band," Kieran noted and sat down. "I listened to them too."

Even better. I didn't often have exciting news to share. "I'm gonna work with the lead guitarist," I said, smiling. "I mean, he's opening a studio in the city, and I'm gonna design their brand." Well, with my team of graphic designers, but whatever. It was my account. Mine.

Kieran grinned. "Look at'chu. Don't burst on us, Ben."

I laughed and opened the next box. Kieran unfortunately loved pineapple on his pizza, which I supposed was good if you wanted to make sure no one else ate your food.

Maggie helped out by opening the last box. "Hon, I got your pepperoni here," she told Kieran. "So tell us more about this project, Bennett. It sounds exciting."

I furrowed my brow and looked questioningly at Kieran, who shook his head and smirked faintly. Extending his hand, he made it clear it was the pineapple pizza he wanted, so I passed it on without a word. I thought he hated pepperoni pizza. It was my favorite, however. And he mocked it when we had pizza in Seattle.

"Oh..." Maggie looked confused. She had a plate ready for Kieran, and he'd already started with a slice. Or two. He had a special way of eating pizza where he put two slices together, toppings facing each other.

Kieran merely stared at her while he ate.

"I can take that, Maggie," Dad said. "We're a pepperoni family."

"Sure—yes, of course." She tried to hide her puzzlement and reminded me of the work story.

So I launched into it, and I told them that my boss was related to this huge rock star. I took ribbings from both Dad and Kieran; they found me funny when I got so animated about this idol of mine. But I could tell Kieran was impressed.

"Oh, I remember now," Dad said, nodding. "I think the kid's from here."

Lincoln Hayes was no kid. He was a rock god, and I was having lunch with him next month. *Lunch.* And yes, I'd learned Mr. Hayes was from here originally, which made sense, with Ellis being from here as well.

Dad tilted his head, thinking. "Didn't he go to prison?"

"Oh yeah." Kieran looked to me. "He did, didn't he? I read something about that."

I waved it off. I'd read up on it, and I was ready to defend the man I may or may not have owned a poster of once upon a time. I'd stolen it from Brianna. She'd been off to uni anyway.

"He was defending the woman he loved. The crime was justified if you ask me."

Maggie giggled. "You are too precious, Bennett. I haven't seen this side of you before."

"I'm full of surprises," I drawled.

"That's true," Kieran said and took another bite.

I shot him a quick look. We were going to act normal. Otherwise, I'd be hit by a brick of guilt every time I looked Maggie in the eye.

"My boy plays the guitar too," Dad said.

"*Barely.*" I shifted in my seat and felt my ears get hot, and I had half a mind to tell him he was embarrassing me in front of my friends.

He frowned. "Now that I think about it, the stick up your—"

"Hey!" I widened my eyes pointedly. We had kids here, and Nate was always listening.

Dad rolled his eyes. "My point exactly. You weren't always this way." He turned to Maggie. "You shoulda seen him growing up. He always had a record in his hand. He wanted to be a critic or something—travel the country and review bands."

"I love the job I have, thank you very much," I said, watching Jess fumble with his slice. "Sweetheart, over the plate. Give him a napkin, Dad."

Maggie smiled at my foolish boyhood dreams, then nodded at Kieran. "He wanted to be a police officer when he was little."

"You did?" I coughed, and a mouthful of pizza slid down heavily. I reached for my beer and took a swig.

Kieran inclined his head. "In my family, you're either a cop or a factory worker. Took me a minute to look outside the family trades. Standing in some assembly line held zero appeal, so..."

He'd make a hot police officer. But good fucking grief, the worry...? Brianna and I never had to worry about Dad growing up; his infantry days had been over for a long time, but it was the environment in which I'd grown up. We lived on bases or in communities where wives and children weren't always lucky enough to have their husband or father come home.

It wasn't much different for policemen, particularly not in cities like Boston.

Dad was the first to leave around ten, and Maggie wasn't far behind. Jaylin was tired and fussy, so Maggie thanked us for tonight and told Kieran not to drink too much. Valid point, I supposed. But since Jess and Nathan were close to passing out, drinking wasn't on our minds.

After helping Jess brush his teeth and getting him ready for bed, I heard Kieran down the stairs, saying Maggie had texted and was wondering if I had plans for my thirtieth birthday yet.

"She forgot to ask earlier," he added.

"I'm having some people over," I replied, guiding Jess to his room. "I'll tell you more soon, but let her know not to make plans for the Saturday after my birthday."

"Will do."

I went through my nightly routine with Jess, followed by a similar routine with Nate. They both got ridiculously inquisitive around bedtime, but where Jess asked what we were having for dinner tomorrow, Nathan asked about space, gravity, and how astronauts went to the bathroom.

I was grateful they fell asleep fast, though. I cherished our little moments, and I did my best to answer all the questions—or say I'd look it up—but when it became time to sleep, I needed it to just happen. I was tired too, dammit.

I remembered when Nathan was about four or five. He went through this phase where he was almost asleep, and then he was suddenly wide awake and needed a drink. Then he'd try to sleep again, only to rush to the bathroom twenty minutes later. It was a constant running back and forth.

When I reached the last step, I saw Kieran in the living room. He had his back to me and was looking at a family picture in the entertainment center. Unless he was captivated by Jess's video games stacked next to the photo, of course.

I approached Kieran, having looked forward to this all night. It wasn't the first time he'd stayed behind to shoot the shit, and it wasn't weird he stayed behind now either. We'd just...be doing other things.

I pressed a kiss to his neck and felt tension leave his shoulders. "We're alone."

He hummed, and I slipped my hands under his tee, drawing them absently over his abs. "You look happy in this picture," he murmured.

Resting my chin on his shoulder, I glanced at the photo. "We'd just come home from the hospital with Jess." I was holding him in the picture—that thankfully didn't express how much that boy screamed as a newborn. Allison stood next to me, her hands on Nathan's head, and he was making a face at the camera. Brianna took it, I remembered. Everything was so different back then. "I worry about Nate sometimes," I admitted. "He becomes more distant toward Allison every time she comes home."

"Makes sense," Kieran replied quietly. "What about Jess? Can he even remember a time when she lived here permanently?"

No. He actually couldn't.

Over the holidays, Allison and I had explained to him that by next summer, she would be home for good. The puzzled look on his face had been as funny as it had been a rude awakening. I only feared Allison didn't take it seriously enough. She knew she was missing out, and yet... She didn't seem to see what a big deal this was.

"I guess we're lucky with him," I said eventually. "He doesn't hold grudges."

"I get it." Kieran turned around. "You're an amazing father."

I smiled and closed my eyes, letting the contentment fall over me. "So are you."

He kissed me carefully, slowly, and took a step forward. I took the hint and deepened the kiss as he walked me backward to the couch. What I craved the most tonight was skin on skin and all the affection I could get, so I started with his T-shirt.

The kiss broke long enough for me to pull the tee over his head, and then he was back. He pushed his tongue into my mouth and unbuttoned my shirt, and I was more than happy to help.

"What the hell?" He frowned, even as his eyes glinted with humor. "You shit. You took out your piercing?"

My what...? Oh. "I looked like a bloody fool with it." Unlike him. I eye-fucked his flawless body, taking in the ink, the nipple ring—he'd changed it to an actual ring too—and his defined yet lean muscles. "My God, you're perfect, Kieran." I nuzzled his jaw and kissed my way down his neck to his sternum. My hands followed, and I became greedier for every second that passed.

How could a man be so fucking sexy? It was incredible. *He* was incredible, and I couldn't get enough.

He sucked in a breath when I flicked my tongue over his piercing and wrapped my lips around it.

Before I knew it, we were tumbling down onto the couch, and he landed on top of me with a feral look in his eyes that drove me insane with lust. In between devouring kisses, we got rid of the rest of our clothes, and I was sure my heart stopped the moment I saw all of him.

"Jesus Christ," I whispered raggedly. "No, wait." I wasn't ready for him to lie down on me again—not yet. I had to see him. I had to stare. I had to touch him. I swallowed hard and sat up, and I put my hands on his hips.

He stayed there on his knees before me, his long fingers disappearing into my hair. I groaned at the sensations and pressed my lips to that V along his abs.

"Tell me I turn you on," he murmured.

I shuddered and slowly wrapped my fingers around his cock. I couldn't look away from it. Even as it made me nervous. I wanted to taste him, to suck him off, but he'd have to guide me. "There's no word for how much," I confessed. The skin around him was so soft and smooth, and combined with how rock hard he was in my hand, even my brain couldn't process how much he turned me on. It was as if I'd been hit in the back of the head with a new universe, and it was all mine to explore. "I'll need you a lot." I glanced up at him.

He swallowed and nodded once. "Every chance we get."

CHAPTER 13

We did take every chance we got.

We didn't even touch our lunch the following Wednesday when I came to his office. Seconds after I'd arrived, we were naked on his couch, kissing and grinding and kissing and touching.

I wanted my mouth on him again. I had to. My first experience with giving Kieran a blow job had almost made me come. He'd settled my nerves and hadn't cared about finesse or my lack of experience.

I raked my fingers down his torso as I dropped kisses below his navel, and he groaned and scrubbed his hands over his face. Then I gripped his cock and sucked him into my mouth, to which he muffled a curse with his knuckle.

The way he reacted to what I did... How responsive he was, how expressive—and that goddamn honesty. *That* was my new drug.

I swirled my tongue around the head, and a spurt of pre-come hit my taste buds. *Good God.* I moaned around him and closed my eyes, getting lost in us. I didn't care what we did; whether we were kissing or he was sucking my cock, the passion was mind-blowing and unlike anything I'd ever felt with anyone.

"Fuck," he panted. "Wait. Ben—Jesus, wait. I bought rubbers."

I licked the underside of his cock and sucked on the head once more, then kissed my way up his body again. "Are you sure?"

He nodded and reached for his discarded trousers on the floor. "I'm done waiting." He grabbed his wallet and nudged me back. "I wanna feel you for the rest of the day."

He tore the condom wrapper and handed me a single-use pack of lube.

I swallowed against the dryness in my throat, goose bumps rising across my arms and shoulders. He didn't want to wait. I was going to fuck him right here in his office. Bloody hell, I couldn't believe it.

I stifled a moan as he rolled the condom down my cock.

"We'll go in there." He nodded at his bathroom. "I wanna watch you in my mirror."

I followed blindly, too turned on to say anything. We didn't have room or time for tact or finding the perfect moment. What we had was a collection of stolen *right here and now*.

He gripped the edge of the sink as I coated my cock with lube, and we locked eyes in the mirror.

I'll be careful.

I kissed his shoulder blade and slipped two wet fingers between his ass cheeks. When I slowly pushed my middle finger inside of him, his eyes fluttered closed, and he clenched his jaw.

"More," he breathed. "I need it. Fuck—I've missed this."

I cleared my throat, a twinge of jealousy spearing me. "Keep that to yourself, Kieran. I don't want to hear about you and other men."

"The only other one, you mean?" He grunted as I pushed in a second digit. "That's not what I meant anyway. I meant—this. Being myself, being able to crave you, getting what I want."

I hummed and placed another kiss along his spine. "Good answer." Then I rested my forehead against his back and focused on feeling him. He was so tight around my fingers, and it was going to take all my self-control not to come in two minutes.

"Fuck, Ben," he moaned. "Give me your big cock."

I whispered a curse and withdrew my fingers. Gripping my cock, I rubbed the head of me around his opening and spread the excess lube. It was the sexiest sight, and I couldn't help but think of when it was me. I wanted him to fuck me more than I thought imaginable.

I pushed inside him as slowly as I could, both for his sake and mine. My brain was a jumbled mess of feelings and sensations, and the only thing I could grasp at was how right this felt. And again...the hunger for him grew. How was that even possible? We locked eyes in the mirror once more, and I held my breath.

"Ben..." The pleasure written across his face was almost too much for me.

My jaw ticked with tension. If I already had to stave off my orgasm, I was in trouble.

"We need more time together," he whispered through clenched teeth. "A whole night. Can—fuck—can you imagine?"

I *had* imagined it. But it wasn't like he could sleep over at my place without raising red flags.

However... "I go to Boston next week."

He sucked in a sharp breath as I pushed in deeper. "I should visit my mother. See how she's doing after her fall."

"You should," I grunted. "You wanna be a good son."

"So fucking good," he groaned. "Fuck, keep going."

"Oh, fuck," I gasped, my eyes flashing open. "Keep going." The searing pain was being doused in fiery pleasure every time he reached deeper. "*Kieran...*" I moaned into the pillow and fisted the sheets.

I didn't know, I didn't fucking know.

After two days in Boston, I was over his careful approach. I was done with the teasing and the sensual play of his fingers. I appreciated it, but I was done. And now... *Finally.* I felt his warm breath against my neck, followed by his lips and open-mouthed kisses.

"You're so goddamn tight," he whispered shallowly. "You have the sweetest ass, did you know? It makes me wanna fuck you six ways to Sunday, call you baby, and tie you to the bed."

I groaned loudly, beyond overwhelmed and desperate. "Do it. All of it." I was done testing the waters too. We'd been doing that for a couple weeks now, and we were better than that. We could go all in and just be raw, animalistic, and rough.

He sank into me with a hiss, and I forced myself to relax. His cock was officially buried in my ass, and part of me still couldn't believe any of this was happening. That we were actually pulling it off.

He wouldn't leave tonight either. He'd told his family he was going to catch up with buddies. In reality, we were going to spend the night together for the first time ever.

"I need to see you." He pulled out carefully, and despite that, I winced at the pain. "Turn around."

I rolled over and yanked him down on me.

He grinned into a messy kiss as he guided his cock back into my ass. "You don't have any meetings until tomorrow afternoon."

"Correct." I breathed heavily, all while trying to keep up with the deep-seated urgency of his kisses.

"And I'm not going back to Quincy until dinner tomorrow," he went on, panting. "We have over twenty-four hours. Just you and me. What do you wanna do?"

I went with honesty. "Pretend that this is it."

He stopped, buried all the way in, and stared at me. Desire mingled with trepidation in his gorgeous eyes, but I didn't waver. I wanted it. It was twenty-four hours.

"That could be dangerous," he murmured. "I already want you too much."

"We're both adults." I reached up and nipped at his bottom lip. "We know the boundaries. Nothing changes when we go home."

He lowered his gaze to my mouth, where he dropped a soft, lingering kiss. "You sound more confident than I am, but I can't resist. We'll pretend." He sealed the agreement with a burning kiss, and I felt his fingers sliding down my arms. First, I thought he was going to thread our fingers together, but then I realized what he was doing.

He took off my wedding band. He took off his own.

He began fucking me harder.

"Nothing changes when we go home."

Nothing would change, but it had been easy to say it before I spent a night with Kieran Marshall.

We woke each other up several times during the night. Just to kiss, to get closer, or to fuck again. We were equally starved for intimacy, and it seemed sleeping in clothes had been out of the question for both of us for more than one reason.

Around eight, I woke up again to him kissing my neck. His morning wood was pressing against my ass, and as tempting as another round of sex was, my stomach was tight with hunger.

"Morning," he murmured.

I yawned and stretched, rolling onto my back. "Good morning." Tilting my head, I stole a firm kiss. "Sharing a bed with you is…" I sighed and stared up at the ceiling.

"Mmm." He brushed his nose against my jaw and stroked my chest. "Sorry if I got too handsy."

I chuckled drowsily and turned on my side to face him better. "It was exactly what I needed, Kieran. I've been…"

"Lonely?"

I dipped my chin.

"Yeah, me too." He pulled me close and hitched my leg over his hip.

"So I take it you're not like this with Maggie?"

He rumbled a sleepy laugh. "That's funny."

I didn't think so. I feared more and more of these thoughts were going to pop up in my head. Because the way he was with me was out of this world, and merely a fraction of it aimed at Maggie was already making me jealous. That wasn't good.

"We should eat," he said, still amused. "Room service?"

There was a magnificent buffet in the hotel restaurant, but I had a feeling that would make him antsy.

"Room service sounds great."

I had another trip to Boston at the end of January, and I was on my own for that one.

I got home late on Sunday, also known as my birthday, and

there was a surprise waiting for me at home. Not only did I not have to pick up a tired Jess and Nate from Dad's, but they were up and alert—at my house—and Brianna was there too.

"Happy birthday, Daddy!" Jess shouted, running toward me in the hallway.

I grinned tiredly and scooped him up. "Thank you, my darling boy." I kissed his cheek, feeling warm all over, and grinned at Nate in the doorway to the living room. He was smirking and holding up a big present. "That's not for me, is it?"

He nodded and walked over. "Auntie Brianna helped us buy it."

Not Allison?

I knew she wasn't coming home—even for my get-together next weekend—but Christ.

As Jess jumped down, I hugged Nathan and kissed the top of his head. "I missed you."

He quirked a grin up at me. "You're thirty now. Is it any different from twenty-nine?"

I chuckled and shook my head. "Not much, no."

Dad and Brianna were next, and I hugged and thanked them for being here. "You didn't have to," I felt the need to add. "It's late. You're not heading back to Seattle tonight, are you?" I looked to my sister.

"I'm here for the week, actually," she said with a smile. "I couldn't miss my baby brother's thirtieth."

This was both wonderful and frightening news. I was prepared for her to meet Kieran for the first time at my little party, and that hadn't worried me. We'd be surrounded by friends and coworkers, not to mention alcohol, so she wouldn't be able to analyze too much. If she was here for the week, however...?

"Well, let's not stand around here all night," Dad decided. "Bri picked up a cake too."

I glanced at her immediately, and she laughed.

"*Yes*, from that place you like so much."

"I love you," I told her.

We gathered in the living room, and while Brianna cut the cake—this fantastic lemon meringue tart from a bakery in the city—I shrugged out of my suit jacket and removed my tie.

It even read "Happy 30th, Bennett!" on the cake.

My chest constricted with the love I felt for my family.

There were more gifts on the table.

From the big box from Nate and Jess, I unpacked a brand-new briefcase that made me misty-eyed. Rather than engraving initials underneath the lock, it read "Nate and Jess's dad."

"Do you like that stuff, Daddy?" Jess asked imploringly. "I wanted to buy a dinosaur."

I smiled. "I love it—"

"Shh!" Nate scowled at his brother.

Brianna chuckled. "Open it."

Half confused, I opened the briefcase to find three smaller presents.

My sister was the best, in short. The boys had picked out something on their own too. There was a tiny plastic toy dinosaur from Jess—a mascot, he said, to remind me of him. From Nate, I received a model of a DNA strand he'd put together in school.

"Maybe you can keep it in your office?" he suggested.

"Of course I will," I replied, swallowing past the emotions. "Everyone's gonna know what a genius kid I have."

He blushed.

Aside from shelling out too much money on the leather briefcase, Brianna had also given me a new wallet, and there was already a picture inside it. It was of her and the boys.

"Your three favorites," she said cheekily.

I laughed under my breath and left my seat to kiss her

cheek. "Thank you, short stuff. You're definitely my favorite sister."

"Dad, you only have one," Nate informed me.

I grinned and sat down again.

"My turn." Dad handed over a plastic bag, and it was such a specific size that I wondered if he was giving me a record.

Brianna must've drawn the same conclusion. "We use CDs these days, Dad. It's been a thing for fifteen years."

I peered into the bag and frowned. It *was* a record. It was mine. I only owned a dozen of them, and I definitely had this. "Uh." No...this wasn't mine at all. I pulled out the record and saw it was a special edition of one I had. "Bloody hell!" It was signed. It was signed by Lincoln Hayes. "How...?" I gave my father a dumbstruck look before I refocused on the record. Where did he get this from? Good grief, talk about mint condition.

"I saw Ellis," he replied. He looked a little smug. "I found the record online, though."

My forehead creased. "I was in Boston for two days. In that time, how did you get to be on a first-name basis with my boss?"

"Nice fella," he said with a nod. "He lives around here, did you know? But I ran into both Ellis and Lincoln at the store." He shrugged. "So I asked."

I shook my head, quite dazed.

"There should be a note," he told me.

There was nothing inside, but when I turned the record over, I saw it.

I was told you'd probably be too shy to ask for my autograph at our meeting. I won't hold that against you. Happy birthday, Bennett.
Lincoln Hayes

PS: My pop used to buy me records when I was a kid. He knew what I could become before I did.

I didn't know what to say. Part of me was positively mortified that my father had done this. I certainly wouldn't have been too shy to ask for an autograph; the reason I had no plan to do so was because it would've been incredibly unprofessional. At the same time...holy shit, I had a signed Path of Destruction record.

"I will cherish this till the day I die," I stated. "But goodness, Dad, sometimes I feel like a teenager around you. Did you have to tell a famous person that your son was too shy to ask for an autograph?"

Brianna started laughing and asked to see the note.

Dad found me amusing too. "Ellis may have mentioned that you'd give me grief for that part."

No kidding.

Kieran cracked up when I told him about the gift a couple days later. We'd arrived home at the same time, so here we stood, on either side of the picket fence that separated our driveways.

"You gotta admit, your little rock-star crush is cute," he chuckled.

I rolled my eyes. "Are you telling me you never idolized anyone growing up?"

"Oh, sure." He scratched his eyebrow with his car key. "Red Sox players, a couple Bruins—"

"Yeah, yeah, I get it. You were only into macho sports. I liked musicians."

He smirked and walked a bit closer, and he leaned forward theatrically. "I jacked off to the players too. Still macho?"

No, but sexy as hell.

I wanted to kiss him. How wonderful would it be to just lean over the fence and plant one on him?

"That may have been the sexiest thing I've ever seen, when you got off in the shower." I kept my voice down, even though no one was around. And that memory...Christ. It made me want more hotel nights with him.

He'd watched me watch him.

I could see that the memory swept Kieran away a bit too, though he recovered quickly and chuckled while he rubbed the back of his neck. "Have I told you you're dangerous?"

I smirked.

The door to my house opened, and I should've seen it coming. I cleared my throat and took a step back.

"Ohh, it's freezing." She hugged her cardigan closer to her body.

"Kieran, you haven't met my sister yet," I said. "Brianna, Kieran."

Kieran smiled politely and extended a hand over the fence. "Good to meet you."

"You too, Kieran." Brianna shook his hand, her smile kind enough. Maybe I was overreacting when I expected her to pull out a couch and tell him to share his life story. "It's been a year and a half of Kieran this, Kieran that from Bennett."

"Oh yeah?" Kieran liked that little tidbit way too much.

"Everyone's out to embarrass me," I said with a helpless shrug.

Brianna snickered. "Am I wrong, then? Have you not spoken a lot about Kieran?"

"Sure I have." I smiled, having no issue admitting that part. "Making friends as an adult is bloody hopeless."

"Ain't that the truth," Kieran chuckled. "Ben's stuck with me now, because I'm not going through that again."

I laughed.

"Well, aren't you two peas in a pod," Brianna drawled, and he and I exchanged a quick, amused look. "Anyway." She nodded at the door. "Nate's complaining about a headache again. Just wanted to let you know."

"Got it. Thank you," I replied. "I'll be right in."

"Everything okay?" Kieran asked.

I inclined my head. "We think he might need glasses. He gets headaches sometimes when he reads for too long."

"Ah." He nodded in understanding. "I won't keep you. I gotta take Jaylin to some dance thing."

I'd heard all about it. She'd begged Jess to start too, and he'd vehemently shaken his head and said that was for girls.

CHAPTER 14

I wasn't surprised to find Maggie and Brianna in the kitchen at my get-together the following weekend.

"You're here as guests," I told them, pointing toward the living room. "Get out there. Everyone has drinks, and they know where to find food." Because I'd strategically set it up on the dining room table.

This was a Bennett-friendly zone with minimum effort required. The beer was chilled in two ice-filled basins, the catered snacks were kept warm on hot plates. It was my birthday party; I didn't want anyone walking around to see if anything needed refilling. Everything was already out there.

The children had their own table to keep them occupied, including coloring books, candy, soda, and board games. Additionally, there was a movie running in Jess's room upstairs. I'd thought of it *all*.

"I was just grabbing these, I swear." Maggie held up a bag of chips.

I shook my head. "You have a problem, hon. There's not a single snack bowl in there that isn't full."

Brianna snickered into her glass of wine.

"Fine," Maggie huffed and set down the bag. "Maybe I have this need to overdo it sometimes."

Yes, *sometimes*. Quite literally. She was the best hostess when they had guests over. Then when it was only Kieran and her, it was a lot different. Or so I'd heard.

"Well, don't look at me," Brianna said. "I'm only here to get away from your coworkers."

I stifled a smirk. My coworkers were just fine. It was my sister who tended to find polite strangers unsettling.

Returning to the living room where the music was louder, I did another scan to see if Kieran was back. He'd disappeared a few minutes ago. At least he wasn't escaping people. He'd found a Red Sox fan in one of my coworkers and a barbecue fanatic in another.

I decided to check in on Ellis. His wife was busy tonight, so he'd asked if he could bring a friend who was new in town. I'd been all for it, since I didn't know that many people in the first place. On the other hand, a dozen people—a few with young children—filled the house without making it feel crowded.

Ellis smiled when he spotted me. We hadn't had the chance to chat tonight, but I was happy to see him more relaxed for once. A couple glasses of wine did that.

"The man of the hour," he said. "I brought you a present..." He frowned and looked around himself. "Where did I put the bag...?"

For goodness' sake. "I thought I said no gifts." And since he'd seemingly forgotten his friend, I extended my hand to the other bloke. He looked...young. Early twenties. He could also be a freaking model. "Hi, I'm Bennett. You must be Casey."

He grinned and shook my hand. "That's right. Thank you for having me."

"I have manners," Ellis said with a wince. "Sorry, Casey."

Casey chuckled. "No worries." Then he pointed toward the hallway. "I think you left it out there."

"Ah—I'll be right back."

While Ellis ducked out of the room, I grabbed a new beer and asked where Casey had moved from. I'd detected a Midwestern accent.

"Yeah, Detroit," he said. "I like the West Coast so far, though. Less...concrete and abandoned houses."

I nodded. "The recession hit you guys hard over there—"

"I have returned," Ellis said, reappearing. He handed over a gift bag to me and picked up his drink again. "I hope you'll approve."

There were two gifts. A bottle of a fantastic whiskey, and then I pulled out something flat and heavy, wrapped in silk paper. A picture frame with... Huh, I tilted my head at the illustration. It was a mockup of an office, black and white except for a brick wall in the background.

"That's your new office," he explained, and my brows went up. "I've been thinking about expanding for a while, and with people like you and Ashley by my side, I'm ready to take the leap."

This was incredible. I assumed that meant he was promoting Ashley, which was great. She'd come far the past year and deserved her own team.

"So, we're moving?" I asked.

He inclined his head. "Not until next year, but yes. Renovations have begun on our new building over on Monroe."

A smile took over my face. "This is bloody amazing, Ellis." I eyed the picture again, and I could see myself there. Especially with the freaking view we'd have at that address. "Have you told Ash yet?"

"Not yet. I'm waiting until the performance reviews."

"I hate those," I laughed. "They always get me nervous."

He quirked a wry smirk. "Bennett, you're my best employee. You're the last one who has anything to worry about."

"Can we get a notary in here?" I joked.

Casey chuckled.

Ellis was plenty amused too.

"Kidding aside, thank you for this." I held up the frame and the whiskey bottle. "I'm gonna go hide the whiskey so no one steals a single sip."

"Good call," Ellis laughed.

I found Kieran upstairs, to my surprise. He was with Nate, the two sitting at my son's desk with a laptop that definitely didn't belong in this house. Well, Kieran was squatting next to Nate's chair, showing him something on the little computer.

"This is so cool," Nate said in awe at something. Then he turned in his seat and threw his arms around Kieran's shoulders. "Thank you so much!"

Kieran smiled and patted Nate's back. "You're welcome, kiddo."

I stayed hidden in the doorway and didn't open the door farther.

"So, I just click here?" Nate asked.

Kieran nodded. "If that's the book you want."

What on earth were they doing?

Nate reached for his calculator. "I have forty-two dollars and sixty cents left. That's...a *lot* of books."

Kieran grinned. "Fill the cart, then."

That was it; I had to know what they were up to. I knocked on the door and opened it fully, and the two looked up at me.

"Dad! Look what Kieran gave me." He scooted off his chair and brought over what looked like a giant calculator, only it wasn't. "I can read books on it and store a whole library in here. It's digital, see? He gave me a gift card so I can buy books too."

I lifted my gaze from the electronic reader to Kieran.

"He can adjust the text size," Kieran said. "I figured it might help with the headaches."

"Oh." I cleared my throat, then put a smile on my face for Nate. "That's a lovely gift. I guess you're busy shopping then, huh?"

"Yeah," he giggled and returned to his seat.

I looked at Kieran again and nodded toward the hallway.

He straightened up, gave Nathan's shoulder a squeeze, then left the room with me. I ushered him into my bedroom, closed and locked the door, and trapped him against a wall. I leaned in and kissed him firmly, slowly, deeply. I slipped my hands up his chest until I could cup his face, and he eventually recovered from the surprise assault and hugged me harder to him.

We had never discussed emotional boundaries.

We should have, because I was learning they were much more difficult not to cross than the physical ones.

"I guess it was a good gift?"

I hummed and kissed the smile off his face, tasting his tongue along my own. "Very thoughtful."

In fact, you care more about my boys than their mother does.

"I have a gift for you too," he murmured. "It's nowhere near that practical, though."

I smiled and dragged his bottom lip between my teeth. "Your cock is definitely practical."

He chuckled huskily, out of breath. "Damn you, I'm trying to be sweet here."

That was the problem, wasn't it?

Resting my forehead to his, I got my heart rate under control while he dug out something from his pocket.

A key ring hung from his finger. Dark brown leather met blackened gold, the design rustic and distressed. There was an airplane, some decorative little gold rings, and a flat charm that read "We met on the way."

"A train might've been too obvious," he said quietly.

I took a breath and accepted the key ring, my mind spinning toward something I wasn't supposed to think too much on. But it was impossible to ignore the future now. How long could this go on? If I were completely honest with myself, I knew I'd fallen for Kieran.

I didn't know how to walk away from that.

We met on the way… Yeah, we'd certainly done that. On the way to what, though? Hardly on the way to work. A mountain of hurt seemed more and more realistic.

"How do you do this without involving feelings?" I whispered.

His gaze softened, and he leaned in for a languid kiss. "Who says I am?"

I closed my eyes and let him seduce me.

We had a few seconds before we had to go downstairs again.

A few seconds where we could pretend we weren't in deep shit.

Life went on.

Despite my growing worries about the future, there was a newfound peace between Kieran and me as well. Or a new level of it. He wasn't in it for the fucking or to have a physical outlet. It was more than that, much more, and it was enough for me.

For now.

He constantly made me see a future where everything could look different.

"Slow down, baby. I got it. I'll pick them up."

Short of breath and soaked from the rain, I got into my car and flipped the call to Bluetooth. "Are you sure?"

I'd missed my train from Seattle, so after a short day of meetings—and no Kieran because he was working from home today—I'd come back to Camassia late. Now I had to go home and change into new clothes too, and then make it to the marina where I was meeting with Lincoln Hayes.

"I'm sure," Kieran insisted. "Mags is at church, so I'll take the kids to McDonald's."

"You're a lifesaver." I puffed out a breath in relief and rolled out of the parking lot by the train station. "Nate's hit a sensitive age, by the way. He wants the Happy Meal but won't go for it because he worries he's too old for the toy now."

"That's bullshit."

"Yes, so if you assume three Happy Meals, he won't have to make the choice."

He hummed. "I'll take care of it. And Jess likes mustard now?"

"The more, the better," I chuckled, hitting the interstate.

"All right, I'll get to it. Kill at the meeting."

"Thanks, love. Talk soon." I smiled nervously and ended the call, only for my phone to ring two seconds later. Allison's name lit up the display. "Hello." At the same time, I received a text from Kieran.

"Hi, hon!" Allison was in a good mood. "Guess who's studying her ass off for finals?"

I grinned at Kieran's message.

Don't fall in love with the rock star. You're mine.

Yes. Yes, I was. I was his.

I cleared my throat, refocusing. "Well, it better be you." I switched lanes to get to the next exit. "What's up?"

She quieted down, which usually only meant one thing.

"You're staying in Chicago over Easter," I stated, and I leaned forward to glance up at the sky. The rain had stopped, and I hoped it stayed that way for a while. The restaurant in the marina was only a short walk from my house; I'd prefer not to drive there.

"I'm sorry," Allison said softly. "I know you were hoping I'd make it home."

No, I wasn't. We had two boys, though. And it wasn't a matter of "making" it home. She just prioritized differently, and this time, she'd done so a month ahead of time.

"You know what, this actually suits me perfectly," I replied. "Then I don't have to worry about Jess and Nathan feeling down when you leave again."

She sucked in a sharp breath. "That's a low blow, Bennett."

I laughed under my breath and gripped the wheel tighter. It was amazing how quickly she could *fuck* up my mood. "Do you realize you haven't even asked how they're doing in almost a week?" I didn't get a response, and I'd reached my street anyway. "I gotta go. I have a meeting." I ended that call too and did a poor job of parking straight.

There's some splendid irony for you... You seem to struggle doing other things straight too.

I sighed to myself, hurried inside, ran up the stairs, and hauled out a new suit from my closet. My very late lunch was in ten minutes; I refused to be late. Thanks to Kieran picking up the boys, I *would* make it on time.

I was out of the house a few minutes later, and the rain hadn't picked up again—thank fuck.

Hurrying down one picturesque street after another, I made it to the marina in record time, and I paused a few paces away from the restaurant to catch my breath. I ran a hand through my hair, made sure I had my plans with me, and then it was time.

"Minor project," as Ellis had called it. Sure, minor. It was minor to help a famous musician make a new name for himself and help him get his brand out there in an industry that judged everything.

A cursory glance at the establishment while I waited for the hostess to arrive made me worry we'd picked a bad place. Lincoln had requested something small and private when we emailed, but this one was also bordering on intimate. It had, however, been one of his suggestions.

The industrial interior didn't erase the fact that there were lit candles on the tables and the other lighting in the room was set very low.

Barely any customers around, which wasn't weird given the hour. It was only three.

Could we even call that a lunch?

A man appeared with a blinding smile.

Pardon me. Host, not hostess.

"Hi there, welcome to Subella. What can I do for you, sir?"

Clever name for a place that served Italian subs, I'd give them that.

"I have a reservation under Brooks," I said.

The door opened behind me, and my heart went *thud*. The teenager in me was starstruck by the appearance of my former idol. *Good fucking grief*. The funniest thing that hit me was that I evidently had a *type*. Because as I quickly took in the well-worn jeans, leather jacket, and bed head of one Lincoln Hayes, I knew I would find the same kinds of clothes in Kieran's closet. The only thing Kieran didn't have was a cigarette stuck behind his ear.

"Bennett?" he inquired.

Time to be cool. I subtly wiped my hand off on my thigh before extending it. "Great to meet you, Mr. Hayes."

"Lincoln," he corrected and shook my hand. I was never going to wash it. "You too, man." He peered around to the host. "Our table ready?"

"Always, sir!" The host had recognized Lincoln too, though I didn't know if it was due to his fame in the nineties or because he came here often.

We were shown to a corner table in the back, passing only six or seven guests on the way, and the host said our server would be with us soon.

"You been here before?" Lincoln asked as he sat down. "I've brought my family every week since we moved in. The Sicilian sub is outta this world."

"No, never been. I guess I know what to order, then." I appreciated his easygoing manner. I might even be able to relax soon.

The server was with us promptly, and we ordered our subs and drinks. Lincoln ordered a soda, so I went with nonalcoholic as well. It was always a good idea to let the client order first.

"So, how's your pop?" Lincoln sat back and smirked.

Figured he'd bring that up...

"Insufferable as always," I replied.

Lincoln chuckled. "Nah, he was sweet. He wouldn't stop talking about you."

"Sometimes he forgets I'm thirty and not ten." I shook my head, only slightly amused. "I hope he didn't get into too much detail about the music critic I wanted to be as a child."

"It may have come up." He grinned. "I take it that dream changed direction?"

Good, we could get back on track. "It did." I smiled. "Working for your cousin has become a dream job. Besides, it's not every day you get to design a brand for Lincoln Hayes.

Speaking of—" I reached down and flicked open my briefcase, pulling out the folder I'd put together for him. "I have some mockups you can bring home with you and look through while you decide on your name."

Personally, I thought he should use his last name. It was already established in his field.

He accepted the folder and thumbed through it briefly. "One of the reasons I don't wanna use my initials, and definitely not just Hayes." He held up one black design where "H" was at the center of a simple, metallic layout. "I don't need a logo that makes street-corner hustlers salivate."

Pardon? I cocked my head, confused.

"H for heroin…?"

Oh. Oh! I nodded once, firmly. "Good call."

"Anyway." He set the folder aside and planted his forearms on the table. "This is where you come in, Bennett. I'm drawing a blank on the name, but Ellis told me you're good at that."

Well, Ellis wasn't entirely correct. "I know what sells. It's not necessarily the name you want, if that makes sense." I paused. "If *your* name were attached to the logo, your brand would sell itself."

Our food arrived, giving Lincoln some time to consider what I'd said.

My sub did look mouthwateringly delicious. Pastrami, thinly sliced olives, marinated artichokes, melted mozzarella, grilled bread—Christ, I was coming back here again. And I was bringing Kieran and the kids.

"Listen." Lincoln cleared his throat. "I recently spent ten years in prison. Everything I knew was gone. I had no plans, no future, and I'd lost the love of my life. Since walking out of those gates a year ago, I've learned two things. One, the love of my life still wanted my old ass." He smirked at that, and I chuckled. "And two, you can never make up for lost time."

The last one was less funny.

"This is my second chance at life," Lincoln went on. "But my first will always be what it was. I can't change that—or take anything back. All I can control is where the first ends and where the second begins. And that's what I want my name to reflect."

I nodded slowly, ideas coming to me. At the same time, I couldn't help but draw parallels between what he'd said and what I was going through in my own life.

You can never make up for lost time.

All you can control is where the first ends and where the second begins.

I knew deep within me that my marriage was falling apart. One day, I was going to ask for a divorce—if Allison didn't beat me to it. Either way, this part of my life was heading steadily toward its end.

The only questions I had were, *when* did it end? And would Kieran be part of my life when I started fresh?

He'd said no from the beginning.

CHAPTER 15

Allison graduated in May. It was a long weekend I spent nauseated most of the time, from the minute our flight departed for Chicago, to the... Actually, it hadn't ended yet, and I didn't see how it could, because she was coming home with us after this was over.

Jess was understandably bored and restless during the ceremony, and Nate had his nose buried in his digital reader.

He did need reading glasses, we'd found out, and he was fucking cute in them. Little black frames that further showed what a tiny adult he'd become. Except for the McDonald's toy he always kept in his pocket these days. He wouldn't leave home without it.

I didn't know the details of what had happened the day Kieran took the kids to McDonald's, other than Jess had come home afterward giggling and shouting, "We had ten Happy Meals! Kieran had Happy Meal also!"

To make Nate relax and order whatever food he wanted,

Kieran had devoured several Happy Meals and said he'd keep one of the toys on the dashboard in his car.

I swallowed queasily and tried to refocus. It was Allison's graduation party at her parents' house, the place filled with family and friends. Never had I felt more like an outsider, however.

People had come up to me all day asking how proud I was of my wife.

I wasn't proud. I probably should have been, but I wasn't.

I pretended, though.

Every now and then, Nate would look up from his book, eye his surroundings, take a sip of his soda, then look down again.

We'd found a good corner to hide out in.

"Dad, when are we going home?" he asked quietly. "I don't like it here."

Me either, buddy.

"Sunday." I combed my fingers through his hair and kissed the top of his head.

"Can we stay at Auntie Brianna's condo tonight instead?" he wondered, hope flooding his eyes. "I couldn't sleep very well last night. Lulu kept jumping up in my bed."

I chuckled. Lulu was Allison's mother's useless little diva terrier.

"That sounds like a plan to me," I replied with a nod. Brianna had thought about selling her condo here for a while, because she spent less and less time in Chicago for work, but I still had my key.

"For the record," Nate interjected, "if *we* had a dog, it wouldn't be like Lulu. Our dog would be *perfect*."

Oh, I'd heard that one before.

"Daddy!" Jess hollered. He appeared from the crowd of guests and ran over with something in his hand. "Why have they done this?"

I peered closer as he opened his hands. He'd found some treats for the kids, and it looked like someone had chopped gummy worms and put them inside partially chocolate-covered s'mores.

My forehead creased.

"I only want the gummy worms," Jess said seriously. "Not the fluffy."

"It's marshmallows," I said unsurely. "I thought you liked that."

"Not with gummy worms!"

"Hey—indoor voice, sweetheart." It was hard not to smile. "It's Mum's graduation party. Snacks are supposed to be fancy."

He sighed heavily and perched himself on my lap.

When either of us was dressed up, like today, I kept my pockets stocked with tissues and Purell. So I put down the treats he was so disappointed in and cleaned the chocolate off his hands before it could end up on our shirts.

"Can I call Jaylin?" Jess asked.

"They're on vacation, remember?" It was Maggie's parents' anniversary, and they'd invited Kieran, Maggie, and Jaylin on a cruise between San Francisco and someplace in Mexico. Kieran had looked forward to that about as much as I had looked forward to this.

Jess sighed again.

What a wonderful weekend it was shaping up to be.

I was going to need more than a summer to adjust to the fact that Allison was done with school.

I'd taken the first two weeks off work at her suggestion so we could "reconnect" as a family and go away together. Well, after three days at a family resort in Victoria, I was thrilled to go home.

Everything had felt fake and out of place, not counting spending time with the boys. We'd visited a water park and a wildlife rehabilitation center, and that part had been fun. I absolutely loved watching my sons growing up to be two so different individuals. Nathan's love for science and, most recently, his obsession with veterinary care for animals were part of a journey I was happy to see him on. He thrived in museums and wherever he could pick up new knowledge. Whereas Jess was all about the next adrenaline rush. In the water park, we'd had to physically tear him away after the eleventh ride on a water slide that made my stomach drop.

At least by the time we came home, Kieran was back from vacation.

He was washing his car when we pulled up, and Nate was the first one to jump out.

Allison and I watched him run over to the Marshalls where Kieran scooped him up in a hug.

I tilted my head. Nathan was speaking animatedly about something in the same way Jess usually discussed pretty much everything in life.

"Well, they've grown close," Allison noted, surprised.

I hummed. I knew they'd shared something since the day Kieran had given Nate the digital reader, which had become even more after their visit to McDonald's, but I was still figuring out the extent. Both of them were weirdly secretive about it, though in a joking way.

It made the image of a fantasy future painfully vivid.

What if Kieran and I had a house together? What if we were a family?

I stepped out of the car and stretched my back a bit.

Nate was on his way back to our side of the fence.

"Welcome home," Kieran said with a slight smile. It wasn't my favorite of his smiles. "Did you guys have a nice vacation?"

"The boys had a blast." I scratched my arm and walked over to the fence. "How was the cruise?"

"Jaylin had a blast," he chuckled. Then he turned on his polite charm for Allison as she left the car too, and a couple minutes of useless chitchat ensued while we unloaded the trunk.

Nate and Jess had already disappeared inside.

Allison followed shortly after, leaving me alone with Kieran.

There was a tightness in my chest I couldn't ease, no matter what distraction I went for.

"Barbecue tonight?" Kieran asked.

I nodded. "Sounds great."

He studied me for a beat and trailed closer. "Do you need a night together as much as I do?"

I needed a lot more than that.

"Probably more," I admitted, mustering a quick smirk.

"Impossible," he murmured. "The jealousy has been insane these past couple of weeks. It legit hurts, knowing you and she..." He cleared his throat and didn't finish the sentence.

I blew out a breath and scrubbed my hands over my face.

Something had to give soon.

He didn't like thinking about Allison and me together? He didn't know the half of it. Living through it was a whole other hell, even though we didn't have sex often at all. It was when I felt like the biggest of frauds.

"Right." Kieran had bitterness written all over him. "With that confirmed, how—"

"What did you want me to say, Kieran?" I asked tiredly. "She and I barely touch—"

"Don't wanna hear it," he responded tightly. "Anyway. Can

we fuck off for a weekend? Go camping or something? Guys do that, don't they?"

I didn't care if guys did that or not; we needed to get away. End of story.

"We'll find time," I answered.

We had to wait first. We had a packed schedule for all of June, with the last weekend being when we celebrated Nate's tenth birthday. Then it was the Fourth of July, I had a business trip, and Kieran had too much to do at work.

Quickies in our offices and stolen moments in our everyday life let us hang on by a thread but no more than that, until we finally got our weekend at the end of July.

We headed out early, backpacks full, and drove up the mountains as the sun rose.

It was as if the rays thawed us out.

Every mile we ticked off, the farther into the wilderness we got, I felt myself being brought back to life. A life where everything wasn't about my boys, work, or finding the next fix.

We didn't talk much on the drive.

The sky was bright blue. The sun climbed higher and higher. Rock music played quietly in the background. Kieran drove, one hand on the wheel, the other on my thigh. Windows rolled down, sending us wafts of pine and moss.

I took a deep breath and let the rest of the world fade away.

Turning my head along the headrest, I stared at Kieran's profile and savored the moment. Every fiber of my being ached for him. He didn't shave religiously in the summer—neither did I, when I thought about it—and he had some sexy scruff across his sharp jaw. Mostly brown, but it glinted ginger and dark blond in the sun. His hair was sun-kissed too. Never neat.

God, how I wanted him. Aside from the boys, he'd become my life.

Kieran threaded our fingers together and brought them close to kiss my fingertips.

All you can control is where the first ends and where the second begins.

"If you could go back..."

I shook my head. "No." Because, foolishly, I had to hope.

"Good," he said, exhaling in evident relief. "Me neither."

We parked by an old campsite not many knew of. We were high up in the mountains, and there was a small freshwater lake that had the most beautiful blue color.

After setting up the tent and preparing a fire, we trailed down to the dock hand-in-hand, something that felt so fucking right I didn't want to be without it anymore.

Kieran had brought his camera, one of those professional ones he'd bought when he was bored.

"Talk about gorgeous," he murmured, peering into the lens.

"Yeah." I looked out over the peaceful water and sighed contentedly. The silence around us was almost as perfect as the scenery. "How cold do you think it is?"

He smiled and took another picture. "Water coming straight from the mountains...? Frigid."

I grinned. "I guess we should find out for sure."

"Oh, we definitely should."

No time to waste, then. I unbuttoned my cargo shorts and took off my shoes. Kieran undressed like Jess. Tee thrown over his head, landing God knows where, pants pushed down with one leg inside out, boots kicked off.

When we were down to our boxer briefs, we walked to the

end of the dock and looked down into the crystal-clear water. It was definitely deep enough to dive in, and the bottom of the lake seemed to consist of smooth, rounded rocks.

"On three?" He shot me a grin.

I sucked in a breath and nodded. The sun felt so bloody good on my skin, and now we were willingly jumping into freezing water.

"One," I said.

"Two." He took a step back to get ready, and I did the same. "Three!"

We ran forward and jumped together, my heart starting to race the second before we hit the water with a loud splash. Okay, it wasn't near-freezing, but holy smokes, it was cold!

He resurfaced before me and was smiling my favorite smile, the one that reached his eyes and was full of happiness, when I swam over to him.

"We needed this." He slipped an arm around my middle and kissed me softly.

"Definitely." I cupped the back of his neck, kissing him back with more passion.

Swimming me backward to the dock, he trapped me against an aged stepladder so we could gain footing. And we made out like teenagers, only we were in no rush for once. Feeling him hard against me, I deepened the kiss and pushed down his underwear. He got the hint and took over, and I threw mine up on the dock as he did the same.

I melted into his hold and closed my eyes. "I missed you."

He shivered as my hands traveled across his back, our kiss slowing down. "I love you."

Hell.

I kissed him hard and let those three glorious words sink in. Goose bumps covered my arms, and I played his declaration on a loop in my head.

"I love you," I whispered, kissing his jaw. "I love you with everything I am."

"Fuck," he sighed. "Say it again?"

I smiled and bit his chin playfully. "I love you."

I'd never seen such contentment on his face before. It was indescribable, knowing that *I* made him feel this way.

"I love you too." He caught my mouth in a kiss that stole my breath. His tongue stroked mine sensually, his every move heavy with promise. "Let's get out of the water."

But we didn't get very far. Kieran went over to his discarded pants and fished out a condom and lube, and then I had him on his back right there on the dock. He grinned up at me, my head shielding his face from the sun, and stole a quick kiss.

"If I get splinters, it's on you."

"I can live with that," I said, kissing my way down his body.

He exhaled a curse as I sucked his cock into my mouth, followed by his fingers in my hair.

I hummed around his cock and watched him shift in pleasure, his thighs tensing, his hips rolling, abs clenching.

"Just like that, baby." He groaned and sucked in a sharp breath. "I wanna come before you fuck me."

Good, because I wanted to see him lose it like this. I redoubled my efforts and hollowed out my cheeks every time I took him as deep as I could, and I stroked the sensitive skin in the crease of his thigh the way he loved.

His grip on my hair always tightened right before he came. He panted out a quick warning, and then my mouth was flooded with his hot release, several ropes sliding down my throat. I continued sucking him off until he collapsed against the wooden boards, and that was my cue. I rolled the condom down my cock and emptied the packet of lube.

"Give it to me." He yanked me down on him, and I pushed inside as slowly as I could muster. Which was a fucking feat because I needed him too much. With his taste in my mouth, I wanted to let go of all inhibitions.

"Fuck, you feel good," I whispered huskily. Grabbing his jaw, I angled him for a hard kiss and shoved my cock deep inside. I swallowed his groaned gasp and began fucking him harder. "Take it for me, love."

"Always," he gritted out. "Jesus Christ, Ben. Harder."

I fucked him harder, I kissed him harder, I grabbed at him harder.

"Do you taste that?" I broke a messy kiss and sank my teeth into his neck.

He hissed, digging his fingernails into my shoulder blades. "Mm, you taste better."

"Now you're just lying." I hooked an arm under one of his legs and pushed in even deeper. That was where I hit his sweet spot, the one that got him going in minutes.

He cursed and spurred me on, and for several moments we were all rough hands and teeth. I licked the length of his neck where a bead of sweat trickled down, and he muffled his moans by biting into my shoulder.

"One day, I want to fill your perfect ass with my come," I murmured, out of breath. He clenched down on me and moaned mindlessly. "Do you want to feel my come running down your thighs, Kieran?"

"Ben—" He screwed his eyes shut and fisted his cock, stroking it roughly. "Oh hell, oh fuck. I think about it all the goddamn time."

I was losing my fight, the orgasm getting closer and closer. The pleasure crackled within me and sent shivers down my spine.

"I'm close, love..." I closed my eyes and ignored my body's protests. I chased the edge and felt the explosions taking over.

The orgasm crashed over me as Kieran's dirty murmurs

flooded my senses. I rocked into him and held my breath. My cock pulsed with each release, and then I felt him coming again too. Hot splashes of come landed across his abs, and I drew in a deep breath, smelling the sex around us.

He was so bloody sexy, I couldn't describe it justly.

Afterward, I collapsed next to him.

My chest heaved with each breath. My heart pounded.

A tremor ran through Kieran, and he rolled over to bury his face against my neck. I circled my arms around him and kissed the side of his head.

"I love you," he muttered drowsily.

"I love you too," I sighed, utterly relaxed. And sticky. We'd need another dip in the lake before getting started on a late lunch. "We should get your Irish ass out of the sun."

His shoulders shook with a quiet laugh. "You're probably not wrong."

This camping trip was turning out to be the perfect getaway, and so much more comfortable than the one we took with Jess and Jaylin. By the time we were ready for dinner, our hair was still damp from our last lake adventure, but our bodies were snuggly warm in sweats and hoodies.

The sun had gone down, and with it, the temperature.

Kieran and I sat by our fire and had a couple beers while we waited for the food to be done. Two thick steaks were grilling above the flames, and deep into the glowing firewood, Kieran had thrown two big potatoes in foil.

Homemade dip, butter, and a salad had been prepared by my personal chef before we left, and it was sitting in the cooler next to him.

How could I not want this for the rest of my life?

This trip was almost going too well. There weren't even that many mosquitos.

I knew a thing or two about trips going too well...

"Remember I used to be secretive about cooking?" Kieran asked, his gaze never leaving the fire.

"Of course."

"I think it's because I gotta keep my lives separate," he went on pensively. "I used to cook with my mother a lot. She's the one who's taught me everything—even how to work a grill. Her marinades...?" He let out a low whistle. "It was kinda our thing. Still is, I guess."

I kept my mouth shut, wanting nothing more than to get a rare glimpse into his past.

"I know you want more, Ben." He looked down and cracked his knuckles while I tried to keep my face composed. "I want more too. But every time I wanna ask Mags for a divorce, I think about the people I'd lose in Quincy." He couldn't possibly know how my heart sank there. *Fuck.* "I think about my brothers, my sisters, my parents, my cousins, all my nieces and nephews..." He cleared his throat and blew out a breath. "Then there's you. You and the boys. You give me air. I can be myself."

I shifted closer and wove our fingers together on his knee.

He wasn't done. "I don't wanna think about my family too much when I'm here because it makes me bitter. They wouldn't approve of you, and it pisses me off. I hate their narrow-mindedness, but I can't change it. So... I don't know." He grew frustrated. "Before you, I was two people—neither of them was true. My parents' CEO son who made it big on the West Coast, and Mags's husband. Now there's a third guy in me I'm getting to know for the first time ever, and it's *me*."

I dropped a kiss to his shoulder.

"What I'm tryin'a say is," he went on, "as long as I keep these three boxes separate, I can borrow more time with you. I can be myself and forget that the woman who raised me prays for gay people to be cured. I can also pretend I'm everything they think I am and go back to Quincy for the holidays and teach my nieces and nephews to play baseball. I can catch a game with my brothers and ignore the slurs. My daughter... Fuck." He looked away and swallowed hard.

"I understand, sweetheart." I put an arm around his shoulders and pulled him to me, and I pressed a kiss to his temple. "I understand where you're coming from."

It was a painful truth.

Considering that he shared so little about his family, it was easy to forget them. In turn, it made it easier to wonder why I wasn't enough. But his family wasn't one entity. It wasn't me versus one person. It was, as he'd mentioned, parents, siblings... I knew he was the godfather of two nephews. It was aunts and uncles and all those people I'd never had to think of. My family, while tight-knit, was tiny in comparison.

I had to think of Jaylin too. Children had survived divorces for centuries, but she risked losing everyone she loved to visit on the East Coast.

"And you're absolutely sure they would...you know."

He let out a humorless chuckle. "Wouldn't be the first time." He paused as he watched our linked fingers. "I had an aunt on my pop's side. This went down when I was two shits high, so I only heard rumors and whispers until I was well past twenty. But yeah, she was gay."

I was almost too afraid to ask. "Was?"

He flashed a wry look. "She was also a chain smoker."

"Ah."

"She died of lung cancer years ago."

I nodded slowly, processing. "But she died alone?"

"My family wasn't there, at least. I don't know if she had anyone. I hope she did."

Me too.

Kieran scooted forward to poke at the fire, and I got the feeling he was done sharing for the evening. My feelings hadn't exactly changed, but I had a deeper understanding now. It helped that we wanted the same thing. God, it really mattered to me. We wouldn't pretend to each other; that was something.

There was one thing left I had to bring up, though. "Would they shun you, for lack of a better word, if you got divorced? I mean—hell, we could live as bachelors as far as… I don't know."

"I get what you mean," he replied, digging the potatoes out of the fire with a stick. "Believe me, the thought has occurred to me, and the short answer is, kinda like homosexuality, it would put my family in two camps. I mean, we live in different times, and I know my family. Some of them would accept me. Most wouldn't. But there would be this rift that I caused."

I helped him plate the steaks.

"I wouldn't say divorce is the same," he said, "but it's the principle. One person's business is everyone's business in my family, and I swear they're all fucking bloodhounds. You can't live with them and keep a secret. So, say Mags and I get divorced. There's Jaylin to consider—we can't ask her to shut up about everything she sees at home, right? Meaning, some of it will reach Quincy."

We would have to stay secret forever, in other words.

"My divorce would be the topic for everyone," he continued. "I can survive that—no problem."

"But…"

"But they're relentless and old-fashioned, so half of them would demand I move home, and the other half would find another way to interfere in my life. I wouldn't be left alone for years."

"Why would they demand you move back to Quincy?"

"Because every man needs a woman by his side," he

mocked. "My mother would probably fly out just to wash my fucking clothes." Then he frowned and sighed. "They would also blame Mags. That she didn't keep me happy—and she doesn't deserve that."

"Are you serious?" I asked in disbelief. "Did your family grow up in the 1800s?"

He chuckled quietly. "They sure as shit belong in the fifties anyway."

My upbringing had been so vastly different that the things Kieran told me were difficult to reconcile. I mean, my own father was a war veteran of the same generation as Kieran's parents. Yet, he'd raised us to be open-minded and accepting.

I pressed another kiss to Kieran's temple. "I love you."

"I love you too, and...and I'm sorry."

It didn't matter. This was the situation we were in, and there was more time to borrow.

CHAPTER 16

Kieran and I found shelter in the norm. People who knew us also knew of our wives, and there was never anything weird about us going away together every now and then. The only one we'd worried about was Maggie, but perhaps she had successfully suppressed her knowledge of Kieran's nature, because she even encouraged our camping trips and, beginning in autumn, our sudden interest in going to football games.

While Kieran had booked us tickets to our first away game, I had taken a crash course in Seahawks facts on the internet to convince Allison I enjoyed the sport.

I didn't, for the record. American football was dreadfully tedious and boring. Five minutes on the clock could last a fucking hour with all the breaks and commercials.

Real football had been a lot more interesting to pretend to follow, but...well, America didn't have that. Not counting the graveyard league where European players came to die.

We took other outings too. Tonight, for instance, Kieran was coming with me to the launch party for Lincoln Hayes's new studio in Seattle.

We wanted to enjoy ourselves and have a few drinks, we'd explained to our wives, so we would crash at my sister's place and come home tomorrow.

It was as bulletproof a plan as it could be, given that Allison and Brianna didn't talk. My sister hadn't hidden her animosity toward Allison's years in a school so far away, and frankly, my wife was a little intimidated by Brianna. I couldn't blame her.

"Wow." Allison came out from the kitchen to see me in the hallway, and she gave me a once-over. "New suit?"

I nodded and adjusted the cuff links. I'd noticed some of my other suits were too big. The scale showed no difference, but I'd started running with Kieran on the weekends. He made me want to take better care of myself.

Besides, the way he looked at me after a run was enough to live on for a whole week.

I glanced at myself in the mirror and hesitated. "Is it too much black?" Both the dress pants and shirt were black. I was forgoing the jacket and the tie, knowing I'd be surrounded by what Lincoln called "industry rats."

"No, you look...very handsome." Allison gave me a small smile. "Now I'm kind of jealous you're taking Kieran instead of me."

I frowned at her. "I asked you first." Knowing full well she'd decline. Her new job was demanding and tired her out. She'd stopped living, claiming she had no energy after work.

Thankfully, she'd gotten her act together where the boys were concerned. For one, she'd taken over driving Nate and Jess to after-school activities. It had resulted in Maggie doing the same with Jaylin. For two, in an attempt to reconnect with Nathan, Allison took the boys out every Saturday for lunch and...such. Tomorrow, they were going to the mall in the

Valley to get Nate new shoes. Jess needed a new lunch box too.

Being a first grader was an adjustment for my youngest, and he'd started throwing tantrums when he didn't understand the teacher.

The lunch box had been the first casualty.

But hey, party time now.

We took my car to the city, and I should've known Kieran was going to knock the air out of my lungs.

"I have to outshine a rock star, baby," he'd said with a smirk.

He'd outshone the world since the day I met him.

Who knew suspenders were so sexy? His jeans and tee had been replaced with a shirt and charcoal pants that made his ass look so fuckable.

"Your ass is mine tonight," he told me.

"Can you read minds now?" I blurted out as I switched lanes. "Although, in my head, the roles were reversed."

He chuckled. "I'll bottom for you any fucking day, just not tonight."

Fuck yes, that meant he was in a mood to go really rough.

I adjusted my cock and tried to pay more attention to the road. We'd booked a hotel room in his company's name, and it was right next to Lincoln's studio. Even so, it would be a struggle to leave the hotel and go to the party when I had this man beside me.

"You didn't tell me it was a goddamn red-carpet event, Ben."

"They're hardly here for us, love." I nudged him to cross the street already. "How else would I promote a musician and get him back into the spotlight?"

He huffed, eyeing the dozen reporters outside the studio. "You're not a freaking promoter."

No, but I'd worked closely with one.

It was a low building for its central location, four stories of red brick, with the black-painted fire escape placed alongside the façade. That was where we found the name of Lincoln's company too, stretching from the top staircase to the bottom, in backlit, brushed steel letters.

"Second Verse Studios." Kieran squinted up at the building. "Did you come up with the name?"

I nodded, hit by a ball of nerves all of a sudden. This had been more than a minor project to me; it was something Kieran had followed and would see the results of.

"Supposedly, the chorus has the message," I said. "But in the verse—that's where we find the story."

To my surprise, Kieran grabbed my hand. We were standing right there on the sidewalk next to all the people who'd been invited to the party. And those who hadn't.

"I'm fucking proud of you, baby."

I smiled widely, humbled and grateful.

He shot me a wink, gave my hand a squeeze, and let go. "Let's head in."

Let's.

As per my firm advice, Lincoln had invited industry people who drew a crowd, not that I recognized any of the ten or so men and women on the red carpet. They were producers and musicians I'd never heard of, but it'd been enough for the promoter to make a few calls and have reporters coming eagerly.

A large security guy stood at the end of the closed-off area, and I gave my name to him so we could pass.

I'd already spotted Lincoln closest to the door, where he was being interviewed by someone. He had his wife next to him, a short brunette who didn't look like she'd given birth a few months ago.

"You did this," Kieran murmured in my ear. "You're incredible."

"Don't give me too much credit," I chuckled uncomfortably. "I designed his brand—I built the concept. The rest... I mean, he has a whole team who made this happen."

"Good one." He draped an arm around my shoulders and clapped me on my chest. "Don't you frequently tell me branding is everything?"

I wouldn't say *frequently*...

"Bennett!" I heard Lincoln holler.

The rush of excitement instinctively made me want to grab Kieran's hand again, until I remembered I couldn't. We walked over to Lincoln and his wife, and I put a polite grin on my face.

"Glad you could make it, man." He shook my hand. "If I'm gonna suffer through publicity stunts like this, I prefer to drag as many people with me as I can."

I laughed.

"I'd say he didn't mean that, but..." Lincoln's wife told the reporter, who snorted a chuckle.

We went through brief introductions, and I didn't mention Kieran as a friend. I stubbornly refused. He was just Kieran, and others could assume all they wanted. Most would see a friend. Lincoln knew I was married. His wife, though— Adeline... She gave us such a cute smile that I couldn't help but believe she assumed we were a couple.

The party was held in the lobby, which consisted of the entire first floor of the building. Kieran and I were met by blaring rock music with an insane guitar riff, and there were servers making rounds with trays of finger foods and cocktails.

"How many were invited?" Kieran asked, taking in the surroundings.

"I think...two hundred people or something like that." It wasn't packed yet, though it would be.

Ellis had still been deciding whether or not he'd show up when I left work earlier.

He and Lincoln evidently shared the same tastes when it came to designing their workspaces. A lot of brick, open areas, wrought iron, and glass. Industrial to the core. The only difference was that Lincoln went darker, and he had vintage instruments in glass cases on the walls.

"I wish we could guarantee we'd only be surrounded by strangers." Kieran nodded at a server, who came over right away.

"Why?" I knew why, but I wanted to hear him say it.

Kieran grabbed us what looked like two whiskey drinks, and the server walked off again. "Because I fucking hate hiding our relationship."

I blew out a breath as my stomach did a somersault. Whenever he said things like that, it was easy to give him time. Too easy. I folded like a cheap suit.

"I love you," I said and took a swig of my drink.

"Love you more." He smiled.

"Your phone's ringing," I croaked into my pillow.

He grunted sleepily and pulled the covers over us. "That's not mine."

Shit.

My head weighed a ton, and it was almost impossible to lift it off the pillow. I reached out blindly and found my phone on the nightstand, and I replied with a half-dead hello.

How much did we drink last night? God.

"Let's have brunch, little brother."

"Stop yelling," I whispered.

Brianna laughed. "Hungover?"

Hungover, exhausted—crap, I had a bite mark on my arm.

"You could say that." I forced myself to sit up, and my feet hit the floor. *Ouch*—my ass had never been this sore before.

"You probably deserve it," Brianna responded wryly. "So, brunch? Half an hour?"

"Ugh." I rubbed at my eyes and squinted. The hotel room was in disarray.

"Ow," I heard Kieran whisper behind me.

"Bennett!" my sister yelled.

I flinched and held the phone away. "My head is killing me. Please be nice." I exhaled heavily, trying to get my brain to function.

Glancing over my shoulder, I saw Kieran stand up and cringe in pain. Holy hell, we'd lost it last night. Two desperate drunks had used each other as scratching posts.

He shot me a look. "I won't be able to sit for a week."

I stifled a laugh, for fear it would kill me. Now I remembered I'd taken my turn after he'd owned me the way only he could.

We were screwed, literally.

Brunch with Brianna would have to wait. I needed a shower and possibly a trip to the hospital.

Time to wrap up the call.

"I can't," I muttered in my morning voice. "It takes a bit longer than that to get to the city."

She let out a soft laugh. "Oh, Bennett. You can bullshit your wife into oblivion, but don't try to lie to me. Hannigan's. You have thirty minutes."

She hung up the phone.

Nausea crawled up my throat, and it wasn't only from the countless drinks we'd inhaled last night.

"What's up?" Kieran yawned.

I lowered my phone and stared at the screen. "My sister swore. She never swears."

You can bullshit your wife into oblivion, but don't try to lie to me.

She knew. Somehow, she knew.

"Fuck," I breathed out.

"Hello, sir—"

"Cheers, my sister's got a table already." I ran a hand through my hair and checked I hadn't forgotten my wallet in the taxi. Refusing to show up without showering first, I had to deal with being five minutes late. It was for Brianna's sake, truly.

Making my way between the tables at the packed restaurant, I reminded myself that I was an adult and that my sister didn't scare me. It was going so-so. In reality, my heart hadn't stopped pounding since she'd ended the call.

Kieran was worried too.

We'd decided that he would take the train home early just in case he would have to get started on damage control.

"Hey, sorry I'm late." I took a breath and chanced a kiss on her cheek before I got seated. She didn't slap me, at least.

She lifted a delicate brow at my clothes from last night. "How was the party?"

Fuck, fuck, fuck. "It was, uh… Did I tell you?"

She shook her head and took a sip of her mimosa. "I read about it on Facebook. Allison made an update and chatted with a friend—from Chicago, I presume. Said you were in the city to go to a work event and that you were crashing at your sister's…

so she had the house all to herself. Isn't that interesting, Bennett?"

"I..." I was saved by a server who came to take my order. I went with a breakfast sandwich with the catch of the day. "And coffee," I added. "Black, a lot of it. Thank you."

I slumped slightly in my seat and scrubbed at my face. My head was still spinning.

"You're having an affair, aren't you?"

My hands fell to my lap, and I swallowed hard. There was no accusation in her tone—or in her expression—just worry.

My silence was enough of an answer for her, and she sighed heavily.

"Bennett... This is so unlike you." She hesitated. "Is it Kieran?"

Jesus Christ, did she have to be right on the bloody money?

I inclined my head because I couldn't find my voice. A hundred different thoughts and questions swirled around my head, but most of all, it was dread that had pushed a metaphorical mute button on me. Dread that my relationship with Kieran had come to an end.

"I had this whole speech rehearsed in my head," she said. "I already had my suspicions, and then reading that from Allison—there was no doubt. And...I hate cheating. I *hate* that you're doing this, but now that you're sitting here in front of me, I can't be mad. I just want to know how the hell this happened because this isn't you, Bennett. I refuse to believe it. There has to be something. You must explain it to me."

Maybe I had a choice. Maybe I could shut her out and tell her to mind her own business. I probably could.

I realized I didn't want to, though. The resentment I held in jest toward my sister whenever we got together was just a juvenile way of showing her she knew me too well. And I missed her voice and her guidance.

"Remember you called him my cocaine?" I asked, and she nodded. "He's not. He's the love of my life."

Then I told her everything.

By the time I got home, I was numb.

I'd texted Kieran and told him we were safe for the time being, that I loved him, and that we'd talk tomorrow. That was all the communication I planned on having with the outside world for the rest of the day.

I wanted a movie night with my boys. I wanted to shut out everything and everyone else in order to process and get my shit together.

"Trust me when I say that I understand you, Bennett. But you need to divorce your wife. She doesn't have to be a pawn in this game you're playing. My personal feelings toward her don't matter. No one deserves to be cheated on. How can you even look at yourself in the mirror?"

If I could somehow get my sister's words out of my head too, that would be great.

She was the reflection in the mirror I'd avoided for a long time. Unless I was with Kieran, and then I only saw him.

"Daddy's home!" Jess shouted when I entered the house.

It was an instant relief to see his cute face, and I picked him up despite that he was less fond of that these days. He was a big boy now, he said. He even called me *Dad* sometimes.

"How's my baby boy?" I blew a raspberry on his cheek.

He giggled and groaned. "I'm not a baby."

"Nonsense. You'll always be my baby."

"Thank God you're home." Allison appeared in the doorway from the kitchen, looking like she'd been through hell. "Nathan's locked himself in his room and won't come out, and *that* one—" she pointed to Jess "—has refused both breakfast and lunch. We couldn't leave the house." She blew out a breath. "I had tickets to a children's thing at the museum."

I lifted a brow at Jess and poked his belly. "Why aren't you eating?"

"I don't want that milk," he complained. "The blue carton is better, but Mum said no."

"You have never said no to milk and cereal before," Allison grated. "Why does it matter what kind of milk we have?"

"Because he gets a stomachache from the regular," I replied and let Jess down again. "Maggie recommended we try an elimination diet, and it's been working. That's why I've bought lactose-free milk the past few months."

"Oh." Allison frowned. "Why didn't I know this? I went with you last week—we grocery shopped together."

I lifted a shoulder. It was the most diplomatic response I could give to yet another thing she hadn't bothered finding out. I'd done my best to share things, but I couldn't give her the CliffsNotes to every single thing. She needed to pay attention as well. She needed to be genuinely interested.

"Sweetie," she sighed, facing Jess, "you could've told me it gives you a stomachache."

I was a little surprised Nathan hadn't. "What's up with Nate?"

Allison gave me a helpless look. "I don't even know. He won't talk to me."

"All right, I'll take care of it." I ruffled Jess's hair and took off my shoes before I headed up the stairs. I knocked on his door. "Nate, it's Dad. Can you unlock the door?"

"It's open," I heard him mumble.

Entering his room, I spotted him on the bed with his face buried in his pillow, which he only did when he was afraid he'd done something wrong. Otherwise, he had no issues standing up for himself and pleading his case with conviction.

"Hey, buddy." I sat down on the edge of his bed and gave his butt a pat. "Why won't you talk to Mum?"

"Because it doesn't matter," he muttered. "She doesn't want to be here anyway."

That broke my heart. "What makes you think that?" As if I didn't know... At the same time, it would be unfair of me to claim she wasn't trying. "She's doing her best, son. I know things are a bit strange now. She's adjusting to being home, and she doesn't know our routines yet." It was much easier during breaks and holidays. Handling school, activities, and everyday responsibilities took time.

"She's doing it wrong," he said, irritated, and he sat up. He'd been crying. "I said to her last Saturday that I didn't want to go out today if she was just going to *be* there."

I furrowed my brow. "I'm not following. What would you like her to do?"

He huffed, frustrated. "She's a babysitter, okay? She just stands there or...like, we went to a bookstore. I wanted a new atlas, and she waited by the register. Couldn't she have come with me? She doesn't talk to us much. We *do* things, but..."

I gave his leg a gentle squeeze. "But you feel she's not really there?"

"Yeah." He exhaled heavily and looked down. "She's on her phone a lot."

Anger flared within me, though I kept that to myself for now. "I'll talk to her, I promise." I paused. "About Jess this morning—"

"I told her," he snarled.

"Hey." I lifted his chin, frowning. "You're angry."

"Yes," he whispered and looked away again. "She doesn't know anything. I told her Jess doesn't like that milk and that he might be allergic, and she said he couldn't be allergic because she'd used that milk in the casserole the day before."

I sighed, understanding. Both of them, but...yeah. Serious communication problems, and I couldn't very well blame Nate and Jess for that. Allison had to accept that she needed to listen a lot. Barging in and thinking we lived exactly like we did before she left four years ago was ridiculous.

The boys and I also needed to be patient with her. The situation was the way it was, and if things were ever going to work...

Fuck, I could hear my sister piping up again. But how the hell could I ask for a divorce now? Allison would fall apart, and the kids would suffer. I genuinely wanted to bridge the gap between Allison and the boys that had appeared while she was away, and I believed it could be done. With time.

We needed to be on the same page where the kids were concerned.

"I'll take care of it, okay?" I murmured. "I see your point, and I understand. I'll talk to Mum."

"Okay," he mumbled.

"Can I get a hug now?" I asked. "I need one."

He fought a smile and scooted closer so I could wrap him in my arms.

"What would you say if we changed into pajamas and watched movies all day?" I kissed the top of his head.

"Can we have candy?"

"Lots of it," I chuckled.

"Yeah." The smile in his voice warmed my heart.

CHAPTER 17

Kieran and I met up the morning after for our run, and I felt better after my day where I'd focused solely on Nate and Jess, making it easier to think about everything Brianna had told me.

The first thing I admitted was that I'd told my sister everything, and I was relieved Kieran had understanding for it.

"I figured you would," he added as we came to the edge of Downtown. "Up the hill?"

I nodded, looking up toward the hill district we had before us. In a sea of green, big estates and mansions popped up here and there. Ponderosa was the district few people could afford to live in but loved to visit during hikes and exhausting runs. It was also where Nathan went to school.

"You said your sister understands our situation?" Kieran questioned.

"Yeah, I mean—" I lifted my shirt to wipe sweat off my forehead. "After telling her about your upbringing and what you stand to lose, it's kind of impossible not to understand." I followed behind him as we met traffic, our shoes crunching against gravel at the side of the road. "She wanted to know that I wasn't doing this out of spite—or that we just wanna get our rocks off."

He snorted.

Thinking back now, it was insane that I'd ever thought Kieran was merely a friend and a quick fix in my search for adventure. As Brianna had elaborated to me—and she'd confessed that she'd missed how deep this went—I was never looking for adventure. I was looking for happiness.

No one made me happier than Kieran. He was the one I wanted to spend the rest of my life with, and I told Kieran this because I was beyond done holding back, and—

He stopped abruptly, right there on the side of the road, cupped my face, and kissed me hard.

Anyone could see us.

"I want that too, Ben."

But we couldn't have it, right? It would never be us.

I caught my breath and swallowed dryly. "That was her first clue. My sister—I asked why she suspected us, and she mentioned that you call me Ben. And that I don't correct you."

Kieran let his hands fall to his sides, and he looked at me quizzically. "You don't like the nickname?"

I huffed a laugh. "I always hated it." I brushed some lint off his hoodie, then nodded for him to keep running. "You can't call me anything else, though. It would be wrong."

"Well, that's good to know," he noted with a frown. "You should've told me."

"No." I picked up the pace. "I like it now—from you. But anyway. That's when she first started to wonder how much you meant to me."

We continued up the hill, the autumn sun warming us up as

the nip in the air tried to cool us down, and I went through everything Brianna and I had talked about. Including the part where she believed I should divorce Allison.

I agreed on that part. What I was doing was horrible, and I had absolutely no excuse. Two wrongs didn't make a right, and no matter how bitter and resentful Allison's priorities the past few years had made me, infidelity wasn't justified. It just wasn't.

Kieran felt the same. "Do you feel guilty, though?"

Not enough, was the best answer. I didn't feel enough guilt to stop. And sometimes—actually, quite often—I felt more guilt toward Maggie. Because even though two wrongs didn't make a right, it did erase my bad conscience. I held a vicious grudge against Allison. There was nothing like that with Maggie. She had never hurt me. The opposite; she helped me with the boys every now and then, and she was a good friend.

What did I do in return? I fucked her husband.

"Jesus, do you have to put it like that?" Kieran asked, breathing heavily.

"Let's be real, Kieran."

"I know, but Christ."

We reached the end of our descent half an hour later. There was a scenic viewpoint with a small parking lot and a few picnic tables where we took a break to guzzle water.

The morning sun turned the bay into a shimmering field of blue and green, and we could see the whole town from here.

"So what happens now?" Kieran took off his hoodie and threw it on one of the tables. "Are you gonna ask Allison for a divorce?"

"Not yet." I detached one of the three small water bottles I had strapped around my hips. "I have to restore the balance at home first." Taking a seat on top of a table, I planted my feet on the bench and uncapped the water. "Allison and Nate aren't close anymore, and they communicate through me. Then I translate to one what the other means."

"That's rough."

It really was. Especially seeing what it did to Nathan.

"I'm afraid of what this entails," Kieran admitted. "You divorce her eventually, and then what? Are we done?"

I didn't want to think about that, much less say anything on the matter. I'd never been so fucking torn in my life. "I can't see myself ever being strong enough to break up with you." That was the painful truth. Just as I didn't want to be his secret for the rest of my days. The mere notion of never sharing a home with him—with *anyone*—and what? Be his side piece?

I would shatter.

Kieran flinched and looked out over the town. "But you know you should," he concluded quietly. "Jesus Christ, it hurts." He rubbed at his chest.

"Hey. We're not there, Kieran."

He sent me a haunted look. "Yet."

From that day forward, I started collecting memories.

It was a desperate move.

I saved everything. Pictures that happened to have only Kieran and me in them, with or without the children. A takeout menu from Subella the weekend Kieran and I took the kids there. A fucking pen from the hotel he and I stayed at when we were "away" at another game.

With Halloween knocking on the door now, I was going all out. Kieran and I had taken the kids trick-or-treating before, but this year we dressed up too.

Kieran and Jess made excellent pirates. Jaylin was a princess and had asked me to be Prince Charming. Nathan was going as a space shuttle.

"You gotta stand still, buddy," Kieran chuckled, helping Jess apply eyeliner.

I smirked and took a photo. Jess froze in place with eyes wide, but he couldn't help but blink.

We were crowding the Marshalls hallway, and Maggie was standing to the side, giggling at the fabulous makeup job.

"There." Kieran grinned and declared his job done, and Jess looked in the mirror.

"We're Jack Sparrow!" he shouted in triumph. And blinked rapidly.

"Aww, you all look perfect," Maggie gushed. "Stand together—I wanna take a picture."

As Kieran and Jess joined the rest of us by the door, I helped Nate put on the top piece, the nose of the space shuttle, that landed on his shoulders.

"You sure you can see through there, Nate?" I asked, giving the plastic shell a knock. He'd gone nuts when seeing it online. He'd pleaded with me, *Please no more papier mâché, Dad.* I hadn't been able to deny him.

"I'm not Nate. I'm Apollo 74."

I laughed. "Why 74?"

"I consider the rest beta versions."

Kieran and I exchanged an amused look at my boy's response.

"Wait!" Jaylin exclaimed. "Prince Charming?"

"Yes, m'lady?" I winked.

"You gotta carry the princess," she stated frankly.

"Of course," I chuckled and picked her up. Positioning her on my hip, I noticed how much lighter she was than Jess.

"Okay, everyone say 'Happy Halloween,'" Maggie sang.

"Happy Halloween!"

"What is she *doing*?" Brianna asked, baffled.

"She's...trying." I winced as I watched Allison throw the basketball to Jess, who almost flew away when he caught it with his stomach.

"It's painful to watch," my sister said.

We were standing at the kitchen window looking out over the driveway where I'd put a basketball hoop above the garage door last weekend. Kieran and I thought it'd be fun to shoot some hoops together with the kids, but I hoped we did a better job than my wife.

I was beginning to feel sorry for her. Nate was right. She was trying. She was trying so fucking hard, but she wasn't listening, and therefore, her attempts failed miserably. She didn't hear me when I told her that it didn't matter what she did with the kids or where, just that she was there *with* them.

The holidays had given me hope, until I remembered she'd always handled those well. When Nate and Jess were home from school, we put more energy into fun activities, and the everyday routine wasn't as important. Then the new year began, the boys were back in school, and Allison floundered.

Next week was going to be easy for her, at least. Nate and Jess would be home for Easter, and Allison had taken the week off work because her parents were coming to visit.

"Can you imagine her being alone with the boys every other week?" I asked.

Brianna sighed and shook her head. "That's an excuse, Bennett. You'd make it work somehow. You just don't want to have the talk with her." She turned and looked up at me.

"You're hurting them. Going behind her back will come back and hurt the boys too."

I tensed my jaw and looked out the window.

"You can't justify infidelity," she continued firmly. "I'm serious." She hugged my arm, maybe to cushion the blow. "There's Kieran's wife too. What has she done to deserve this?"

Absolutely nothing.

"What's the alternative, Bennett? You stay married and act as the translator between Allison and the boys?"

"You're the psychiatrist. I was hoping you'd tell me."

She snorted.

She didn't have to tell me that I knew what I had to do. I did know, and time was running out.

"Anyway," I said, needing a new subject. "We talk about me too much. How's it going with that bloke you were seeing?"

Judging by the faint blush that bled across her cheeks, things were going well.

"That good, huh?" I smirked.

"I don't want to talk about it." She got snippy and returned to her seat at the table. I followed suit after refilling our tea. "Okay, fine, he's been asking why I'm not introducing him to my family."

I pretended to gasp. "Are you hiding us?"

"No! I'm just..." She released a breath, visibly frustrated. "How do I know it's worth it? I'm not used to serious relationships."

I knew she wasn't. The story of her life was that she overanalyzed the men she dated, and it got to the point where they ended things with her. Occupational hazard, she joked sometimes, though I knew she was hurt.

"Do you like him?" I asked plainly.

She nodded and took a sip of her tea.

"Then you need to stuff the shrink who analyzes behaviors

into a closet and trust that a twitch doesn't mean someone's lying," I told her. "If a guy wants to meet the family of the woman he's dating, chances are he's serious."

"I *know*," she bemoaned. Next, she flashed me a look. "For the record, I haven't had regular patients in years."

Yeah, yeah, semantics. She was all about research and clinical trials or whatever she called it. She met with focus groups and ran test studies with other teams of doctors.

Brianna and I heard a scream coming from outside, and the topic was forgotten as we rushed outside to see Jess on the ground.

"I'm sorry, baby!" Allison cried out.

I squatted down next to Jess and inspected his knees. Both had received scrapes, and he had blood trickling down his legs. Poor boy could barely breathe, he was crying so hard.

"It'll feel better soon, sweetheart. I promise." I gathered him to sit on one of my knees so I could carefully brush off the tiny pebbles. "Let me see your hands?"

He showed me his palms, where he had some minor scrapes too. "Oww, D-Daddy!"

Glancing over at Allison, I could see her own hurt plain as day, and it ran much deeper than the cuts and scrapes Jess ended up with one way or another several times every year.

Sensing that I wanted to talk to Allison, Brianna squatted down next to Jess too.

"Darling, how about you and I go inside? You know I never come up here without my bag."

Jess let out a sob and nodded pitifully.

"That sounds great, doesn't it, buddy?" I brushed some tears from his cheeks. "I bet she has some new Band-Aids."

It was sort of her thing.

"I do!" Her eyes lit up for Jess's sake. "All kinds of cool colors." She poked his belly. "Just for you."

That calmed him down some, and he grabbed her extended hand so they could go inside.

One down, one to go.

I walked over to Allison just as she broke down in tears, and I wrapped my arms around her.

"I don't know what I'm doing wrong," she cried. "My own sons hate me."

"They don't hate you, hon." I stifled a smile and kissed the top of her head. "Jess will forget this in ten minutes."

She wept harder, hugging my middle, and I sighed, having no fucking clue how to get through to her.

In my periphery, I saw Kieran and Maggie returning home from breakfast in the city with her parents. Jaylin looked like she was in a bad mood. Actually, so did Kieran.

"Just...remember that he's our Jess, not Magic Johnson."

Allison smacked my chest, and I couldn't help but laugh.

Then she looked up at me and tried to hold her scowl.

"You have to listen to them," I murmured. I cupped her face and wiped away her tears. "I'm not telling you to be interested in astronomy. I'm telling you to be interested in Nate's interest in astronomy. He just wants to share his excitement and teach us what he reads."

"I'll try..." She reached up and kissed me, and I cringed inwardly, knowing full well that Kieran saw it.

A door slammed.

We'd been through this before and would go through it again and again and again.

We got jealous every time we had to be husbands to our wives.

"I'm trying!"

"No, you're not!" I yelled. "It's getting *worse*, Allison!" How could she not fucking *see* it? "You've just wasted two months of the summer to work overtime when you could've spent that time with Nate and Jess!" I got heated and couldn't sit down any longer, so I started pacing in the living room while I ranted and got out the shit I'd kept bottled up for months and months. "Nate once told me you act like a babysitter, and I couldn't find a more apt description. For chrissakes, you've been home over a year now, and not only have you drifted further apart from Nathan, but you're disconnecting from Jess too. And he loves everybody!" I threw my arms out in frustration. "You haven't been to a single game since he started playing soccer, and you missed Nate's play at school."

"I was working!" she screamed.

"Then don't fucking complain when the boys don't want to spend Saturday with you!"

She flinched as if she'd been slapped, but she was back to seething in no time. "This wouldn't have happened if we'd had kids the way we'd planned—"

"Bring that up one more time, and I walk out that door," I growled furiously. "I'm dead fucking serious, Allison. It was the last time you used that against me."

She gnashed her teeth and glared.

She wasn't happy. It was clear as day. I wasn't happy either. The difference was my unhappiness lay with her. She was miserable because family life didn't live up to her expectations.

This fight had been brewing all throughout August, so I'd asked Kieran and Maggie to keep the boys tonight. And now... Fuck, I couldn't do this anymore. I couldn't be married to someone who'd made me feel like a single parent—and continued doing so when she was home.

"This isn't working." Saying it out loud, and the acceptance hitting me instantly, was such a relief.

Allison paled and stood stock-still.

I shook my head and scrubbed at my face, exasperated. "I work full-time, I shoulder the biggest responsibility with the kids, I take care of the house, I help them with homework—"

"So do I! I help them with homework too!"

"You give them the answers," I snapped. "Are you bloody serious? You give them the answers and don't explain shit! You treat everything like it's a chore, and the faster you can get it over with, the better. Because now that you're done with school, you wanna play catch-up in your career too. But I gotta ask, Allison—when will you put your family first?"

She had no response.

When numbness took over, I slouched back in a chair and stared at the ceiling.

Allison was stewing on the couch. Every now and then, she'd defend herself and once again say she'd tried. She was doing her best, but it wasn't easy to work full-time and be a mother too.

That one gave me a chuckle.

The absurdity of it all was that she didn't understand. She didn't hear herself. Christ, what had I been doing the past five years? Oh, right, working full-time and being a parent.

We were both too bitter to ever make this work. Even if we'd wanted to, there wasn't a chance in hell.

"I've been having an affair," I said at the ceiling.

And so that cat was out of the bag too.

I felt nothing. No jitters, no fear, no worry...no guilt.

"What?" Allison choked out.

"For the past..." I puffed out a breath and squinted, tapping my fingers together to count. "Damn. Two years."

Two fucking years.

"Are you—oh my God, I can't believe you." She fell apart and sobbed. "You act so high and mighty—"

"I certainly don't," I replied calmly.

"—and you have the nerve to preach about good parenting, all while you're fucking around—"

"Parenting has absolutely nothing to do with how I've been as a husband," I said. "You want to ignore the years I tried to reconnect with you? Fine. You want to pretend I haven't done everything in my power to make us work? Be my guest. Call me a shitty husband, let this one thing erase everything I've done—I don't bloody care anymore."

I was so tired. In the end, I was always going to be the bad guy. I'd knocked Allison up, and intentions hadn't mattered. To this day, she liked to throw that in my face. Now she knew I'd cheated on her too, so I saw no reason to defend myself. I'd given up. I didn't care.

She was never going to understand what *I* had been through.

The cheater was the villain in every story.

So why the fuck bother.

"Who is she?"

Good Christ. "It doesn't matter."

"Is it Ashley from work? Or Maggie?"

My head shot up, and I stared at her incredulously. "Have you completely lost touch with reality?"

"Then who is she?" she yelled.

I didn't reply.

CHAPTER 18

Kieran had just woken up the morning after when I knocked on their door.

The sheer hotness he displayed put a rock of want in my gut —from the low-riding sweats and his ink and piercing, to his messy hair and sleepy eyes—until I felt the need to remind myself that he'd shared a bed with his wife.

I'd slept on the couch.

"Morning," he yawned. "A little early for our run, isn't it?"

"I'm not going today," I said, clearing my throat. "Are the boys up?"

"Not sure about Nate. Jess and Jaylin are watching cartoons in her room." He took a step closer and frowned, and he touched my hand briefly. "Everything okay?"

I shook my head. "No. I don't know. Maybe. Allison and I broke up last night."

That sure woke him up. "Jesus," he whispered. "Are you —I mean... Shit." He ran a hand through his hair, then hauled me inside his hallway and closed the door. "What can I do?" He hugged me to him and pressed a kiss to my neck.

Leave your wife and be with me.

"Nothing." I eased out of the hug. It was too much right now. "We're, uh, we're gonna tell the boys right away."

"Okay." He nodded and stuck his hands down in his pockets. "Will you tell me everything later?"

"Yeah." I didn't want to be irritated with him. I really didn't. "You have nothing to worry about." I assumed that was why he was eager to know the details. "I told her I'd had an affair, and she asked who the woman was."

He frowned. "That's not why I asked. I'm worried about *you*. I wanna be there for you."

"But you can't," I whispered. "You have your own family."

He flinched.

"Please go get Nate and Jess for me," I said.

I spent the day putting out fires.

Nate had been dead silent when Allison and I told them we were getting divorced. We went through all the clichéd lines we'd found online. Mum and Dad getting divorced didn't mean we didn't love each other; we just loved each other in another way. We were still a family, and we would make this work. The boys would get two Christmases, two rooms, two birthdays—all that shit.

Jess was upset. He was angry. He was sad. He threw a crapload of toys down the stairs and screamed at us.

I took care of it because Allison said she was too upset to do it.

Nate wasn't as easy to get through to, though eventually he

opened up and asked if it was his fault we were getting divorced.

"Definitely not, Nathan." I hugged him as he let go of the emotions he'd bottled up. "Don't ever think that. Christ—my sweet boy, this could never be your fault."

"But I have had issues with her," he croaked.

I felt my eyes well up at the same time as I smiled at his adult manners. "Still not your fault," I whispered, brushing my thumbs under his eyes. "When you struggle with something, the rule is you come to us. Right? You did the right thing, and that isn't why Mum and I can't live together. We've... Feelings change between grown-ups sometimes."

"I know," he mumbled. "Linda and Peter have divorced parents too."

I nodded, remembering when Linda's mother called to tell us. She and Nate were fairly close, so Linda's mother had wanted to give us a heads-up. Peter was another friend of Nate's, and his parents had lived separately for years.

"We'll make this work for us, Nate," I murmured. "Do you trust me?"

He nodded. "You will live here, right?"

That question led to the next couple of fires I had to put out. Allison and I had agreed that it would be better for her to stay at the house, because it would be the one place our sons were the most comfortable already. It was their home. But unlike her, I had a wonderful relationship with both Nate and Jess, and I could create a new home easier than she could. My financial situation was also much better.

Over the next few days, Allison and I stayed home from work, and I didn't speak to Kieran much. He understood I needed space to deal with all this, though I could tell he was anxious about what this meant for us. For him and me.

Truth was, I didn't know. I couldn't think about that.

"Jess is asleep." Allison joined me at the kitchen table one night and slumped down, looking as exhausted as I felt. "Nate's...quieter than usual. He wanted to be left alone and watch TV."

"He'll come around." I finished my coffee and then leaned back in my chair.

Allison took a breath and looked out the window. "I could have cheated on you in Chicago. I didn't, but...there was a guy. We talked a little. He was into me, and when he asked me out, I considered it."

I gave her a dry look, wondering why she was telling me this now. Did she honestly believe I cared?

"But I could never betray you, Bennett."

"Jesus." I didn't know whether to laugh or cry. "Do you think infidelity is the only way to betray someone? You're not seriously that daft."

She shot me a glare. "Did you just call me stupid?"

Well, that *was* the definition of daft.

"Let's review our marriage once and for all, shall we?" I sat forward and ticked each thing off my fingers. "In college, I accidentally got you pregnant when we were both three sheets to the wind. It was a mistake that gave us our son, by the way. But it was a rough pregnancy, and you had to drop out early. I worked, went to school, and took care of you. I *didn't* go to parties and have fun with friends. You gave birth and stayed at home. I worked, finished school, got started on my career, and took care of you and Nathan." Did she see it yet? No? "You mentioned a second baby, and we agreed to have one more so you could go to school later. I kept working, I kept taking care of you and now two boys. And then...you finally got to resume your studies. You picked a school that was halfway across the country, leaving me alone with two young boys, a full-time job, and the house. And you bitched and you moaned and you complained about every fucking thing, and I didn't understand because I don't know what it's like to miss out on life and have a kid."

"Are you done?" she asked irritably.

"I'm not, actually." I kept ticking shit off. "While you were away at college, you had zero responsibilities. You lived with your parents, you went out on the weekends, and your daily calls home to check in with us became weekly calls and sporadic text messages. And it was like this for four years, Allison. For four years, I singlehandedly raised our children, all while managing my career and a house we bought together when we were happy." I leveled her with a serious look. "I met someone who could see how lonely I was. Someone who understood me. We started an affair. I have no excuses, but you know what? I have no remorse either, because you haven't given a flying fuck about us for years."

She stalked out of the kitchen without an expression on her face, without saying a goddamn word.

Kieran turned thirty-one on September 19th, and it was the first time our families got together since Allison and I had begun our divorce proceedings.

Calling it awkward would be the understatement of the century, but it was a good decision to have his birthday dinner at a restaurant. The kids behaved better there, and we all tried harder in general.

"So what does the festivity schedule look like?" I asked, cutting into my steak. "Are you flying out to Boston?"

"Nah." Kieran answered while helping Jaylin remove the pickles from her burger. "I reckon we'll wait till Thanksgiving. The only reason we flew out last year for my birthday was because I turned thirty."

"Now you're no longer special," Allison joked.

"Exactly," Kieran chuckled. "We had dinner with Mags's folks yesterday. That's enough of festivities for me."

"I'm so glad I'm an only child," Maggie said, amused. "Our phone's been ringing off the hook all day." She nodded at Kieran. "It's like his brothers and sisters forget he's not home during the day."

True, having a birthday on a weekday was sort of pointless.

Conversation died out, and it was ridiculous. There were plenty of things to talk about, but we didn't go there in case someone got offended or uncomfortable. Such as, how was my house hunt going? It showed promise, thanks. Had I gotten a bank loan approved? I had, and it felt great. Had Allison flipped out when I told her she'd have to buy me out of the house? Oh, you bet.

That'd been a fun fight.

After getting it thrown in my face that I had been nothing but a lying, cheating husband with zero understanding, I showed her what it was like when I didn't have understanding. Half the house was legally mine. If she wanted to stay there, which she did, she could buy my half.

Her parents were helping her with the loan next week.

"Nate," Maggie said, desperate for a safe topic, "how's fifth grade treating you? Is it fun?"

"I'm somewhat pleased with the challenges," Nate replied with a nod.

Jess showed off his brilliance too, with ketchup on his nose and by saying, "Second grade is funner."

"I love you, my little goofball." I had to give his cheek a smooch. And hand him a napkin. "Wipe your nose."

The following Wednesday, I brought Chinese food to Kieran's office. He was on the phone, so I sat down on the couch and began eating.

"Perhaps it's time for a second branch, then," he said. "I'll run it by Shawna and get back to you." He rose from his seat. "All right, talk soon." After ending the call, he loosened his tie and joined me on the couch. "Fuck, I'm starving." Right as I was about to shovel some noodles into my mouth, he grabbed my jaw and kissed me hard. "How are you feeling?"

I shrugged. "Still numb." I went back to eating, and Kieran sighed and opened another container. "I think I found a place."

"Yeah? In Downtown?"

I nodded. Part of me actually wanted to leave the district and maybe buy a condo in the Valley, but it boiled down to the boys. Aside from Nate going to school up in Ponderosa, everything they knew and called home was in Downtown, so the listing I'd looked at was for a house a few streets away from where we lived now.

"I'm worried about us," Kieran admitted. "You seem distant. And if it's just—you know, if you're struggling with this divorce shit, I completely get it. But if there's anything more than that, I need to know."

The food in my mouth went down like a chunk of lead. "I don't know, to be honest. I'm kind of savoring this numbness because I know everything will hurt the second it's gone."

I loved Kieran to stupid measures; I missed him with every fiber of my being. I also knew what I couldn't have, and it was more than hurtful. It made me angry with him.

"It's better we don't talk about it right now," I said. "I'm gonna focus on Nate and Jess and get us a new place. Then we'll see."

"All right," he replied warily and set down his container again.

Yeah, I wasn't hungry anymore either.

Shortly before Christmas, I asked my boss if it was okay I changed things around so I continued my meetings in the city on Tuesdays instead.

He had no problems with it.

I needed space. I needed peace and quiet. I needed to shrink my world. Right now, everything was a mess. I couldn't relax at home because Allison was hostile the moment the boys left the room, and there were moving boxes everywhere. I couldn't confide in Kieran because every time he said he wanted to be there for me, it felt empty. Or filled with conditions.

Brianna was finally happy and in love with a man I was meeting for the first time this holiday, and I didn't want to bother her with my shit. I'd done that too much as it was.

My father was already helping me with Nate and Jess.

Tuesdays wouldn't grant me a total escape from Kieran; after all, he commuted to the city every day. But Jess and Jaylin had both continued with swimming classes and had started in a new group this year, one that practiced on Tuesdays as well as Thursdays. In other words, I wouldn't need to come up with an excuse to hurry home after work. I had to leave regardless, to take Jess to practice.

Today was one of those days, in more ways than one. Tuesday. Rain mixed with snow. Winds were harsh and wet. And it was *one of those days*. A client bailed on a project my team had spent weeks working on, resulting in a phone conference with my boss's legal team. Allison called around noon to say she couldn't get back to Camassia in time to get Nate to his dentist appointment, so I had to call my father, who was more than happy to take Nate, but I also knew it brought him a lot of pain. He shouldn't be out in this weather with a hip that already gave him so much grief.

My train home at the end of the day was delayed, and I ended up on the later train that Kieran took too. *So much for avoiding him*. I informed him of the switch of days, and I lied. I lied right to his face and told him it was my boss who'd changed it from Wednesday to Tuesday, and I didn't think Kieran believed me.

We didn't talk much on the way home. He pretended to work, and I used my phone as a cover.

To make matters worse, Jess was in a crap mood when I picked him up. On the way to swim practice, he complained about everything. His clothes didn't fit right, his lunch today had been gross, he wanted to cut his hair, he didn't want to wear a seat belt, and he hated both Allison and me because we were *stupidheads*.

Then, of course, he was all grins and giggles when he jumped into the pool with his friends.

I dragged my tired ass over to the café, ignored the humidity, and ordered a cup of coffee.

Maggie was there already, and she quirked a wry smile. "Have you learned nothing, Bennett? Coffee in this heat?"

"It's that or fall asleep standing." I slumped down at her table and prayed she didn't want to talk too much.

"Rough day?" She switched on the concern, another thing I didn't want.

Sometimes, when I was feeling particularly bitter, I tried to come up with things that were bad about Maggie. That she would somehow deserve what was going on behind her back.

I was a horrible human being, and not only had I not been able to think of anything, but the guilt was eating me up every time she did something kind.

"You could say that." I nodded with a dip of my chin and shrugged out of my suit jacket. "When are you leaving for Boston?"

All I knew was that they'd canceled on Thanksgiving because they'd been sick, so now they were heading east early for Christmas. Jaylin would miss the last practice next week.

"Sunday," she answered. "We'll help you move in to your new house when we get back."

I shook my head. "That's sweet of you, but I plan on being done by then." I got the keys between Christmas and New Year's, and I wasn't going to waste a minute in my old house.

"How can I help?" Maggie asked, the worry written all over her. "I know I spend more time with Allison, but I consider you a very close friend, Bennett. If there's anything I can do, please don't hesitate."

God. I nearly choked on the guilt. It churned in my stomach and crawled up my throat with nausea, and I couldn't take it. I swallowed down some coffee and shifted in my seat, and the new angle made my keys dig into my thigh, so I put them on the table instead. *I consider you a very close friend, Bennett.* She shouldn't. I was a despicable friend to her.

"This is nice," she commented with a careful smile. She reached out and touched the key ring Kieran had given me once. Her husband. She touched the airplane gingerly and read the words softly. "'We met on the way.' From a friend?"

I nodded once. "Long time ago."

I figured Allison hadn't told her about my affair. It wasn't surprising; she'd asked me to keep that to myself. But otherwise, it would've been easy for Maggie to guess it was from the "other woman."

Holy fuck, what had happened to me? For more than two years, I'd had an intimate relationship with a married man. While I was married myself. I'd fallen in love with a man whose promises had an expiration date.

You win, Maggie. He's yours.

I cracked. And I gave up. When they came back after the holidays, I was ending things with Kieran.

CHAPTER 19

I had a feeling this was going to be an awful year.

I pressed a hand to my shoulder and stretched my neck. I'd hurt it yesterday when we carried furniture upstairs. Thank goodness for Chris, Brianna's boyfriend. Not only a great guy who clearly adored my sister, but he was in that stage where he wanted the approval of my father and me, so he'd insisted on helping me around the house the past two days.

My new house didn't look much different from the other place, except this one was painted white with pale yellow shutters, and there was a guest room on the first floor. It was now my bedroom, which left the boys in charge of the upstairs. Well, sort of. The room in between theirs was turning into an office slash gym. If an exercise bike and my badminton racket counted as a gym.

Brianna had helped me pick out all the new furniture. She'd also put up pictures on the walls and turned the stairs into a timeline of the boys' lives. Photos of them as newborns graced the wall above the bottom step, and with each frame, they got older.

I took the steps slowly, studying each of the black-and-white photographs, and stopped near the middle. Jess was six, Nate was nine. It'd been a great year. I'd grown closer to Kieran...

Looking down at my wrist, I saw it was almost midnight. Kieran, Maggie, and Jaylin would be home now.

Nate and Jess weren't coming back for another few days. Allison had taken them to her parents' in Chicago—the first year I hadn't joined them—while I got my house ready.

I liked my house, but it felt incredibly empty, despite the new and the old that filled up the place perfectly. It was the boys. They were missing; they hadn't left their mark here yet. The porch was too big, too clean, and the backyard had no toys scattered about, even in the dead of winter.

The fridge and freezer hadn't been flooded with drawings or notes from school. Jess hadn't gotten toothpaste all over the sink upstairs, and Nate's books stood neatly in his shelf without bookmarks and Post-it notes stuck between the pages.

I missed them. And I wondered how the hell Allison had gone four years with infrequent visits, sometimes several months without seeing them. Here I was, moping when it'd been four days.

Christ, everything made me mope. I'd been gone on business for longer than four days more than once. This was just the new me, I guessed.

Someone knocked on the door, causing me to frown. Could it really be Kieran at this hour? Brianna and Chris had headed back to the city, and Dad was undoubtedly asleep. Trailing down the stairs again, I aimed for the door and looked through the small window there. Shit, it was him.

He looked relieved to see me.

I couldn't even begin to describe how I felt. The love and the hurt and the pitiful yearning rushed around inside me.

"I feared you'd gone to bed," he said as I let him in. "I texted."

"Oh. My phone's in the kitchen."

He glanced around in the hallway and into the kitchen. "Looks kinda the same, doesn't it? I mean—I like it. But the design, I mean. Never mind." He chuckled, coming off as uncomfortable. "Hey."

"Hey yourself." I cleared my throat and locked the door. Now was the time to be resolute. I wasn't going to throw myself at him. "I expected you to crash the minute you got home."

He removed his coat and kicked off his shoes. "Not without seeing you first."

Fuck.

"Will you give me a tour?" he asked.

"Sure." I could stall for five minutes. Nodding toward the living room, I let him walk first. Just like at the old house, the left part was where I had the couch, chairs, and TV. The entertainment center was the one thing that still needed attention. It was mostly empty, with boxes of DVDs and photo albums on the floor. The other half of the room was the dining area.

"It's hard to believe you have your own place," he mentioned quietly. He ghosted a hand along the edge of the dining room table and ended up at the patio door. "Damn, this is nice. The deck looks new. You have a hot tub here too, huh? Lucky bastard."

If he wanted one, he could order one in five minutes. He wasn't known for his frugality.

"This is gonna be paradise in the summer, Ben."

I hummed, coming up to stand next to him. It was too dark to see much of the yard now.

"Can my housewarming gift to you be a new grill?" he

joked. He'd spotted my old one on the deck, something he'd teased me about in the past. I wasn't the grill master. He was.

I mustered a stiff smile.

I figured he'd been trying to keep things light on purpose when he so quickly ran out of steam. He blew out a heavy breath and stared out into the darkness.

"We're over, aren't we?" he whispered.

I swallowed hard, feeling my chest crack. I couldn't speak. Not a single word would come out, so I only nodded and looked down.

"Fuck." His voice broke, and I lifted my gaze automatically. Only to see his eyes welling up and two tears rolling down his cheeks. "I knew it was coming, but—" He coughed into his fist and wiped away the tears quickly. "*Fuck.*" He turned away from me.

His reaction caused an onslaught of emotions for me too, and I couldn't keep them inside anymore. My vision blurred and burned, and tears followed rapidly.

"I can't stand the secrecy anymore," I admitted thickly. "I can't keep doing this to Maggie, and I can't share you. I just can't, Kieran."

"I know." He turned to me again, and he gave up on wiping the tears away. He wrapped his arms around my shoulders, and I let out a muffled sob as everything inside me shattered. "I love you so much, baby," he croaked. "I'm sorry for everything I've done. I know I've hurt you."

I screwed my eyes shut and hugged his middle.

He cupped my face in his hands. "How can I let you go?" He pressed his forehead to mine and let out a stuttering breath. "You're the love of my life, Ben."

I whimpered, tears burning their way down my face.

"I don't know how to live without you," he said, sniffling.

"I don't either." I eased away and wiped my cheeks. "But

I'm just gonna grow bitter. I want you next to me, not hiding away at some hotel."

"I want that too." He shook his head and covered his face with his hands. "Fucking hell. I'm so sorry."

Not sorrier than me.

"I need space," I whispered hoarsely. "Give me a few months, at least." I had every intention of burying myself in work and focusing more on Nate and Jess. I suspected he would do the same for a while. After that...maybe we could salvage parts of our friendship, but I couldn't see it now. I didn't even know how we were going to pretend in front of Maggie and Allison. Our kids were so close that it would be impossible to avoid each other completely.

Yeah, this year was going to be fucking awful.

"Nate, can you get the mail for me, please?" I asked, grabbing the last bag of groceries before I shut the trunk. "Jess, be careful! You can't run on ice."

March was starting off with a goddamn storm, burying every trace of spring under four inches of snow. Jess was delighted. Nate and me, not so much.

Not that anything delighted me these days.

"How many minutes until my friends come over, Dad?" Jess asked, tugging at the door.

"Use your key, buddy. It's locked." I walked up the path, and Nate closed the gate behind us. "They'll be here at seven."

"That's forever," Jess groaned.

I thought the opposite. But the boys had been asking for a while now when they could have some friends here for a sleepover, so I'd agreed to this weekend. Jess had three classmates coming over, and Nate had invited a new friend from school who wanted my boy to join the lacrosse team.

If he'd go to tryouts this year, I'd be pleased as punch. It was difficult to get Nathan interested in sports. Every now and then, he signed up to play soccer, but he'd yet to finish a whole year.

This new boy, however—Timothy—seemed to be a good influence on Nate. It helped that Timothy shared the same love for science, and they both attended tech group, a project on a trial run at their school. Every week, they met up to do experiments and...probably dissect frogs.

"Where do you want the mail, Dad?" Nate asked.

"You can leave it here on the table." I started unloading the groceries into the fridge and freezer. "Can one of you call Grampa and tell him dinner is at six?"

"I'll do it!" Jess hollered.

With the groceries stowed away, I flipped through the mail and frowned at a flyer we'd received. It was for a protest in the Valley. "Huh." Apparently, they were closing the express train between Camassia and Seattle. The local train had so many stops, it would save time to take the car.

I knew someone who had to be pissed about this.

I was only in the city once a week, so I could survive. Kieran commuted every day.

I took a breath and waited for the familiar stab of pain to fade.

It had been an okay day, and I had a weekend full of distractions ahead of me. I wasn't going to think about how much I missed him.

We saw each other in passing, of course. At the store or when Jess and Jaylin played. And it hurt every time. It hurt to pretend, which we had to do when Maggie was near. We had to pretend like we wanted to get together soon and that work had been the reason we hadn't met up in months. We had to pretend we were in high spirits.

There was one thing I'd learned about Kieran since we ended our relationship, and it was that the smiles he'd given me before were very different. Because I'd always loved his smiles and felt like there was affection in them. Now, though...? Now I knew the smiles he gave Maggie. They were emptier. It was the same with how he addressed people. How he spoke to them, how he behaved. Those select few who were in his closest circle got his full attention, and he would walk through fire for them. I saw and heard and felt it when he talked to Nate and Jess. Jaylin too, of course.

I didn't know I'd been in until I was out.

Around seven, friends of the boys began trickling in.

I'd set everything up for Jess and his mates to be in the living room. The table was full of unhealthy snacks and soda, and the DVD player was ready for whatever they wanted to watch.

After Jess's friend Max arrived, it was Aurora's turn.

"Jess!" I called. "Aurora's here." I grabbed her overnight bag for her while William, her father, helped her with her jacket.

"Daddy, I can do it myself," she complained.

I smirked at William, knowing what that was like. The kids no longer wanted our help, especially when they needed it.

"Are you sure you know what you're getting yourself into?" he asked me, amused.

I let out a laugh. "No one can be as bad as Jess, I figure."
He grinned.
Jess came running out. "Hi, Aurora!"
"Hi, Jess." Aurora beamed.
It took less than two seconds, and then they were gone.

"You have our number," William said. "Don't hesitate to use it. I can't fathom the madness you'll live through tonight." He paused. "Although, you've earned plenty of cool points, so perhaps it's worth it. Aurora's been talking about this all week."

"Don't give me too much credit," I chuckled. "I'm banking on them passing out when the sugar rush is over."

"It's the hours before that I'm worried about," he laughed. "Have a lovely evening, Bennett. And I mean it, call if you need assistance."

"Will do." I didn't even have to close the door before the next person arrived. It was Timothy this time, and now Nate didn't have to wait by the stairs anymore. The two had big plans to play trivia games in Nathan's room, and of course, they'd have snacks too. Nate had already brought one too many bowls up.

The last guest was Jaylin, and my heart beat a little faster when I saw her jump out of Kieran's car.

Why hadn't he told Maggie to drop her off?

"Bennett!" Jaylin squealed.

A big smile broke out. I was incredibly happy to see her. "How are you, my darling?"

"I'm good!" She rushed forward to hug me, and I was more than happy to pick her up. Unlike Jess, she still allowed it. "I think you live in the wrong house. You're so far away now!"

"It's less than five minutes away," I chuckled, peppering her cheeks with kisses. "Are you excited about the sleepover?"

Judging by the cute rambling she launched into, she was. She was eager to show me her new pillowcase with a princess on it, and she told me she had matching pajamas. I tried to take in every word, I truly did, but it was difficult with Kieran standing in the doorway.

"Can I get a hug before you run off, monkey?" Fuck, his voice... It hit me right in the bloody heart every time.

I stood there, uncomfortable and fucking weak, as Kieran

hugged Jaylin and murmured something to her. He told her to be good, and I missed the rest.

She disappeared into the living room shortly after that.

I wanted to say something—I wanted to say a *lot*—all while I wished he hadn't turned up at all.

"It's gonna get crazy here, man," he said. "You sure you wanna go through with it?"

He was acting normal. I was any other parent of his daughter's friend.

"You're not the first one to say that," I replied. "I think we'll live."

He nodded and took a step back, ready to leave. "Call if you need anything."

"Okay."

I needed something. Just a glimpse of the old him. Christ, how frustrating. Had he moved on so easily? He was completely unreadable. He looked tired, that much I could see.

As he turned to leave, the words left me without permission.

"How did you move on?" At least I'd managed to keep my voice low.

He half turned and furrowed his brow at me. "Huh?"

I wet my bottom lip, suddenly anxious. I shouldn't have said anything. "You're…just normal. You seem fine."

At that, he let out a flat chuckle and smirked faintly. "Lifetime of practice, Ben. If I was dead inside before you, it has nothing on now." He gave me a two-finger wave and walked down the porch. "Mags will pick her up tomorrow."

I cursed under my breath and ran a hand through my hair.

I spent the evening in the kitchen with Dad—well, when I wasn't in the living room for one of the hundred reasons four young children might summon me.

There'd been a lot of spillage...

"I had you drinking out of a sippy cup until you were twelve," Dad said pointedly.

No, he certainly hadn't.

"That's child abuse," I joked. "More coffee?"

He peered into his cup. "I could go for another refill."

I fetched the pot and gave us refills, then emptied a bag of chocolates into a bowl. If I couldn't drink whiskey tonight, I wanted to get my own sugar rush.

"So how are you doing, son?"

I decided to steal his standard line. "I'm on the right side of the grass, so I can't complain."

He made a face and popped a candy into his mouth. "It's less satisfying when a kid gets vague."

"Good thing I'm not a kid, then."

He grunted.

I wouldn't know what to say if I were to be honest. Dead inside was a fitting description. I'd never been much of a crier, and aside from a few rough nights here and there, I got by with emotional death.

"You didn't leave Allison because you didn't get along," he stated thoughtfully. "You left because you didn't love her no more, and yet..." He gestured to me. "You've been acting like a heartbroken puppy for months."

Lord, not him too. "I get enough psychoanalyzing from Brianna, Dad."

He narrowed his eyes at me. "You were also always a shitty actor, Bennett. Now, maybe Allison never noticed anything because her head wasn't where it was supposed to be, but I ain't blind. What's her name?" He leaned forward. "Or his name."

I shot him an irritated look. I didn't want to be disrespectful toward him, so I'd appreciate if he stopped digging into my brain.

"Is it Ashley at work?" he guessed. "Or Kieran?"

"For fuck's sake." With my elbows on the table, I planted my face in my hands and wished I could be anywhere but here. "You do realize Kieran is married to a woman, yes?"

Dad let out a gruff laugh. "So was I."

My head shot up, and I stared at him in shock. Was he at long last confirming something I'd wondered about as a teenager?

"So were *you*," he added. "I know you had your suspicions about Thomas and me. So did your sister, and she didn't shy away from asking."

"I didn't shy away," I replied, frowning. "I just...I didn't know what to make of things. You were married to Mum back then." This had been long before I was even born, so my mother hadn't yet turned into the flighty runaway who later on left us to see the world with her friends.

"Times were different." He twisted a candy wrapper between his fingers, a wistful look on his face. "We could never be together, Thomas and me. It wasn't in the cards for us."

I loathed that entire way of thinking to the point that it made my blood boil. Perhaps it made me a fool, a naïve romantic, but a fool nonetheless. I just wanted to believe love was greater than social structures and obstacles. I knew very well that my father and Thomas couldn't have been together in public back then, but, see, *that* was a valid reason to live a secret life. Not today in modern society. During war? Sure. Hell, Thomas's upbringing couldn't have been easy. A black man—from Georgia, if I remembered correctly—enlisting to bring home money to support a family who depended on him. My father got drafted. He'd had plans to join the family trade and work at a lumberyard. Then he fell for the army life, and evidently, he'd fallen for Thomas too.

"So, you both wanted to be together, and nothing happened," I said. "That's terrible, Dad."

"I never said nothing happened," he replied with a wry smirk. "I said we couldn't get the life we wanted."

Oh. Well, good. "It makes me horrible to be happy about that, doesn't it?"

He lifted a shoulder and took a sip of his coffee. "The harsh reality of life is that our happiness is rarely free. Someone always suffers for it." He paused. "You had an affair with Kieran that ended, I assume."

I hesitated, then figured, fuck it. "Yes."

"Allison and Maggie suffered for that."

Maggie didn't know, but I got his point.

"Your mother left to be happy," he went on. "You and Bri suffered. Allison went to school out of state. You and the boys suffered. We like to talk about the sacrifices we make. It's less fun to discuss our decisions that others have to pay for, but they do happen. Every damn day."

Kieran wouldn't be honest with his wife and family.

I suffered.

My father was right.

"I wish I could tip the scale, though," I murmured. "I don't like hurting others. I still feel guilty for going behind Maggie's back."

"But you'd do it again, wouldn't you?" Dad tilted his head, observing me. "Just being frank, my boy."

I sighed, knowing he was right there too.

"For what it's worth," he said gruffly, "I'm rootin' for you. That's the cold, hard truth. My son's happiness at the expense of someone else's? I wouldn't even hesitate."

His statement was as heartwarming as it was uncomfortable.

It was the type of honesty people didn't generally talk about. We all knew, in hard times, we would sacrifice others to save those we loved. But times weren't that hard now, and I didn't want to be a monster.

Without justification.

CHAPTER 20

"Jess!" I called. "Please come back here." My fingers kept tapping against the keyboard, and I sent off another email. Jess appeared in the doorway to my office. "I told you not to bother anyone, sweetheart." I nodded at the couch where Nate sat. "Go do your homework instead. Mum told me you have a quiz on Friday you can practice for."

It was Allison's week, but more often than not, she worked late. The last person to complain was me, except for the days I had to work extra too and Dad couldn't watch the boys.

"I can help you," Nate offered Jess.

"Thank you," I mouthed to him. "I'm done in about an hour, boys. I think we've earned some McDonald's today."

"Yes." Jess fist-pumped the air. "Are we sleeping at Mom's or at home?"

Firstly, at least Allison was home enough to further Americanize Jess. I was only slightly miffed about his recent switch in how he pronounced Mum. Secondly, it bothered me that the house they'd always called home was now "Mom's."

"She's going to call when she's on the way home, so we'll see how late it is," I answered.

They'd closed the express commute in May, despite protests, and people weren't happy. It hadn't been profitable enough, according to Amtrak. Allison was understandably pissed off too, and now she was stuck in traffic two hours at best every day.

I got more time with my boys, though. It helped that my new office was bigger than the old one, because I'd been able to decorate the other half with Nate and Jess in mind. We were also in the heart of the Valley, so if they needed anything, Nate could duck out and get it on his own.

"I want seven hamburgers," Jess declared.

I snorted, waiting for the cars to pass. McDonald's was just across the street, and I was starving.

"Dad, can I get an extra burger with mine?" Nate asked quietly.

"Definitely." I gave his neck a squeeze. When we moved in to the new house, I'd learned about the bottom drawer in his desk. He collected McDonald's toys, so I hadn't stopped ordering Happy Meals for him. I could understand it wasn't enough for him anymore, though. Those burgers were tiny.

"Bennett?"

I glanced over my shoulder and saw a man I definitely recognized but couldn't place. Almost black hair, blue eyes, significantly younger...

"Casey," he said. "I was at your birthday party a couple years ago."

"Of course! I remember. You came with Ellis. How are you?"

"Good, thanks." He smiled. "You guys also heading to McDonald's?"

"I'm gonna have seven burgers," Jess informed him.

I chuckled. "Yeah, I worked late. Way too tired to cook." The cars had passed by now, but Casey seemed to be waiting for the light to turn green. I didn't want to be rude, so I stayed. I could be a good role model for the boys.

"I hear ya," Casey replied. "Everything good with you and your family?"

"Yeah, sure." It was a lie. It was always a lie these days when someone asked how I was doing. "The family shrunk," I admitted. I could do that, at least. "Allison and I got divorced."

"Oh. Sorry to hear that." He frowned. "I don't think I met her."

No, Allison had been in Chicago then.

The light finally turned green, and we crossed the street and entered a fairly empty McDonald's. It was why we came to this one and not the one at the mall, which was a deafening experience throughout the day.

I didn't quite know the protocol here. As Casey ordered his food and I heard he wasn't taking it to-go, I wondered if I was supposed to invite him to sit with us. I didn't know him. On the other hand, the absence of Kieran in my life had left a big void. I'd never be able to fill it to the point where I was as happy as I'd once been, but I didn't have many mates. Or any.

Man up.

After ordering for the boys and me, I cleared my throat and faced Casey. "There will be a seat available at our table if you—I mean, unless you're meeting—"

"I'd love to," he was quick to say. "I spent the past three days with only a newborn as company. So if you don't mind, yeah. Count me in."

Well, then. I could do this. I gave myself a mental pat on the back.

"And that might've come out wrong," he said thoughtfully. "What I mean is, I just had my first child, and I miss talking to adults."

I grinned. "Congratulations. Been there, still looking for adults to talk to."

He was about to say something, but our food was done at the same time, so we brought our trays to an empty table.

"Coke for you?" I asked Jess. In turn, he faced his brother and asked what Nate was having. Sprite was his answer, which became Jess's answer too.

"No ice, please," Nate said.

I filled three cups with Sprite, one without ice.

Casey couldn't decide what to choose. "I guess water will do. Damn Pepsi discrimination."

"Oh, I don't think I've ever met one of you," I joked in wonder. "I thought you were a myth."

"Ha-ha," he snarked. "I'll have you know it's the best pop on the market."

"It's certainly not," I laughed.

We returned to the table and sat down, and I told Nate to put away his phone. His first phone. Part of me still couldn't believe it. Brianna had given it to him for Christmas.

"I was just texting Kieran," he defended.

I frowned. Why were they texti—

"Do you like being a dad?" Jess asked Casey. "Is it a boy? Boys are the best."

"It's a girl, actually." Casey smirked. "She's sort of awesome too."

"And both your best friends are girls," I pointed out to Jess. Then I turned to Casey. "How old is she, if you don't mind my asking?"

"Almost three months." The way his eyes lit up showed everything from love and joy to the mandatory parental exhaustion. "You're a parent, so I can show you pictures, right?"

"Of course," I said with a grin.

He brought up his phone, the same type of iPhone I'd recently bought. "I've learned that not many people who don't have kids enjoy looking at pictures," he said, smiling awkwardly. "Okay, here's my Haley."

The baby girl in the picture was incredibly cute, but it made me miss Jaylin. I only saw her briefly at swim practice these days, and it was an extra good day when she launched herself into my arms.

"She's adorable," I murmured. "Three months—they're cute at that age, but I do not miss it."

"Right?" Casey tucked away his phone and widened his eyes. "I made the mistake of waking her up yesterday."

I winced in sympathy and took a bite of my burger. "We only make that mistake once," I said around my food. "When she sleeps, you and her mother sleep. Make it a rule."

His smile was forced. "It's just me now, but I have help from my family. I don't know what I would've done without them."

"Bollocks, I'm sorry." I felt like an idiot.

He shook his head. "You couldn't have known. But let's change the topic. It feels really good to talk to someone who won't throw up on me."

I cracked a poor joke in an attempt to relax him further. "You haven't seen me drunk."

It worked. He laughed.

Nate turned twelve in June, and it was the first time I summoned the courage to invite the Marshalls over for a birthday barbecue. Allison couldn't make it, but she'd celebrated Nathan last weekend when her parents came to visit.

I invited my new friend Casey too, along with Dad, Brianna, and Chris.

Dad manned my new grill, a purchase I had made one hundred percent with Kieran in mind.

He was always there, on the edges of my stream of consciousness, in my dreams, in my stupid heart.

Every time I saw him in town or when we picked up Jess and Jaylin at the same time, the stitches I'd managed to partially close the wound with were ripped open, and I had to start all over again.

When was it going to become easier?

Although, right this second was kind of peaceful. The Marshalls hadn't arrived yet, and I was holding little Haley while Casey made what he called his world best nonalcoholic margaritas for kids. Jess was over the moon.

"Brianna, are you sure you don't want to give me a niece?" I asked.

She laughed a little too hard, I thought.

Casey came out onto the patio with drinks for the children, and Jess gushed at the prospect of drinking like an adult.

Mildly worrying for the future.

Nate had three friends here, and they were excited to try margaritas too.

When the doorbell rang inside, I instructed Nate to get the door. It was his day, his guests. My heart didn't flip-flop at all. I was cool, calm, and collected.

"She's weirdly quiet in your arms," Casey noted, frowning at his daughter. "Love me more, you little screamer."

"What can I say, I shut people up," I laughed. In this case, it was my wallet. Haley was chewing on it. "Do I make you speechless, munchkin?"

At that, she dropped my wallet and reached for her dad.

Figures.

"Hi, Jaylin!" Jess shouted across the backyard.

My head shot up, and I watched Maggie and Kieran step out on the deck. Nate was close behind, holding a big gift bag.

I barely registered that Casey took Haley from me.

Kieran had lost weight. So had I, but I was gaining some of it back now. Our gazes met, and it was a sucker punch. *I miss you so fucking much.* I hated that I missed him. I hated that I wasn't enough.

He broke eye contact and eyed Casey before clenching his jaw and turning his focus to Nate.

Maggie was all smiles today though, and I reintroduced her to Casey, in case they didn't remember each other from my thirtieth birthday. I functioned on autopilot because my mind was with Kieran and Nathan. They had disappeared inside the house, and wasn't there something I could get? Surveying the table, I hoped for an excuse to head in. Potato salad, Brianna's parmesan chips, salad, condiments—the fries! I was going to check on the fries in the oven.

"Excuse me a moment." I went inside and crossed the living room. They weren't in the kitchen, so I headed up the stairs instead.

"Oh my God, where did you *find* this?" I heard Nate exclaim. "It's older than I am!"

"I found it on eBay," Kieran answered, amused. "You reckon it'll go on the shelf?"

"*Duh.* This is so cool. Thank you, Kieran."

"You're welcome, buddy."

As I reached the landing, I peered into Nate's room and saw them hugging. Then Nate walked over to his desk where he put what looked like a small toy on the shelf where he kept the books he was currently reading. The little toy was from McDonald's, and it was bloody old. Unless Mr. Potato Head was making a comeback. He'd officially turned to collectibles. And it was something he shared with Kieran.

"What did you get from your mom and dad?" Kieran asked curiously.

Damn straight, I stayed hidden.

"I got a new bike from Dad," Nate answered. "Mum gave me clothes and roller blades."

"That sounds fun."

"I have to show you the bike later," Nate added excitedly. "Dad and I are gonna go camping this summer, and we're bringing our bikes. We're going all the way up to Coho Pass."

I smiled to myself.

Kieran let out a low whistle. "Color me impressed. It's uphill the whole way."

Nate snickered. "I know. I told Dad we'll be standing up most of the time." He went back to Kieran and sat down next to him on the bed. "Why aren't you and Dad friends anymore?"

Fuck.

He'd asked me once before, but it'd been easy to blame work then. Too much time had passed now.

"I did a shitty thing." Kieran's answer sent shock through me. Never in my life would I have guessed he'd say that. Holy shit, didn't he know he could lie to kids? "I was a bad friend, but I hope we can hang out more someday. I miss him."

"Huh. He probably misses you too," Nate replied frankly. "Maybe Casey can hang with you then? I like him. He's very nice."

I dared a peek to see Kieran's face. His features were drawn tighter.

"Right. Casey. Is he here a lot?"

I was torn between rolling my eyes and smirking. Sue me, it felt good to witness his subtle jealousy.

"Sometimes." Nate shrugged. "He and Dad run together when Jess and I are at Mum's."

"I see." Kieran cleared his throat. "I don't wanna keep you from your party. You should go back to your friends."

"All righty. Dinner will probably be done soon too."

I ducked into Jess's room as Nate went for the stairs faster than I expected, and I breathed a sigh of relief that he hadn't heard me. Or worse, spotted me. He was too smart for his own good, and he would've known I'd been eavesdropping. There was nothing like being judged by a preteen.

I had no such qualms where Kieran was concerned, and by the time he left Nate's room, I was leaning against the wall between his and Jess's rooms.

Kieran did a double take when he saw me, then narrowed his eyes and cursed. "How long have you been here?"

"Long enough," I replied. "I'm not dating Casey. We're just friends."

"You and I started as friends once too."

I rolled my eyes and pushed away from the wall. "So if you get what you want, I'll never meet someone. That seems nice."

"If I get what I want..." He chuckled darkly and dragged a hand over his face. "When the fuck did I ever get what I wanted, Ben?"

"That's the fucking problem," I whisper-yelled, instantly furious. "Before you know it, it's thirty years later, and you'll look back on a life that made you miserable. But hey, as long as you didn't hurt your family's feelings, right?" I shook my head and went down the stairs. Why I had stayed in the first place was beyond me. There'd been no point in discussing anything with him.

God-fucking-dammit. It'd been too soon to invite him and Maggie over. The hurt wasn't merely too close to the surface; it still consumed me.

CHAPTER 21

"Dad! It's green!" Jess called.

Shit. "Sorry, buddy." I started driving again and glanced in the rearview, surprised no one had honked. I wasn't fit to drive today, too distracted and scatterbrained. Ellis had even noticed at work, and he'd told me to go home early. "Are you excited to spend the day with Jaylin?"

"Yeah."

Good talk.

Thank God Kieran hadn't gotten off work yet. Otherwise, I wouldn't be so casual about driving Jess over to their house. After the dream I'd had of Kieran last night, it felt like we broke up yesterday. When, in reality, we were approaching one year. One year of trying fruitlessly to get over him.

I could still see us. Even more so after the vivid fantasy that had played out in my sleep. We had a house together, went on vacation together...

Kieran continued to walk through my consciousness like a ghost.

Or maybe I was the ghost, because it sure as fuck didn't feel like I was alive.

When we reached the street I knew so well, I made sure to check if Kieran's car was in the driveway. It would've been just my luck that he was sick or something. Alas...

There was an unfamiliar car in Allison's driveway, on the other hand.

"Did Mum buy a new car?" I asked dubiously.

"No. I dunno."

Perhaps she'd met someone. It was strange she was home this early, though. The past couple of months, I had seen the boys after school almost every day. They'd had dinner with me before Allison picked them up on her weeks. She always had a deadline, it seemed.

I parked outside of Kieran and Maggie's house, and I reminded Jess to bring his backpack. Before they did anything fun, both he and Jaylin had homework.

Jess complained about it until I reminded him it was the last week of homework, as next week was the last before winter break.

Maggie was as happy as ever to see us, and she ushered us in and told us there were cookies in the oven.

I could smell them.

"Bennett!" I heard Jaylin yell.

I smiled instinctively and peered into the living room. "Hey, darling. What're you up to?"

"Come." She waved me over. "I'm watching movies of us."

A glance at the flat screen showed me Kieran and another man running through sprinklers. Jaylin was sitting on Kieran's shoulders, and she couldn't have been more than three or four.

"What's this?" I asked.

Maggie passed me in the doorway with milk and cookies for the kids. "When she misses Kieran, she sometimes puts on home movies."

I furrowed my brow. "Where's Kieran?"

"Tacoma for business. You know, why don't you join us for a bit? I'll get you a cup of coffee."

I checked my watch. I wasn't picking up Nate at a friend's house for another two hours...and I wasn't sure I could pass up the opportunity to get a glimpse into the life Kieran lived on the East Coast. Unless they were in Maggie's parents' backyard on the TV now. I didn't recognize it. The other guy in the video, however, looked a lot like Kieran.

When Maggie returned with beverages for us, and more cookies, I sat down in a chair while Jess dragged his backpack to the couch.

"Cheers, hon." I took a sip of my coffee and smiled when Jaylin crawled over to squeeze herself in to sit with me. "How's my favorite girl in the whole world?"

She giggled. "Good. I woke up with the sniffles, but I feel better now."

"Glad to hear it," I chuckled.

Turning to the home video, I watched the clip from someone's backyard end, and a new clip began. It went from summer to Christmas. A kitchen was packed with people, and no one was quiet.

"Another crazy Christmas at the Marshalls'." It was Maggie's singsong voice that filtered through, and it must've been she who held the camera. "Everyone's waiting for Angela's turkey and Kieran's mozzarella biscuits. Brent, can you stop that? You flippin' antagonist."

Brent had to be one of Kieran's brothers. They looked to be close in age and had the same eyes and smirks.

"How many brothers and sisters does he have?" I wondered.

"Four brothers and two sisters," Maggie replied with a wry grin. "It's a madhouse every time."

"Daddy is almost oldest," Jaylin supplied helpfully.

Maggie nodded. "Uncle Brent and Aunt Angela are older."

I was sucked into the video again. Kieran came into view with a big pan, and the woman next to him had to be his mother. He dipped down and kissed her cheek and said something we couldn't hear, but whatever it was, it made his mother laugh and whack him with an oven mitt.

Kieran's grin made me take a deep breath. It was so genuine and full of hell-raising.

The entire scene could've been taken straight from a holiday comedy. Kids running around, grown-ups bantering, the table packed with food, a patriarch at the end of the table who had a rolled-up paper ready in case anyone got too mouthy.

I did notice the change in Kieran's accent. It was full-on working-class Boston with a fair bit of Irish.

The next clip took place on Christmas morning. The living room floor was buried under gift wrapping and toys. Kieran was bickering with his sister, whose name, Jaylin told me, was Grace. Brent was in a corner with four kids. That woman, Angela, had her own litter of children.

"Those two by the tree," Maggie said, "that's Connor and Desmond, the two youngest. They look up to Kieran a lot, and I think they might move out here next year."

"Oh?" That had my attention.

Maggie smiled. "They want to work for Kieran."

I wondered what Kieran felt about that. He'd told me he didn't want his different lives to mix.

"I take it they're close?" Another sequence began, one where Kieran—with Jaylin piggyback riding him—was making snowballs out on the street. The other brothers were there too, though there were clearly two teams.

"I'd say he's closest with Brent," Maggie said pensively. "Then maybe Des. But I mean, they're all so close."

I nodded slowly, understanding more and more about him. His brothers and sisters were no longer faceless. They had names and matching eyes and children of their own.

It was a hard pill to swallow. At the same time, some of my bitterness evaporated. It became harder to resent Kieran.

God, I missed him.

We continued watching home movies from Quincy for another hour, and then I couldn't really take it anymore. My brain was chock-full of images of his family and how he seemed to come to life when he was with them. He'd been the same way with me, in a softer, more affectionate kind of way, but I hadn't seen any version of that Kieran in a long fucking time. He wasn't here, in the pictures on the walls where he lived, and he wasn't at barbecues or any other occasion.

Why did he even live on the West Coast anymore?

Maggie didn't strike me as the woman who would refuse to leave Washington.

While she told the kids to go up to Jaylin's room to do homework, I brought my coffee cup out to the kitchen.

Jess and Jaylin did their homework together often enough, and I was idly curious how that worked if they were left alone. When they were at our house, they sat in the kitchen. Otherwise, nothing got done.

"Do you talk to Kieran at all these days?" Maggie asked, entering the kitchen. She looked unsure about something.

"Of course," I lied. "We meet up for a beer sometimes when I'm in the city."

She hummed and leaned against the kitchen counter. "Would you tell me if he had an affair?"

I almost dropped my mug in the kitchen sink. "What on earth? Where did this come from?" *Please don't say because of me, please fucking don't.* I wasn't sure I'd be able to lie to her face if she asked point-blank if I'd had a relationship with him.

"I can't help but think—" She let out a ragged breath and put a hand to her chest, as if to calm herself down. "He won't touch me, Bennett. We haven't—I mean, it's been almost two years since—Christ." She stopped herself as her cheeks colored. "At first, I thought it was work stress. Especially recently with the expansion in Tacoma, but then he started sleeping in the guest room, and he offers the stupidest excuses. The times he's worked late and spent the night in his office—I buy that. He's been working so hard. But now I can't help but question everything. Is he really sleeping at his office? Is he working late so often? Because what I come back to is, no one accidentally falls asleep in the guest room for two months, almost every night, because he was watching the news in there. He's never done that before."

It was information overload, and I took a step back and ran a hand through my hair to gather my thoughts. Could I guarantee Kieran wasn't cheating on her again? Of course not. If anything, it was the likeliest scenario. And it pissed me the fuck off. It felt as if he were cheating on *me*.

I didn't want to believe that about him.

"What do you think?" Maggie asked hesitantly. "Should I confront him?"

No. I was going to do that. He wouldn't be honest with her, regardless.

"I'll talk to him after the holidays," I said. "I don't think you have anything to worry about, though. He wouldn't jeopardize his family." The last part was certainly true.

Maggie hugged me, visibly relieved. "Thank you, Bennett. You're a great friend."

I truly wasn't. I was the lowest of men.

It was Allison's turn to have the boys on the 24th and 25th, and in order to keep myself from sinking into a pit of despair, I'd come up with a brilliant plan. I refused to accept this Christmas as the worst I'd ever had, so my father and I stayed busy. We ate junk food, decorated the tree, watched movies, wrapped presents, and prepared for a big surprise for the boys when I picked them up on the 26th.

Brianna had wanted to be here this year, but Chris was taking her on a cruise, where Dad and I knew Chris was going to propose.

Despite my efforts, Christmas Day wasn't easy. Jess and Nate called around five in the morning, both upset, because they'd realized we couldn't do our Christmas tradition of having hot chocolate by the tree and playing the song.

To make matters worse, Nate called again after breakfast to say, "Mum's new boyfriend just got here."

How had I never heard of him? Allison was free to date whomever she wanted, but when the kids were involved, I would've liked a goddamn heads-up.

I trudged on. And I texted plenty with Nate to keep their spirits high. Thankfully, they loved their presents from Allison, so all hope wasn't lost. Jess called to tell me about his new action figures, and Nate was happy about his tickets to a science fair next spring. The clothes Allison and I bought for them together every Christmas were less exciting.

"We did good, son," Dad said and sat down on the couch with a satisfied grunt. He looked around the living room, decked out to the max with decorations, then settled for the big box of assorted chocolates on the table. "Who did you get these from?"

"Second Verse Studios." Ever since my team and I had gotten Lincoln Hayes's production company branded, they'd sent chocolate and whiskey for Christmas. Ellis, Ashley, and I sent similar items to our clients. This year, it'd been gift baskets with wine and cheese, and I had one in the kitchen. I wasn't going to miss out on good cheese.

As I sat down in my chair, something small and furry nibbled on my foot, and I grinned and picked up our newest family member. A black, ten-week-old Lab mix I'd adopted. The boys would hopefully agree on a name for him tomorrow.

They'd asked for a pet for as long as I could remember, and now that Nate was old enough to come and go as he pleased, I figured it was a good time. When I worked long hours, the puppy could be with my father, and Nate could take the little furball out after school. Soon enough, Jess would be able to shoulder more responsibility as well.

"When everyone leaves me, at least I have you." I smooched the pup's little face, and he wagged his tail and pawed at my cheeks.

"That didn't sound bitter at all," Dad drawled. "And what am I, shit under your shoe?"

"I can't cuddle you like this." I held the pup to me and got spoiled with nuzzles and puppy licks. In my pocket, my phone vibrated. Could be the boys, although I hoped they were asleep by now.

It wasn't them. It was Kieran.

I hope you had a good Christmas. Not a day goes by where I don't want to call and say how much I miss you.

I swallowed hard at the onslaught of emotions and flicked a glance at the clock above the TV. It was late on the East Coast. Hell, it was almost three in the morning there.

I pressed my lips to the top of the puppy's head, where his fur was the softest, and ignored the fact that Dad was observing me. I'd certainly learned where Brianna got it from.

"Answer him, boy," Dad murmured.

"How did you even—" I was cut off by his laugh. I didn't think I'd been so obvious that I deserved laughter. Clearly, I was wrong. "I wouldn't know what to respond with," I muttered. "He says he misses me."

"And you miss him."

I shook my head. "Doesn't matter. I won't go down that road again. I haven't recovered from the first time."

"There are other roads, Bennett," he pointed out patiently. "You miss his friendship too."

That was true.

Seeing him in the home videos had continued to take away my anger, which helped. What Maggie had told me helped even more. It was selfish, I knew, but the fact that Kieran was pulling away from her offered comfort.

I didn't believe he was cheating either.

Perhaps I was ready to see him more often. Just talking to him—I missed that as well. Or all the times we'd gotten together and done something with the children. The children were safe, to boot.

I went with it and typed a response before I could think twice.

We could take the kids to the skating rink when you get back.

He replied within seconds.

I'd love that. I can bring snacks.

I dragged my teeth across my bottom lip, hesitating. But fuck it.

Lemon bars?

My heart did a ridiculous flip-flop thing at his answer.

Always.

The coast is clear! Rescue us!

I chuckled at the text from Nate and hurried out to my car. I'd instructed them not to change into regular clothes, which I hadn't done either. It was going to be a day spent in pajamas.

Dad had stayed the night, so before I left, he'd gotten started on breakfast. I would've prepared the pancake batter myself, but I had a puppy to clean up after.

How long did it take to get them to piss outdoors?

At three minutes past seven, I parked outside my old house, and I saw Jess run from the kitchen.

The car I'd seen in the driveway once before was here now too. I assumed it was the boyfriend.

Jess ripped the door open and smiled widely. "Hi!"

"Hi? That's not what we say on Christmas morning, sweetheart." I pretended to be offended and scooped him up with a grunt. "Jeesh, how much turkey did you have yesterday?" I rubbed his belly, and he laughed. "I don't like how fast you're growing up."

It was unbelievable that he turned ten next May.

"I'm a grown-up now—lemme down," he said, still laughing. "And it's not Christmas morning."

I let him down again and was happy to correct him. "It actually is Christmas morning. I had a talk with Santa, and he was willing to make a change for us this year."

"Santa," he giggled and rolled his eyes.

Nate appeared in the hallway with two bags. One that he always brought to and from our houses, and one with what I presumed were Christmas gifts.

"Good morning, Dad." Nate smiled sleepily.

"Merry Christmas, buddy." I combed back his messy hair with my fingers and kissed his forehead.

Allison joined us too, looking like she'd just woken up. "Morning. It's a bit early, isn't it? We haven't had breakfast yet."

"I'll save you the cereal and take them now," I replied. I was admittedly still displeased with how she'd handled things yesterday, introducing our children to her new boyfriend without my knowledge. "We ready to go, boys?"

"Yes!" Jess ran out right away.

"Hey! Excuse me, young man. Can Mommy get a hug first?" Allison asked incredulously. "You're never this eager to leave Daddy's house."

I cleared my throat pointedly. She wasn't bringing that up in front of them. Fucking hell. That type of comment was why Nate and Jess sometimes felt guilty for wanting to be at my place more, and it caused the rift between them and her to grow. Simply put, she made them uncomfortable, and I wouldn't have it. I'd told her numerous times.

She met my gaze and flinched, then plastered a smile on her face as she said goodbye to the kids. "I understand you're excited to open more presents. I love you both so much!"

All was right in the world—for the moment—when the three of us were in my car, seat belts on, motor running, and doors locked. Next stop, Puppyville.

"Did you have a nice Christmas with Mum?" I asked in the rearview.

"Frank likes metal music." Nate looked disgusted.

Jess started headbanging.

Frank, huh. I prayed that wouldn't become a thorn in my side. Truth be told, I was relieved Allison had moved on, but I would be her worst nightmare if the person she moved on with wasn't a good influence around the boys.

"Some metal can be good." I did my best to be diplomatic. "Jess, you and I know how to rock it to Iron Maiden, don't we?"

"Number of the beeeast!" Jess did the sign of the horns like I'd taught him.

I grinned.

Nathan rolled his eyes and looked out the window.

"Was he nice, at least?" I hedged.

"I suppose." Nate shrugged. "He said I'm a genius."

One point for Frank. Good.

"He said I'm funny!" Jess boasted.

I smiled and relaxed a little. "Does he have kids of his own?"

Nate nodded. "Two daughters, but they're in college."

That was interesting. I'd have to investigate more later. We reached our street, and I pulled into the driveway. "Okay, so we have some rules for today." I unbuckled my belt and peered back at the boys. "We're turning back the clocks twenty-four hours, and it's officially Christmas today."

Nate snickered. "Okay."

"Rule number two," I said. "There are heaps of presents under the tree, some from me, some from Grampa, some from Auntie Brianna and Uncle Chris. But you'll only get one before breakfast, and you have to share it."

That made both of them skeptical, possibly because they rarely liked the same things.

They would like this one, though.

In fact, the other stuff we'd gotten them would probably be forgotten.

"I don't like rules much," Jess whispered to his brother.

I laughed under my breath and left the car. Opening the door on Jess's side, I added, "Last rule. No shouting when we get inside the house." With my youngest's windpipes, the puppy could be scarred for life.

"I hardly ever shout," Nate said and paused. "And now I realize that was for Jess."

Smart boy.

I helped them with their overnight bags and the gifts, and I exchanged a nod with Dad in the kitchen window. He was ready.

"Grampa's here," Jess said happily. Then he opened the door, and I was incredibly impressed that he kept his greeting to his grandfather at a moderate volume.

"Do you have the gift, Dad?" I called.

"Right here," he replied from the kitchen. I grabbed Jess's shoulder so he wouldn't walk farther in. "Are they ready?"

"I'd say so." I let Nate pass me, and I quickly pulled out my phone. I was going to film this.

The boys looked at each other quizzically, but a second later, little paws skidded across the hardwood floor in the kitchen, and the puppy jumped out into the hallway.

Jess gasped and turned to me with wide eyes.

I grinned, capturing the whole moment.

"Oh my gosh," Nate whispered, kneeling down on the floor to greet the pup. "Is it really ours, Dad?"

"He sure is." I gave Jess's shoulder a gentle squeeze. "You wanna say hi to the pup, buddy?"

Jess gulped, overwhelmed, and nodded shakily. Then he sank to his knees next to his brother and carefully patted the puppy on his head.

"So soft," he whispered. So this was the way to silence him—good to know. "Nate, we have a puppy."

The puppy was soaking up the attention but was in no way interested in cuddling. He wanted to play and nip at fingers.

Nate yelped and laughed, withdrawing his hand.

"His first set of teeth are sharp, boys. Be careful."

"What's his name?" Jess asked. He was recovering from his shock, and I could see the excitement building up.

"That's for you two to decide," Dad told them. "And before you fight over it, I suggest you each write three names on a piece of paper, and then we can discuss them without shouting."

Good idea.

"Was it a good Christmas present, boys?" I asked.

They nodded furiously, and I felt ten feet tall.

CHAPTER 22

The Marshalls came home the first week in January, and I'd already been warned that Jaylin demanded to see the puppy immediately. So she came over the same evening they got back, and she had Kieran with her.

"Jess!" I hollered. "Jaylin's here."

Kieran didn't look happy. Just...broody and fucking sexy. That rat bastard.

"Who pissed in your cereal, sunshine?" I frowned.

Jaylin was already gone, darting up the stairs like a kid on crack. She'd soon realize what she came for wasn't up there. The puppy, who now proudly carried the name Duke after someone who'd walked on the moon, was only allowed down here. No Lego he could choke on, no McDonald's toys he could chew on.

I was going to buy a gate when the first step on the stairs wasn't Duke's personal Everest.

"The hellion who just ran past you," Kieran said. "She pissed in my cereal."

"My sweet princess who can do no wrong? No way." I smiled innocently. Most of all, I was just glad there was less tension between us. It felt neutral. And good to see him.

Kieran shot me a look and trailed into the kitchen. "Please tell me you have coffee."

Damn, his accent was something else when he'd just returned from Boston. He reminded me a little of those two actors in *Good Will Hunting*. Not quite as rough, but close.

"I have coffee." I walked over to the coffeemaker while he slumped down in a chair and shrugged out of his leather jacket.

"When you posted the video of the boys—when they got the dog...? I swear, the minute Jaylin saw it on Facebook, she pushed away the brand-new bike my parents gave her and screamed at the top of her lungs."

I winced.

"Spoiled rotten is what she is," he muttered.

Jess and Jaylin stomped down the stairs, where Duke was waiting for them. It caught Kieran's attention, and he turned in his seat to glance out in the hallway.

"He's cute."

"I take it you're not getting one." I brought two cups of coffee to the table and sat down across from him.

Kieran faced me again and lifted his brows. "After her reaction? Fuck no. I was actually considering it. I saw the video first and thought, you know, maybe it could be a good gift for her next birthday or whatever. Then she acted the way she did, and..." He shook his head. "She's reached a weird age. She's so fucking defiant and mouthy sometimes."

"Thank God boys are different." I blew some steam off my beverage and took a tentative sip. "I reckon my troubles with Jess won't come until he notices girls."

I wasn't sure Nate would ever give me the same types of problems.

Kieran sighed and leaned back, and it was as if he just now noticed how bizarrely normal our conversation was. Or rather, the lack of discomfort in how we acted toward each other.

"It's good to see you, Ben," he murmured.

"You too." And it really was. Just to have him here in my kitchen put me at ease. How strange. The last time we spoke, really spoke, the air around us had been full of hostility and bitterness. I could sense some caution from his side, but that wasn't weird. And I hoped this next topic didn't fuck things up. "Are you being unfaithful to Maggie?"

His eyebrows shot up. "Excuse me?"

"She came to me," I elaborated. "I was dropping Jess off to play with Jaylin when you were in Tacoma, and Maggie asked if I knew anything—if you were having an affair."

He sighed heavily and cracked his knuckles absently on the table. "I guess I can see why she'd be worried, but no. Not since you. I wouldn't—I mean..." He trailed off and frowned to himself. "No, I'm not cheating on her."

He was going to say something else initially, I was certain.

"You think she'll confront me?" he asked pensively.

I shook my head. "Not based on the reaction I got when I told her I could ask you."

He let out a tired chuckle. "Makes sense. She used to be headstrong and ambitious. Now a doormat could walk all over her."

Maybe she wasn't the only one who was a pale image of what she used to be. I knew I used to be happier, especially when I had Kieran. And Kieran himself... His genuine grins from the home videos haunted me.

None of us was happy.

I swallowed the burst of bitterness with my coffee and reminded myself it was egotistical to think I'd come before his family. A family that was big enough to start their own football team.

"Have you thought about dating?" Kieran asked carefully.

I shook my head and finished my coffee. "Hopefully when I feel better, but I'm not there yet."

I didn't even know what gender I'd date, much less a specific person. I was objectively and generally more attracted to women, but since Kieran, I hadn't looked at another person that way. It was as if all types of attraction had just fizzled up and died. No one drew me in. My sex drive was pathetically low, and the only one I dreamed about was the motherfucker sitting across from me.

It was my turn to ask. "If *you* could go back…"

He knew what I was talking about. "Maybe—for your sake. I hate having put you through this. It fucking kills me to see—" He cut himself off and blew out a breath. "For my own sake? No. You're my 'If I could have just one more day' person. You know what I mean? I was at a bad place before I met you, and I remember thinking, 'If I could just have one thing for myself, something that made me happy for a single moment…' And there you were, and I had you for a short second, and it wasn't anywhere near enough, but I got what I asked for."

The hurt made a swift return, spreading across my chest. His words were so final. We were never getting back together; we were never becoming our own unit, a family, a team. Because he got what he *fucking* asked for.

Something died inside of me. Something I thought had already died. Hope. If only a sliver of it. It was gone.

"What about you?" he wondered, and the tension was back. I could feel it. I could almost cut it with a knife. We weren't ready to be friends at all. We weren't going to go skating with the kids.

"Yes," I heard myself say. "I would go back, Kieran. If I

knew then what I know now, I would find another seat on that train."

"*Yes. I would go back, Kieran. If I knew then what I know now, I would find another seat on that train.*"

I bolted awake in a cold sweat. My lungs burned, and I gulped in air as the memory of Kieran's face flitted past in my head. The hurt in his eyes, the understanding, the remorse, and finally, how he'd shut down.

I cursed and shifted to the edge of the bed, then glanced at my alarm clock. The digits glowed red in the darkness and told me I wasn't supposed to get ready for work for another two hours.

I'm sorry, Kieran.

Oh, it was going to be that kind of day.

For the past few months, I'd gone back and forth between regretting what I'd said and...thinking I hadn't been blunt enough. Today, I was full of regret.

I couldn't think of a time in my life I had been this conflicted. I was constantly pulled between what I felt and what I logically thought. I couldn't get my heart to understand what my brain told me. I *knew* Kieran. I knew he had good intentions. I knew he wasn't a coward. I knew he wanted what was best for those he loved. And yet...

But my hurt had a valid point. He was going about things the wrong way. He was protecting people's feelings and ignorance where it wasn't deserved. In my opinion. And then my brain chimed in again. *You didn't grow up with his family. You don't know how much they've done for him.*

"Fuck," I exhaled exhaustedly. Back and forth, back and forth.

The house was empty, so I had only Duke to distract myself with. After my shower, I took him for a long walk and watched the rest of the town wake up. Then I dropped Duke off with my father before I took the car and got ready for a day in traffic.

I had meetings in Seattle all day, plus a lunch with my sister.

My early start did cut me some slack, however. The traffic wasn't as bad as it usually was, though I still bitched to myself about Amtrak closing the express train. Again, I didn't envy Kieran and Allison who went through this every—

"Dammit," I said, pulling out my phone. I'd forgotten to call Allison. A text would have to suffice now. She was at work, and my first meeting was in ten minutes.

Reminding you that Jess has a dentist appointment tomorrow at ten, and Nate wants help with his science project. Which means he's insecure about it, so please tell him you're proud of him and that the teacher will recognize his progress.

She replied as I entered the restaurant.

Can you take Jess? I can't leave the city that early. I know how to help Nathan, Bennett. You don't have to feed me lines.

"Could've fooled me," I muttered under my breath. The hostess greeted me, and I told her my name and that I had a reservation for two under Brooks. She showed me toward my table, and I responded to Allison again.

It's your week, Allison. I can't cover for you every bloody time. I'll figure something out with Jess tomorrow, but you must start putting our sons first.

When I had lunch with Brianna later, I got to vent some of my frustrations to her. Allison was another topic that made me torn. She *was* making more of an effort in front of the kids; she was more present these days. But the minute they were an inconvenience and got in the way of her work, I had to jump in.

"Not to be a dick, but her boyfriend is almost better with the boys," I said around a mouthful of pasta.

"Frank, was that his name?"

I nodded. "I've only met him twice, but he seems like a good bloke." Jess was fonder of him than Nate was, but my eldest was finicky. The important thing was that Frank understood the children came first, and it brought me some comfort every time the boys came home with a funny anecdote that involved Frank. It was all I wanted, for them to have a grown-up they could turn to when I wasn't there. No more, no less. "Anyway. How are you preparing for, what was it you called it, your last birthday?"

She rolled her eyes at my smirk. "I'd rather not discuss it, thank you very much. Jess's birthday is a much better subject."

I chuckled. The fact that Jess turned ten in just a few weeks was definitely a topic worth discussing, because Allison and I were throwing him a big party in my backyard. Well, she was in charge of decorations, at least. But my sister's thirty-ninth birthday was something we hadn't covered at all, including what she planned on doing that day.

"Come on. Where will we bring a gift?" I asked. "You coming up to Dad or—"

"I suppose we can do a dinner here," she said, disinterested. "Chris has been asking too, but with the wedding planning, and work, and...ugh."

I smiled. "You're happy. You try to whine, but I see it."

She gripped her fork a little tighter and raised her bitch brow.

I laughed.

She was too funny about her obvious hatred toward turning forty next year.

"When's your next meeting?" She went for another topic change.

I grinned and wiped my mouth on a napkin, then withdrew my phone from my pocket. "In…" Holy shit. Twelve missed calls. Panic seized my chest. Had something happened to one of the boys— "What on earth?" *Maggie* had called me, of all people. Twelve freaking times. *Oh God, Jaylin.* I swallowed hard, worried all over again, and hit redial.

"Is something wrong?" Brianna asked, concerned.

"I don't know yet." I frowned.

Maggie answered with a hoarse, "Finally! I've been trying to call you for an hour, Bennett."

"I know, I just saw—sorry, hon. I keep it on silent. What's wrong?" I could hear she was crying, and I needed her to tell me what was wrong right fucking now. "Is it Jaylin?"

"It's Kieran," she sobbed, and my heart stopped. "That— that bastard!"

A breath gusted out of me, and I ran a hand through my hair. The frustration grew rapidly. If she called him a bastard, he must be safe. Right?

"He's in Quincy," she cried. "At the hospital."

My fist hit the table with force as my patience ran out. Brianna jumped and put a hand to her chest.

"Tell me what happened," I demanded. "Is he okay?"

Around me, I could see lunch guests glancing our way.

"You can go see him if you want," Maggie snarled through her sobs. "He just ruined our family by telling his parents that he's gay!"

"*Jesus Christ,*" I exhaled.

"Tell me what's wrong." Brianna reached across the table

and put her hand on mine. "You look like you've seen a ghost, love. Is it one of the kids?"

I shook my head, dazed.

"Why's he in the hospital, Maggie?" I forced out. To Brianna, I mouthed, "Kieran."

"Oh." Her lips formed the word.

Maggie continued weeping, only anger allowing her to push the words out. Or so it sounded. "His brothers put him there, of course. Did-did you know, Bennett? Did you know about K-Kieran?"

That's what she— *"That's* what you want to know?" I asked in disbelief. "That's your greatest concern? Whether or not I knew Kieran was gay? For the love of God, Maggie—"

"He wrecked my family!" she screamed. I held the phone away and caught Brianna's quizzical look. "I think he'll survive a few stitches."

Stitches wouldn't put him in the hospital, and Kieran wouldn't seek medical attention for anything minor.

"Text me the address of the hospital and any other information you might have," I told Maggie. I was grateful my sister jumped into action and asked for the check. "Do you understand, Maggie?"

"I understand," she cried. "No one cares about me."

I suppressed a sigh and pinched the bridge of my nose.

My dad's words came back to me. Sometimes we sacrificed ourselves. Sometimes we sacrificed others. Either way, someone was always going to suffer.

It was Maggie's turn.

I handed over my credit card to the waiter and hung up the phone, then rambled anxiously to my sister about what I'd learned. *Kieran's in the hospital.* Nausea churned in my gut, and I had to stop a few times to press a fist to my mouth. His brothers had abused him. I couldn't believe it. In this day and age. They were his motherfucking family. *Kieran's in the hospital.*

"Let's step outside, darling." Brianna ushered me out of the restaurant.

Hysteria crept higher. I couldn't believe it, I couldn't believe it, I couldn't believe it.

The May sun shone down on us, and the street was crowded.

"Who does that?" I rasped. "For almost twenty *fucking* years, he's kept that a secret to protect their goddamn bigotry." The rage exploded within me, and I turned to the nearest brick wall and sent a fist flying straight into it.

"Bennett!"

"Who *does* that?" I yelled. "He's their brother—their goddamn *son*!"

"Bennett!" Brianna hissed. "Oh my God, your hand."

I didn't feel anything but crippling fury, and I wanted to—I wanted to—*hell*. I screwed my eyes shut, dizzy, and bent over slightly. The pain hit me in pulsing waves, and I didn't know what hurt the most—my hand or the image of Kieran. Oh God, I'd pushed him away. I'd made him feel guilty. I'd avoided him when he needed me the most.

"Fuck," I whimpered.

I barely registered that Brianna was guiding me in between two buildings. Then she said something about being back soon. Tears welled up and spilled over. Kieran. That hurt the most. He was alone. He was in the hospital all the way across the country, and I didn't know if he had anyone with him.

I had to get to him. I had to be with him. Maybe he needed me.

The clicking of heels alerted me to Brianna's return.

"I told him I regretted we ever met." My voice broke, and I

turned away from the mouth of the alley where people flooded the sidewalk. "I pushed him away, Brianna."

"Bennett, love, you have to pull it together," she pleaded with me. "Your hand is broken."

"I have to get to Boston," I croaked.

She nodded and reached up to undo my tie. "A friend of mine has a clinic not far from here. Once your hand is taken care of, we'll get you a ticket. Okay?"

I shook my head. "My hand can wait." I was such a fucking idiot. "I...I..." Shit, I had to think straight. Priorities. Nate and Jess. Meetings— "I have to cancel my meetings and go home. Make arrangements for the boys."

"Don't be daft, little brother." She wrapped my tie around my hand, and I winced at the sharp bolts of pain. Next, she tucked a Ziploc with ice in it underneath the temporary wrap. Did she go back to the restaurant for the ice pack? "Dad and I will take care of Nate and Jess. You're going to get your hand fixed, then you wait at my place a few hours, and then you take the red-eye to Boston. You'll be with him first thing in the morning. Don't argue with me."

I sniffled, and I didn't argue with her.

CHAPTER 23

I arrived in Boston the following morning, bleary-eyed and with nothing but the clothes on my body, a bottle of painkillers, and a mind-numbing headache. Well...I had a new splint to my name too, attached around my wrist, stabilizing my whole hand up to my middle and ring fingers. Brianna's doctor friend had taken me to get X-rays, revealing two fractures along my knuckles. I wasn't allowed to use my hand for a while, and I was supposed to keep it elevated.

The last part wasn't going so well. Neither was the first part, because I couldn't open the bottle of meds one-handed.

And I probably shouldn't have washed down two tablets with a vodka on the plane.

I hurried to the cabstand outside the airport and jumped in as soon as it was my turn.

"Quincy Medical Center," I said, trying to open the pill bottle again.

The driver eyed me in the rearview. "There're hospitals much closer, man."

"It's not for me." Christ. I used my teeth and managed to get the cap off. "Please just go."

This time, I downed two pills dry. Then all I could do was wait. I must've been a sorry sight. My suit didn't look like it'd just come out of my closet, my tie was gone, my hair was a mess, I had shadows under my eyes, and the wrinkles of worry and annoyance were probably etched into my forehead permanently at this point.

The city of Boston disappeared from view, a city I'd come to know well by now. A city I actually loved but never had gotten the chance to enjoy. A city full of history and Kieran-related curiosities. How many times had I been in a cab toward Westwater Hotels headquarters, passed a bar, and wondered if Kieran had been there?

I'd since then learned that he didn't get out of Quincy much growing up. When they went into the city, it was a special occasion. He'd mentioned his mother's favorite restaurant was in the North End.

I'd had dinner in the North End many times, often wishing Kieran had been with me.

Now he was in the hospital.

And his phone was still dead, I confirmed as I dialed his number for the tenth time since yesterday.

Thank God for my sister. Not only had she taken the day off to be there for Nate and Jess, but she'd managed to wrestle some more information out of Maggie. I knew where Kieran was; he'd been moved to recovery as of sometime last night. Apparently, Maggie and Kieran's mother were crying on each other's shoulders over the phone. In turn, Kieran's mother—who hadn't been to see him—was getting her information from Grace. If I wasn't mistaken, that was Kieran's youngest sister, and I prayed she was on his side. Or hadn't abandoned him.

Half an hour later, I was as restless as I was exhausted. My foot tapped rapidly as the driver entered hospital grounds, and I specifically told him the emergency room.

"I don't want to end up in the maternity ward or something," I muttered.

The driver hummed and made a turn, following the signs. "I think that closed. Years ago."

Whatever, we'd made it. I looked out the window and figured this had to be it. Then I paid the cringe-worthy fare, cradled my injured hand close to me, and darted for the entrance.

I'd half expected a Friday-night type of cacophony. Instead, it was a Thursday morning, and I could walk straight up to the closest desk and ask where I could find Kieran Marshall.

Two nurses perked up, though one was buried in paperwork and charts. Another one helped me and asked about my relation to the patient.

"He's my brother," I lied.

Please don't ask to see my driver's license.

The nurse checked the computer. "He's in recovery on the second floor. Elevators are over there—" she pointed to my left "—and he's in room six."

I nodded and thanked her, then hurried to the elevators.

Seconds felt like an eternity until I stood there, right outside his room, and stared at a door that didn't have a window big enough so I could see him. I saw the foot of a bed, that was it.

Just go in.

Nerves tightened my stomach, and I took a deep breath. I opened the door and stepped inside, having no clue what to expect. To be in recovery, there had to be something to recover from. It couldn't be cuts and scrapes. They would've just sent him home. Hell, he wouldn't have come in the first place.

Each step closer to his bed revealed more of him. The drape between his bed and another was drawn. No one else was here—no other patient, no family. No beeping machines, thankfully.

I swallowed hard and took a punch to the gut when I saw his face. *What did they do to you?* I blinked back my emotions and cleared my throat quietly, not wanting to wake him up. Someone had tucked him in—maybe a nurse. How injured was he under that blanket? His face was partly swollen, with bruises dominating his right eye, his jaw, and one cheek. Butterfly bandages held together a cut across one eyebrow, and his bottom lip was split.

Family wouldn't do this.

I rounded the bed and silently moved a chair closer to him. I couldn't tear my eyes away from his form even for a second, and his injuries had me speechless. It was impossible not to judge. I tried, I fucking tried, but this wasn't okay. Ever, under any circumstances. I didn't care what goddamn generation his parents were from, or how traditional the brothers' upbringing had been.

I sniffled and leaned back in my seat, one foot resting on my knee, and forced myself not to check his injuries further. I feared he was hurt more under the blanket. Broken ribs? How many more bruises?

Then again, no amount of bruising would take away the pain he'd suffered internally.

I thought of the home movie I'd seen. His happy grins and wolfish smirks.

With an elbow on the armrest, I pressed my thumb and forefinger against my eyes and exhaled tiredly. A yawn escaped me the moment I was no longer bothered by the hospital lights, so I stayed in that position a couple minutes.

The pain in my hand was dulled by the meds that also seemed to make me sleepier.

I should've tried to sleep on the plane.

I yawned again and let my good hand fall to my lap. I squinted briefly at the lights in the ceiling.

Then I saw Kieran shift in his sleep, which was followed by a flinch and a low groan.

I sat forward, my heart rate picking up.

He grunted and withdrew his arms from under the blanket, and he cracked his eyes open with pain flitting across his face. When he faced me, it took a moment for him to realize. Then the confusion cleared, and he swallowed hard.

"You're here," he whispered hoarsely.

"I got a call from Maggie yesterday," I murmured.

He rolled his eyes as they became glassy. "Of course. I figured Ma would call her." He tried to sit up, but a wince stopped him, and I was out of my chair right away. "It's okay."

"Nothing here is okay. Where does it hurt?"

"My ribs."

I cursed and helped him raise the back of his bed a bit. "Are they broken?"

He shook his head. "Just bruised."

Just.

"Who did this?" I whispered.

"It doesn't matter."

"Tell me, Kieran."

He sighed and leaned his head back against the pillow again. The defeat and abandonment were written all over him, and it fucking killed me.

"Mostly my big brother. Brent." He cleared his throat as his eyes welled up again. "Mark got a couple hits in too."

"I'm so sorry." I slumped down in my seat again and grabbed his hand.

He gave me an empty little smirk. "You didn't do this."

"I pushed you away." The guilt nearly bowled me over. "I told you I regretted we ever met."

"I needed to hear it," he whispered.

"But it wasn't true," I argued. "I could never—" I choked up and had to take a calming breath. "It was my bitterness talking. Meeting you is one of the best things that ever happened to me."

The look in his eyes softened, and he gave my fingers a squeeze. "When did you get here?" He frowned. "How did you get in?"

"I took the red-eye. And I may have lied and said I was your brother."

His mouth twitched in amusement. "I reckon you're about to meet Grace and Des, then. My youngest brother and sister," he clarified.

I already knew who they were, having "met" the family through a TV.

I cocked my head. "Why?"

"Grace is a triage nurse here, and she's working right now. She's keeping tabs on my room to make sure...the others don't get in. She got pissy with me when I said I didn't wanna press charges."

The *others*. As he'd predicted, his family was now split into two camps.

I stared at my feet, feeling horrible about everything. "I hate that this happened to you. If I'd offered better support—"

"Hey. This has been brewing for years, Ben."

I glanced up at him.

He smiled sadly. "I can't tell you how many times I've worked myself up to tell them, especially after meeting you. You wouldn't let me hide behind excuses—you spoke out loud the things I already knew and tried to ignore."

"I never wanted you to lose your family."

"Neither did I, but that wasn't up to you or me. It was a choice they made."

I sighed heavily and rested my forehead on his hand. "I'm still sorry."

He hummed and slipped his hand free, only to weave his fingers through my hair, and it felt too good for words. A shiver ran down my spine, and I stole a selfish moment to enjoy the pleasure. To enjoy being next to him.

It was a short-lived moment, though. The door was pushed open, causing me to tense up and lift my head.

A young carbon copy of Kieran entered the room, followed by a woman. A nurse. It had to be Grace and Desmond.

Desmond eyed us before settling his stare on me. "Who the fuck are you?"

God, he sounded like Kieran too, except his accent was much rougher.

"He's a friend, Des," Kieran said wryly. "Calm your tits."

Friend.

"I'm Bennett," I said. "You must be Desmond and Grace."

"I don't know if we must, but we are." Des frowned at us for another second, then reprioritized and focused on his brother. "How you feelin'?"

"Like someone kicked me in the ribs," Kieran drawled.

Grace hurried to Kieran's side to check his healing. "Has the pain spread?"

Kieran shook his head.

I sat back and stayed quiet. This was the first time I was witnessing Kieran interact with his family, and I wasn't going to miss it. Desmond, who couldn't be more than twenty, had clearly taken on the position of Kieran's bodyguard, and I found that impossibly sweet. Grace didn't look much older, yet she cared for her big brother with an age-old practiced, motherly touch.

"Still can't believe you didn't fight back," Des muttered. "You coulda taken Brent before Mark got there."

"No, he was smart," Grace murmured. "The kids were watching. They're so mad at Brent."

I glanced at Kieran, curious. And fucking worried. I couldn't relax in my seat.

"It was after dinner," Kieran told me. "I told them I was gonna divorce Mags and that I'm gay, and Brent dragged me outside." He paused, in pain as Grace checked the bandage around his torso. When she carefully lifted the stretchy fabric, I spotted what I assumed were ice packs. "Trust," he told Des, "I was gonna get him. That cunt gets high and mighty about queers but has no issue cheating on Theresa every fucking week. Ouch."

"Sorry," Grace said with a wince. "I'll change the gel pads in a bit, but it looks like the swelling is going down. That's good."

Kieran drew in a deep breath and looked my way again. "I saw the kids in the window. Brent's and Mark's. I didn't want my nieces and nephews to see me beat their pops."

Admirable. Impressive. I wasn't sure I'd be able to do that. Grace was right, though. It was a bloody smart move, because children didn't judge sexuality. They judged violence. They judged their fathers for beating up their uncle.

"I'm proud of you." I squeezed his hand briefly.

That earned me another frown from Des.

Kieran had placed his attention elsewhere. "What the fuck happened to your hand?"

Oh. "I, uh…" I looked down at my injured hand. "A brick wall ran into it."

Desmond snorted, suddenly amused.

"Was it recently?" Grace asked softly.

"Yesterday," I replied. "After I spoke to Maggie. I guess I was a little angry."

Kieran's eyes flashed with understanding, knowing there wasn't much on this planet that made me violent. He'd probably also figured out that Maggie wasn't his best friend at the moment, and therefore wouldn't defend him. Not that she didn't have every right to be royally pissed, but lately, I kept coming back to the fact that she knew. She'd known he was gay. She'd entered a marriage with someone who used to date her very male friend. Did she think it'd been a phase? Was she a good partner to have enabled this charade?

There were too many circumstances for the answers to be black-and-white, but one thing was certain. Maggie wasn't completely innocent.

"I assume it's fractured if you were given a splint," Grace said. "Try to keep your hand raised above your heart. It'll help with the swelling."

"I will, thank you." Despite that I'd heard it from a doctor, there was a kindness to Grace that made it impossible to brush off her advice.

She turned to Kieran again and adjusted his blanket. "You need to get some rest, big brother."

"When can I leave?" he asked.

"I told you. Tonight at the earliest," she answered. "I'll do my best to keep you here if the doctor wants to move you to another floor."

Kieran mustered a charming smile. "Or you could let me leave early."

She patted his shoulder. "Yeah, no."

Around noon, it hit me that I hadn't eaten in almost twenty-four hours, not counting a highly repulsive meal bar Brianna had forced me to eat at her place after I'd gotten my hand fixed.

Kieran was starving too and didn't want to go near hospital Jell-O, so I stepped out to get us some real food.

I smuggled in burgers, fries, and shakes, and we quickly learned that Kieran couldn't eat the burger without reopening the cut on his lip.

"Maybe you stick to the fries and the shake," I suggested.

"Maybe," he muttered reluctantly.

Grace checked in with Kieran every now and then.

Des came back for another visit in the afternoon. He was the one who kept in touch with the rest of the family, and he didn't look happy.

"Let me guess," Kieran sighed. "Everyone knows now."

Des nodded once. "Ma's been calling everyone, cryin' and whatnot. She's at church now with Angie."

"I'm sure they'll find the perfect guidance there," Kieran replied flatly. "Anything from Pop?"

Des shook his head. "Hasn't said a word. Brent and Mark stand firm. They won't accept this."

Fuck them, I wanted to say. But I didn't. Maggie had told me Kieran had once been closest to Brent, and Kieran would need time to grieve.

"You'll have Con on your side, bro." Des grabbed a chair and sat down on the other side of Kieran's bed. "He's just... I mean, you know he's looked up to both you and Mark. But I'm talking sense into him."

Kieran covered Desmond's hand with his own fleetingly. "I appreciate what you're doing, kid. You and Gracie—it means the world to me."

"Yeah, well." Des huffed and leaned back, one foot perched on the edge of Kieran's bed. "Fuckin' yesteryear gobshites. Can't wait to get outta hea'."

I bit at a cuticle on my thumb and smiled at their exchange.

"Don't push 'em away completely," Kieran told him. "They're still your family."

"Then they can fuckin' act like it," Des said irritably. "Buncha hypocrites, if you ask me. We can forgive adultery and be all hush-hush about Aunt Siobhan's gambling problem and Mikey being a boozehound, but someone comes out as queer, we start waving our bibles around? Fuck that."

I truly, truly liked Desmond.

"It's good I have you two," Kieran said. "You call it like it is. Only...Ben's better with words."

Des gave me a once-over, then looked to his brother. "Ben sounds British."

"You don't gotta talk like he ain't in the room," Kieran chuckled. "Enough with the attitude. He's a good guy. I've told you about him before."

He had?

"You have?" Des asked. "Oh! Wait, *he's* the guy Jaylin's mad about?"

Just like that, I was ten feet tall again. I could count on my princess.

"The one and only," Kieran replied, amused.

Des furrowed his brow at me. "Before you came around, I was her favorite."

"What can I say, I wear people down with my British charm," I answered. For the record, I wasn't that British, goddammit. It was something the Irish had gotten into their heads. "Anyway." I faced Kieran. "Where are you spending the night? I thought I'd step out in a bit to find a hotel."

"I wanna go home tomorrow," he said. "I'm not sticking around here, and I gotta deal with Mags."

"You sure you don't wanna try to talk to anyone?" Des asked hesitantly. "At least Connor—I think he needs to hear from you."

Kieran nodded. "I'll call him from the hotel." Did that mean he was staying with me? I hoped so. "I wanna get outta Quincy, though. Ma said I was sick, someone's struck Pop's mute button, Brent and Mark think I'm better off dead, and Angie wouldn't look at me. I ain't stayin'." His family could rot, for all I cared. Jesus. Kieran addressed me next, and he looked a little uncertain. "Do you mind if I stay with you in the city?"

"Of course not, l—" Probably not smart to call him love now. I was a fool. "I'll go book us a room."

"Thank you."

CHAPTER 24

Desmond drove us toward Boston that evening, to the waterfront hotel that had become my home away from home whenever I was here. The same place Kieran and I had spent our first full night together.

I hadn't slept in...ages, my hand was throbbing with pain, Kieran was hurting a million times that, and I was ready to be behind closed doors with him. I needed to take care of him. I needed to be able to hold him and hug him without strange and curious looks from his siblings.

Grace was in the car too, seated next to Des. When she'd finished her shift, she'd gone to their parents' house to pick up Kieran's belongings, and there'd been a box of childhood memories waiting for them.

They were seriously cleaning Kieran out of their house, and I was done pretending to give them the benefit of the doubt. Fuck the whole "But I didn't grow up with them" bullshit. The harm they were inflicting on Kieran today was worse than the punches Brent and Mark had delivered yesterday.

"I'll call Maggie when we get to the hotel." I kept my voice down, even though I knew they could hear me in the front. "We'll get Jaylin on the phone for you, okay?"

Kieran didn't look away from the window, but he nodded slightly.

I couldn't imagine what was going through his head.

"Look, Brit boy," Des said, giving me what I assumed was supposed to be a hard stare in the rearview. Didn't he know I only found him endearing for being protective of his brother? "Here's the deal."

"The deal is that when your big brother called me Brit boy a few years ago, it was funny," I told him. "When you call me that, it doesn't change the fact that I just want to hug you. Which I would've done by now if you weren't so standoffish." I earned a soft snort from Kieran and a giggle from Grace. "I have nothing but respect for you, and if you wish to keep up this tough front another while longer, that's fine by me. I know why you do it. Just—you have nothing to worry about. I'm on Kieran's side."

Desmond scowled at the others' mirth. "I'm just sayin'. My lease expires in December. That gives me eight months to convince Grace and Connor to move with me to your neck of the woods. And when we do, I'm taking back Jaylin."

I stifled a smile. "Bring your A game, kid. You're gonna need it."

"I find you both adorable," Grace said and looked back at me. "I'm glad Kieran has you, Bennett. And I'm looking forward to getting to know you better."

"Likewise," I murmured.

She smiled and held up a bottle of painkillers. "Make sure he takes two of these every four hours, okay?"

I nodded and accepted the bottle. "Will do."

She also handed me a paper bag. Inside were a handful of cooling gel pads, and she explained how to activate them.

"If you can avoid an early flight home tomorrow, that would be good," she added. "He really needs to sleep a lot, and sitting up for five hours on a plane, not to mention the stress coming in and out of airports—it might be too much."

"We'll stay an extra day," I decided firmly.

I wouldn't mind getting some extra sleep too.

"Goddammit," Kieran cursed from the bathroom.

I was there in a heartbeat. "Can you please let me help you, you stubborn fool?"

He groaned. "I guess I don't have much of a choice. It's open."

I'd already seen the bruises that covered his torso—when he got dressed at the hospital—but they still took my breath away the second time. It was a miracle nothing was broken.

Grace had been clear that the severe contusions and internal bruising were bad enough and that Kieran wasn't allowed to sweep this under the rug. Last night, they'd found traces of blood in his urine, and the doctors had confirmed that his kidneys had received some bruising as well. When Grace told me all of this earlier, I'd almost flown into a panic again.

He needed to go easy on himself, and I was going to make sure he followed the instructions. No unnecessary moving around, no lifting.

He was standing at the counter with a towel wrapped around his hips when I joined him, and it looked like he'd been struggling to put the bandage back on. Two of those gel pads were on the counter.

Parts of his tattoo along his rib cage were so darkened by the contusions that I couldn't distinguish it from the bruising.

There were so many things I wanted to say. I wanted to hold him to me, I wanted to say I despised many of his family members, I wanted to kiss his shoulder while I attached the soft brace, I wanted to comfort him.

Instead, none of that came out, and he wouldn't look at anything but the floor anyway.

"Are you hungry?" I asked quietly.

He shook his head.

"Do you want to talk to Jaylin?"

He cleared his throat and let out a shuddering breath. "I'll wait till tomorrow."

"Okay." Standing behind him, I stared at his reflection and waited for him to lift his gaze. "Kieran...I don't know what to say, but I'm here for you. Anything you need. Let me do it."

"I'll be fine—"

"*No.*" I grew desperate; he couldn't shut me out. I refused. "It's me, Kieran. We don't bullshit each other. Don't pretend any of this is okay."

He swallowed hard and turned around carefully. "You're right." His voice came out thick and gravelly. "I've seen my brothers' hate before. Brent—when his girlfriend left him years ago. He had this look in his eyes, like he wanted to murder someone."

I cupped his cheek and brushed away some hair that had fallen in his eyes.

"I was on the receiving end of that look yesterday, and I can't get it out of my head."

"Fuck," I whispered. "I'm sorry, sweetheart. And I'm...*not* sorry about saying this. He's a fucking dick. I've been trying to keep that to myself, but Jesus Christ, I want to throttle him."

Kieran offered an empty smile and walked out of the bathroom. "You could probably take him. The chip on his shoulder is big because he knows he ain't shit. He got offended when I didn't fight back."

"Part of me wishes you had," I admitted and followed him out. "Even though..." The kids.

"I know." Kieran slowly slipped into a pair of sweats before discarding the towel. "What are the rules on alcohol tonight?"

"Neither of us is allowed to have any." And didn't that just suck.

"Great," he muttered. Walking over to the windows, he pulled back the blinds, revealing one of the best views Boston had to offer. The waterfront was stunning at night, with its glittering lights from the boats in the water and the tall buildings. "Can you kill the light?" He nodded at the nightstand on one side of the bed.

I walked over and turned off the light, then joined him at the window.

Kieran let out a slow breath and looked out at the city. "There's relief too."

"Tell me." I ached to hear some good news.

"I don't feel like a fraud," he confessed. "I don't have to pretend anymore."

My shoulders lost a bit of tension at that, and I reached out in the darkness and squeezed his pinkie finger.

"It's like being unshackled." He glanced up at the buildings that stretched higher than us, and the city lights reflected in his eyes. "It'll be so fucking hard to get past this, Ben, but..." He closed his eyes and sighed. "For the first time in my life, I can live on my own terms."

Unable to help myself any longer, I shifted closer and pressed a kiss to his shoulder.

"I mean it. We seriously shouldn't be doing this," I said.

"Yes, we should." Kieran put on his shades and exited the elevator. "I'm being careful, see?"

Not careful enough, damn it. I cupped his elbow to offer a bit of support as we crossed the hotel lobby. It was huge, and people were coming and going in every direction. A Friday at a hotel attached to a convention center was crazy. Some were drained after a week of meetings, some were checking in for weekend seminars, and then add tourists to that.

"I promised your sister I would take care of you," I told him, half irritated. "This isn't what resting looks like."

"I'm asking for one hour, Ben. *One*. I wanted to do this when we were here together, but I was too much of a chickenshit to go outside with you. Even like this, like friends."

I got it; I fucking got it. We were friends. I heard it the first time he'd called us friends. Message received.

"One hour," I muttered.

We stepped outside and were met by the beaming sun and a clear blue sky. Kieran inhaled deeply, and I narrowed my eyes when he twitched at the pain. Okay, perhaps I was turning into a mother hen. I should relax and focus on his mood. He was in higher spirits today, and he'd been nagging about going out for ice cream since breakfast.

I'd done my best to stall. I'd even used the hotel's laundry service to have my suit and underwear dry cleaned. I'd also taken my time in the shower, brushed my teeth for half an eternity, until he banged on the door and told me to grow up.

"I look like a hobo," he said, "but I feel hella good. Let's savor the moment before I'm back to heartbroken."

I wasn't sure it was physically possible for Kieran Marshall to look like a homeless person. Despite sweats, a hoodie, and a battered face. His shades concealed the black eye, at least.

"We should get a taxi," I said.

"The boardwalk is literally around the corner, Ben."

It *literally* wasn't. It was a five-minute walk at best, which was five minutes too many for him.

I didn't stand a chance against him, though. We walked carefully and somewhat slowly until we reached the strip of boardwalk that followed the river. Plenty of people had taken their lunch outside, and it took us some time to find an available bench. Once I did, I put my freaking foot down. He was in pain, and no amount of ice cream was worth it.

I told him to stay put while I bought the bloody ice cream.

"You're cute when you're pissy!" he hollered after me.

I pretended to stay pissy.

But he wasn't entirely wrong. I could be cute.

There was a plaza near the harborwalk where I found food trucks and little shops, and one of them had ice cream. I bought two soft-serve vanilla cones and hoped that would satisfy Mr. Brightside and his sweet tooth.

He was practically lounging on the bench when I returned. Face tilted toward the sun, arms draped along the back of the bench, and one foot propped on his knee. In other words, completely the opposite of what Grace had instructed.

"Kieran, you're supposed to keep your back straight."

He hummed. "Don't kill my buzz."

Perhaps I should switch out our meds. His were clearly better than mine.

I sat down next to him and extended one of the cones, and he accepted it with a lazy smile.

"Thank you."

"How are you feeling?" I wondered.

"Right now, fantastic," he replied. "It's like a whole hallway of doors has opened up. Shit I can do that I couldn't before. It's the principle—not that I wanna do all those things, but just being able to if I did."

I looked away from him as he started eating his ice cream, because there was an indecent sight if I ever saw one.

"Give me an example." I shrugged out of my suit jacket and leaned back.

"I can sit here with you, for one," he murmured. "I'm forty minutes away from where I grew up. I have cousins and old friends who come to the city all the time—they could be right here on the boardwalk, and I don't have to care about it anymore." He paused, and the arm he still had behind me crept higher until his fingers gently scratched my neck. "I can do this."

Goose bumps rose across my neck, and I shivered at the sensations.

He wasn't finished. "If I were so inclined, I could also check out your ass in those pants when you go buy ice cream."

I smirked to myself as a river of contentment flowed through me.

"I don't have to look over my shoulder anymore," he said quietly, more serious now. But his fingers kept playing with the hair at the back of my neck. "I'm free."

Unshackled.

I let out a long sigh, more relaxed than I'd been in a long time, and tasted my ice cream.

"I would never go back, Kieran."

He swallowed audibly and squeezed my neck affectionately. "Me either. Never."

The moment was too perfect as it was, no other words necessary, so we fell silent. We just sat there, two blokes who were friends but probably not just friends, and ate ice cream in the Boston sun.

Despite the hurt that had been caused all around, despite the situation with Kieran's family, coming home was like the end of a vacation.

I'd bought luggage to fit Kieran's stuff in, and he didn't want to look at it, knowing it was filled with photos and trinkets from his childhood. Things his mother no longer wanted in her house.

My sister had once again come to the rescue and driven my car to Sea-Tac, and I spotted her near the exit as soon as the crowd of arrivals dissipated.

"This way, love." I brushed my hand against Kieran's back to change his direction. He followed silently, not in the mood to talk. The flight had been painful for his ribs, and the past few days' events sent him on an emotional roller coaster.

I'd warned Brianna already when I filled her in on everything. She knew what to expect. She'd also advised me not to ask too many questions and merely be there for him. It would be a while before he could tell up from down.

"Hey, boys." Brianna smiled and snuck in for a quick hug.

I held her a bit longer than that. She had no idea how grateful I was for everything she'd done, but I'd make sure she found out soon.

"It's good to see you." I kissed her cheek and stepped back.

"You too—both of you." She touched Kieran's arm. "Jaylin's at Bennett's house. Dad's watching them. She can't wait to see you."

Kieran mustered a small smile. "I appreciate it, hon."

He was nervous and anxious, I could tell. He'd told me he worried about scaring Jaylin with his injuries, but Brianna had prepared her. Daddy had been in a minor accident and had some bruises on his face. All Jaylin wanted to do was hug him and make sure he got better. Apparently, they had a sweet routine that involved napping, cartoons, and pancakes.

"You guys ready to drive me home?" Brianna asked.

"Yes, ma'am," I replied.

I'd known Kieran had nothing to worry about. The minute we arrived home and stepped out of the car, Jaylin darted out of the house and into Kieran's arms.

He scrunched his face in pain at the impact but made no sound.

"I missed you, Daddy."

"I missed you more, beautiful monkey."

I gave them some privacy and headed inside with the luggage. What followed was twenty minutes of mayhem, with Jess talking a mile a minute about what I'd missed, Nate telling me that his teacher was asking the wrong questions on a test, both of them inspecting my fractured hand, little Duke jumping up and down, and Dad asking what had happened in Boston.

I offered an abridged version for now, more interested if anything had happened with Maggie. Because Kieran hadn't spoken to her even once, which was slightly enervating. In a situation like this, I needed information and answers. I needed to map out the future and make a plan.

All I knew was that he'd asked if he could crash on my couch for a few days.

As if I would say no.

"How did it go at the dentist?" I asked Jess.

"Fine." He shrugged. "I got a sticker."

"They want to monitor him for a year or two," Dad said, offering a better response. "Then they'll see if he needs braces."

I nodded. "Thanks for taking him."

Jess grew bored and announced he was going to play with Duke in the backyard.

Dad peered out the kitchen window. Kieran and Jaylin were on their way in, and she was gesturing to her eye, to which Kieran said something and touched his black eye. Some of the fainter bruises had already started fading or yellowing. "You take care of him now, you hear?" Dad looked at me pointedly.

"Yes, sir. Of course." I didn't want to be in the way or complicate Kieran's healing, so I wondered if maybe I should turn the office slash sad excuse for a gym upstairs into a guest room. It would only take a bed and possibly a dresser. The gym equipment could go in the closet, and the desk could stay where it was.

I wanted him comfortable here.

Jess had started sleeping longer, something I sure as hell appreciated, though eight was still early on a Saturday morning. When he tumbled down the stairs, I didn't want Kieran to feel like he had to get out of the way so Jess could watch cartoons.

It was a good plan, and I had the whole weekend now.

"When did the boys get here?" I asked, curious.

Dad frowned in confusion. "Wednesday. Since I took Jess to the dentist. Why?"

Jesus Christ, I had to deal with that ex-wife of mine. It'd been her week until today. "Allison shouldn't have taken advantage like that," I said. "Brianna was only supposed to cover for her the day I left for Boston."

Nate, who lingered in the doorway, piped up. "We told Mum we wanted to be here. She said it was okay."

Oh. What was the protocol for that? It was simpler in the beginning. Strict days to create structure for the boys. Now they were growing up, and it made sense they were granted more freedom to choose where to be. At the same time, they'd drift. I knew they would. They'd want to spend less and less time with Allison.

I'd have to talk to her—later. Not now. Now I wanted to focus on Kieran and Jaylin.

They were here, in my house, where I'd once upon a time had foolish daydreams, in which this was their home too.

CHAPTER 25

"And he scores!" Jess yelled, then ran a victory lap in the backyard.

I chuckled, out of breath, and dug the football out of the rose bushes. Safe to say, I was done holding back from now on.

"Can I play, Bennett?" Jaylin asked.

"Of course, princess. Get over here," I said. "Let me just go get us something to drink first."

That was code for, "Let me see if your parents are done fighting."

Maggie had turned up an hour ago to talk a few "practical things," so I had ushered all the kids out to the backyard for some football. Nate and Duke were relaxing in the shade on the patio, and books and Jaylin's Barbies filled the table.

Jogging across the lawn and up the steps to the patio, I wiped some sweat off my forehead and then ducked inside and made sure to close the door behind me. No shouting this time; that was a plus. Last time I'd snuck in to check on things, they'd been yelling in the kitchen about promises made when they were younger.

"Jaylin won't go to school in Seattle," I heard Kieran say firmly. "Our divorce shouldn't cause her unnecessary suffering, so if you wanna move to Seattle to be closer to your parents, you'll be moving away from our daughter."

Shit. I lingered in the living room, too nosy. Couldn't be helped. I wanted to know. Kieran and I had been home all weekend, and it wasn't until today he'd talked to Maggie. It just struck me as odd.

"She needs me," Maggie argued. "Every child needs a mother."

Well...

"I'm not saying Jaylin doesn't need you," Kieran replied flatly. "I'm saying if you wanna stay close to her, you gotta stay in Camassia. This is where we agreed she would grow up."

"We agreed on many things," Maggie shot back. "You said you wanted this for life. You said you could suppress those urges—"

"I was a fucking kid!" Kieran growled. "I knew I wouldn't have support anywhere. It was being myself *by myself*, or pretending to be normal." He let out a harsh breath. "Look. I've told you—I didn't want this. I didn't wanna hurt you, or for you to pay the price for my—"

"But I did!" Maggie cried out. "I'm losing everything, Kieran! I'm losing my husband, my family—"

They kept interrupting each other. "You wanna talk about losing family?" Kieran asked in disbelief. "Would it be better if we went back to what we had? Huh? You want me to go back to pretending to be someone I'm not just so you can feel good about yourself?"

Silence.

I hung my head, wishing I could help somehow. Just yesterday, Jess had expressed how he couldn't wait to grow up, and both Kieran and I had looked at each other with this "If only you knew, kid" expression. Because now more than ever, we knew how easy it was to be a child. Everything was black-and-white until you grew up and saw gray everywhere.

There were millions of rights and wrongs in our lives, and blame could be placed with all of us. Which made disputes difficult to solve, much less get past.

"I knew you weren't happy with me," I heard Maggie say quietly, sniffling. "It used to make me bitter."

"I'm familiar with bitterness," Kieran muttered.

I wanted to ask Maggie why she hadn't wanted what was best for the man she supposedly loved. It wasn't a simple situation, but I found the question valid nonetheless.

"I can't believe we're getting divorced," Maggie whimpered. "I meet these women at church—they've been divorced or remarried, and I thought, that will never be me."

"Mags," Kieran said tiredly. "There are worse things than getting divorced today. You're not this old-fashioned woman your parents want you to be. You used to have so many goals—"

"Oh God, I haven't even thought that far." Maggie got upset again. "I don't know how to take care of myself. You're leaving me without giving an ounce of thought for—"

"*Easy*," Kieran warned. "First of all, give me some motherfucking credit. I'm not ditching you on the side of the road. Of course I will take care of you while you get on your feet. The house—take it. I don't care. We'll share custody of Jaylin. You have a prestigious degree that you've never used. Maybe it's time." There was a pause, and I took a few steps closer to the hallway to hear better. "I get that you're afraid, Mags. You've closed yourself in for years, and starting over is terrifying. I'm starting over too, and I'm doing it without most of my family. But I owe it to myself. And frankly, I'm done hating my life. I've tried for almost thirty-three years to fit into this box everyone I love thought I should be in."

My chest swelled with pride, love, and ache to be with him. He'd come so far in just days. Maybe he'd known for years; he'd already told me I had said out loud what he'd worked so hard to suppress. But even so, to be vocal about it now… I admired him immensely, and I was sick of hiding it. Or giving him a watered-down version of what I felt.

I returned outside, not wanting to eavesdrop anymore, and wondered how the fuck I was supposed to pretend I wasn't still head over heels in love with that man.

Bad news probably traveled faster than good news, and by the time we'd celebrated Jess's birthday and then Brianna's birthday, I could bet everyone we knew—and then some—was aware of the latest divorce gossip.

Maggie stayed at their house, though she went to Seattle when Kieran had Jaylin.

To be perfectly honest, I was as happy as I was anxious. Happy because I received a glimpse of what it could've been like to share a home with Kieran and Jaylin. Happy because we had breakfast together every other week, the five of us, and happy because I got to be close to Kieran for when his moods took a nose dive and he needed comfort.

The anxiousness increased every day, though, because I knew it was time borrowed. Kieran was only staying with us until he found a new house, and he was studying the listings in the paper every weekend.

By mid-June, I could tell Kieran was getting restless. He'd grown frustrated with public listings and hired a Realtor one rainy Wednesday.

I stood by the windows in the living room and looked out at the downpour.

The kids were with their mothers, and we'd planned on having a relaxing evening with beer and barbecue. We both needed a night off. Plus, Kieran was almost fully recovered, and it was something to celebrate, I thought. My hand was practically good as new too.

"Still raining?" Kieran asked, appearing in the living room.

"Yup." I left the window and stopped somewhere in the middle of the room. "Should we order in?" Either way, I wasn't changing out of my sweats and tee. Work was slow, so I had the next two days off. I was actually going to use that time for doing nothing in comfortable clothes.

"No..." He looked like he wanted to mope. It was sort of cute. "I really wanted to try the garlic rub I bought."

My grill master.

My kitchen had never seen so many marinades, glazes, and spice rubs before.

Kieran made his own seasoning mixes. Next to him, I was a novice when it came to cooking. And I thought I'd gotten better. Judging by the boys' reaction when Kieran cooked dinner, I hadn't made enough progress.

"How did it go with the Realtor?" I asked.

"Could've gone better." It was his turn to walk over to the window and look up. "I'm mostly worried about Jaylin."

I knew he was. She'd been more anxious lately. She'd handled the news of the divorce remarkably well, and she had the understanding of someone much older. But she felt uprooted and didn't know where her home was anymore.

"There are no good options in Downtown," he said. "The few listings I've seen—" He shook his head. "One house was good—big backyard and newly renovated kitchen—but I don't need four bedrooms for just Jaylin and me."

Stay here. Give us another chance.

I had to make my feelings known to him. If I didn't, I'd regret it for the rest of my life. Then I had my sister in my head, and her reminder to go easy on Kieran. No pressure, no major plans for the future. Christ.

"Fuck it," Kieran muttered. "We're doing the goddamn ribs. You have that big umbrella, right? We put it over the grill."

I had something better; I had a canvas awning, and I should've thought about that earlier. It covered the whole patio when fully extended.

"We should put that Jacuzzi to use sometime too," Kieran noted and passed me on his way to the kitchen. "The kids used it wrong."

Yes, they had; they hadn't used the jets or wanted the water very hot. But my mind was stuck on us using the hot tub together, and I wondered if I could…well, flirt. In a subtle way. No pressure, just letting him know…over a few beers, in the Jacuzzi… Lord. I rolled my eyes at myself. When had I ever been subtle? Or suave, for that matter.

On the other hand, he had never cared that I wasn't smooth in my approach before.

While Kieran worked his magic in the kitchen, I extended the canvas ceiling over the patio, blanketing the area in dark blue and pitter-patters from the rain hitting the fabric. Then I wiped down the table and chairs, rolled the grill closer to the edge of the deck, and removed the top from the Jacuzzi. We'd just filled it the other week for the kids' sake, and they didn't want it as warm as grown-ups tended to. So I turned on the heater, knowing it would be a couple hours before the temperature was more adult-friendly.

I was going for a cozy, discreetly romantic atmosphere, and I was nervous about it. At the same time, I knew I had to do it. I would be awkward and probably make him uncomfortable, but he needed to know.

Candles would be too much, right?

It wouldn't be dark for at least three hours, and we had patio lights. Yes, candles would be too much. And certainly not discreet.

From the shed next to the hot tub, I grabbed the cushions for the chairs and—

"Well, fuck." Kieran stepped out with a lazy grin. "This is perfect. We're getting our barbecue. Now we just need some music." He turned on the grill.

Wonderful, nothing set a romantic scene like Dropkick Murphys... I assumed that was what he would put on. He lived and breathed Irish rock, and I liked it too, I truly did, though it wasn't something that screamed romantic date.

This isn't a date, idiot.

It could turn into one...

To my surprise, it was the radio he put on in the living room. One of the stations I listened to a lot, with mostly singer-songwriters. It was the only station I played in my car, and Kieran wasn't a huge fan.

When I was done on the deck, I headed inside again and figured I could watch Kieran cook. I had nothing else to do, and he hadn't complained about my stalker tendencies before.

The second I set foot in the kitchen, I could tell something had changed drastically. Kieran had his back to me, hands planted on the counter, head hung in defeat, and the sight put me on edge. He'd been in good spirits a minute ago.

"What's wrong?" I asked.

He tensed up and cleared his throat. "Nothing, just —nothing."

"Okay, liar." I understood he'd gotten tired of the times he crashed, but avoiding it wasn't going to solve anything. "Should I ask again?"

He sighed heavily and scrubbed a hand over his face before he turned around. "Sometimes I forget, that's all. Then I'm standing here, trying to remember the ingredients for something, and I think, I'll just call my mother."

Ah. Understanding dawned, and I approached him carefully. Sometimes he didn't want me to get close; he'd brush things off and claim he was fine. "And then you remember," I murmured. At his nod and open expression, where I saw the hurt plain as day, I closed the distance and hugged him to me.

The assertive shit-stirrer from Quincy had become a skittish animal, and I didn't like it one fucking bit.

A few days ago, he'd told me it was hard to mourn someone who wasn't dead. There was no closure, and nothing felt final enough. He was constantly torn between calling his family to either beg them to accept him or to tell them to go fuck themselves.

"You'll be all right." I tightened my hold on him. "It'll take time, but you'll be all right. You have me. And my family. And Des and Grace."

He let out a breath and rested his forehead on my shoulder. "I don't know what I would've done without you."

"You won't have to find out either," I replied quietly. "I'm not going anywhere."

He shivered as I ran my fingers across his neck, and he hugged my middle a little harder.

It'd been a selfish idea to think I could...what? Seduce Kieran? Sometimes I couldn't believe myself. He wasn't ready for anything remotely close to that. What he needed was a friend, someone who let him process things at whatever pace he wanted.

I was going to be that person, end of discussion. So while we ate, my thoughts changed direction. I refocused and considered the living arrangements we had at the moment.

"Maybe it will be too stressful for you to move now," I mentioned, taking another scoop of mashed potatoes. I didn't know how much butter and parmesan Kieran had used, and I didn't want to find out. It was too good for words.

"What do you mean?" Kieran sucked barbecue sauce off the edge of his thumb. Not distracting whatsoever.

"You're already dealing with divorce proceedings, what your family did to you, work, Jaylin, and...you know. You have a lot on your plate, so perhaps you should stay a while longer."

He frowned. "I don't think being more of a burden will make me feel better either. Besides, Jaylin needs her own room soon. She feels unsettled."

"She does need her own space," I agreed. "Sharing with you and Jess is ridiculous when the guest room could be hers. Almost as ridiculous as the notion of you being a burden."

Kieran mulled over what I'd said, and the rain continued beating down on the canvas ceiling, a sound I admittedly enjoyed. I didn't want the evening to end. *It's barely started. Slow your roll.* Oh, rolls. I grabbed another one and bit into it. Homemade by my personal chef and dripping with garlic and butter. I was in heart attack heaven.

"You're right," Kieran said eventually. "I feel better now and don't need as much privacy. Jaylin should take the guest room, and I'll sleep on the couch. It's not like I haven't fallen asleep there some nights anyway."

Was he serious? Was he twelve? "Kieran," I said slowly, "we've had our tongues up each other's—" What the bloody hell was I actually saying? I froze and felt my ears get hot, much to Kieran's evident amusement.

"Up each other's what, Ben?" He sat back and folded his fingers across his stomach.

I blew out a breath and coughed. "What I mean is, we're adults. You won't catch anything if we share a bed."

Good fucking grief, I was mortified. Kieran's low laughter didn't help me either.

It also didn't help that I couldn't get the image of him out of my head. More accurately, the time we'd showered together and he'd gotten down on his knees behind me to tongue-fuck my ass.

I blinked and looked down at my food. "Apologies," I said stiffly. "I shouldn't have said that."

"I kinda love that you did," he chuckled. "Think about that often, do you?"

I shot him a glare.

Instead of erupting in guffaws, which it sort of looked like he wanted to, he eased off and held up his hands. "Don't bite my head off. *I* think about that moment often, and I could use an ego boost." He did what? He thought of— "Kidding aside, I'm not sure it's wise I get too comfortable here." Oh great, he'd been kidding. Cheers. "I'll think about it, okay?"

I nodded once, having lost the desire to talk about it anyway.

I let a huge helping of dessert comfort my bruised heart. Kieran had made my favorite, lemon bars in cake form with lemon meringue frosting.

"You're too good at this," I mumbled around a mouthful. Fuck, a perfect blend of sweet, rich, and tart. Each bite took one workout from me. I'd gotten better at exercise the past couple of years, but having Kieran under my roof was going to erase the definition my chest had gained and the biceps I'd worked so hard for. They weren't that impressive to begin with, but still noticeable. Then he'd started cooking around here, and I had no self-control.

"I like doing this stuff for you," he murmured. Glancing up from my plate, I saw he was leaning back and looking relaxed. Sipping his coffee, dessert finished. "When Mags and I lived in Savannah and she was still in school, we used to joke about it. That I would stay home and cook, and she would have a career."

The opposite had happened. It made me curious, though. "Have you thought about working less?" He was certainly in a position to do so if he wanted.

"No," he replied pensively, "but I have thought about opening a small office here in town. Much of what I do doesn't require seeing a bunch of people on a day-to-day basis. I have my meeting days like any other, but I could save a lot of time if I could work closer to home a few days of the week."

I bet.

"I saw some listings at the Realtor earlier," he mentioned. "There's a new office complex in the Valley—over by Fifth and Elm?"

I nodded. I drove past it on my way to work—when I wasn't in the city. "I think it sounds like a good idea," I responded. "Like you said, it doesn't have to be every day."

"Exactly."

I took a sip of my coffee. "Is that something you're going to involve your brother in?" That Desmond was eager to move out here was becoming abundantly clear. He texted and called Kieran often, asking about things he might need to know, from public transit to the cost of a pack of cigarettes.

"Partly, definitely," Kieran answered. "Once he's been housebroken, I want him to be my eyes and ears at the headquarters and the new office in Tacoma."

I chuckled at his wording. "And what about Connor?"

Kieran grew hesitant. "He hasn't decided if he's moving here or not."

Having gotten to know Desmond a bit better by now, I was sure he'd arrive with both Connor and Grace. As far as I knew, Grace was getting increasingly tired of the rest of the family's attitude, and Connor missed Kieran but struggled with the venom the others spat. He'd looked up to Mark very much, and now the man was turning on the other brother Connor viewed as a role model—Kieran.

"From what you've told me, he seems like a man who will make his own path," I said. "Wasn't it initially Connor's idea to come out here and work for you?"

Kieran nodded. "Then they found out I'm gay."

Well. I had faith in Des and his protective manner.

"Anyway," Kieran said, and I sensed a topic change. "Wine, whiskey, beer?"

"Cake," I said.

He laughed.

CHAPTER 26

Kieran sank into the hot tub, and I avoided looking at him until his too-sexy body was underwater. He could be an underwear model in those Hugo Boss he wore.

"Fuck, this is perfect," he sighed contentedly.

I hummed, agreeing, and sipped my whiskey.

Darkness was falling, as the rain continued to. Combined with the jets from the hot tub, the constant, low sounds were almost lulling.

Kieran placed his whiskey in one of the cupholders and draped his arms along the edge of the tub, and okay, I looked. I couldn't not look. He was too beautiful and indecently hot for words.

Perhaps I had issues.

Only a couple bruises lingered on Kieran's body, and they were thankfully fading. One across his right shoulder, and the other below on his rib cage.

Goddamn, how I missed him. Even here, now, when he

lived in my house. Even when I saw him every day and spent most of my free time with him.

"Remember the times we went camping at the lake?" Kieran asked.

I nodded and finished my drink. Not the best topic, if I was being honest. I felt too raw.

Kieran left his underwater seat and submerged himself in the middle of the Jacuzzi. Resurfacing, he pushed back his hair and wiped the water away from his face. "Not counting being Jaylin's dad, I've never been happier than when I was up there with you."

I stared at him, suddenly terrified. Hope threatened to explode in my chest, and I couldn't take another downfall.

"That's why I don't think it's a good idea I stay here much longer." He cleared his throat and averted his gaze to the water. Then he mustered up the courage to look me in the eye again. "You're still everything to me. If you want me to be just your mate, I'll need some distance. I hope you get that."

I swallowed hard and flushed as heat spread throughout my body. Was I hearing him right?

You're still everything to me.

It looked like he was about to return to his seat, and my body reacted on reflex. I couldn't have him move a single inch away from me, so I met him in the middle, and I took in the sight of him. The way he clenched his jaw when he was on edge and anxious, how his gaze flickered with uncertainty.

He made my pulse shoot through the roof.

I lifted a hand from under the water and cupped his cheek, to which his jaw ticked, and he closed his eyes. My forehead met his, and I watched him swallow hard. Then I pressed my mouth to his and felt my hope soar like a fucking rocket. Kieran's breath hitched. I kissed him again and again, soft, pleading kisses, until he finally got it and kissed me back. The low groan of surrender that emanated from his chest ignited my entire being.

"You're not going anywhere." I kissed him hard and wove my fingers into his hair. "You're staying here with me."

He shuddered and slid his arms around my midsection. "You want us?"

I didn't know if he was talking about him and Jaylin or him and me together, but the answer was the same. "More than anything."

He whimpered into the next kiss, and a forceful urge to take charge surged forward. The relief nearly floored me. I couldn't describe the whirlwind of emotions that raged inside of me, but I could express them. And I took it all out on Kieran.

As we made out like teenagers, I backed him into his seat again and hovered over him.

Every now and then, we slowed down and merely looked at each other. I brushed some waterdrops from his cheek, feeling the scruff under the pad of my thumb.

My heartbeat went on a roller coaster.

I kissed him again, the hunger growing within, and tasted the remnants of whiskey on his tongue. He hummed and tried to pull me down on him.

"I missed you," he whispered. "More, baby—please."

Desire flooded to my cock, and I slipped my hands down his stunning body and gripped the waistband of his boxer briefs.

"Wait—" He broke the kiss, voice ragged. "I want it all this time. You're clean, right?"

"Yeah." I wet my bottom lip and stared hungrily at him.

He nodded and took a breath. "Lemme get some oil."

Fuck. I backed off and dragged a hand over my face. "Hurry." The thought of fucking him without anything in the way—I would come in under a minute. I needed to calm my ass down.

To his credit, he was back within seconds, with a bottle of

baby oil, and he handed me the bottle while he threw back the last of his whiskey.

"I can't go yet," I said, setting the bottle on the edge of the tub. "I'll come too fast."

His eyes flashed with the predatory obscenity I'd missed for so long, and he pulled me close to his body. "Good," he murmured huskily. "You'll get off twice, then." He nodded at the seat he'd occupied. "Sit down and let me take care of you." But before he let me go anywhere, he pulled down my boxer briefs, causing my cock to slap against my lower abdomen. "Jesus Christ. How can anyone be so perfect?"

He was insane.

I sank into the water again, the jets bringing the surface to life around my shoulders.

Kieran removed his underwear too, then lowered himself into the hot water and moved closer. He kissed me slowly, his tongue coaxing mine out in sensual strokes.

"Did I tell you I've missed you?" he whispered into the kiss. "Life without you is just survival."

I sucked in a breath as he touched my cock, wrapping his fingers around me. "Same here. I missed you so much."

He deepened the kiss and stroked my cock unhurriedly, and I lost my original plan. The forceful need to take, to claim—it was just gone. All I wanted was to lose myself in the pleasure he gave me. For now, anyway. It was one of the things I loved with us, the sexy pull between give-and-take.

"Are you sitting in the middle of the seat?" he asked.

"Huh? Yes."

"Lean forward a bit."

I did as told, and my eyes flashed to his when I felt a strong jet. Kieran grinned like the hellion he was, and I couldn't stop the moan. Holy *fuck*, that felt good. The sharp airflow teased my ass perfectly and sent me into this desperate frenzy where I just wanted more and more.

Kieran held me in place, continued to stroke my cock, and kissed me breathless. "Feels good, doesn't it?"

"Yes," I panted. "I need more."

"Anything for you. Turn around."

I swallowed dryly and got up on my knees on the seat, and Kieran told me to hold on tight. I learned why right away; he hauled me up to the surface with a firm grip on my thighs, and a chilled blanket of air settled across my back.

I gasped a curse as he buried his face in my ass and pushed his tongue inside me. "Fucking hell, a little warni*hnngh...*" I moaned, completely swept away by the indescribable euphoria.

My cock strained and ached. To relieve the pressure, I planted one forearm against the edge to support my weight. Then I was stroking myself to the tempo Kieran set with his skilled mouth. Goose bumps rose on my back, and it became increasingly difficult to stay quiet. Or, at least, not to let any nosy neighbors hear anything.

I swallowed another moan when he breached me with his tongue over and over. It was sensational yet only made me more desperate.

"Fuck me," I breathed out. "I want your cock, Kieran."

"I won't last—"

"I don't care, just give it to me before I come," I growled.

He hummed and licked the length of my ass, then finally stood up and grabbed the oil. Jesus, we were going without condoms for the first time. I was going to feel all of him; he was going to come inside me.

I whimpered like a needy fucking slut.

The second he brushed against my sensitive opening, I thought I was going to blow. He was rock hard and had no patience, which suited me perfectly. He rasped out a warning; it was gonna be quick and hard, and he was almost apologetic about it. I shook my head. Fast and hard was exactly what I craved.

He positioned himself and gripped my hips, then pushed inside in one excruciatingly painful thrust, but it was accompanied by the intense, fiery pleasure I'd missed for over a year. I shot straight into a fog where only he and I existed, where everything was about us getting each other off.

Kieran's sharp groan shook me to the core, and then he was fucking me hard and deep. My muscles protested, and the heat of the water and the cold of the air became uncomfortable. But I couldn't stop. I wouldn't allow it. I rubbed my cock as fast as I could and gnashed my teeth to stave off the orgasm.

"Jesus fuck, baby," he gritted out. "I can't be without you again."

"Deeper," I panted. "Don't stop. We won't—never."

"Promise me," he growled.

"I..." My eyes nearly rolled back. I was right on that precipice. "I promise." The words left me in a shallow gust of air before I lost it. I tensed up all over and erupted, and the orgasm surged through me like electricity.

Kieran rocked into me a few more times before he lost it too.

This was going to be *our* bed. *Our* home.

I wanted the sheets twisted around us, the covers on the floor, and clothes thrown over my lamp on the nightstand. Like they were right now.

Gathering Kieran's hands above his head, I pushed in deeper and kissed him with all the passion I had.

"You belong here," I muttered breathlessly. "You and Jaylin."

"With you and the boys." He grunted at a particularly hard thrust and grazed his teeth along my bottom lip. "I—fuck—it's all I want."

Me too.

"I love you," he murmured.

I shivered and buried my face against his neck, and I began fucking him harder. "I love you too."

He groaned and slipped his hands free to run them up and down my back.

When we needed more, he rolled onto his stomach and got on all fours. I kneaded his ass cheeks and watched my cock disappear inside him, inch by inch, with nothing between us. We glistened with oil and pre-come, and I couldn't stop staring. I gripped his hips; he gripped the headboard. I pounded into him, still watching, still eye-fucking. He moaned and met every thrust.

"Oh Christ," he panted. "Right there. Fuck me."

I slammed in and ground against him, and he let out a long groan and clenched down around me. The pleasure spiked and pushed me toward the familiar edge.

"Almost there." I screwed my eyes shut and held my breath, chasing, chasing, chasing. "*Fuck*."

Kieran came before me, without warning, and it sent me over. The smell of him, of us, and his tight ass clamped around my cock—I didn't stand a chance. My orgasm crashed into me, and my thrusts became erratic and all about filling his ass with my release.

As the high slowly faded, I drew in a dry breath, my lungs burning and my throat parched.

Kieran hissed when I withdrew my cock. Collapsing beside him, I pulled him close to me and waited for my heartbeat to slow the hell down.

"I'd almost forgotten how good you fuck," he murmured hoarsely.

I chuckled, out of breath, and smacked a kiss on his lips. "Please continue to stroke my ego, my love."

He smiled lazily and went in for another kiss, a slow, teasing one with his magic tongue. "I'll stroke you every day if you keep calling me that."

I grinned as another bout of relief sank in. We were finally happening. "It's us now," I whispered, and the humor faded. "You're staying here. You're going to tell your Realtor tomorrow that the only thing you might be interested in is an office in town."

He sighed and cupped my cheek, his thumb ghosting over my bottom lip. "I promise you, the only move I want to make is out of this wet spot."

I let out a laugh and scooted closer to the edge, and he was quick to follow. "Better?"

"Much." He smirked and slipped an arm around my middle. "I'm gonna spend the rest of my life with you. How can I not feel fucking fantastic?"

My smile probably couldn't get any wider, and I felt goddamn cheesy, but I didn't care. I rolled on top of him and kissed him hard. We deserved this moment, for everything we'd been through.

"I love you, Kieran."

"So fucking much." He nipped at my stubbly chin and palmed my ass. "When I came out to my family, I didn't have the balls to hope for this outcome, but I've wanted it for longer than you could possibly guess."

I brushed some hair away from his forehead and kissed him softly. "Can I ask what triggered you to tell your family the truth?"

When my hand slid down his jaw, he turned his head and

kissed my fingertips.

"I saw you in town. In the Valley—you were having lunch with that guy. Casey?"

I nodded.

"It wasn't jealousy," he went on. "Okay, it was a shitload of that too, but most of all, it was this suffocating feeling that the world would always go on without me. Eventually, you would find someone else. And...I couldn't cope anymore. I bought a plane ticket the day after."

I shook my head, still struggling with how his parents had handled things. And three of his siblings whom he'd been so close with.

"For the record," he said, lifting a brow, "you can't tell me Casey's straight."

I chuckled and rolled off him again, propping my elbow on my pillow. "No, he's bi. And certainly not a threat to you."

Kieran huffed, bloody adorable, and held on to me. "Bi is a fucking threat, Ben. You're one of those men who don't know how criminally hot you are."

I grinned. "Keep going."

That earned me a growl from him, and it was his turn to pin me to the mattress.

My pulse kicked up a notch or twelve as I stared up into his predatory gaze.

"You're supposed to reassure me," he said with accusation in his tone.

"I've already told you he's not a threat," I laughed. "He's a good mate, one who's been on the receiving end of nothing but my moping about *you*." It was what Casey and I had done; we'd met up for lunch to complain like old ladies. He'd bitched about his love life, and I had bitched about Kieran. "He and I... There's nothing there. It hasn't even come up or been hinted at—from either of us. I think we stumbled upon each other at a time where we only needed a friend, and it's stayed that way."

That seemed to relax my jealous man, though I couldn't deny it was sexy as hell when he got possessive.

"I think you'll like him," I mused. "He writes a funny blog about a lot of things we can relate to."

"Such as?"

"Parenting." I widened my eyes at the horror.

He finally cracked a smile.

"Can we talk about how long you've wanted me now?" I wondered.

"Longer than you deserve right this second," he chuckled and ended up next to me. Then he sighed and gave me a quick kiss. "The first time we met up after work, I knew you'd be trouble. By the second, you'd become the one who could both make me and break me."

I gathered his hand in mine and kissed his palm. "No more breaking for us."

He hummed. "Unless we're talking headboards."

"Oh, *deal*."

CHAPTER 27

So...Wednesday ended on the best note possible. Thursday was taken straight out of a fantasy, and that was it? The wedded bliss was over now? Because unlike yesterday, when I woke up to a blow job and spent most of the day in bed with Kieran, I woke up alone this morning, and he didn't respond when I called his name.

I left the bedroom, grumpy, and rubbed the sleep out of my eyes.

There was sound coming from the kitchen, though. I was sure of it.

After trudging down the stairs, the first thing that hit me was the blinding sun pouring in through the kitchen window. And then I saw Kieran at the stove, with his back to me, and he had headphones on.

He poured something into a skillet, the butter sizzling, and it didn't take more than a few seconds for the smell of pancakes to flood the kitchen. My stomach growled in hunger. My mood improved insanely fast.

Kieran jumped slightly as I put my hand on his lower back, but I was more focused on looking over his shoulder where he was making pancakes. They looked fucking amazing.

"Morning." He removed his headphones, and I heard the faint sounds of Flogging Molly from them. "Should I get an apron that tells you to kiss the chef?"

"Unnecessary." I snuck in a kiss and hugged him from behind. "I could get used to this, but let the record show, I prefer waking up next to you."

He chuckled. "Mmm, me too. But you'll have to suffer sometimes so I can make us breakfast."

I smiled against his neck, seeing our future ahead of me. "Will cooking become your thing?"

"Fuck, yeah." There was a grin in his voice. "Consider it my territory if you clean."

"Done. I'm a bit of a pro with the vacuum."

And Kieran was an utter mess when it came to keeping things tidy, so this actually worked out wonderfully.

Making myself useful, I made us coffee and brought in the paper. Merely whipping up some pancakes wasn't enough for Kieran; no, he had to create a feast. There were extra buttery ones, blueberry, chocolate chip, and a couple with bacon bits. Then a bowl of whipped cream, whipped butter, and syrup for the table.

"When's your pop coming over with Duke?" Kieran asked, getting seated.

"Hopefully after we've devoured all this." I plated a bacon pancake and an extra buttery one. To start with. "Have I told you I love you today?"

Kieran snorted. "You're easy, baby."

"I'm *hungry*, is what I am." I cut into the bacon one first, and then I had vanilla sweetness and salty bacon exploding on my tongue. "If I'd had this before I met you, I would've said it was better than sex."

His eyes danced with amusement, and he took a sip of his coffee and looked out. He nodded at the window. "Your pop's here."

"Hide the food—" Or not. My suggestion was met by laughter.

"I'll get him a plate," Kieran told me.

Fine.

Dad let himself in, and soon we had Duke rushing into the kitchen. He barked and wagged his tail and tried to jump up on my lap, but he wasn't quite that skilled. I smiled and patted his head as my father appeared in the doorway.

"Morning, boys. Something smells great," he said.

"Good morning, sir. Have a seat," I replied. "Kieran made breakfast."

"I deduced that when I said it smelled great."

I wasn't even going to pretend to be offended.

Kieran set a plate at the head of the table, along with a cup of coffee, and I couldn't help but notice he'd gone a little quiet. Was he nervous? Oh—did he not want family to know about us yet? We hadn't discussed it. We'd talked more about turning the guest room into Jaylin's room, and we'd agreed to go shop for furniture today before we picked up the kids. There hadn't been time to approach anything else, due to all the fucking that we'd prioritized.

While Dad treated him to breakfast, I gave Duke fresh water and found him a bone in what had become his cupboard. Sweet Nate, sometimes he used his allowance to buy Duke extra treats.

"What're your plans for the day?" Dad asked us.

Kieran seemed a bit stuck, so I answered as I took my seat again.

"We're gonna pick up some stuff I've been meaning to buy for the backyard." I locked my feet with Kieran's under the table, hoping it would relax him. Shit, maybe it would make it worse...but the small smile he sent me was reassuring.

"Yeah?" Dad devoured half a pancake in one go.

I nodded. "I want a hammock."

Kieran's gaze flashed to mine then, and I smiled. The picture of him and me, and the kids, in the hammock that summer was one of my absolute favorites, and I could finally dig it up from my desk drawer in my office and frame it. Again.

"Sounds like a plan," Dad said. "You got a nice spot for one between the apple trees." He stifled a belch and lifted his coffee mug. "You two gonna tell me you're together, or do I have to wait for an invitation to a coming-out party?"

Kieran dropped his fork.

I was less surprised and more than a little amused. I was used to my father noticing things by now. Things I'd always believed I was subtle about.

I raised a brow in question at Dad, curious.

He jerked his chin at Kieran. "He's wearing your college tee, and you're playing footsie under the table like a couple girls."

I grinned around a mouthful of pancake.

Kieran let out a breath, weary. "You're okay with it?" He glanced hesitantly at my father, who frowned in confusion.

It hit me that Kieran hadn't been nervous about going public. He was scared out of his mind of facing more rejection. My heart ached for him, and I cursed his useless fucking family to the ninth circle of hell.

"Why on earth wouldn't I be okay with it?" Dad asked. Then he shook his head and patted Kieran's hand. "Welcome to the family, son."

My father could have all the pancakes he wanted.

"This is a stupid idea."

"Sometimes a stupid idea is the right one." A particularly cold crosswind blew past us as we reached the street on which we used to live, and I yanked up the hood on my sweater. "Besides," I added, "I'll have to face her at some point. Might as well be now."

We'd spent the whole day getting Jaylin's new room in order once we realized that children talked. Kieran and I wanted to be official, and even though we had no plans to make out in front of the kids right away, we didn't want to hide either. We'd done that for years already. But, if the kids knew, so did their mothers.

Perhaps not Allison. Maggie, though. Jaylin was closer to her than Nate and Jess were to Allison, and I wanted to be there when Maggie found out. It was the right thing to do. Because just as the children had different relationships with our exes, so did Kieran and I. He had never been close to Allison, but Maggie and I were friends. Or used to be, if this conversation went as Kieran predicted.

So we had stopped assembling Jaylin's new desk and were now on our way to Maggie's house to tell her about us. In an attempt to stall, Kieran had suggested we walk. He was no doubt hoping we'd miss Maggie and that she would take off to Seattle before we arrived, though I happened to know she wasn't going until tomorrow. It was one of the things that had become an established routine since Kieran and Maggie separated. She wanted to be close by the first night of "Daddy's week," in case Jaylin got upset.

My stomach knotted with nerves as the house came into view.

I had conceded on one point. We weren't going to say that we'd had an affair. Kieran claimed no good would come of it; it would only hurt Maggie further, and I admitted he had a good reason. We didn't live in a fairy tale, and not every truth would set us free.

We were already free.

I checked my watch. We had two hours before we had to pick up Jaylin, who was with a friend. Nate and Jess had left Allison's early to spend the day in the city with my sister. With the wedding approaching, Brianna wanted to make sure the boys had nice suits since they'd be in the wedding.

"You okay?" I asked.

"Huh? Yeah." Kieran seemed surprised I'd asked. "Ben, Maggie and I didn't love each other the way we were supposed to. We both wanted convenience and an easy way out. She wanted a traditional core family, and I wanted...the same. It looked great on the outside." He nudged me with his elbow. "First thing she told me after I said I wanted a divorce had nothing to do with her feelings being hurt. It wasn't even the second or the third or the fourth. She's lost her comfort, and that's scary. But it'll pass."

It was mildly reassuring. I wasn't going to believe we were doing Maggie a favor, though with their marriage in the hands of lawyers now, I did hope she'd find someone eventually who wanted her for who she was, not for the image of *traditionally acceptable*.

I let Kieran walk first, and he chuckled at how weird it felt to knock on the door instead of just going right in.

Maggie opened it a few seconds later, dressed in yoga pants and a sweatshirt, looking like she'd been working out. "Oh. Hey. I have some more boxes for you. It's mostly clothes and photos."

"Cool." Kieran entered as she backed up, and Maggie sent me a small smile.

"Hi, Bennett. Good to see you."

"You too, hon." I was a prick. She was about to hate me, wasn't she?

"Can we talk?" Kieran asked.

Maggie furrowed her brow but nodded and gestured to the kitchen.

We passed a stack of three moving boxes in the hallway and headed into the kitchen, where Maggie offered to make us coffee.

"No, I'm good," Kieran said and sat down. "We won't take up much time."

The nerves made a swift return as I sat down next to him.

"All right, what do you want to talk about?" Maggie sat down across from us and slid her gaze from Kieran to me. She was curious about why I was here, I could tell.

Kieran shifted forward in his seat a bit and bounced his knee restlessly. "Since the kids will be with us next week, we wanted you to hear this from us instead of from Jaylin." He cleared his throat and cracked his knuckles. Such a telltale sign of his discomfort. "It's about us—Ben and me."

Maggie sat back and folded her arms over her chest, and one eyebrow hitched.

Jesus Christ. Here we go. My heart started pounding.

"We're together," Kieran said.

I sent a quick skyward glance and braced myself for Maggie's anger.

She spluttered first, and she stared at us blankly. But as the seconds ticked by and neither of us laughed at what she probably hoped was a joke, her eyes grew wide.

"I don't want you to get upset with Ben," Kieran murmured. "He wanted to do the right thing and tell—"

I put a hand on his arm and shook my head. "Don't." The last thing I wanted was credit for something that might earn me one brownie point when I'd lost hundreds. I'd been desperate and halfway into a depression when I met Kieran, but I'd been fully aware of who I was hurting.

Kieran sighed and leaned back.

"You're serious," Maggie whispered. She didn't look angry as much as she looked like she was going to be sick. "The two of you? *You*, Bennett? Since when are you gay?"

I opened my mouth to respond, only to close it again. What was I supposed to answer? This wasn't about my confusing sexuality. I'd never thought of myself as anything other than straight, but then Kieran came along, said, "Hold my whiskey," and made me fall head over heels.

"I didn't understand my feelings for a long time." It was the truth, at least.

Maggie shot Kieran a snide look at that. "I'm sure my ex-husband-to-be was more than happy to explain things."

Kieran's expression flattened, and he took a deep breath.

Maggie shook her head and averted her gaze. "I can't believe this. Ten years of marriage down the drain because you couldn't keep a simple promise."

"Sim—" I hadn't heard her right. Right? "Do you think any of this has been *simple* for Kieran, Maggie? It wasn't a promise he couldn't keep. It was pretending to be someone he wasn't that became too much, though I'm sure your *encouraging* him to keep up this charade prolonged your marriage."

"Your turn." Kieran spoke under his breath and shook his head subtly at me. "Don't bother."

Actually...

"He lost most of his family for this," I told Maggie. Because I had to get that out. "His parents won't talk to him, his brothers *put him in the fucking hospital*. I was there to see him. I saw the bruises and how he could barely move. Don't call that simple. I—" Christ, I hadn't intended to get worked up. "I'm extremely sorry you got caught in this, Maggie. I feel awful about it. You didn't deserve to get hurt. But this wasn't simple—for either of us. We're done lying, though. To others and ourselves. We've fought it—Kieran much more so than me—but we're done. It happened. I love him with everything I am, and I wouldn't change that."

I would never go back. Ever.

Kieran took my hand under the table, maybe to shut me up, maybe to...just hold it; I wasn't sure. I had nothing more to say anyway. I did feel guilty for having hurt Maggie, but I couldn't cope with an alternative where she got to keep the image of a perfect family and Kieran and I were miserable.

I couldn't.

"You can go," Maggie said, refusing to look at us. "Both of you—out, please. My family's ruined, so excuse me if I'm not jumping for joy at your...*union*."

I clenched my jaw but said nothing.

Kieran glanced at me, then nodded at the hallway. *Let's go.* I stood up and followed him out, and when he grabbed two of the boxes waiting for him, I picked up the other one.

Then we left and started to walk back home.

My head was a jumbled mess, though that was nothing new. And not all bad either. My life before Kieran had been almost as black-and-white as my childhood; there'd been an easy answer to everything. It was either yes or no, sometimes *maybe later*. But I'd learned firsthand how incredibly dull life was without nuance. I didn't want my existence to be predictable and easy anymore. With Kieran and the children, I felt more than ready to take on uncertainties and adventures.

It made me think. Did we lead uncomplicated lives with the people we wouldn't trust to go to war with? Had I avoided picking fights with Allison because I'd known deep down we weren't strong enough to survive them?

I blew out a breath and adjusted my grip on the boxes, and I glanced over at Kieran. "Are you okay?"

He appeared to be deep in thought, and I brought him back. He inclined his head. "Just thinking you might be the first person ever who gets me. There isn't a thing I wouldn't do for you, Ben. I was blind for too long, and now—" He shook his head. "I just wish I'd seen it sooner. Or hadn't been such a fucking coward to pursue happiness. To pursue you."

I smiled and walked a little straighter.

I'd go to war with him any day of the week.

CHAPTER 28

"I can't believe we pulled it off with so little time." Kieran hugged me from behind and rested his chin on my shoulder, and we both stared at our day's work. A boring guest room slash office slash gym had turned into a princess's badass lair.

Jaylin loved black and purple, so that's what she'd gotten.

Her Barbies, books, magazines, and movies filled a shelf that took up an entire wall. Her clothes had found a home in a new armoire that Kieran had cursed at least a dozen times while assembling. She had a new desk, a new bed, and on the nightstand was a new lamp that was black with purple satin bows on it. A teenage girl with black hair and a lot of eyeliner had helped us in the store.

This weekend, we were hanging Jaylin's baby pictures where Nate's and Jess's were on the staircase.

"Should we summon the punk princess?" I asked and turned to kiss his cheek.

He nodded.

We'd told Jaylin she wasn't allowed up here until we were done with "something," so she was downstairs watching a movie.

Brianna would be here soon with the boys too.

Telling Nate and Jess about Kieran and me probably wouldn't cause much reaction. Their mother had a new partner, and they knew not everyone wanted someone of the opposite gender. In retrospect, I could see why my father had been the one who pushed a bit harder to normalize same-sex relationships when we were kids, for which I was grateful today.

Kieran wasn't worried about that aspect either. Jaylin had come home last year with a book about two moms who had a baby together. We could thank her teacher for that one, though Kieran admitted with a wry smirk that Maggie had been against the book. Not because she had anything against other sexualities, but because it hit too close to home, and she'd lived in denial as much as Kieran had.

"Monkey," he hollered down the stairs. "Can you come up here a second?"

We waited while Jaylin paused her movie and scrambled off the couch, and then we saw her walking up the stairs.

"What's up?" She fiddled with one of her pigtails. The rubber bands at the ends had purple skulls attached to them. At this rate, her favorite store in a couple years would be Hot Topic.

"Ben and I wanna show you something," Kieran replied. He nodded at her room, where the door stood open.

Jaylin did a double take at the sight of it, then rushed inside to look around. "All my stuff is here, Daddy. Oh my gosh, look at the lamp! I love it!"

Kieran sent me a nervous smile before entering the room. "It's pretty cool, isn't it?"

She nodded, wide-eyed. I could tell she liked her room. I

could also tell she was confused, because the plan was for them to get a place of their own.

While Kieran sat down on the edge of her bed, I stayed closer to the door, opting for the desk chair.

Kieran patted the spot next to him for Jaylin. "We're not gonna move again, baby."

She sat down with a wary expression. "We're not?"

He shook his head. "What do you think about us staying here with Ben, Nate, and Jess?"

At that, she looked over at me.

I smiled gently, suddenly nervous as hell. "This would be your home too. You'd share the upstairs with the boys."

Her brows knitted together. Her frown was all Kieran. Just like her hair, her eyes, and her cheeky smirks. "Where's Daddy gonna sleep?"

Kieran cleared his throat, and we exchanged a quick glance, to which I nodded.

"In the bedroom downstairs," he answered. "With Ben."

Poor girl, we'd confused her further now. She scrunched her nose and became skeptical. "You're gonna share? But you have a million things in the attic, Daddy. It's never gonna fit in Bennett's room."

I let out a laugh. She wasn't lying. Kieran had left his old house with a *lot* of gadgets. He'd been adorably bashful about his spending ways. Then he'd lit up when I had suggested we turn the garage into something useful. We never parked our cars there anyway, and I wouldn't say no to a pool table. The only reason we'd put his moving boxes in the attic for now was because the garage door needed fixing. It didn't close properly.

"We have a plan for the million things." Kieran took her hand and dropped a kiss on top of it. "What I'm trying to tell you is that Ben and I going to be sharing a room as parents do. We're not only friends anymore. We love each other."

Jaylin's mouth formed a silent "oh," and she blushed furiously as her gaze flicked between Kieran and me. "You kiss and stuff?"

Kieran stifled a smile, somewhat. Well, he tried. "We do."

She squeaked in embarrassment.

I realized I was holding my breath, so I exhaled and wondered when she was going to ask if this was why her mother and father separated. Then I became unsure. Perhaps she wasn't old enough to even have that question.

"My daddy's your *boyfriend?*" Jaylin asked me, still recovering.

"Yes, darling." Amusement—not to mention relief—trickled in when her reaction was so innocent and age-appropriate. At ten, or almost ten, she found boys gross. Unless it was Jess. Now she was learning that I was willingly kissing a boy, and that was positively abhorrent.

"But girls are so much better," she grated. "We're not jerks."

I grinned.

"I'm gonna let you hold on to that opinion until you're thirty." Kieran kissed the top of her head. "Are you okay with this, though? Me and Ben together and us living here with them?"

She nodded slowly, processing for all she was worth, and a crease appeared in her forehead. "We smell better too."

Well, I couldn't quite agree there. I thought Kieran smelled bloody amazing.

Kieran winked at me over her head and hugged Jaylin to him. "I don't smell bad."

"After you run, you totally do," she huffed. "You stink."

Safe to say, we wouldn't have any major issues with Jaylin. She'd probably blush and be embarrassed when she saw us kiss or hold hands for a while, but she was clearly more focused on other things. Such as boys being smelly jerks.

"Hallelujah!" was Brianna's reaction to my new relationship. Then she kissed Kieran's cheek, my cheek, and apologized for having to dash right away. Her parting words were, "Chris and I have reservations, but I'm so happy for you, and I'll arrange the seating chart for the wedding."

That was good to know, I supposed.

After stowing away Nate's and Jess's new suits, it was time to continue the coming-out train before Jaylin spilled the beans, and I'd been right not to worry. Jess had a similar yet opposite reaction to Jaylin. Girls were gross! He was happy that I'd picked a boy instead, although he wasn't immune to squirming in embarrassment at the sight of displays of affection. And all I'd done was squeeze Kieran's hand.

My sweet Nate was relieved purely for innocently selfish reasons. With Allison meeting Frank, there'd been natural changes at their house. It happened with any new relationship. Things changed, like routines and rules, and Nathan wasn't fond of that—whether it was good or bad. But he knew Kieran. He *liked* Kieran. Kieran was good people.

I could count on my sons to turn the whole conversation into an anticlimactic event, where they—shortly after they'd said they were fine with all this—asked what we'd have for dinner.

They stared at Kieran when they waited for an answer.

Kieran appeared to be waiting for the other shoe to drop, but he managed to say tacos. Actually, it sort of came out as a question, and the kids approved. Then Kieran ducked out of the living room, and I followed him into the kitchen where I found him releasing a heavy breath and scrubbing his hands over his face.

"I think coming out to my family gave me PTSD," he joked weakly. "I should'a known the boys wouldn't care."

Ah. *I* should have known Kieran would be tense for this conversation too. I walked over to him and hugged him to me. "I remember when they came home once after you took them to McDonald's. Jess thought it was hilarious that you'd ordered a Happy Meal for yourself." I kissed his neck, recalling how at ease Nate had been. "Nathan, though—you gave him such a boost of confidence that day." Cupping Kieran's cheeks, I eased away a few inches to look him in the eye. "You showed him it was okay to order whatever the hell you want from the menu. You showed him that just because his friends had started ordering *grown-up meals*, he could set his own pace. And he's looked up to you ever since."

Kieran relaxed and closed his eyes, resting his forehead to mine.

I *loved* that he and Nate still carried on their Happy Meal tradition. Kieran bought old collectible toys off the internet and snuck them to Nathan every now and then, and he lit up every time.

"I love you," he said, taking a deep breath.

"I love you too." I gave him a quick kiss. "You know, someone once told me that one of the few things we can control is when our second life begins. I want to do that with you and the children now."

He cracked open his eyes and smirked affectionately. "Was that someone a rock star you had a hard-on for as a kid?"

"I—" was surprised he knew who'd said that. "I certainly didn't have a hard-on for him."

Kieran snorted a chuckle and kissed me hard. "Maybe your memory's just shit, then. You've told me that story several times."

"Oh," I replied dumbly.

"You're cute as fuck." He went in for another kiss, a slow,

deep one that stole my breath. "Want me to dress up like a rock star for Halloween?"

"*Oh*. That's, uh…" I swallowed hard. Imagining Kieran in tight leathers, his sculpted torso on display—well. I cleared my throat. "Perhaps not a Halloween for kids."

He grinned and pinched my ass. "Will I see you in Bruins gear then? I can help you with the jockstrap."

Fucking hell, he seduced me too damn easily. "Consider it done."

"Perfect," he murmured against my lips. "But first, we're starting our second life with tacos."

Yes, sure. That too.

"You ready to lose a bet, baby?" Kieran called up the stairs. "We gotta go."

"On my way." I threw a clean pair of underwear for Jess into the bag and left his room. On my way down the stairs, I adjusted my tie and ran a hand through my hair. Damn, we were late. "For the record, I would've won if Allison hadn't canceled on Nathan's birthday party."

When Nate turned thirteen last week, Kieran and I had made a bet on whether or not Allison would figure out he and I were together. As far as I knew, Jess and Nate spoke of us all living together, but I wasn't sure they went into the kinds of details adults were particularly interested in. In Jess's eyes, it was much more important to share what candy he'd eaten on the weekend than, say, mention his dad had a boyfriend.

Life had been busy with work the last month, so I hadn't had the chance to talk to Allison in person very much. I had, on the other hand, left a voice message. But I knew she missed those on occasion.

In the kitchen, I grabbed a few bottles of soda and some snacks, and I saw Kieran had stepped outside to greet my father. Everyone was dressed to the nines today, but Kieran took the prize in his three-piece charcoal suit. I was going with the dark blue suit Brianna had picked out for me, and my tie matched Kieran's outfit, something she'd made sure of. Same with Kieran's tie being the same shade as my suit. My bossy sister was bossy and also very much a romantic. The latter was all because of the man she was marrying today.

Once I was done, I left the house and locked the door.

"Looking sharp, sir," I told Dad. He was going to walk Brianna down the aisle in his formal army uniform, and I wasn't going to shed a single tear at the two of them. If I kept telling myself that, perhaps it would become reality.

"You too, son," he replied. "We ready to go?"

I nodded. "We're taking Kieran's car." Because he'd upgraded his this summer, to a black SUV I'd told him we probably wouldn't need. I was wrong. The only way for the whole family to travel together was in his monstrosity. Jess and Jaylin could sit in the far back. Nathan and Dad would be comfortable in the regular back seats, and then I'd sit next to Kieran and his smug smirk while he drove.

"Did you grab the camera?" Kieran asked me.

"Yes. Did you get the gift?"

"Already in the car," he answered. "The boys' suits too."

Okay, good, we were ready. Duke was getting spoiled by one of Dad's neighbors, I had packed Jaylin's dress, drinks and snacks, the gift, and I'd brought Dad's spare cane in case he needed it. He was leaving town without his, which was just a pride thing. I understood he wanted to give Brianna away without help, but there was the party afterward. He was going to be in pain.

The drive to Allison's and Maggie's was only a few minutes

long, and then it was time to pick up the kids. Kieran went one way, and I went the other.

How many times had we stopped on either side of the fence to steal a moment together before we went home separately?

Never again.

"She's gonna bring it up," Kieran told me. "Gut feeling."

"I don't see why she would." I frowned and knocked on the door.

Kieran disappeared out of sight, though I heard him laughing. Did he know something I didn't? Otherwise, I saw no reason for him to put fifty bucks on Allison choosing this very moment to ask me if Kieran and I were together.

It was Frank who opened the door, and Allison and the boys were behind him in the hallway getting ready.

"Morning, man." Frank smiled.

"Good morning, Frank. I see you guys've been busy."

He chuckled. "They've been up since seven. Jess is excited about the cake."

Of course, he was my son.

Frank excused himself to get started on breakfast for him and Allison.

Nate was ready to go. He gave his mum a quick hug on the way out and passed me to join Dad in the car.

"I'm almost ready, Dad!" Jess called nervously. "No, not like *that*, Mom." Allison was trying to make his hair nice, and I could've told her it was a lost cause. Actually, she should know that by now. Nate had inherited my hair; it was a bit wavier but fairly easy to tame. Jess... Poor boy was stuck with a mess of whorls and cowlicks.

"I'm sorry. I don't know how you want it," Allison said.

"Like *Kieran* does it," Jess protested. He was close to throwing a fit, so I intervened.

"Sweetheart, we can fix that at the church," I told him.

"We're arriving early so you can get dressed without rushing." And to minimize the opportunities to spill. "Kieran will help you with your hair." Because his messy hair was similar.

Jess huffed and ripped the comb from Allison's fingers.

"*Hey.*" I threw him an irritated look of warning. "Be respectful, Jess."

He sulked. "I'm sorry, Mom. Can we go now?"

I stepped to the side as he put on a hoodie, and after giving his mum a hug, he ducked out. I could hear Kieran and Jaylin somewhere outside too.

"We'll be back on Sunday," I said to Allison. "Are you guys home around four?" This was technically her weekend.

"Yeah, no problem," she answered. "By the way, while I have you alone..."

Fuck. No.

She took a few steps closer and hugged herself. "The past couple of months, I've noticed Jess talking more about Kieran." She looked up at me, hesitant. "Aren't you worried he might get too attached?"

"Who?" I quirked a brow.

"Kieran, of course—while he's staying with you. And, you know, since he's gay."

This was not the way I thought this conversation would go. So Kieran wasn't actually correct. Allison didn't suspect me. After all this time. After the stories the kids shared. Hell, she was neighbors with Maggie! Did the two never talk anymore? Allison couldn't possibly be so removed from reality.

I had to be clear. "Let me get this straight." Oh, the irony. "You're worried Kieran might be too attached to me?"

She furrowed her brow and nodded. "Of course. Aren't you?"

I couldn't help but chuckle. "Well, I should certainly hope

he's too attached to me. It would've been a painfully one-sided relationship otherwise."

She blinked, then shook her head quickly as if to clear it. "Wait, what?"

I smiled. "Kieran and I—"

"We gotta go, Ben!" Kieran hollered from the car. "We've got one Nate and two cranky ten-year-olds who need to change too."

Oh, joy. Jaylin was also in a mood. It was going to be a lovely drive to Seattle.

"I'm not ten yet," I heard Jaylin snap.

"I'm not cranky!" Jess shouted.

"Okay, he's not cranky, and she's not ten yet!" Kieran yelled.

I laughed and turned back to Allison.

She was staring at me in shock, no mirth found whatsoever. Pardon me, I thought Kieran's exchange with the kids had been funny.

"You and him?" she questioned. "You're together? As in— you're together?"

My amusement faded, and I nodded once. "We are, yes. I understand it's a surprise—it was to us too." Sort of, technically, in the beginning. "It took me a long time to realize how I felt." Sort of, technically, in the beginning.

"Jesus," she mumbled, touching her lips. "Here I was, thinking your next partner would be that Ashley woman you work with."

It wasn't the first time she'd brought up Ash, and it was just as strange now. Ash and I had virtually nothing in common, though we worked well together for bigger accounts, plus we were both happily involved with others. She'd been married for a few years now.

Sometimes, we believed what we wanted to believe as well. It could be convenience. Allison felt it was reasonable and easy to suspect a coworker of mine, and perhaps that was partly why she didn't ask if Kieran had been the one I'd had an affair with when I was with her. Time was also a factor. Hurt, bitterness, and anger had expiration dates. We'd let each other go and didn't care as much, so long as the boys didn't suffer.

"We have to go." I rubbed the back of my neck. "Now you know, though."

She snorted. "Yeah, thanks for the heads-up." She gave me a wry look. "You do whatever makes you happy, Bennett, but since it involves our sons, maybe you tell me a little sooner next time." She had to be joking. "Jess and Nate have been acting like you guys are a family for weeks, and I didn't understand. I was under the impression Kieran was staying with you guys until he found his own place."

She wasn't kidding.

"Since when does that matter to you?" I asked curiously. "You introduced Frank to the boys before I even knew he existed."

Allison had no response to that, aside from looking annoyed, and I truly had to go.

"We'll be back on Sunday," I said. "Call if you won't be home."

A big church wedding had never been my sister's style. I could've pictured her getting married at city hall or perhaps a destination wedding in India. But this part was for Chris's family's sake. A little over two hundred people filled the church, and I was the last one to take my seat.

"How's Jaylin?" Kieran asked hesitantly.

"It's fine. She was just nervous." I slipped my hand into his as violins started playing. A low murmur traveled through the church, and everyone turned to see the wedding party enter.

I was ready with my camera.

"It was sweet of your sister to include her," Kieran said, keeping his voice down.

I thought so too. Brianna wasn't getting married with a maid of honor by her side. She'd asked the boys—and recently Jaylin—to be there with her instead.

I grinned widely as I saw Nate walking first, Jess and Jaylin only a couple feet behind. They looked so cute in their suits. Which I wasn't allowed to call Nathan anymore. He was a teenager now; he was almost taller than his aunt, and he'd become frustrated when I had—in his opinion—taken too many pictures.

Jess soaked up the attention and smiled for everyone. Now that Kieran had gotten his hair "just so," life was good again.

Jaylin grinned shyly as she passed us, and Kieran and I continued taking photos. Me with the camera, him with his phone.

"She's too adorable for words," I murmured.

"So are the boys," Kieran responded quietly.

Dad and Brianna were next, and I got a lump in my throat. I had the best sister a bloke could ask for, and I was incredibly happy for her.

"You're beautiful," I mouthed as we locked eyes.

She beamed behind her veil.

Dad looked proud as hell.

"I didn't think shit was gonna get emotional," Kieran whispered.

We straightened and sat forward when the wedding party had passed us, and I glanced over at Kieran. Thank fuck, he was a little misty-eyed too.

Kieran wove our fingers together, and we watched Brianna kiss Dad's cheek before taking Chris's hand.

"I love you." I squeezed Kieran's hand.

"I love you too."

The minister opened the ceremony with a talk of new beginnings. How life was a journey with stops along the way, and that it wasn't about how far we came before our final destination, but that we were surrounded with loved ones who'd shared our journey.

It was a speech for Brianna and Chris, who hadn't met as kids, who hadn't been there for each other through college. They'd met along the way. Like Kieran and I had, which was why it was difficult not to take the speech personally. Particularly for Kieran. I felt him tense up a bit when the minister spoke of the importance of family.

I squeezed his hand again. He tightened his grip and released a breath.

We were family. I was his family. He had my sister, my father, and my sons too. Two of his brothers and his youngest sister would move here at the end of the year. We were going to build something better, something that never let go of him.

"I'm going to force you into one dance with me later," I whispered.

Kieran mustered a sideways smile and shook his head. "No force needed. Just don't get pissy when I step on your feet."

I was looking forward to it.

He did step on my feet a couple times, and I'd never cared less. At an estate outside of the city, in a ballroom that looked more like a posh greenhouse, under a glass ceiling with ivy and chandeliers, I got to dance with Kieran.

We were so full, from amazing food to all the impressions of the day, so we didn't talk much. Yet, we managed to convey everything we needed. He squeezed my hand and nodded at the door, and I followed his gaze to see Nate dart out of the ballroom.

I chuckled under my breath, and Kieran smirked.

Nathan had been asked to dance by probably all the girls his age, and he'd had it. He'd warned us already, in his adult way, that he might escape for some "bloody privacy" soon.

The band started playing a song that was slower than the last one, and I quirked a brow in silent question.

One more?

Kieran smiled and pulled me closer, our foreheads touching.

I'd never found such contentment in a public setting before. There was freedom in the whole experience, being able to dance with the love of my life at a wedding. Something I hadn't thought would matter so much before.

It put me to ease that Kieran seemed to enjoy it too. Because I would've understood if he'd be wary of this initially. Having spent a life in hiding...it would've made sense that he still glanced over his shoulder here and there. Instead, he had an appetite for it, whether it was kissing me in the doorway to his office when I stopped by with lunch or we went out for dinner in Camassia. Perhaps because he'd deprived himself of it until now.

I sighed, relaxed, and closed my eyes.

"We're gonna start our own traditions, right?" Kieran murmured.

I hummed. "Many of them." I knew he was thinking about his family. I'd caught his pensive expressions, and the grief that sometimes lingered, throughout the evening. With the number of siblings, aunts, and uncles he had, he'd probably attended a lot of weddings.

"Good." He kissed me. "It's getting easier."

I opened my eyes and stroked his cheek. "You don't have to reassure me, love. I know it still hurts."

He nodded minutely. "It does, but then I think about everything we can do. You and me. All the Christmases and Easters and birthdays—we'll make them ours. I want our house to be the place where everyone gets together."

I kissed him quickly and tried not to get choked up as our entire future became so incredibly vivid. "Fuck yes," I said instead. "We'll start with a Halloween party for adult friends so we can get fall-down drunk as rock stars and hockey players."

Anticipation and happiness ignited in his eyes. "Then Christmas when my brothers and sister get here."

"An Easter egg hunt in the backyard for the kids, obviously."

"And a Fourth of July barbecue."

I closed the distance and kissed the smile off his face. "Love you."

"Mmm, love you too. You have no idea how much, Ben."

CHAPTER 29

On December 22nd that year, I watched Kieran and Connor hug in the sea of arrivals at the airport in Seattle.

With help from Desmond, Kieran had convinced Connor and Grace to move before the holidays instead of after. We had traditions to begin, and everyone had to be there.

"Con needs this," Grace murmured and wiped a tear from her face. "He's struggled a lot this year."

It looked like they all had. Desmond had lost a bit of weight, and Grace was visibly exhausted.

"Brent gave us a final lashing before we left," Des revealed. "I almost throat-punched him."

I shook my head, and part of me was angry that Kieran was letting Jaylin go to Boston for New Year's. Maggie was still his parents' most precious daughter-in-law, and she'd been invited over the holidays. So Maggie would fly out with Jaylin on the twenty-eighth.

Kieran said he was only relieved, because he wanted the kids to be kept out of the drama. This way, Jaylin would still have a relationship with her cousins.

Still. Jaylin was a clever girl. In a few years, she wouldn't buy the hollow "Daddy's fighting with Nana and Pop-Pop" excuse.

Kieran was right, of course. I wanted the children to be protected from grown-up bullshit for as long as possible too. It was just my bitterness that reared its head sometimes. After everything they'd done to Kieran, they didn't deserve shit.

They'd clearly been rough with Connor too. Abuse wasn't always physical. Kieran pulled away from the hug slightly, only to cup the back of Connor's head and say something we couldn't hear. Connor nodded and wiped at his cheeks, and Kieran hugged him again.

"I'm glad you guys are here." I put an arm around Grace's shoulders for a quick squeeze, and she smiled gratefully. "Kieran's been counting the days."

"So have we," she laughed softly.

"Seriously," Des chuckled. "It's a second chance at life, for fuck's sake."

Kieran and I knew a thing or two about that.

It wasn't only big family traditions Kieran and I wanted to start. Everyday life consisted of the little things, and we had new family members to grow closer to. For Kieran, it was Nate and Jess. For me, it was Jaylin.

Nate put it best one morning, when Kieran had announced he was taking the kids to find us a tree and I wasn't allowed to tag along. Nathan had pushed up his glasses and said, "So, like, you could say we're a five-ply rope in this family. Each ply needs to be tended to. Because you want to do something that's just ours, and Dad will do something else where you're not allowed to come."

Kieran's new *little tradition* was to get a tree with the kids. It'd been an afternoon just for them; he'd picked them up from school and headed out with lemonade and sandwiches.

We'd decorated the tree together the next weekend.

On Christmas morning, it was my turn. Nate and Jess woke me up around five, and I grunted sleepily and told them to wake up Jaylin. Then I detangled myself from Kieran, yawned, and got dressed in a pair of sweats and a Red Sox tee.

I was in the kitchen making hot cocoa when I heard the kids failing at being quiet on the way down the stairs. Nate was explaining the meaning of the song while Jess rambled about Grampa's *old bestest friend,* Thomas.

I smiled to myself and carefully rotated my left shoulder.

We'd spent the past two days getting Des, Grace, and Connor settled in their new place in the Valley. Kieran and I had taken out a loan to buy the loft, and once they got settled into their own apartments, however long it might take, Kieran was going to put in an offer at the loft next door and turn it into a local office. He'd finally decided to just open a small branch for his business here in town.

With four mugs of cocoa and too much whipped cream ready, I carried a tray into the living room where the kids waited expectantly on the couch. My place was still on the floor, and someone had pushed out the table for me, plus brought out my guitar.

"Don't forget to tell the story too," Jess reminded me.

"I remember," I chuckled.

Jaylin was seated in the middle of the couch, and she smiled sleepily at me. "I've never heard it before."

"It's a good thing you're here now." I winked and handed

her the last mug. Then I got comfortable on the floor while they fanned out Nate's duvet. And didn't spill, thank goodness.

As I tuned the guitar, Duke looked up from his bed by the tree, blinked slowly, then went back to sleep.

I eased into the familiar music. "So your grandfather wrote this song for his unborn son."

"The son is Dad," Jess whispered.

I cracked a grin and shook my head. "Once upon a Christmas," I started, strumming on the guitar, "a young man sat up all night and watched his pregnant wife as she slept. His son would be born in a few weeks." I hummed with the tune. "The young man prayed for words of wisdom. Words he could one day give his son. He prayed for advice, and then he remembered his best friend."

"Thomas—I told you about him," Jess told Jaylin.

"No spoilers," Nate chastised.

"He spent the night before Christmas thinking of his best friend and everything the young man had learned from him. He sat by the tree and wrote in his journal what he imagined his best friend would tell him now." I tinkered wordlessly for a minute and cleared my throat. I still wasn't the best singer. "Oh, but James, you have your own book in the Book of James… As the body without the spirit is dead…so faith without deeds is dead, so my James…" I hummed some more, the lyrics hitting me differently this year. "You tell your boy one day…what a good deed is."

Maybe things had changed for my father too. The message of doing good deeds had gotten lost in the memory of *"I'd rather someone else suffers than you, Bennett."*

People had gotten hurt since I last sang this song for Nate and Jess.

"James, you tell your boy one day to…see not the color of a man's skin…not the clothes he wears on his body… My James, you tell him to share his bread and drink. Tell him to share his bread and drink..."

"I like your voice, Bennett," Jaylin said softly.

I peered down at the guitar and smiled, reminded of her presence. Maybe that was my job now, more than ever. For Kieran and me to teach the kids about good deeds. At this point, school was easy. But eventually, all three might face problems because they had two dads.

That thought was scary. It always was for a parent. Knowing you couldn't be there to protect them at all times. I released a breath and finished the song, but I wasn't quite there anymore. Kieran and I had been so consumed by establishing our relationship and planning for a bright future full of traditions and adventures that I'd completely forgotten the struggles we might have to take on from others.

There were a lot of people in the world like Kieran's folks, people who spat hatred and judgment.

Were our children going to take hits because we wanted to be together?

How was that fair?

And I was supposed to do what? Tell them to turn the other cheek? Was that a good deed?

Perhaps I wasn't a very good person then, because I fucking refused.

I would never tolerate intolerance. I would never treat bigotry with respect, and I wasn't sure I could teach my children to do that either.

The kids had gone quiet behind me, and when I looked over my shoulder, I noticed two things. The children had fallen asleep where they sat, and Kieran was standing in the doorway.

After setting down the guitar, I stood up and grabbed Jaylin's and Nate's mugs. Jess had already put his on the table.

Then I tucked the kids in under Nate's duvet and kissed their foreheads before I met Kieran in the hallway.

He probably saw I was troubled.

"Am I a good person?" I asked quietly.

He frowned, then nodded at our room.

Once we were behind closed doors, we sat down on my side of the bed, and he gathered my hand in both his.

"What brought that on?"

"Just..." I made a vague gesture toward the living room. "The song. I don't know if you heard—"

"I did." He kissed my knuckles. "It's possible I took a picture of you guys too."

I smiled, even as I felt the doubt clouding me. "When I sang that song to the boys before, I never thought twice about good deeds and what makes a good person. And after everything that's happened—with us—and the people who got hurt... I don't know. And then I thought about the narrow-minded idiots who walk freely everywhere. The chances our kids run across them are pretty fucking high."

He hummed and nudged my elbow lightly with his. "I don't think you need to share your bread and drink with those morons in order to be a good person, baby. You don't owe them any wisdom either. People are free to hate too."

My forehead creased.

He quirked a wry little grin. "One of the reasons I love you is because you think in those terms. You worry about the big picture and ask the universe-sized questions, but no one's keeping score, Ben. I think we like to believe there is, but in the end, I'm gonna meet the same death as my parents. They've done good and bad. I've done good and bad."

I nodded slowly, picturing my dad saying similar things.

He continued. "The schoolyard bullies who one day might

corner Jess and say his dads are fags—ain't a whole lot we can do about that, except prepare Jess."

"Right," I said, because this was my point, "and I have no desire to teach Jess to just take it. To turn the other cheek and accept being bullied."

"Who says we will?" He cocked a brow.

"Well..." *Everyone* said that. "Don't tell me you haven't had a teacher who told you not to stoop to their level."

"Oh," he chuckled. "The high road and that bullshit. Sure. Then I grew up." He shrugged. "If someone gives our boy a beating, he will know how to hit back. Trust." The rough-around-the-edges Boston kid made an assertive appearance, though I was more focused on the fact that he'd called Jess ours. Warmth spread all over. "You don't buy into that shit, Ben. Do you?"

"What?" I asked dumbly. Buy into what?

"Never mind," he said. "You know what a good deed is? It's flying across the country when I was in the hospital because you weren't sure I had anyone. A good deed is raising your sons selflessly the way you've done. You've given them everything. A good deed is supporting me while I got out of my funk. It's about being there for those you love and to help others when you can, it's about getting my sister an interview at Brianna's friend's clinic, and it *will be a good deed* when we prepare our children for reality. They will know how to defend themselves and stand up for what they believe is right."

It was amazing how quickly Kieran could calm me down. More than that, how well he centered me and made me look at what was important. And the truth was, being a good father and a good partner far exceeded the opinion of an imaginary scorekeeper.

"You're right," I said. "You're sort of smart for an Irishman."

He grinned. "That Irishman could mop the floor with your English ass."

I clapped him on the shoulder. "Cleaning—a fitting job for—"

"Oi!" He pushed me back onto the mattress and crawled over me while I laughed. "I wouldn't finish that sentence if I were you."

I grinned up at him. "Can I kiss you for good luck or should I rub your leprechaun?"

He shook with silent laughs and dipped down to kiss me. "That was a good one."

I chuckled into the kiss and ran my hands up his back, feeling much better. Thanks to him. "Merry Christmas, my love."

He hummed in pleasure and pecked me once, twice, three times. "Merry Christmas, baby."

Later that day, at a more respectable hour, Kieran was in his element. He was surrounded by loud children who were running around playing with their new toys, there were spiked hot drinks, a lot of yelling between Desmond and Grace, and I was the recipient of the exact words, "I love you, but get outta my kitchen."

Safe to say, he didn't want my help with the turkey—or anything else for that matter. So I grabbed two cold beers and joined my father on the couch in the living room.

"Did I hear him ban you from the kitchen?" Dad chuckled.

"Can you believe that?" I shook my head in amusement and took a swig of my beer.

Brianna and Chris were here too, and they were currently looking at the pictures I'd put up from the wedding. They deserved their own spot on the wall next to the entertainment center, and one of the pictures was slightly enlarged. It was of Kieran and me when we'd danced. The wedding photographer had captured a perfect moment. My head ducked, a grin playing on my lips, Kieran's beautiful laugh frozen in time, our hands clasped.

"Not too close to the TV, Jess," I hollered. He was playing tug-of-war with Duke and his new chew toy, and they'd already knocked over one glass of soda today.

"He's almost stronger than me now," Jess huffed, out of breath. "Good boy, Duke."

Glancing over at the dining room table, I studied Nate and Connor for a bit. They seemed to have connected quite well. Connor was quieter and calmer than the other Marshalls, and he was into computers. Nathan ate that right up, and now they were playing a board game with questions about technology.

"This is a wonderful picture, Bennett." Brianna pointed to one of Nate and Jaylin from the wedding. She'd wanted to dance but had been too shy to ask anyone, so Nate had taken one for the team. He was a good brother.

All the pictures were amazing. They'd gotten lucky with their photographer. "My personal favorite is the one of you and Dad after you and Chris had your first dance." It wasn't on the wall, though. There'd been too many to choose from, so that one had ended up in a frame in my office.

"That's a great one," Chris agreed with a nod.

Dad had no comment. He merely sat there in silence, sipped his beer, and smiled every now and then.

"Nooo! Put me *down*, Uncle Des!" Jaylin shouted. "I will punch your butt!"

I spluttered a laugh and turned my head just as Des waltzed into the living room with Jaylin thrown over his shoulder.

"I have a kid to sell," he offered. "Any takers?"

"Jerkface!" Jaylin started banging her fists over Desmond's back and ass, to which he laughed. "You can't sell me!"

"I suppose I can give you five dollars for the princess," I said.

"That's a fine offer," Des replied.

"Bennett!" she screamed.

I winced and feared the windows might break if she screamed any louder. Desmond grinned and started tickling her —God, what a bunch of hell-raisers they all were—and then dumped her on the couch.

Jaylin yelped, only to squeal with laughter as her stomach flipped. "Do it again," she demanded.

I snorted into my beer.

Dinner was even crazier.

It was a good thing we'd bought a new dining room table, because even if we could've fit at the old table—though barely— Kieran and Grace had made so much food that we couldn't see the surface anymore.

Nate was seated between Connor and me, and he leaned close to speak in my ear. "I think Jess is a Marshall."

I let out a laugh and shared his comment with Dad at the head of the table, and he laughed too.

Nate probably wasn't wrong. As the Marshalls had raised the volume with their mere presence, Jess had come to life with a whole new default mode. Indoor voices had ceased to exist entirely, and he'd eased into the role of Desmond's antagonist like a champ. If Jaylin poked Des in the ribs, Jess upped the ante to get a rise too. Jaylin would narrow her eyes and take it even further.

Kieran was on my other side, also at one of the short ends,

and he nodded at my father. "You wanna do the honors and cut the turkey, sir?"

"Oh no," Dad said. "This is your feast, son. Yours and Grace's. You go ahead."

Kieran and Grace exchanged a glance, and she decided to make a toast while her brother took care of the turkey.

As she stood up and raised her wineglass, the rest of us lifted our drinks too.

"First of all, I wanna thank Kieran and Bennett for welcoming us to the West Coast," she said, and I tipped my beer bottle at her. "You have a wonderful family, and we're blessed to be part of it." The next part was for her brother. "The family we choose is sometimes better than the one we were born into, big brother. And sometimes, we get a little bit of both," she added with a cheeky grin, "but either way, I've made my choices, and I could not be happier. And looking around me today, watching you, seeing you with Bennett, I'm confident you feel the same."

Kieran leaned over and kissed her cheek. "Fuck yeah, I do."

"Hear, hear," Des and Connor exclaimed.

Grace beamed and held up her glass. "*Sláinte mhaith.*"

A round of cheers rang out, followed by Jess asking "what the shit" that meant, and I stared at him with wide eyes.

He pointed to Des. "He said that before!"

"No, I didn't," Des replied with a frown. "I said what the shite. Ya gotta learn, kid."

Sweet Jesus.

"Maybe we don't go full throttle the first year," Kieran told Des. "Take it down a notch—at least until gay marriage is legal and I can trap Ben properly."

Grace guffawed.

"That's the sweetest proposal I've ever heard," Brianna laughed.

I was...overwhelmed. Amused beyond words, in love, and

utterly defeated. The Brooks boys didn't stand a chance against the Marshall manners; we just had to enjoy the ride.

Nate looked over at me, seemingly as shell-shocked as I was, and I could only grin. And kiss the side of his head.

"I'm dizzy," he chuckled quietly.

"You and me both, son."

Around midnight, the last people had left, and the kids had passed out in various stages of food coma and exhaustion.

Brianna and Chris were spending the night at Dad's place, and after an hour's wait, Camassia's only taxi service showed up to take the three youngest Marshall siblings home. Ten minutes later, Kieran and I collapsed into our bed and refused to touch each other.

I feared I would explode at the slightest pressure.

"Today was..." I had no words for how I would much I would cherish the memories this Christmas had given me.

"It really was," Kieran murmured. "I haven't been this happy in...ever."

I found his hand in the darkness—

"Just don't touch my stomach," he whispered.

I smiled tiredly. "Wouldn't dream of it."

We let out a collective sigh of contentment, and I closed my eyes.

To think, five years ago, Kieran and I had chased the opportunity to meet up for beers for the first time. Five years. He'd texted me merry Christmas. He'd been in Boston. I'd been in the middle of microwaving hot chocolates for the boys and me. Now we shared a home and had merged our families.

"That wasn't the proposal, by the way," Kieran said

drowsily, halfway to sleep. "You'll know when I ask you to marry me."

I used the last of my strength to lift our hands and kiss his fingertips. "Maybe I'll propose first."

"Nuh-uh," he yawned. "I'm calling dibs."

I chuckled, something that made my stomach clench, and that fucking hurt. "We're not ten, love."

"Nope..." He shuffled around, and soon I felt the duvet over me and his body heat right next to me. "We're thirty-three, and I still call dibs." He kissed my shoulder. "Let's have sex tomorrow instead."

"Or the day after," I said. "I don't think I'm leaving this spot anytime soon."

"Christ, me either. Deal—day after tomorrow. We'll fuck like bunnies."

"Ouch," I groaned through a laugh. "Don't be funny, please."

"Sorry." Judging by the grin in his voice, he wasn't sorry at all. "Night, baby."

"Good night," I yawned.

EPILOGUE
A FEW YEARS LATER

"That's fine," I said, making a note in my calendar. "I'll be out there on the 19th anyway. I'll talk to them then."

Outside my office, I could hear that Jaylin was here. She asked my assistant if her dad was available, something that never failed to put a smile on my face. She'd never called me Dad in person, much like Nate and Jess only called Kieran by name, but we were more than happy about them referring to us as their parents to friends and teachers.

After wrapping up my phone call, I told Jaylin it was okay to come in.

She popped her face in first, as if to make sure it really was okay to enter. "Hi."

"Hi, darling. What brings you by?" I checked my watch. I'd thought she'd be at the beach now. It was where Kieran and Jess had decided to spend the day, while some unlucky others had to work.

"Nate wanted to go to the comic book store, so I tagged

along," she explained, taking a seat across from me. Her backpack ended up in the other chair. "He just dropped me off."

"Ah." That made sense. The fact that Nathan had recently gotten his license was a bit of a mindfuck, but we tried not to think about it too much.

"I wanted to talk to you about something," she went on hesitantly. "But you can't tell Dad."

I'd been waiting for this. Maggie was getting remarried in Seattle next weekend, and none other than Kieran's parents were invited to the wedding. So for the first time in basically ever, his mother and father were coming to Seattle. Desmond and Connor had been on a strike where the family was concerned since Kieran was no longer welcome; Grace saw them once a year for Thanksgiving. And Jaylin...well, she'd come up with excuses the past couple of times when Maggie was heading back east to visit. Since they'd be so close next week, I had no doubt they'd reached out to their granddaughter.

"It's about your grandparents, I assume." I sat forward and clasped my hands on the desk, and she nodded. "Whatever it is, I'm sure you don't have to keep it from Kieran, sweetheart. He wants you to be able to see them whenever you want."

She looked flustered about something. "I want to confront them," she admitted. "Especially Nana. Everything is so fake now when I see them. That's why I canceled before. It doesn't feel right."

I understood her. Jaylin was growing up so fast, and this year she'd taken a big interest in politics. She was also headstrong beyond words, and she looked up to Grace and Brianna a lot, two women who prided themselves on standing up for what they believed.

"You mean, confront them about why they won't see your father?" I asked to make sure.

"Well, yeah. How long do they expect me to believe it's a

stupid fight that's keeping them apart?" She became annoyed. "They can't treat Dad like that and then think the rest of us can go on like nothing's happened. It's dumb as shit."

I pressed my lips together to hide my smile. "I understand where you're coming from, trust me." I phrased myself carefully. "Think about your mum for a minute first, though. It's her big day—she's getting married and probably doesn't want a big fight at the reception—"

"Nana and Pop-Pop will be in town for almost a week," Jaylin pressed. "I could talk to them before they go home or something. Either way, I won't pretend anymore. I refuse." She paused. "I thought Pop-Pop was gonna come to his senses when you and Dad got married last year. He asked a million questions when we talked on the phone." I remembered; she'd told me before. He'd asked Jaylin if Kieran was happy. "Now he's mostly in a bad mood, and Nana's still...ugh. Blah. She's the worst sometimes. She gets so judgy! What happened to not casting stones or whatever the bible says?"

I chuckled under my breath. This sweet girl—what had I done to deserve having her in my life? She amazed me every day.

"Look," I said, smiling gently, "if you want to confront them at some point, your father and I won't stop you. You have to do what you believe is right. But I ask that you don't let this interfere with the wedding festivities. Your mum has enough on her plate as it is."

Because, bless her, she'd met a man through her parents' church who had eight children. A local guy who lived here in the Valley—whose parents were close with Maggie's. He was good for her; Kieran and I had done some snooping, but we completely understood Jaylin for preferring to visit rather than live in the middle of that chaos. She lived with us most of the time nowadays, though she and Maggie snuck out for dinners and whatnot several times a week.

Jaylin sighed heavily and pushed her side bangs away from her eyes. "I agree on one condition."

I raised a brow. "I didn't know this was a negotiation."

She pursed her lips. "I don't go down to Seattle until the day before the wedding. That way, I don't have to spend time with Nana and Pop-Pop and pretend everything is okay."

Hmm. "Don't you guys have a bunch of things planned?" I asked. "You were going to a spa or something."

She slumped back in her seat and threw the back of her hand across her forehead. "Don't make me gooo!"

I laughed.

"It would've been fine if it were just Mom and me, but there's gonna be like twenty women!"

"Plenty of people to hide behind so you don't have to talk to your grandmother, then," I pointed out cleverly.

She huffed. "That's just the spa day. Then there're a gazillion other get-togethers."

I shook my head, amused. "Maggie will want you there by her side, darling. I'm sure you can find a way to avoid your grandparents. You have my permission to lie and say you're not feeling well if they get pushy."

Jaylin dropped her hand and squinted at me. "Promise?"

"I promise," I replied with a nod.

She stood up and extended her hand. "Deal."

I chuckled and shook her hand firmly. "Always a pleasure doing business with you, princess."

"I know, right?" She sat down again. "What's for dinner tonight?"

"Lamb chops," I answered. "We're going to try to cheer up my boss."

"Is Ellis sad about something?" she questioned.

I wasn't sure, to be honest. "He's going through a divorce," I murmured. "We thought he could use some company."

Part of me wondered if Ellis was in a funk for other reasons. He and his wife had never seemed particularly close or affectionate toward each other. And, a few years ago when I told him about Kieran and me, he'd had the strangest reaction. He'd made a joke, saying, "For a moment, I'd feared you were dating Casey."

He'd used the word *feared*. Why would that be a fear? Unless... But I wasn't allowed to ponder that for Kieran, who had taken a liking to calling me a gossip. In my defense, now that I was so happy with my own life, I cared more about other people's happiness. Funny how that worked.

Everyone was home when I pulled into the driveway, and I noticed Kieran's car had been washed. That usually meant Jess wanted money and was ticking off chores he could do for extra cash. Perhaps our lawn had been mowed too.

Nathan's car was parked on the street, and there was no money to collect there. Nate washed it religiously every other week.

Music and laughter traveled from the backyard, and it got louder as I entered the house. I wondered which of the kids had friends over. Kieran had insisted on a real, in-ground pool last summer, resulting in too many of Jess and Jaylin's friends wanting to come over on weekends.

Kieran was in the kitchen, bobbing his head to the beat of the song as he prepared something on the kitchen counter.

I snuck up behind him, and he jumped slightly as I pressed a kiss to his neck.

"Jesus, baby."

I smiled and peered over his shoulder. "Hello, my love." Fuck yes, he was making his baby potatoes with herbs and garlic. I was a big fan.

"Hey. I missed you today." He turned around in my arms and kissed me. "Did you read Casey's blog post? It was funny."

"I haven't had the time yet. How was the beach?" I felt his cheek. It was a little rosy.

He hummed and turned his face to press a kiss to my palm. "It was nice. Connor showed up after lunch, and we jumped from the pier."

"Jess too?" I was impressed. He'd been summoning his courage all summer, it seemed.

"He didn't wanna come home," Kieran chuckled, and I grinned into another kiss. "By the way, my daily reminder. Six days—just you and me."

"Mmm, can't fucking wait." Anticipation rushed through me, and I deepened the kiss and pressed myself closer to him. Six days until it was just him, me, and the narrow roads along the Amalfi Coast in Italy. Two whole weeks. A dream vacation to celebrate being married for one year.

Neither of us had proposed. Not really. But the day same-sex marriage became legal in all fifty states last year, we'd looked at each other and just known we were thinking the same thing.

Two weeks later, we'd walked out of city hall with wedding bands we were never taking off, wedding bands with a few words engraved on the insides that were just for us.

We would never go back.

MORE FROM CARA

In Camassia Cove, everyone has a story to share
Lincoln & Adeline
Ellis & Casey
William

Cara freely admits she's addicted to revisiting the men and women who yammer in her head, and several of her characters cross over in other titles. If you enjoyed this book, you might like the following.

Auctioned
MM | Suspense Romance | Hurt/Comfort | Trauma

At twenty-one, Gray Nolan became a human trafficking statistic. He and seven other young men were taken aboard a luxurious yacht where they would be auctioned off to the highest bidder. Tortured, shattered, and almost defeated, he watched his new owner step out of the shadows in a swirl of his own cigarette smoke.

Noah
MM | Hollywood Romance | Hurt/Comfort | Age Difference | Standalone

In 48 hours, Noah lost everything. He walked in on his girlfriend with another man, and the next day a plane crash ripped his family away. Gone was the carefree man who'd lived his life in the fast lane of the film industry, leaving a forty-year-old shell that dwelled at the bottom of a bottle. But one person could relate—only one. Noah's sister's stepson who hadn't been on the plane. Julian showed up on Noah's doorstep one day, and it was a good day to start picking up the pieces of what was left of them.

Uncomplicated Choices
MM | Comedy Romance | Family | Single Dad | Standalone

When life gave you lemons, you found out who stayed and made lemonade with you. Or something to that effect. And the day Ellis kidnapped me—or rather, he borrowed a yacht and didn't know I was sleeping below deck—he'd definitely been handed too many lemons. We were practically family, so I owed it to him to stay and make sure he was all right. Apparently he was trying to decide whether or not to divorce his wife, so it was truly not the best time for me to develop a crush.

MORE FROM CARA DEE

Check out Cara's entire collection at www.caradeewrites.com, and don't forget to sign up for her newsletter so you don't miss any new releases, updates on book signings, free outtakes, giveaways, and much more.

ABOUT CARA

I'm often awkwardly silent or, if the topic interests me, a chronic rambler. In other words, I can discuss writing forever and ever. Fiction, in particular. The love story—while a huge draw and constantly present—is secondary for me, because there's so much more to writing romance fiction than just making two (or more) people fall in love and have hot sex.

There's a world to build, characters to develop, interests to create, and a topic or two to research thoroughly.

Every book is a challenge for me, an opportunity to learn something new, and a puzzle to piece together. I want my characters to come to life, and the only way I know to do that is to give them substance—passions, history, goals, quirks, and strong opinions—and to let them evolve.

I want my men and women to be relatable. That means allowing room for everyday problems and, for lack of a better word, flaws. My characters will never be perfect.

Wait...this was supposed to be about me, not my writing.

ABOUT CARA

I'm a writey person who loves to write. Always wanderlusting, twitterpating, kinking, cooking, baking, and geeking. There's time for hockey and family, too. But mostly, I just love to write.

~Cara.

Get social with Cara
www.caradeewrites.com
www.camassiacove.com
Facebook: @caradeewrites
Twitter: @caradeewrites
Instagram: @caradeewrites

Printed in Great Britain
by Amazon